The Independent Contractor

by
Richard Connolly

AmErica House
Baltimore

© 2001 by Richard Connolly.

All rights reserved. No part of this book may be reproduced in any form without written permission from the publishers, except by a reviewer who may quote brief passages in a review to be printed in a newspaper or magazine.

First printing

ISBN: 1-58851-206-1
PUBLISHED BY AMERICA HOUSE BOOK PUBLISHERS
www.publishamerica.com
Baltimore

Printed in the United States of America

Dedication

This book is dedicated to my family,

the most consistent source of joy and pride in my life:

my wife, Mary,
children, Mark and Lisa,
mother, Evelyn,
sister, Elaine,
son-in-law, Adam,
and daughter-in-law, Donna.

Acknowledgments

It's likely that no book today could ever be written without help, and mine is no exception.

As such, I would like to thank:
my wife and best friend, Mary,
for her understanding, encouragement,
and insightful comments on the manuscript;

former Criminal Defense Attorney Jim Moran of Hingham;
the Massachusetts State Police,
especially Bob McCarthy and Detective Lieutenant Dick Lauria;

the contractors who allowed me to borrow freely from their lives;

Paula Saltman, Jeanne Logan, Maureen Zemina,
and Attorney Robert MacIntyre
for help with medical office practices or Medicare issues;

Bruce Spitzer of Fleet Bank, Boston, MA
for electronic banking procedures;
and Architect Richard Heym of Richard Heym Assoc., Boston, MA.

Special thanks to all who read the manuscript through its many permutations, most notably, Louisa Cunio.

Edward Cunio for designing the cover.

Chapter 1

The prosecutor approaches the stand for his cross-examination.

The only defense witness, a dignified woman who is noticeably nervous and shaking, is also the defendant.

The prosecutor glares at her before questioning. Then he begins.

"Isn't it true, Mrs. Andes, that your husband wanted to pick out the colors for the kitchen cabinet countertop, and you wouldn't let him?

"Isn't it also true, that you had to ask his permission to spend an extra $700 for puck lights, even though you worked full time?

"He wanted a ceramic tile floor in the kitchen, didn't he, but you insisted on hardwood. Isn't that right, Mrs. Andes?

"You thought he was trying to control you, didn't you?

"You resented it, didn't you? Answer me, Mrs. Andes, didn't you? You killed him, didn't you?"

"Objection! He's badgering the witness."

"Overruled!"

"Yes! Yes! Yes! Yes! Yes! Yes! Yes! Yes!" the witness sobbed hysterically. "I did. I admit it!" she said, as she broke down on the stand and had to be removed from the courtroom.

"I have no further questions," the prosecutor said with disgust.

"The defense rests, Your Honor."

Twenty minutes later, the jury returned with its verdict. "Not guilty, Your Honor, by reason of remodeling insanity."

Karen Andes had made legal history with the Remodeling Defense.

The jury had been carefully selected: all had homes they remodeled. Even the victim's family members sympathized. They had remodeled their homes, too.

Can you believe it? What's next, the Personally Annoying Defense?

****

"Hey, Benjie. Is my car fixed yet?" the owner of the luxury, foreign and domestic car dealership in Hingham, Massachusetts, called out to his mechanic working in the bay.

"Yep. It's all set. I swapped the flat for a new tire and changed the oil and filter. Anything else you want done?"

"No. That's it. What was wrong with the tire?"

"Had a nail in it. Looked life a roofer."

"A roofing nail? Where the fuck did a roofing nail come from? I haven't been around any roofs."

"It could have come from anywhere. Didn't you have some work done on your house awhile ago?"

"Yeah, so what?"

"Could have come from there, was by the edge of the driveway near the lawn, and you didn't see it."

"I didn't think of that. Maybe you're right. Fuck it. I've got to go. Where are the keys?"

"In the ignition."

"Great. Thanks for the help. Make sure you tell Gayle I went to the bank. I'll be gone for a couple hours and should be back by two."

Gayle Armstrong was the owner's office assistant, a nice woman who was not too bright and hand picked for the job by the boss himself. Her most obvious characteristic was her substantial breasts, which would endanger all but a glass blower when caught in her loving embrace.

Still, she was pretty good on the state-of-the-art computer system installed at the dealership. Although a plodder in most things, Gayle had a good sense of humor and teased The Boss about his fumbling. "Too bad you don't have an H&P key on your keyboard," she said. "It would really help you."

"No. I don't have one. What is it?" he asked.

"A hunt and peck key," she answered smartly.

The Boss and Owner, Anthony Romano, liked his women dumb but titillating, and Gayle filled the bill exactly. He probably had her around for show, like the latest model car on the floor, and failed to notice her other qualities beyond the beautiful body and passable face.

She had been with Tony Rome, as she liked to call him, since he purchased the dealership in the early 1990's, when she was in her late twenties and had found the job through a classified ad.

Even though both were single – Gayle because she had not found the right guy and Tony because he was not searching for a mate – rumors about the Armstrong-Romano connection occasionally surfaced. No one had ever seen them together outside the dealership, and Gayle always went home on time.

Romano was a well-built man, nearly six feet tall, with a full head of thick, fairly straight black hair, dark brown eyes, an Italian complexion, thin legs, hairy back and chest, small ass, and weight appropriate to his height, as the personal ads would say. He shared Gayle's love of jewelry and wore several rings on his fingers and a gold necklace with a dangling unicorn horn. Tony wasn't Adonis, but he did attract female attention.

THE INDEPENDENT CONTRACTOR

He drove off to do his banking in Cohasset, the rich, respectable, and Republican community he now called home and the opposite of its next-door neighbor, the seaside Town of Hull where his mother and father still lived. It was only a short ride for Tony to visit them, which he customarily did at least once a week, usually in the morning before he went to work. Both were retired and living on Social Security and his father's small pension.

Tony liked to think of himself as a man who never forgot his roots, which were tangled and not what one might expect of a man so financially successful before he was forty. Romano had grown up in Hull and would do – then as now – almost anything for a buck, including running errands for neighbors, shoveling snow off sidewalks, delivering newspapers, mowing lawns, stocking shelves in a liquor store, clamming, or hauling lobsters with his uncle, a great guy who drank too much.

Although he was an only child who received a lot of attention from his financially strapped parents, Tony couldn't concentrate in school, had failing grades, and longed to be elsewhere – out on the beach, the water, or behind a cash register.

For the most part, Romano's school years were uneventful, except for the time in his sophomore year when he and a friend were accused of breaking into Hull High School and vandalizing the property. One of the kids Tony hung around with ratted him and the friend, but all the police did was question, fingerprint, and release them. It was quite a scare, which is exactly what the police intended.

Romano was a poor student at best and definitely not college material. After he graduated from Hull High School in 1978, Tony found a job at an auto garage in nearby Cohasset. There, he quickly learned the automobile business and how to work on cars, saved a few bucks, and bought himself his first automobile, an older muscle car that needed only some bodywork.

Within a year, Romano changed jobs and went to work for a much larger dealership that sold new and used cars and also had a repair shop. He soon discovered in an age before computers that no one kept a close eye on the large tire and battery inventory, which afforded him the opportunity to sell a few on the side. He quickly and quietly developed an interesting and specialized clientele.

In no time at all, Tony had a nice little business going for himself, a rightful supplement for the many long hours and hard work he put in for the owner doing whatever was asked of him, always without question. He continued to live with his parents in their small home, helped them out around the house, shopped for groceries, and never missed a room and board payment.

By all accounts he was a good son or, as his mother liked to say, a good boy. He was also a good and loyal friend.

Ten years later, life at the dealership was different for Romano because he had moved up to a senior sales position and had become intimately familiar with every facet of the company's operation. Tony was the dealer's jack-of-all-trades and a highly trusted and valued employee, and his membership at the South Shore Country Club helped with sales.

One day while getting a haircut, Romano read in a 1982 magazine a rare article on Novi lobster boats, which was the closest thing to research Tony ever came in his life. The piece had been written by an old salt from Nova Scotia and was far more technical than Tony had the ability to grasp.

He did discover, however, that the boat departed from many of the accepted, western world practices for powerboat design and construction and that some people thought the Novi had been thrown together, didn't measure up, or was good only in sheltered water.

The author blew away these notions, of course, but Tony liked the idea that the Novi had a reputation for being a maverick. He also loved the boat's look with its nearly plumb stem and strong sheerline that rose sharply to a very high bow where a raised deck and trunk cabin, called a cuddy, provided standing headroom in the forecastle.

That distinctive feature kept the ocean spray out of the boat when it was moving windward in a chop or eliminated the likelihood that the nose would go under a wave in very heavy seas.

Since time and tide wait for no man, a lobster boat's speed greatly mattered. The wide stern of the boat and the narrow bow, both of which came under criticism, helped the Novi get speeds of up to sixteen knots. It was a tradeoff of good bearing aft – and better sea worthiness – for speed.

Romano was surprised to learn that the frame of a lobster boat built in Nova Scotia would be made of softwood because there is little oak or cedar growing there. Oak, in fact, could be a disadvantage because its tannic acid would quickly rust the galvanized boat nails.

Nova Scotia boat builders incorporated spruce, hackmatack, yellow birch, and maple into their craft and made use of whatever materials were available. Softwood and hardwood were terms that applied to the cone or nut, respectively, from which the tree grew, not a quality or property of the wood itself.

Boats – like life – can be a series of compromises you accept and learn to live with the weathered author of the article concluded. Romano would have no need to worry about the seaworthiness of a bargain he was looking for and about to find.

THE INDEPENDENT CONTRACTOR

Shortly thereafter, Tony acquired from some Cohasset guy who was getting out of the business a hardly used, thirty-five foot Novi with one hundred and seventy-five traps, which he subsequently would set somewhere along the rocky coast between the Towns of Hull and Scituate.

This venture was small enough for him to work it alone, part time, while turning over some hard earned cash, which, like his other dealings, went largely unreported. When he wasn't using the boat himself, Tony let his cousin, the son of his hard drinking uncle, take it out with a friend.

His agreement with Joey was never broken. "Make sure my parents get a few lobsters, take care of the boat and its equipment, don't forget about your mom and dad, no drinking on board. You break, lose, or use anything, you replace it, including the fuel."

The red and white lobster boat, which was moored in Cohasset Harbor, forced Tony to make one concession to honesty. His buoys, traps, and boat all showed the last four digits of his social security number, 4622, which was legally required of all lobstermen in order to avoid friction over who owned the gear.

In addition to the number, his buoy had to be displayed prominently on the boat for all to see, and its colors were described on his lobstering license.

The distance from his home in Hull to Cohasset Harbor was not much more than four or five miles and a very beautiful, fifteen minute commute. The harbor was an especially serene place where pleasure craft and lobster boats intermingled.

In the middle of a winding road traversing the harbor was a large restaurant with a magnificent view, especially from the bar lounge. To its left was a small, fashionable hotel where many famous guests playing at the nearby South Shore Music Circus stayed during the summer months.

On the right, an old, weather beaten, decaying, former boat yard stood on a white water inlet. Its commercial boat building days was long since gone, but it was still being used for repairs and restorations. Its small entrance was fewer than five feet high, and to its left inside the building was a rectangular hole in the floor that had been patched.

The hole had once been used during Prohibition to smuggle booze in and out of the building.

Next to the boat yard building was an ugly, rusting, out of place Quonset hut loaded to the brim with tools and equipment. A third, more recently built but equally tasteless structure was used as an office.

The magnificent location, despite its blight, had caught the attention of developers who were interested in building expensive condos. A counter movement was already underway to get the boat yard shop declared an historical building, which would put an end to any further development but hasten a restoration project.

The foaming waters that alternately rushed into or out of the harbor from the inlet at high and low tides were a favorite place of kayakers who could be watched from a rocky ledge at the mouth of the inlet or an arched bridge above it.

The harbormaster's hut was perched on this rocky cliff, at the base of which stood the pier and parking area for small trucks, vans, and cars. In good weather, you could sit on a bench in the lovely park fronting the water and gaze out on the boats, the entrance to the harbor, the magnificent homes surrounding it, and the human or commercial traffic going by.

To get to his regular job, Tony needed no car because the dealership provided him with one, and the out of pocket savings was considerable. Anyone who knew Romano would admit that he worked very hard, always hustling, helping a friend with his take out restaurant on Nantasket Beach, painting a house or two in his spare time. As long as he was paid in cash, Tony could be counted on to be there when you needed him.

Romano knew that he could go on as he had indefinitely but was itching to make his money more easily. His chance came one night after he delivered a new car and went to the pub at the ancient Red Lion Inn, located in Cohasset Center. Tony had a beer, talked to some guys he knew, grabbed a bite to eat, and settled in to watch Monday night football all by himself.

A short time after the game started, a guy walked into the pub, sat down at the bar on a stool next to Romano, and ordered a beer. The stranger made a few comments about the high priced players, and he and Tony were soon in a conversation.

"What do you do for a living?" asked the stranger who was in his mid forties and wearing an expensive, dark blue pinned striped suit.

"A little bit of this; a little bit of that. Mostly cars. Fixing them, delivering them. Stuff like that," Tony said guardedly. "How about yourself?"

"Me? I do importing and exporting. I have a container ship moored in South Boston. I'll be here for about a week before heading back to the Caribbean."

"Really? What are you hauling?"

"Well, it's not sugar or molasses, I can tell you. No rum either, but other things," the stranger added suggestively.

"I didn't think so, but you can never tell. I know something about molasses," Tony said with reservation.

"You do? What about it?" the stranger asked, apparently interested.

"There was a great flood of it in Boston, I think near the North End, and twenty-one people were smothered in it. Something like two million gallons poured from a wooden tank. My mother told me about it."

"That's interesting. What a way to go. When did it happen?"

"Around 1919. I guess they originally thought it was sabotage by the Germans, but it was the wooden tank, which had thin walls that broke. They were under specifications."

"Was your mother alive then?"

"Fuck no, but my grandmother was and told her. She remembered the Titanic, too. After each one, they changed the regs. Ah, getting back to this exporting thing, ever do any cars?"

"Yeah. I've done some cars but not many. I wouldn't mind doing a few more."

"Any money in it?"

"Oh, yeah. There's money in it. Real money."

"Real money? I mean, what are we looking at here?"

"Heavy markup. Very serious stuff."

"Can I buy you a beer?"

"Yeah. I'd like that. By the way, the name's Al."

"Well, how do you do, Al? Pleased to meet you. Call me Tony," Romano said while shaking Al's hand. "Hey, Mike. Two Bud Lites at the table in the corner."

Al and Tony picked up their cigarettes and half empty glasses and moved to the booth in the front right corner of the pub. Mike placed on the table two bottles of beer, each capped with a fresh glass. "Might as well drink up," Tony suggested.

For the next two hours or so, the pair put down five beers between them, and both were in a mellow and less cautious mood. They talked mainly about sports and women, but every now and then came around to the subject of cars.

"Look, Al. On this car thing. How serious are you about exporting cars – used cars, if I understand you right?" Tony finally asked.

"I'm very serious. From what you said, you're in the car business, and maybe we can work out a little something together." Each man looked the other carefully in the eyes, attempting to assess him or divine what was going on in his head.

"What kind of deal you got in mind?" Tony laid out for openers.

"I think somewhere around six cars for starters. We'll see how it goes and take it from there."

"I think I can handle that. What's the arrangement?"

"Simple," Al said while leaning forward on the table. He looked around the room before continuing. "You pick up the cars and deliver them to me at the Conley Pier in South Boston. You go through the entrance at the end of Farragut Road in your hauler and drive over to where the ship's moored.

"I issue a bill of lading for household merchandise, put two cars in one container, and bring it aboard. There's nothing else for you to do once we've got all the cars in containers. No questions asked coming or going."

"What about security?"

"No problem. I've got the best security money can buy," Al said with knowing irony. "All you have to worry about is your take, which depends on what we ship."

"What do you mean?"

"Let's say we grab a car worth $40,000 here. Depending on where it goes in the Caribbean, we can sell it for $50,000. Luxury import taxes can be more than the cost of the car. In Argentina, you can double the 50 because there is not domestic production of cars. Naturally, out of that, we have other payments to make, so it's not all pure profit. Like any business, we have our overhead, you know."

"I'll probably have some expenses on my end, too," Tony mentioned offhandedly.

"Of course you will, but there will be more than enough left over," Al assured him. "Another thing. Boston's perfect for what we're doing. It's the only port on the East Coast that does not have drive on facilities. No one's expecting exported used cars. A few here and there are no big deal."

"Who handles the cars once they're in a foreign port? How do you get them through customs?" Tony asked in rapid succession.

"You don't really need to know, but I can tell you this much. Those countries down there are very poor, but there's a lot of money at the top. It's perfect. The people working in customs don't have much, and a few extra dollars is a lot of money to them.

"All they do is read the bill of lading, which will say the container has household goods in it, you know, shoes, consumer electronics, general merchandize, or whatever. That way, we keep the customs tax down without drawing any attention.

"The containers are put on trailers and driven off. It's nice and clean," Al Sanderson explained. "Christ, we could slip the guy his own death warrant, and he would sign," Sanderson said with a laugh.

"What about the missing cars? Won't someone be looking for them at some point?"

"By the time the cars are reported missing, they'll probably be on their way to the Caribbean. No state agency is interested in recovering stolen cars from a foreign country. There are, I guess, no investigative procedures in place. State and federal jurisdiction is let's say, a problem that works in our favor.

"Then there's the manpower shortage, limited resources, the whole thing. The thinking is let the insurance – not the government – take care of the claim. It's that simple."

Tony heard the "we" and "our" part of the bargain very clearly. Al had already decided to include him in the deal. Romano tapped his fingers on the table, finished the beer in his glass, and thought to himself for a moment while dragging on his cigarette.

Stealing cars was new to him, but Tony foresaw no problem doing it. In fact, he was unintentionally well trained for the task by the dealership, routinely – and legally – broke into cars when their owners left the keys inside, and had access to the master keys for many different makes.

Romano had even had some tempting, lucrative offers before to steal used cars for their parts but turned them down because the risk was too high. The many large malls that populated the South Shore were a handy resource. He could store the cars on the back end of the dealership lot where no one would notice or care.

"So what did you think? It's all rum, mangoes, bananas, coconut, and spices in the Caribbean? There's a lot of money down there, Mon," Al said smiling broadly, "and guys who are dying to spend it."

"I like your offer. Why don't we get the fuck out of here and go visit some ladies I know."

"Who's driving?"

"It's your call. I think I'm along for the ride."

On the way to the lady friend's house, Al filled Tony in on how to handle his transaction. "I suggest that you get your cars the day before or even the day they're shipping. Be careful with the God damn plates and dispose of them one at a time in different places."

"Sounds like you have some experience."

"Let's just say I done it once before. That's the trick. You don't do something like this every day, only every now and then. It's better that way. Everything stays quiet. There's nothing too big for someone to notice."

Tony could certainly relate to that strategy.

"Have you done any travelling?" Sanderson inquired.

"Not much. Vegas, Atlantic City. Detroit probably don't count," Tony answered dryly.

"I mean outside the country."

"No, not at all. What's it like?"

"Let me put it this way. Most Americans have no clue how good it's here. You go to the Caribbean or South America, and you can't believe what you see. All them islands are beautiful but extremely poor by our standards. Corruption is a way of life, a means of survival. The begging's so bad on some of the islands it's hurting tourism.

"I've spent some time in Venezuela where everyone has his hands in your pockets, you know. You order a taxi at a hotel and the concierge gets a cut. The taxi takes you to a restaurant or a nice shop, and the driver and the concierge get a cut again. Everyone's on the take, but they don't see it that way. It's cultural and institutionalized.

"There are two groups: those who have everything, and those who have next to nothing. They live in one room shacks in the mountains and with six to eight small kids to support."

"It's interesting, I suppose, but who really gives a fuck?" Tony asked.

"Right. Really. Anyway, most of the Caribbean islands have terrible roads they call white knucklers. They could use a few pricey sport utility vehicles, if you know what I mean."

The two newly formed partners arrived at a small house in Stoughton sometime after twelve that night. The girls were a bit miffed at the late hour, but they liked Tony and let him and his newfound friend in. After some small talk and a few good laughs, Tony paired off with Liz, a thirty-two year old, divorced southern belle he met through the dealership several years ago.

Her bedroom was roomy, nicely decorated and furnished, and very feminine. Liz liked a puffy bed with lots of odd size pillows, delicate perfumes, windows with lacy curtains hanging in swags, boarded wallpaper with tiny, colorful flowers on a dark background, and woodwork painted a glossy white.

Tony gave her the small oriental in front of the four-poster bed. The brass candleholder with a base in the shape of a boat's propeller on the bureau was also a gift, and Liz lit the fresh candle in it before turning off the lights and tightly closing the door.

If she had had her way, Liz would have seen Tony more often because he had been very good to her, but she knew that he preferred work to a deeper relationship. He never gave her money, always nice things she could use around the house. It was the respectful thing to do since he did not want to run the risk of making her feel cheap, and he really liked her as a woman and a friend.

Liz was petite, and her hair was dyed a pretty reddish-brown and kept very short, almost like a man who needs a good haircut. She also had large brown eyes with long lashes, thin eyebrows, a tiny nose, and a small mouth.

Romano called her his little pixie that liked a little Dixie and laughed at his friends' pun on the little Dixie part.

Tony removed his gold jewelry and placed it carefully on the dresser. From behind, Liz helped Tony remove everything else before taking him by the hand, pulling down the covers of the bed, sitting with him on the edge, then gently lying back waiting for Tony to kiss her. As he did, he untied her bathrobe, reached around to her back, and deftly drew Liz towards him.

It had been a while since Liz had been with a man – Tony was the last one – and her first gentle kiss of him quickly became more fervid. He loved the hushed sound she made, rhythmically, as they kissed, sensed her craving for more, but decided to take his time.

Tony undid her pajama top, slowly, subtly, one button at a time, and drew it aside. With the back of his hand, fingers spread, he traced from her neck to her waist and up again without fondling her breasts, breaking the sensuous kiss, or parting their barely touching, swirling tongues.

After a few minutes of pleasurable, anguished teasing, he proceeded past Liz's middle and momentarily pressed the palm of his hand firmly between her legs, continuing until he felt the waistband of her pajamas, which he gently pulled and removed with a minimum of help from Liz.

Her deep moan was muted by Tony's lingering kiss, but he could feel her fingernails digging into his arm. "I can always tell when you really want me," Tony said softly, as he gently stroked her hair with his left hand. "You have this very pretty smile on your face. It's almost invisible, but I can see it even with the candle."

Liz stared at him with hazy eyes and became more inflamed, but it would be some time yet before they both slipped under the covers and Tony into her. Some things in life were worth waiting for and required patience, and lovemaking was one. Being around him or in his arms made her feel, for the first time, like a real woman.

Al had been left on his own and with the minor challenge of explaining his marital status. He and Liz's older roommate got along just fine because they were both direct about their needs and intentions. They were lusting and thrusting before Liz and Tony.

Sanderson and Romano left the house just before two o'clock in the morning, returned to Cohasset Center, and parted company shortly thereafter with a promise to stay in touch.

The next day at work Tony called Dazzie Clarke, his boyhood friend and a trusted member of his distinguished clientele. Exactly one week after their accidental meeting, Tony delivered his product to Al Sanderson as promised.

The entire transaction went as smoothly as he had predicted, and one month later Tony's ship came in.

The money was more than Romano had ever seen all at once, and he used it to fix up his parents' home, which needed a new furnace, roof, insulation, and exterior paint job. Naturally, he paid cash for all the repairs, and – just as naturally – the contractors took it without question.

Over the next two years, Romano and Sanderson did eight other deals, all as successful as the first, but Tony now had a major problem on his hands: what to do with all that cash. Incredibly, he kept it in a green garbage bag under his bed because, quite simply, he had nowhere else to put it.

Tony's search for cars had taken him once in awhile to the back streets of South Boston where housing prices were beginning to fall after the recession started in 1990. There were several good buys to be had, especially in the more industrial area near the Gillette Razor Company corporate headquarters.

Southie had two sections: the upper and lower ends that came with accompanying attitudes. While the first extended, roughly, from Dorchester Street along Broadway, eastward to City Point, the latter demarcation went from the same streets, westward to Broadway Station.

Realtors favored the newer designations – East and West Side – to the older and grouped First, Second, and Third Streets of the lower end, West Side, into a new subdivision known as "City Side" because of its physical proximity to Boston. Townies sneered at the name.

Romano had no problem putting down the minimum required for a triple-decker on West Third Street in St. Vincent's Parish. His plan was to fix up the three apartments with the money he had made on the auto exporting adventure and turn them into condos, which he could rent until the real estate market got better.

Tony hired all the subs directly rather than using a general contractor because he knew he could save money. More importantly, Romano did not want to meet a general contractor's payment schedule, which would call for large payments most people would not make in cash. His new acquisition may have been in the lower end of South Boston – City Side – but even there one could not escape attention.

Once again, he paid cash for all the work, and, once again, the contractors took it with no questions asked. They were just as willing to set aside the old fashioned, metal window counterbalances, which he used to weight his lobster traps, and didn't mind the increasingly frequent visits by Dazzie Clarke who had his own money and reasons for being at the site.

Clarke, like Romano, had the unmistakable look of someone who had grown up hard or in the city. Hull was much like South Boston in that respect, a place unto itself with many of its residents struggling to keep everything all together.

Dazzie fit right in but had a much more severe – almost perverse – look about him than Tony did. The contractors liked Daz because they thought he was a funny bastard. One day he complained to them about his own boss. "I'll tell you how much of a cheap prick this guy is. The fucking guy shits every other day to save money on toilet paper. I'm telling you the fucking truth."

The subs soon directed Daz to certain bars on East and West Broadway where he could buy more than a beer and a good time.

Tony was now one year past The Big Three O and a little bit too old in his mind to be living with his parents. He purchased and financed in the traditional way a one bedroom, water view condo at Weymouthport, a complex that had Webb State Park as a front yard and the Back River in the rear. From his apartment, he could see the Hingham commuter boat pulling out or returning.

Romano also bought furniture for his condo at an expensive, higher end store in Weymouth and relied on Liz's good taste and sense to make the apartment comfortable, functional, and attractive. His mother would miss her good boy but not his money because Romano continued to pay rent and help out even though he was no longer living there.

All Tony asked was that the door to his room remain locked. Without his help, his parents would have trouble getting by, and they thought it best not to inquire.

Tony liked his job at the dealership; especially since his side dealings had proven to be so lucrative. "Here I am," he would think to himself, "this little guy who doesn't know shit, and I'm worth over half a million on paper." Not quite, but getting there.

The guiding principle in Tony Romano's life was that you could never have enough money, and he was open to more opportunities. He didn't have to wait very long.

"Tony, Al Sanderson. Any chance we can meet later at the Venetian?"
"Yeah. What time?"
"Let's say seven o'clock."
"Done. See you then."

The Venetian in Jackson Square was a well-established Weymouth eatery that specialized in great food at good prices. Although there was a regular clientele and most patrons knew or recognized each other, new faces came in all the time.

Seven o'clock on a Thursday night meant a long wait and a drink or two at the bar. Al had arrived early and put his name in for a booth in the smoking section, which was in the left rear corner near the kitchen and noisy swinging doors.

Al was sitting on a stool sipping a beer and watching the news on the television behind the bar when Romano arrived a bit before seven. Tony barely had time to order his beer when Al's name was called for a booth.

Once seated, they ordered, and quickly got down to business.

"I have a once in a lifetime opportunity I thought you would be interested in," Al began.

"Yeah. I'm listening."

"And when I say once in a lifetime, I mean exactly that. This deal will never happen again, Tony, ever."

"I get the picture, but I'm missing some details."

"You put up $200 grand, which is different, I know."

"I take it it's not cars this time."

"Nope. No cars this time. Something else. Imports."

"Imports. Ah huh."

"Imports for which I'll need your lobster traps."

"My lobster traps. I think I get your drift. What kind of time we looking at?"

"Not this run, although it's clean. The one after. We'll need some room to set things up. Can you handle it?"

"The two hundred I can do with a little time. I have a building in Southie I can re-mortgage. Funny, I was planning on doing it anyway. The rates are getting better. I follow these things now that I'm a landlord."

"I don't know, Tony. I'm getting worried about you. You're becoming a fucking capitalist," Al chided playfully.

"And you, sir, are becoming a good judge of character. I've gone from landlord to investor since I met you."

They both had a good laugh and ordered another round of beers before digging into their meals.

"You have to look at it as a business, nothing else. I've been working on this thing for a long time. See, the market for coke's saturated, and the Columbians are pushing heroin because they have, well, you know, the infrastructure already in place.

"Now, heroin has a bad rep, people dying, AIDS, addiction, all that. So the word goes out that you can smoke or line it, which is safer, and, they say, not addicting. I think that's bullshit, but just the kind of thing good marketing can do.

"Anyway, a nickel bag on the street is worth $20 today and is forty percent pure. If a guy has a $200 a day coke habit, we can cut it by eighty percent."

"What do you mean? What's a nickel bag?" Tony pressed, understanding money but not economics.

"Just a term. It used to mean five dollars for a one-dose bag. Back then, you would get only five percent heroin, but now it's forty percent."

"How come?"

"With all the shit they used to cut it, it wouldn't burn, so you couldn't smoke it. With the price of coke falling, the producers can now move heroin and make a huge profit. We're looking at $200,000 a kilo wholesale, dockside. We're paying $50,000."

"Why now? Why didn't they do it before?"

"I'm told they didn't have the facilities or chemists and that the cocaine market was just too good to change. You know, it was their cash cow. The people I'm in touch with have a Syrian chemist working for them with the right expertise. They are now in the early stages of production and want to break into the heroin market and diversify. So, they're testing the waters. That's why this one deal will never come along again."

Tony shook his head. "Al, you really are unbelievable."

Three months later at three o'clock on a Sunday morning in early April, a five hundred and fifty foot-long container ship with an eighty-foot beam and twenty-eight feet of fully loaded draft travelling eastbound at eighteen knots approached the BB Buoy off New Bedford, Massachusetts. A call to the Army Corps of Engineers was made on Marine Channel thirteen for a pilot to board the vessel to pass through the Cape Cod Canal. The tide was almost high.

Once aboard, the pilot radioed back the name of the ship, its deep draft, regular net tonnage, the flag under which the vessel was flying, the general cargo being carried, its last port of call, and its next, Boston. The ship entered the canal, continued at ten miles per hour, passed under the Bourne and Sagamore Bridges, and dropped the pilot off at the CC Buoy before heading into the waters of Cape Cod Bay on a northerly course towards Boston.

The vessel, no longer on radar, slowed down about three nautical miles offshore near the Town of Duxbury, temporarily turned off its deck and running lights, and passed Scituate and Cohasset. A short time thereafter, the ship turned its lights back on and headed for the B Buoy, which was eight miles off Nantasket Beach in Hull. Knowing the ship's ETA – estimated time of arrival – the local agent in the Port of Boston had previously arranged to have another pilot board the vessel to navigate the harbor.

That same morning about half an hour before sunrise Tony boarded his lobster boat and headed out Cohasset Harbor – which had become so heavily silted that navigation at low tide was becoming nearly impossible – towards the shallow and rocky waters beyond.

The weather this morning was unseasonably warm, and the ocean as smooth as glass. Romano respected the sea and knew it could turn on you quickly without warning. Many, many ships had gone down over the years in the rocky shoals off Scituate and Cohasset, and the entire coastal area of Massachusetts Bay had once been considered amongst the most treacherous waters on the Atlantic Coast.

He was wearing thermal underwear, jeans, a sweater, windbreaker, and hat, a rubber apron, and knee high rubber boots.

Tony's cousin, Joey, had been using the boat and had previously set out sixteen ten-pot trawls, for a total of one hundred and sixty traps in all. Tony wasn't looking for Joey's set; he was after one trawl of his own.

His lobster boat, the Novi, had a flat, wide-open stern where the traps were launched. Its rear was low to the water and without much freeboard, a distinct advantage because the traps were easier to haul or launch. The boat's draft was not much more than three to four feet, which allowed it to operate safely in shallow waters.

Tony loved the sea and lobstering. Countless times he went out alone, trailed his buoy in the water, dropped the first baited trap, and watched the remaining nine slide off the transom every fifty feet, until the second buoy of the haul slipped into the sea. Then he would set the second haul, the third, fourth, next, and last.

He would carry two pairs of rubber gloves to protect himself from bait that could become poisonous from sitting in brine or any sea urchins, crabs, dog fish, cod, or sculpin – a spiny and slimy trash fish – that would periodically get caught in his traps. The second set of gloves he left on the manifold of the engine to keep them warm in cold weather.

Like all lobstermen, Tony would set his traps according to a compass heading South to North in order to avoid crisscrossing another man's gear on the seabed.

He paid attention to safety and regulations and was careful not to become entangled in the three-eighths inch or quarter inch rope, called pot warp that connected a haul of traps and its two distinguishable buoys. Unlike nylon, the rope didn't stretch and would sink to the bottom.

Romano had heard more than one story about guys getting caught in lines and being pulled to the depths by several hundred pounds of gear. Lobstering could be a dangerous business, and it was definitely not the romantic line of work pictured by the seascapes or postcards.

THE INDEPENDENT CONTRACTOR

About four miles out, he saw his buoy, slowed down, and grabbed it with a boat hook. He then brought the buoy onto the boat, put one end of the line over the pulley of the starboard side davit, which was out over the side of the boat, spun the other end several times around a drum-like device attached to the engine, engaged it, and started hauling the first trap up from the bottom.

When the trap reached the pulley, Tony reverse spun with his left hand the rope on the drum, and with his right grabbed the trap to lower it into the boat. Under normal circumstances, Tony would then haul the second trap according to the same procedure as the first, which is emptied and re-baited while the second is being hauled up.

The first trap would be set aside near the cabin, the second in front of it, and so on. The traps in the haul would be reset in reverse order, first on, last off. A man working alone could usually set one trap in two to three minutes, depending on a number of factors, like weather, sea conditions, time of the year, etc.

Meantime, the lobster would be checked for size. Keepers' claws were banded, and the animal stored in an aerated tank of seawater. Females with eggs – seeders – and undersize lobster would be thrown overboard.

Today was not a normal day, and Tony was not hauling lobsters. He removed from the trap the first of three, water tight, one-kilo packages, which he stored in the tank. He moved quickly through the haul and headed inland with the traps on board.

He soon found a haul that Joey had set, recovered and reset it, and moved on to two more. Of the thirty traps he hauled, he took fourteen lobsters, which would be considered a pretty good catch – on a percentage basis – any day of the week.

Before he headed back to Cohasset Harbor, Tony placed on the bottom of light weight, insulated containers several layers of the water tight packages, and on top of them rags wetted with salt water. Next came two lobsters at the very top, covered by another layer of rags. Tony could have used seaweed as cover, but he did not have time to collect it.

When he reached the pier by the park, Romano transported the containers from the lobster boat to an unmarked mini van he had borrowed from the dealership. No one on the pier asked him any questions about the catch because lobstermen were traditionally secretive about what they had caught and where. His cousin, Joey, showed up with coffee and took the boat out again to re-bait and set Tony's haul closer to shore. It was nearly eight and no longer dark out.

Romano then drove a short distance to Cohasset Center where he picked up Sanderson after Al had made a phone call from a pay booth. The two then drove to a garage in Boston's South End, making excellent time because there was almost no traffic on the Southeast Expressway. They waited until another van with two guys in it drove up and parked next to them as had been arranged.

"You got my lobsters?"

"Yup. You got the money?"

"Yup. Let's see the lobsters."

Sanderson then opened the side of the mini van, took the lid off one of the containers, removed the rag, and picked up and shook a lobster for everyone to see.

The buyer removed a second layer of rags, found what he was looking for, and checked out the product, which was pure heroin. "Seems ok. Your money is on the back seat of my van."

Tony helped the two men move the lobsters from his mini van to theirs while Sanderson transferred the money. "These guys are fresh out of the water and should keep for awhile. Enjoy the feast," Tony said. "Right," one of the two called back.

Sanderson returned to the mini van with a medium size suitcase, which he did not open again until they were on the Southeast Expressway heading towards Weymouth. "Better do a heat ditch at the Furnace Brook Parkway exit, just in case," Sanderson advised Tony.

Satisfied that they were not being followed, Al undid the locks, raised one side of the suitcase enough for Tony to see, and quickly closed it. Tony and Al both looked at each other – wide eyed – and shrieked with wild delight over the millions in the suitcase.

They were giddy and drunk with excitement and laughed all the way to Tony's condominium at Weymouthport.

There they split up the money and their partnership. Each would go his own separate way and get out before drawing attention, unlike a professional whose greed would eventually be his undoing. Sanderson put his share of the money back into the suitcase, while Tony put his in a green garbage bag, which he placed under his bed, a favorite hiding place.

"It's been fun knowing you, partner," Tony said while shaking Al's hand. "Now you go out and get that dealership you've been talking about," Sanderson said in return. "And take good care of yourself."

"Same here."

When Tony closed and locked the door behind Sanderson, he ended a strange but exciting chapter in his life. Once again, he had a money problem, one much larger than before. Who would ever believe that he was sleeping over a garbage bag containing two million dollars? No one, and for that very reason the money was safe for now.

It was all so easy, maybe too much so, but that was the way it went. He was no dumb fuck after all. Hey! Shit happens, even to guys like himself.

Tony cast a lean and hungry look at South Boston again. Time for another purchase, but on the upper end, maybe a six-unit house. Romano found one on East 6th, St. Brigid's Parish, bought it, and fixed it up in the same manner as before. He was taking a chance that his money wouldn't be noticed in the town where everyone knows your name and what you had for supper last night.

By early 1993 Tony had his dealership, which fell into his lap much like the export – import deal. A district representative of a major, luxury car manufacturer had visited the dealership not knowing the owner was out. He spoke to Tony instead, and the two went out to lunch that day to talk some more. Romano was a rare breed in the automobile industry because he knew the business and also had money. Typically, a guy with the money threw in with one who knew the business to buy a dealership jointly. Tony was both.

The deal was struck, and on the day the papers were signed, Tony Romano showed up at his attorney's office in Boston carrying under his arm a brown paper bag containing $500,000, which he gave to his attorney. The lawyer, in turn, produced a certified check for that amount in the name of the manufacturer.

The rest of the deal was financed, and the cash was placed the same day in the attorney's escrow account in a downtown bank. As required by federal law for any cash amount over $10,000 or a suspicion of money laundering, a CTR – currency transaction report – was issued by the bank and left on file where it drew no attention because the deposit was only one of many similar types the attorney or his firm had made over the years.

Tony was now a legitimate businessman whose dream of owning a dealership had come true.

When Romano turned from Jerusalem Road onto Atlantic Avenue, he suddenly realized that he had been daydreaming. He slowed down to take a sharp right onto a bridge that crossed over an inlet.

A short distance from the bridge was his street, which was really a long, private, pea stone driveway that led to a magnificent, L-shaped contemporary on a cliff overlooking the ocean. Much of the original house was gone, but not so much as to create a problem with conservation, the septic system, or state regulations.

As he pulled into the driveway, Romano stopped to take his mail out of the street-side mailbox and placed it on the passenger seat before continuing.

Tony got out of his car, inspected the driveway for additional nails, found none, then let himself into the house, reset the security alarm, and went directly to a locked room next to the kitchen.

Romano sorted out his mail and tossed into a box several statements – all from different banks – he did not bother to open. His home office was very neat and contained a large desk for his computer, printer, phone, and files. He also had a fireproof safe built into the cabinets and bookshelves behind the desk.

While he was working, Tony could gaze out on the Atlantic in all its unpredictable beauty. It could be mesmerizing.

Everything had worked out better than anyone could ever expect. When the recession ended, Romano's investments in South Boston really paid off because housing values skyrocketed along with the rents, which were no longer under rent control. In fact, Southie had become one of the hottest markets in the city and was in the cross hairs of future economic development that threatened to change its way of life.

His nine condos were worth $200,000 each at minimum.

Romano had parents that were still healthy, money, a business, valuable income property, an expensive house in an exclusive neighborhood, friends, and a woman who loved him, all pretty much in that order. Not bad.

The business, rental property, and house were real assets that could be sold and, along with any liquid assets, constituted his sizeable and appreciating estate.

Tony then turned on his personal computer to do his banking electronically in the privacy and security of his home. He printed out some invoices to bill the dealership for goods or services that were never received or performed and would later place them in the files at work.

The invoices had been folded carefully, giving them the appearance of having been sent through the mail. Several were printed on different paper, and all appeared to be very legitimate, right down to the cent. He then invoiced the dealership and electronically paid the bogus companies.

There was nothing peculiar about his habits at work because he was on and off the computer system all the time or looking into the files.

He also knew that Gayle would simply go about her work and not ask any questions. Although she also had access to the computer system and the accounting package, she did not know everything about the dealership. She had limited access to the books and never saw a balance sheet, profit and loss statement, or the paid invoices. She was a data entry clerk when it came to that aspect of the business. Her small, glassed in office was next to Romano's, which she was in and out of it just as much as her own.

Tony was worried that spreading equal payments evenly over all the accounts at the same time wouldn't look good, so he front-loaded them instead. The older the account, the more money it contained. It was a practical matter, and Romano was very much a practical man.

The amount transferred wasn't much by Romano's recent standards – about $600 a week – but it did add up over time. As a percentage of the millions coming into the company annually, it was nothing. He was careful not to round up the amounts paid and knew from his attorney that banks routinely monitored accounts for suspicious activity. Patterns were detectable.

He had set up checking accounts at twelve separate, small banks to distribute "the pocket change" and religiously emptied out in person a different one each month. In that way, no teller was likely to recognize his face when he came in for his once-a-year cash withdrawal.

Because no single account ever exceeded $10,000 or contained less than $100, he thought it would be a waste of time to balance his bank statements. He knew how much he had – over $50,000 – and kept it all in his head. All he had to do was check his balance before withdrawing.

Payday was a few clicks away and a marvel of simplicity. Like most people with personal computers, he used the same password – his initials and month and year of his birthday – for everything so that he would not have to remember it.

Romano laughed at the thought of stealing from himself and the government. The respectable life was, after all, dull and not adventurous, and he got a real kick out a little larceny every now and then. He had been at it for several years.

This technology stuff was really something almost magical. He could connect to his office computer to check on orders, inventory, bonuses, or whatever, right from his home office. It was just like being there but without the distractions.

Tony looked around his office and wondered for a moment what had ever happened to Kevin Sweeney, that guy who completely designed, specified, and coordinated the remodeling of his house eighteen months ago and had helped him set up his home office.

Was it possible Kevin and Al Sanderson knew each other? They were both in Caracas around the same time or could have crossed paths in Barbados or St. Maarten. Tony remembered the stories each had told him about the wonders and woes of the Caribbean, and they appeared to be remarkably similar.

"No way. Sweeney was too much of a straight arrow. A real upstanding guy. A good guy and a hard worker. You have to give him credit. He helped me get an incredible house!" he said to himself. "Too bad about the framer. Ah, fuck. It was only business."

Chapter 2

"You no good, goddamn, son of a bitch bastard," the handsome, senior executive growled at no one in particular as he looked down at the flat tire on the driver's side of his shiny, new, black BMW, which had been purchased in cash at Tony Romano's dealership. He spoke slowly enough for a stone engraver to take notes.

Disgusted, he slammed the car door and went back into the house to call a tow company to come and fix the flat. Normally, he would have changed the tire himself because he liked working on cars or with tools, but he didn't have time today and was supposed to be at work before eight to prepare for an important corporate presentation later that afternoon.

He reasoned that by the time he had changed his clothes and taken out his tools he could have had a tow company do the work. Meanwhile, he could go over his presentation once more at home and upload it from his laptop to his boss at work.

The boss would understand. No big deal. What the hell, such things happen to everybody every day. Besides, it was only five forty-five, and he wouldn't be all that late, if the traffic on the infamous Southeast Expressway going into Boston held up.

The early morning was cool and gave the first hint of the New England Winter that was soon to come, and the landscape was no longer ablaze with the magnificent colors of autumn that Monday of the first week in November 1998. Of all the days to have a problem – not a big one to be sure, but an irritating one – today had to be it.

The moist air coming in from the Atlantic made it seem even colder in this beautiful, seaside community with its many private and majestic homes overlooking the ocean. The Town of Hingham, which was a mere eighteen miles south of Boston, had once been a boat building, fishing, and farming community but had long since abandoned those commercial traditions to the new money professionals who worked mainly in Boston.

Many of them, it was rumored on the South Shore, scoured nearby eighteenth century graveyards in search of last names to use as first names for their male children.

Still, Hingham was the perfect place for the irritated executive whose tire was flat this morning. He raced into the house, grabbed the phone book from a shelf over the built in desk that was installed with the cherry cabinets when he and his wife did over their kitchen several months ago, and called a tow company.

"Central." A harsh female voice bellowed after a few rings. "Can I help you?" she asked in a monotone.

"Hi, I'm calling from Hingham. My car's got a flat, and I need to get it fixed. Can you help?" If you were calling from Hingham, it was supposed to mean something.

"Depends."

"Depends?" he said, his voice rising. "On what?"

"Well, on how backed up we are, sir, and where you live," she said – with the emphasis on "sir."

"Listen, it's only a goddamn flat, and I've got a spare. I need a tire change, not a fucking tow."

"Hey! Cool it. I don't have to listen to that."

"Look, I'm sorry. I'm a bit pissed off. It's not you."

"Alright. Just calm down. It's early. Where do you live?"

"Are you familiar with the Historic District past the South Shore Country Club?"

"Yes, I am," the voice answered indifferently.

"Well, we're the first left, after the intersection with the tracks, heading towards the harbor. Number 18. The BMW's in the driveway."

"Ok. I can send a truck down, but it won't be right away."

"When will it be? I've got to get to work. I'm really in a hurry. I'll even pay extra."

"I understand, sir, but we can't get there for at least half an hour. Besides, we don't charge extra for good service. Maybe we should," she said with a good laugh.

He could feel his face flush. These goddamn service people have you over a fucking barrel and simply don't give a shit, but there's nothing you can do. "Yeah, right," he said in a way to let her know he didn't like the joke. "Do you take credit cards?"

"Yes, we do," she said with the same perfect balance between courtesy and contempt.

"Great. Do I give you the number now or when you get here?"

"Either way."

"Why don't I give it to you now? That way you'll have it."

After he gave her the credit card number and expiration date, he listened carefully as she read it back.

"You got it. We're all set," he said. "I'll see you when you get here."

"Have a nice day." Click.

"You fucking bitch! Have a nice day! Jesus! Hope she chokes on her coffee and cigarettes. Have a nice day. Blah, blah, blah."

About an hour and a half later, a tow truck pulled into the driveway. A short, heavy set guy wearing backwards a Red Sox baseball cap and sporting a thick beard and long hair tied in a pony tail bounded out of the truck, leaving the engine running. He noticed the flat tire.

The driver, Tony Romano's best friend, Dazzie Clark, walked up to the door of the breezeway and with a stubby finger poked the doorbell. A moment later, a svelte, very attractive woman, impeccably dressed in a dark blue tailored suit, opened the door.

"Hi," she said pleasantly. "Can I help you?"

"You drive the BMW?"

"Me? No, my husband does. Just a minute. I'll get him."

"Jay," she called out, "it's for you. The truck is here."

"Great, I'll be right there," Jay said from the family room off the kitchen.

Jay Parker's wife, Lauren, noticed that the driver standing outside was blowing on his hands to keep them warm. "Would you like to come inside?" she asked politely.

"Sure, thanks. Getting colder out," Clark said as he took one last deep drag on his cigarette, flicked the butt onto the driveway, and then stepped into the mudroom.

"Nice place you've got. Great kitchen."

"We love it, too. We had the kitchen redone this spring and added the family room and bath. We had a lot of work done."

"Oh, yeah? Who was the contractor?"

As she was about to answer, Jay appeared at the entryway of the mudroom. "Hi. I'm Jay. Would you mind taking the spare out of the trunk? I'm just finishing up some work and will be with you in a minute."

"Sure, no problem," Dazzie said flatly as he took the car keys from Jay and headed outside.

Jay returned to the family room, sipped on his second cup of coffee, checked his E-mail, and uploaded to his office the revised presentation and some notes. It was going to be a big day for him, and he knew it.

Lauren went into the new bathroom to put on her lipstick and comb her hair for the last time before heading off to catch the commuter boat to her job at a software startup located in a warehouse in South Boston. The daily trip had become something of a social event, and nearly all the passengers knew each other by name.

She was heading in late this day and told Jay that she had to register the children for the after school enrichment program. Judging from the inside of the house, no one would have guessed that children – three of them – lived there at all because it was so neat and tidy.

"What time will you be coming home tonight?" Lauren asked Jay.

"I really don't know. I may go out with some people from work after the presentation. I'll call you."

Their children, twin girls and a boy who was the youngest and a second grader, were finishing breakfast at the angled island that separated the family room from the kitchen.

The island was a big hit with them, especially when their mom was baking cookies. They would twist on the rotating stools, help mix, measure, lick the bowl or spoons clean, or watch, their little faces propped on both elbows and waiting for the first batch of chocolate chip cookies to come out of the new, built in double oven.

From where they were sitting, the children also had a perfect view of the custom-built entertainment center in the family room. Their parents, however, did not allow them to watch TV often and had very strict rules about it. School came first.

The family room was in the rear of the house off the kitchen, had a cathedral ceiling with four remote controlled skylites, a dozen recessed lights, indirect lighting on the ceiling, and the obligatory floor to ceiling field stone fireplace. French doors adjoined a multi-level deck that lead to a fully landscaped brick courtyard and in-ground kidney shaped pool. To open up the area, the contractor had installed a steel beam, which had been configured by a female structural engineer, a rarity in the construction industry.

She and Lauren had really hit it off mainly because they were both professional women with young children. The engineer had been divorced recently but was making it on her own with a resolve and spirit Lauren admired.

Almost as if on cue, the children slid off their stools and went into the family room to kiss their father goodbye. Lauren picked up after them, wiped down the polished granite counter, and neatly folded the dishcloth before hanging it on the inside door of the cabinet under the double bowl sink.

"Hey! Hey! Watch out for the computer. You'll trip or break it," he said as they fluttered about like moths in a mitten.

"Come on, kids, or you'll be late for school," their mother called from the mudroom.

"See you later, alligator," the boy said to his father.

"Make it soon; you big baboon," his dad answered. The children giggled at what was now becoming a delightful tradition: rhyming good-byes from their father.

"Bye, Dad."

"Bye. Do well in school now. I don't want to see any bad grades. Hugs and kisses." Lauren then kissed her husband goodbye and offered him good luck on his presentation. "Thanks," he responded. "I should do fine."

The children were standing about in the mudroom putting on their outer clothes. Each had a separate cabinet – there were five in all – to hold their lunch boxes, books, backpacks, small playthings, or whatever. It was an idea the contractor suggested to make use of a space that would have been otherwise wasted.

They left in the family's new Land Cruiser, which the children loved. Occasionally, Lauren drove the kids to school in order to have a few extra minutes with them before starting her day.

The public school system had an excellent reputation, which was one more reason why property values in the community were so high. She and Jay were very pleased with what they had seen so far.

Lauren had once been a stay at home mom after the birth of her twins, Brianna and Danielle. She loved being home with her daughters, but the routine of endless feeding, diaper and clothes changing, and house cleaning soon bored her.

The other young mothers she met did, too, with their constant complaining about their husbands or mindless discussions about the color, content, and texture of their infants' bowel movements. With so little time to herself, Lauren had difficulty continuing the small accounting business she had started for extra income and outside stimulation. She missed the gym and hated what nature was doing to her body without her thrice-weekly – Monday through Friday – workouts.

After three years of being super mom and having Stephen, she returned to her career and a new job with a start up software company in the City of Waltham, which was west of Boston off Route 128. She also got back to the gym and looked great.

The bell soon rang, and Dazzie stepped inside the mudroom. "Hello. Hello, sir. Your car's ready," his voice echoed.

Jay got up from his chair in the family room and headed towards the door. "Hi. That was fast. How much do I owe you?"

"Ah, let's see. That's forty-five dollars."

"Whoa! What? I'm in the wrong business. Forty-five dollars for fifteen minutes? You've got to be kidding. That's fucking theft."

"Hey, I don't set the rates," Clark protested, holding up the palms of his hands and shrugging his shoulders.

"Where did you leave the tire?"

"In the trunk. Has a roofing nail in it."

"A nail? Where the hell did a roofing nail come from?"

"I don't know. Must have been from when you did the house. Decent job, by the way."

"Yeah. We had a guy from Weymouth do it. His name is Kevin Sweeney. He's real good, but we had some issues. The usual."

"Never heard of him."

"Really? Everybody around here uses him."

Jay then reached into his left breast pocket for his burgundy leather billfold and pulled out his personal credit card, oddly enough, the only one he carried at the time.

Clark paused for an awkward moment and said he couldn't take the card.

"Why not?" Jay demanded.

"Beats me. Something about the card being maxed."

"Maxed! That card's not maxed. Something's screwed up. Do you take checks?" Jay asked, his voice rising along with his frustration.

"No, sir. Cash or credit."

"Shit! All right. All right, I'll pay you cash then. I can hit an ATM on the way to work."

Dazzie took the cash Jay handed him and stuffed the bills in his pants pocket without counting them. "Need a receipt?"

"No, don't bother. You should have told me about the card before you did the work."

"Hey, it's no difference to me. Sorry."

"Yeah. Bye."

Driving off, Dazzie wondered aloud, "Where the fuck do these people get their money? It's really hard to believe."

Jay wandered around the house to check things out before leaving and snapped his fingers while crooning, "Those fingers in my hair. That sly, familiar stare, that strips my conscience bare, it's witchcraft," in a passable imitation of Sinatra, his favorite singer.

He found his keys were right where he had left them on the built in desk in the kitchen. That arrangement – another very good one suggested by the contractor – had resolved at least one problem Jay had had with Lauren: her nasty habit of putting his personal things where she wanted them to be.

Parker then checked himself out in the oval mirror hanging in the mudroom and liked what he saw. Double breasted, light gray suit looks good; colorful tie knotted perfectly in a Windsor and hanging slightly below the belt; thick, black, wavy hair combed back without a path, a hint of gray at the temples. "Here's looking at you, kid," he said with a lisp and a laugh.

THE INDEPENDENT CONTRACTOR

Jay took his tan London Fog coat out of the mudroom closet. After buttoning up, he put on his hat – a narrow brimmed Stetson with a gray band and small red feather – that was still being made and had been given to him by his father, an alcoholic who no longer drank.

Not many guys had the balls to wear such a hat, but Jay could and did so proudly. He picked up his brief case, set the security system, and dashed out the door towards his car, which was parked in front of the left bay of the two-car garage.

Things were back on track. It was still early, around seven-forty, and he wouldn't be all that late driving into work. Depending on traffic and road conditions, the trip could be an hour or more, but no one could tell because The Big Dig was well underway in Boston.

The ATM was on a main road along the way, so Parker stopped for a cash withdrawal and then headed for his morning coffee and bagel at a drive in kiosk in Weymouth, the next town over from Hingham.

When his order came up, Jay got his frequent customer ticket stamped, paid, and left on the stainless steel counter his eleven cents change from the two dollar bills he gave the waitress. He smiled; his next coffee would be free.

The traffic on the Southeast Expressway was moving, and Parker made near record time going through Braintree, Quincy, and Milton before slowing down after *The Boston Globe* plant on Morrissey Boulevard in Dorchester.

Parker flipped open his cell phone to call work and let his secretary know he was on his way but stuck in traffic. When the call did not go through, he tossed the phone on the passenger seat where he had placed his briefcase.

Jay liked listening to the NPR station on his radio, which offered excellent news coverage and heavy classical music. He flipped between that station and a second that played more often his favorite composers: Mozart, Beethoven, Vilvaldi, Puccini, and Bach.

From his frequent day trips to New York City, Jay had discovered from the cabbies the soothing properties of classical music. They were trained to listen to it, one told him.

Weird how the contractor who had worked at his house listened to classical music, too. Interesting guy, that one. A bit unusual, but interesting nonetheless.

Jay hated being late for anything or unprepared. He was already running about an hour behind his plan and could easily see that he might not get into work by nine-fifteen. No problem; everyone there would know from his earlier e-mail – sent before he left the house – what the situation was.

When Jay and Lauren moved from Connecticut to the Boston area, they were happy that they had made the right decision. Sure, they had heard about the traffic jams, but what major city didn't have them?

Boston was a fabulous, first class city. It had great restaurants, Hanover Street in the North End – famous for its Italian food and culture – The Boston Public Library, the Museum of Fine Arts, the theater district, heart throb Keith Lockhart conducting the Pops at the Hatch Shell on the Esplanade every Fourth of July, the refurbished Frog Pond on Boston Common, the Swan Boats in Boston Garden, Fenway Park, Bunker and Beacon Hill, the U.S. Constitution, Bulfinch, Olmstead, The Freedom Trail, the Aquarium, the Science Museum, internationally renowned medical and financial centers, Fanueil Hall, Quincy Marketplace, the harbor, Newbury Street in the Back Bay, the world's highest concentration of schools of higher learning, and history everywhere. There was something for everyone.

It was a great and exciting place, but they preferred their house in the suburbs with its convenient location and close proximity to Cape Cod. They also knew that Boston had its underside, too: crime, dirt, noise, congestion, and segregated neighborhoods.

They hadn't heard much back then about the planned Big Dig, which would soon become "the largest, most complex and technologically challenging highway project ever attempted in American history," as the billing proclaimed. City planners had decided to suppress the old, ugly, and decaying Central Artery, which had divided the city along the waterfront for forty years.

The original cost of construction – somewhere around two billion dollars – was now over seven times as much. A river of federal and state dollars was flowing into the city, and there was plenty of work for the contractors and job security most had never seen.

Republican Jay knew first hand about cost overruns when he and Lauren remodeled their house. Every time they turned around, it was something else, and the contractor's suggestions – as good as they were and appreciated then – added more to the cost projections. Still, they had wanted the extras and could easily afford them.

Kevin Sweeney wasn't the sole reason for the changes. Both Jay and Lauren had had trouble visualizing from the blueprints what the space was going to look like. Once the walls were up and things in place, they could actually see how the room was going to turn out. Then the opportunities began, as did some communication problems between Jay and Lauren.

The Big Dig was not the only large-scale project that pulsed the area. Across Boston Harbor in Winthrop sat an enormous, new facility with its single most recognizable feature's being twelve huge, egg shaped sewerage sludge digesters that readied waste for transport and conversion to a product known as Bay State Fertilizer. The Boston Harbor Cleanup was the first time in the country's history that such a large public project was funded directly by private citizens: the politicians had actually failed to get to Washington in time to file for federal assistance. Some feared that the cost of being connected to the system would soon equal property taxes.

Between the cleanup and artery suppression, the best and brightest construction, design, and engineering minds in the world were assembled in Boston.

As Jay passed The Big Dig's huge steel cranes and their cables near South Station, they seemed to him like masts and rigging on wooden ships, a poetic idea he toyed with for the next several minutes. He was pleased that the city would name a new harbor tunnel after the Hall of Fame baseball player, Ted Williams, instead of a politician.

Nearing his exit at South Station, Jay changed lanes, stopped at the lights at the end of the ramp, and reached for his cell phone on the passenger seat.

"Hi, Cindy, it's Jay. I'm right at Kneeland Street and should be there within the next twenty minutes.

"Fine," Cindy said. "See you when you get here."

When the light turned green, Jay headed up the street towards the Financial District and pulled into a parking garage. On the third floor, his reserved space was waiting for him, a nice perk that came with the title of Vice President of Marketing.

After a short ride down in the garage elevator and walk across the street, he landed in the lobby of his employer who occupied most of the modern high rise and zipped to the top floor.

"Hi, Jay. Where've you been?" the office receptionist inquired. "Eleanor's waiting for you in the conference room."

"Thanks. Is Andrea with her?"

"I think so. They seemed like they were going over your presentation."

"Great. I'm late," he thought, "but no one's been held up."

"Morning. Hey, what's up?" Jay said more than once as he worked his way towards his office, briefcase in hand.

Immediately, Cindy popped into the doorway. "Better get into the conference room quick. They've been waiting for you."

"No problem. I'll be there in a minute. Any fresh coffee on?"

"I'll get it for you. Anything else you'll need?"

"No. I'm all set," Jay answered as he hung up his coat and hat in his office wardrobe. He reached over his desk, picked up a pink, hand written message on the leather bound blotter, frowned, and put it down.

With no opportunity to enjoy the harbor view, Jay headed for the conference room at the end of the corridor and breezed into the meeting. "Good morning, good morning," he said cheerfully. "Got my presentation, I see."

"Well, no, Jay. We didn't." What's going on? This is not like you."

"You didn't get my presentation?" he asked incredulously. "I uploaded it to you about seven-fifteen this morning. Are you sure? Did you check your e-mail?"

"Yes, I'm positive I never received it," said Eleanor, his boss and president of the world-class investment firm. "In fact, the only thing that came in from you was the note you sent to Andrea. We knew you were going to be late."

Suddenly, Jay went pale and could feel the sweat on the palms of his hands. The notes he had sent to Andrea? He hadn't sent her any notes; they were for Eleanor, her eyes only. No wonder Andrea Wilson was shooting daggers at Jay. She was sitting upright near the end of the oval table, arms folded, legs crossed, wagging a high heal on her toe, and remaining deadly silent. He had recommended that she should be moved to a different area of the company, and now she knew.

Jay kept his cool, and neither Eleanor nor Andrea noticed his discomfort. In fact, Jay liked being the center of calm in a bad storm, much as he had done when he weathered his drunken father's thunderous tirades and vicious beatings as a child living in Pittsburgh.

Parker's beautiful home in Hingham was a far cry from the tool shed he converted into a bedroom to stay out of Jay Parker Sr.'s way. There, at least, Junior could get a good night's sleep without having to listen to his father's heavy shoes dragging slowly down the long hall of their apartment or his father's fingernails scraping against the hallway wallpaper to steady himself, sometimes with one hand, sometimes two.

No matter how secure he felt in the tool shed, Jay could not escape the late night screams of his mother or little sister, especially when Parker Sr. needed two hands for his terrorizing trek. While a two-hander meant that his father was dead drunk and about to pass out, a one hander made him loveable but more unpredictable. Junior could never figure out which was better or worse.

Nor could he forget the mangled doorframe leading from the dining room into the kitchen. Senior ripped it off one night when his wife barricaded herself – as she usually did – in the kitchen. The bitch had been slapped around for that one. "There. Let her try closing it now."

Let him try closing the lid of her coffin years later. He couldn't, of course, because he wasn't there for the funeral. Parker Sr. was so overcome with grief over his loss that he sat in the living room the morning of the service and drank himself into a stupor.

Had it not been for the kindness and charity of a next-door neighbor, the gathering of relatives and friends at the Parker home after the funeral would never have happened. No one asked where Mr. Parker was that morning or who had set the dining room table and provided the food. No one had to.

Jay's heart might be pounding and the sweat beading, but he always landed on his feet. There wasn't much he couldn't take, and nothing galvanized his thinking better than an anxious moment. Yet, something was wrong, very wrong he felt in an eerie way, but what? Fuck. What is going on?

"Perhaps you two would like to take a few moments to discuss matters privately," Eleanor suggested.

"Sounds like a plan," Jay said, relieved by the interruption.

Chapter 3

"Hi, Mr. Evans. This is Kevin Sweeney, the contractor, calling."

"Oh, hi, Kevin. How are you?"

"I'm fine. We have an appointment at eight-thirty this morning, and I wanted to let you know that I'll be leaving my office in a few minutes."

"That's terrific. Michelle and I are looking forward to meeting you. Take your time. We're in no hurry."

"Thanks. It will probably take me ten or fifteen minutes to get there, which is a bit earlier than we had planned."

"No problem. See you then."

Before leaving his office, which was in the basement of his Weymouth home, Sweeney crumpled a few Post-It notes and threw them into the wastebasket. He liked to keep the area neat and especially hated having papers with handwritten notes all over the place. It was too easy to lose important information, and Kevin wrote everything down rather than trust his memory.

The hardware and software sitting on his custom-made desk was worth more than $15,000, and he knew how to make it sing. In a way, his whole life was on that computer. The information on the Post-Its definitely was, because Kevin had already entered it into CAT, the mnemonic name for his contact, activities, and time management software.

The laptop computer he owned was in the desk draw. Kevin took it only to a client's house to measure it up using an architectural drafting program. He would not need it today.

Sweeney's wife, Marie, knew that the condition of his office was a good indicator of what was going on in her husband's business: chaos or calm. Seldom was it in between.

Kevin never overdressed for a sales call and was wearing a soft, open neck, plaid shirt, tan Farah slacks, and a white, loosely knit, V-neck sweater, all recently bought for him by his wife. "You have to look professional," she would always say.

The colors were muted and non-threatening. He also wore a short, Woolrich jacket and his black Rockport shoes, which were shined.

The drive to the Evans house was not very far, six miles at best, but no one ever measured distance in miles. Everything was time.

Along the way, Sweeney crossed over the Southeast Expressway, turned right at the first intersection, and passed the coffee kiosk where he usually stopped for his morning regular. Not today, however: don't want coffee breath when talking to a prospect.

He had to swerve slightly out of the way of an oncoming, black BMW that turned sharply into the kiosk driveway. "Can't imagine what it must be like to live that way," Kevin said to himself. "Always in a hurry, late for work. Major pressure day in and day out."

He definitely did not miss the morning commute to his former high tech job off Route 128 in Bedford, which was west of Boston. He did miss the people and the excitement, though, and probably would have gone back in a heartbeat to the floundering ship the company had since become. Realistically, he knew that call would never come.

Sweeney soon found himself on Commercial Street, outside Jackson Square, Weymouth, and followed it into Hingham where the road changed names to Fort Hill Street.

The name of the street was not the only thing that changed; the houses did, too – from being smaller, more crowded, somewhat less well kept, and closer to the road in Weymouth to larger, more open, and set back further in Hingham.

Along the way, Kevin passed the golf course by the railroad tracks that had become a huge public controversy. The Commonwealth wanted to revive the defunct Greenbush Line, as the system had once been known, and extend public transportation to the coastal region of the South Shore.

Most communities welcomed the idea, except Hingham, which objected to the commuter trains' potential impact on the downtown, historic district and had sued to stop the project. Hundreds of millions of dollars and many construction jobs were involved in the outcome.

A few streets down, Sweeney turned left to an older part of town with houses that were mindful of its maritime days. He passed a house he had once worked on, a duplex that was unusual because it had been built more than two hundred years ago when most homes were single family.

Kevin would never forget the cat – or rather its skeleton – which he found in the downstairs wall of the duplex. It was the one time he could ever recall that the portentous, "You never know what you might find in the walls" adage rang true. More often than not, the warning was an exaggeration the contractors used to serve notice to homeowners that the cost of the work was never certain and there were bound to be extras.

Sweeney slowed down as he checked the house numbers, which went from 63, 59, 57, and finally to 51 on the right. Some had prominently displayed plaques on them indicating the date when the houses were built –

1820, 1831, 1817, and a real fossil, 1756 – and for whom: Capt. Stanley Coates, The Hon. Joshua Lambert, etc.

He pulled his car into the narrow driveway on the right hand side of the house, which was partially hidden from the street by several overgrown bushes.

Unlike most contractors, Kevin did not drive a truck, which was the ultimate symbol of someone who was in the residential construction business. He also had no cell phone or pager because he found them to be dangerous and annoying distractions.

He would rather listen to classical music or the German tapes he kept in the car or let his mind wander. His concentration was so great that he once forgot to watch where he was going while putting in a tape and had a minor car accident with his neighbor.

Whether Sweeney had difficulty accepting the fact that he was now a building contractor instead of a well respected, highly paid, middle manager in high tech, he never volunteered, and no one ever asked. He showed few of the trappings of the business.

His car was a snappy, late model, four-door, Pontiac Grand Am SE with rear seats that could be pulled down to carry a few, eight-foot two-by-fours or other building materials. It was a great feature of the car and the very reason he bought it.

Number 51 was a nondescript, white New England colonial with black shutters, some tell tale, rust stained clapboards, curling roof shingles, and fieldstone foundation, a small house compared to its neighbors. Someone had added to the building years ago, and the work was poorly tied into the original and sitting on a brick foundation.

Approximately twenty-five feet behind the house on the right side at the end of the driveway sat a small barn – now a garage – that was quite handsome but needed much repair.

After getting out of his car, Sweeney walked up to the barn, peered into the windows, and checked around outside some more. Satisfied by what he saw, Kevin then stepped onto a solid granite stoop, shifting his briefcase, large white binder, and rolled up blueprints to the other hand, and rang the bell in the recessed, front doorway.

"Hi, you must be Kevin. I'm Stewart Evans. Come on in. Can I get you some coffee?"

"Hi Stewart. Thanks, I'd love a cup," Kevin answered as he stepped into the vestibule, its wide pine floorboards squeaking as he did.

Stewart closed the door behind Kevin and nudged it shut with his knee and shoulder. "The door's a bit tight, and one of the items we wanted to talk to you about. Here. Let me help you with your things," Evans said, as he removed the blueprints and binder from under Sweeney's arm.

"So I noticed," Kevin answered, "but that's what these classic, older homes are all about. I like all the imperfections. Makes the house more interesting and charming. Thanks. You can leave those materials in the hallway or someplace nearby. We'll get to them later."

"Sure. Well, I don't know about the classic part, but you're right. It does have charm, which my wife and I really like. Let me go get her."

Evans walked down the short hall, leaned onto the narrow, cased opening of the kitchen, and told Michelle that Kevin was there.

"I know," she said. "I'll be with you in a second. I just need to clean up a bit. I don't want him to see a mess."

"He doesn't care about a mess. He's not here to clean the house, you know."

Michelle looked at her husband firmly, and then smiled. "Take him into the living room. I'll bring the coffee."

Stewart showed Kevin into the living room, which was in the front of the house but to the left of the hallway. The room had a fireplace, a low, beamed ceiling, and wainscoting and was very tastefully decorated with a mix of traditional furniture and – Sweeney was certain – real antiques.

"Would you like to sit down?" Evans asked.

"No, actually I would prefer to stand. May I look around a bit?"

"Oh, sure. Be my guest. Let me show you around. We can't go into the kitchen yet. Michelle's afraid you'll see some dirty dishes."

Kevin laughed. "If it will help, tell her I truly don't care."

"I already did, but you know how it is."

Sweeney went immediately to the built in bookcase on the wall dividing the hallway from the living room. Three recessed lights that Stewart quickly switched on illuminated the area.

"Do you read much?" Kevin asked as he cocked his head to read the titles or glanced more closely at the framed pictures of the family.

"As much as I can. My wife's the big reader. She's always got a book going, sometimes two or three. I can't read like that. I'm a start to finish guy, one book at a time."

"Same here," Kevin said, running his hand along the wood counter top of the cabinets below the bookcase. No dust, he casually observed.

"How about you?"

"I love to read. Mainly biographical history, seldom fiction."

"Really? I do, too, but once in awhile I like a good Clancy or a Ludlum," Evans offered. "Let me show you the rest of the house."

At the rear of the living room was a large cased opening into the dining room that felt small but comfortable. The furniture was old, imposing, but in excellent condition and similar to many sets he had seen when Sweeney went to visit his grandmother or her brother and sisters.

They were Irish immigrants, city folk who paid a little bit more than what they could afford and looked for quality with lasting value. Their furniture was neither cheap nor expensive and held up well over the years.

The leaded crystal sparkled in the couple's lit china cabinet, which also contained some interesting pieces in addition to the Royal Daulton place settings.

"I like those little blue and white rabbits," Kevin mentioned to Stewart.

"They belong to the children. My mother gave each one a rabbit every year at Easter. It's quite a collection. The process of making them look old and cracked is unique. You can still get them but have to hunt around in the specialty shops."

"Interesting. How many children do you have?"

"Two, but they're not children any more. Two adults. My son is twenty-six, and my daughter twenty-four. He's living in Boston, and my daughter is planning to move out soon."

"Hey! Same again. My son's living in Vermont and my daughter is finishing her Master's at the New England Conservatory of Music. She wants to teach and will probably be gone with her first paycheck. They're about the same age as yours."

"What does your son do?"

"He's a professional artist and is actually working in his field. Both my children are artists, which is something of a surprise to my wife and me. It's funny how they turn out. They are really great, and we enjoy them now more than ever."

"Your lucky they turned out so well. These days, who knows."

"It wasn't luck," Kevin gently corrected. "It was a lot of hard work, if you know what I mean."

"I do. Same here, and definitely worth it."

Just then, the swivel door from the kitchen opened about a foot, and bumped Kevin who then stepped out of the way.

"Can I come in?" Michelle asked.

"Oh, sure," Stewart replied, as he stepped back, too. "Kevin, I'd like you to meet my wife, Michelle."

"Hi. Pleased to meet you," he said, extending to her his hand, which she shook firmly.

"I'm pleased to meet you, too. Sorry I wasn't here sooner."

"No problem. I understand. All the women want the house perfect when someone comes in. Most of the men don't care."

"Well, I care," she said, again glaring at Stewart.

"I've been showing Kevin around, and we were just talking. He has two children. His son's an artist, and his daughter, a musician."

"Really? How very interesting. Two artists? Must be a fun place," Michelle implied, wondering how the artistic personalities got along with each other and their parents.

"It is, or I should say, 'was.' My son moved out about six months ago, and my daughter is getting ready to leave. It's been awful. I really, really miss him, and I was the one who couldn't wait to see them go. It's as though something has been ripped out of me."

Michelle was genuinely touched but very surprised to hear a man she had just met speak so tenderly of his son. "Of course you miss him. We miss our son, too, and Lori won't be around much longer. All of which, by the way, brings us to the very reason we wanted to talk to you."

"Great. Shall we get down to business?" Kevin suggested, and the two looked at him and nodded eagerly.

"Sure. Where would you like to start?" Michelle asked.

"Anywhere would be fine. It doesn't really matter."

It did matter, and Kevin was deliberately encouraging them to talk, getting them to loosen up. He knew that the small talk in the end was really big talk, that the minor details held clues about their thinking, attitudes, and real plans for the project. All he had to do was listen and observe very carefully, watch and wait.

Sweeney was enjoying himself, and the couple seemed like very nice people. Although their house was tired on the outside, the inside was well appointed and beautifully kept and furnished. It even had a nice smell.

Stewart and Michelle were approximately the same age as Kevin and his wife, a very good sign because they could feel comfortable with him. Their having so much in common with Sweeney might be an advantage because the couple would be more likely to identify with him than a younger contractor.

On the other hand, they might be more sympathetic to an inexperienced guy who – like their own children – was also starting out. He wasn't sure or worried about it. He would be, as usual, himself.

At this point, Sweeney had a very good handle on what the Evans were all about and could make a lot of assumptions that most likely would be true. They didn't know it, but Kevin had found out much more about them than he had given up about himself, although he was not uncomfortable with anything he had said so far.

THE INDEPENDENT CONTRACTOR

He was searching for an edge.

"Usually, what I like to do is walk through the house, and you can tell me anything that comes to mind about your plans. The big picture or the little details, you know. Whatever."

"Ok. Well, you've already seen the living and dining rooms. If you'll follow me through this door, I'll show you the kitchen, where most of the problem is," Michelle said.

"Sure, but one other thing. Where did you get the dining room set? I especially like it."

"That set belonged to my grandmother. It was stored in the barn for years because the person, my aunt, to whom it was promised, had no place for it in her house. Eventually, my aunt gave it to me because she and her husband had no children, and we've used it ever since. The living room set belonged to Stu's mother."

"Interesting. Where did your grandmother live?"

"In Dorchester off Gallivan Boulevard. Over by St. Brendan's," she answered in the almost automatic response of place, street, and parish people from the city use to indicate where they lived. "Stu and I are both originally from Dorchester."

"Really?" Kevin said with some surprise. "I grew up in Southie. Fourth and H. A few doors up from Gatie. Something told me you were from the city," Sweeney asserted realizing he did not have to use the church's official name, Gate of Heaven. Anyone from the city would know Gatie.

"Well, we are. Irish, the whole bit. Small world. Here. Let me show you the kitchen," Michelle said as the pushed open the swivel door.

"The kitchen is a problem for us," Stewart said. "Michelle and I have talked about it, and I think we would like to enlarge it either to the back of the house or maybe the side. We would like to put in some nice cabinets but not go, you know, overboard."

"Sure. I understand. Generally speaking, you're much better off if you can work with the space you have instead of extending it, especially out.

"There's a formula you can follow: for the cheapest space, go down; for the most expensive, go out; and for the most cost efficient, go up. The problem with going down is that the space there is not considered 'living' for resale purposes.

"Going out can give you what you want under most circumstances, but all the trades are involved. Up is the most cost effective, but you don't appear to have that need.

"Bear in mind that the space you create by going out or up is considered 'living' for resale purposes and will probably add value to your house,"

Sweeney explained, fully aware that this couple – like most home owners – was expecting free advice.

"Based on what you have told me, the work you are planning on doing most likely will be a good investment. A pool, for example, probably would not."

They didn't know that Kevin's counsel, which seemed very good and insightful, was standard operating procedure for him: tell them enough to demonstrate your expertise but don't give away the store.

A less experienced contractor would have given the Evans a lot of good design ideas with no assurance of getting the job. Sweeney focused instead on their emotional needs, not the physical space, and was technical enough to satisfy Stewart without confusing Michelle.

Sweeney figured that Stewart was like all men who assume – falsely – that they know construction simply because they are men.

If Michelle were money conscious like her Irish grandparents, she would most likely be concerned about over-pricing the house for the neighborhood and not getting the most value. Renters who moved from the city to the suburbs to buy a house and raise a family had a different attitude towards money than residents who had always lived there.

"Well, that's something we certainly didn't know," Stewart said as he turned towards Michelle. "We weren't sure of which way to go. This actually helps."

"Is there a bathroom on the first floor?" Kevin asked.

"Yes, there is, but I wouldn't exactly call it a bathroom. It's over here," Michelle said as she opened the out swinging door to the bathroom. "As you can see, it's pretty small."

"Sure is," Sweeney said. "It will probably have to go with the new scheme or be worked into something nicer and more functional."

All of a sudden, Stewart remarked, "Damn! We've gotten so involved talking to you, Kevin, that we forgot about the coffee. Would you still like a cup?"

"Sure. Cream no, if you will."

After looking at the room in the rear, the three went upstairs to the bedrooms, which, like the downstairs rooms, were cozy but small. "We're not sure what we should do here," Michelle said. "Technically, there are three bedrooms. We thought we might be better off with two larger bedrooms, especially now that we don't need the one extra."

"I have a few ideas, but I'd like to think about them first before passing them along," Kevin said with some encouragement. "I see you have access to the attic."

"Yes, we do, but there is not much you can see up there. Mostly boxes, some clothes. The usual. Is there anything else you would like to see?" Stewart asked.

"One thing. The basement. Shall we?" he said, gesturing towards the stairs.

Michelle, Stewart, and Kevin carefully descended the stairs, which were both narrow and steep. Kevin went into the basement himself, looked around for a few minutes, was impressed by its clean appearance and smell, and returned to the kitchen.

"What do you think?" Michelle inquired. "It's pretty dreadful down there."

"Not at all. I don't see any water problem, which is good. I think you have a beautiful house with lots of possibilities."

"I figured you'd say that. Everyone wants to work on this house," she said, unintentionally letting Kevin know that other contractors had been there, too.

"May I be blunt?" Kevin asked. "Your house is beautiful, but it needs a lot of work. Whether you can even do these other things you're planning is something that I can't determine because current codes, zoning, your fieldstone and brick foundations, the septic system, and balloon frame structure of the house raise issues that need to be resolved.

"Therefore, I'm going to give you some homework to do. Let me get my briefcase." Kevin then went into the living room to get his briefcase, the plans, and the binder, and returned with them to the kitchen.

He took out a document that contained a lot of questions for the Evans to ask town officials. "Don't be intimidated. The instructions are easy to follow, and all my clients do this research on their own before going any further. It will save you a lot of time and aggravation, and maybe even some money."

Kevin deliberately handed the questionnaire to Michelle. "Stewart, I don't mean to offend, but you may want to let Michelle do the research. I have found that women are much better at it than the men. I'm not sure why. Maybe they have more patience and like getting into the details."

"Fine. Sounds good to me."

Michelle looked at Stewart approvingly. "He really doesn't have the time, and I do. This is great. I really appreciate it."

Sweeney then handed Michelle a very distinctive pen commemorating his company's tenth anniversary. "I don't know if you plan to talk to other contractors. Everyone is hustling, and I have no problem with that routine. I don't want to become involved in a project that's poorly planned or have you spend money on designs that can't be built."

"One thing that would help tremendously. Do you have any idea of what all this will cost? Could you give us a ballpark figure because we have no clue," Stewart said.

Revving up to his favorite argument, Kevin said, "Let me put it this way: would you buy a car on the basis of its cost per pound?"

"Ah, no, of course not. That would be silly because you would not know what you'd be getting," Stewart answered.

"Precisely. It might be interesting information but not particularly useful. Well, the ballpark figure and the cost per square foot of living space are the same thing. What's worse, there is no industry-accepted definition of living space."

Michelle's eyes widened. "Then how come everyone else says all we have to do is carry something ridiculous, say $80 - $100 a square foot, for example, to come up with a figure?"

"You know the deal," Kevin said, shifting into fourth gear. "The more living space that's included, the lower the cost per. The less, the higher. The whole approach is terribly misleading, and I simply won't do it."

The two looked at each other before Michelle asserted, "Kevin, we're going to need to know how much we're getting into this project, financially, before we go much further. We need some idea. Anything."

"I agree but know a better way to do it. I like to show my clients various projects I have worked on and let them know how much $100,000 or $75,000 will buy. What you need to know is how much you can afford, not what something's going to cost.

"You need to know how much you'll finance or have in your hand and go from there.

"I'd be happy to take you with me some Saturday morning to several of my client's homes. It's a lot of fun, and they love talking about what they did and why." Overdrive.

"That does sound like fun," Michelle said. "I love looking at other people's homes. Are you sure they won't mind?"

"No. They won't mind at all. It's all part of my relationship with them. Naturally, I try to visit different homes instead of the same ones all the time. It works out great."

"Can I help you with your things?" Stewart asked, noticing that Kevin appeared ready to leave.

"Sure, but do you have a few more minutes? I'd like to show you something else."

Kevin then rolled out and placed on the kitchen table a set of blueprints for a project he had recently completed. "These plans are a good example of the work we do but are not really similar to your project. They're all generated on my computer, which makes them very easy to change.

"Except for a complete redraw, I am usually very generous about the number of changes I will do for a client because I would rather make them on paper than in the field."

Sweeney then went through the plans, which were in color.

"The color really makes it easy to see what's going on," Stewart said. "Very impressive."

"Thank you, but that's not all. Let me show you my project organizer, which is what every client gets and is identical to the one I keep in the office," Kevin said while setting aside the prints and opening up the two inch thick, three ring binder.

He turned immediately to the color-coded Table of Contents then the tab for Carpentry Specifications and Materials.

"As you can see, each phase of the project is broken down according to the subcontractor who will be doing the work.

"The carpentry specification is the most comprehensive and difficult to develop. It's broken down, in turn, into categories like demolition, framing, roofing, windows, interior finish, and so on, according to specific regions of the house, like the bathroom, master bedroom, or family room.

"Not only is the work carefully identified by phase and location but the materials are, too. You'll notice that each has a line item identifying its cost. For this client, there may have been one hundred and fifty line items on the carpentry alone. The material costs for each might add another twenty."

"This is unbelievable. It looks like a huge amount of work. I mean, it's almost scientific. Who does it?" Stewart observed and asked in rapid fashion.

"I do. It's a system I developed that's very precise, but it's not science. There's some art to it, too.

"Let me just show you one other thing. Here's the Project Cost Projections where all the line items are totaled. It's not uncommon for this spreadsheet to be twenty or more pages long.

"What's more, you can take out line items for items you don't want to do, such as a skylight, and identify its material cost, the time to frame the opening and install the unit, then the cost to insulate, sheetrock, and paint. It's all there."

Kevin was doing all the talking at this point, but he had the rapt attention of both Michelle and Stewart.

"I have another analogy I would like to make. Here's the traditional way things work. Let's say you wanted a very special cake made for you, and you took a picture of it to several bakers.

"What you'll get back from them is three or four different prices for something that looks the same but may not taste the same, weigh the same, or feed the same number of people. Nothing will be the same from one baker to the next."

"I think I know where you're heading with this," Michelle said.

Kevin smiled. "Ok. Tell me."

"What's missing is the recipe. If they all had the same recipe, they could all make the same cake. The only thing that would be different then would be the price. We could then compare price and other variables like location, reputation, or, you now. Am I right?"

"Oooh. I'll say. Very, very good. You're the first person I have talked to who put it all together so quickly. Now I'm the one that's impressed."

Everyone laughed, and the chemistry between them all seemed right. "Since you've stolen my thunder, here, I'll just finish up the thought. The picture of the cake is the same as the blueprints for the project, and the recipe is the specifications," Kevin quickly added. "It's that simple, and the secret to controlling costs."

"This is all very, very interesting. I hadn't thought of it that way," Michelle said slowly.

"You've opened up our eyes to a lot of issues," Stewart said. "Thank you for taking the time and being so patient. It's a very, very impressive system."

"You're more than welcome. It's been fun. Thank you for considering me."

"Absolutely," said Michelle. "What's the next step?"

"The next step is for you to do your homework and call me with the results. I'll then send you a proposal for the design phase of the project along with my references.

"You'll probably need a surveyor – you're a bit close to your neighbor on the left – and I can refer you to one. Either way, you have my card, which has my Web site address. Make sure you check it out."

"Definitely. Thank you. I can't wait to get started," Michelle said enthusiastically. "And thanks for the pen."

Having concluded their business, Michelle and Stewart walked Kevin to the door. "You'll be hearing from us soon," Stewart said. "It's been great."

After nudging the door shut behind Sweeney, Stewart turned to Michelle and asked, "Well, what do you think?"

"I like him. I like him a lot. He's very personable and the one contractor who really seemed interested in us, not only the house. I just hope we can afford him because he comes so highly recommended. The two women I talked to raved about him."

"I liked him, too. He's very straightforward and has a lot of confidence in himself."

"I agree, and he's very professional and knowledgeable."

"He's very quick. I really like him. He's, shall we say, different? That binder that he showed us, its details were incredible. None of the other contractors have anything like it, not even close. In fact, I can't think of a single contractor who would want us to know as much.

"Everything's there in black and white."

As Kevin backed out of the Evans' driveway, he began thinking to himself. He was very pleased with the way the meeting went. Nice ebb and flow, good mix of personal and professional, left on an upbeat note.

Although he had identified himself as a contractor when he first called, Sweeney was fairly certain that neither Stewart nor Michelle now saw him that way. When he had started the business, Kevin wanted to differentiate himself from the competition and heavily stressed that he was a construction consultant, not a builder or contractor.

This strategy did not work well because the public was slow to see the difference. If you wanted to get some work done at your house, the first thing you would do is locate a contractor. If you needed a lawyer or doctor, you knew where to look or call.

Most likely, you had no idea that a construction consultant even existed. Having someone advocating on your side during a construction project was probably a service you would want, but you might never have heard of it. Kevin decided to blend in, then stand out, and the new strategy worked. The concept was still new to practically everyone he met.

Sweeney liked Stewart but knew that Michelle was the key, and she had responded to him very well indeed. Kevin was always respectful of the men, but deliberately aimed his presentation towards the women. They were the ones who were motivated to do something with the house.

More often than not, the men didn't care or simply went along to please their wives. Things would change quickly once the bids came in, and then the contractor would have the husband's complete attention.

Sweeney hated the glib, "Give them the sizzle, not the steak" approach and actually gave Michelle and Stewart something of substantial value when he handed her the questionnaire. He was doing them a favor; one that they would feel unconsciously obligated to return. It was a nice way to keep the door open.

If Michelle did the research, Kevin could safely assume the she and Stewart were not tire kickers who were wasting his time. Until that commitment was made, the project was not likely to go ahead.

Kevin had not asked either Stewart or his wife what they did for a living but knew he would find out eventually. She had more time than he did. Was she working? Any clues from the books? Maybe.

The subject of their budget or how much they were willing to spend had also not come up, as it never did in the early stages of a project. How did they feel about money?

Stewart and Michelle were both conservative. Kevin had picked up on the comment about not going "overboard" with the cabinets. Michelle had probably done the math for a three hundred and twenty square-foot kitchen addition and was shocked by the $25,000 to $32,000 price range.

Kevin had clients who paid that much for the cabinets alone.

Their expectations were unrealistic, but they may come around. The project organizer was a real eye opener, but they didn't seem put off by that project's total cost, which was over $125,000.

Did the Evans have money? The antiques aside, the evidence was there that they did.

Sweeney suspected that Stewart's mother had died, perhaps recently, because of the way he talked about the rabbit collection in the china cabinet. Past tense: gave. Was he an only child who had inherited his widowed mother's estate?

Kevin thought so from the pictures, one of which showed Stewart, Michelle, and an older woman who looked like she was in her mid eighties, taken in some kind of facility. Stewart already had her living room furniture.

Was there anything left after assisted living? Of course there was. Savvy children whose parents had assets knew how to protect them and their inheritances at taxpayer expense, all very legally.

With their money worries probably behind them – the Evans had two expensive, late model cars in the garage; the children were out of college – Michelle and Stewart were most likely looking to get more out of their lives together.

Sweeney had handled the ball park figure well and avoided committing to a number that was low enough for him to get the job – but not make any money – or so high as to preclude him. What a strange irony, Kevin thought, the public distrust contractors but not their ballpark figures.

Michelle was charming, clever, and attractive, but Sweeney scrupulously avoided letting women know what he thought about them. Even so, they always seemed to sense that Kevin was a man who truly enjoyed women, took them seriously, and found them interesting.

If Michelle and Stewart Evans liked him, genuinely liked him, Sweeney would probably get the job. Kevin was fully aware that the decision to hire a contractor was emotional, not rational. In the end, the clients always subconsciously hired mirror images of themselves.

The relationship between the couple was mature and sound, even though Michelle spoke to Stewart with darting eyes and knowing smiles. They were at ease with each other, and neither was trying to be top dog or deferential to the other. There was also none of the endless correcting of one another that some couples engaged in, a sure sign that communication in the household was poor.

Over the years, Sweeney had been in countless homes, talked to many homeowners, and was an astute observer of the interaction between husbands and wives. Despite all the bleating about equality in modern marriages, he found that most were still very traditional: the man's work came first, and he controlled the money; the woman made the decisions but subordinated her career to the husband's and taking care of the family.

Most of what Sweeney saw was a snapshot in the everyday life of his clients. Generally, it was great fun and an opportunity for him to draw comparisons to his own life and laugh.

Wanting to make his rounds, Sweeney headed for the main road and passed a small, triangular park near Hingham's quaint, downtown center outside the harbor. Abraham Lincoln's great, great, something or other had once lived in Hingham, and a bronze, sitting statue of the venerable Abe – not the ancestor – had been erected in the park.

The monument bore the inscription, "With malice towards none, with charity for all."

"Now, there was a world class worrier," Kevin thought, "Not many in this town are. Must be nice to have it so easy."

He then snaked by the South Shore Country Club. Not missing the chance to add to the quality of town life, Hingham had acquired and improved the ailing facility to provide "additional recreation opportunities for residents while preserving the suburban character of this historic seaside community."

A moment later, Kevin crossed the tracks and drove to Weymouth. As he passed through Jackson Square, he noticed on his left the Korean War Memorial with its standing, granite statue of an armed soldier. The memorial was very similar to the one he had seen many times at Castle Island in Southie, and he reflected on its meaning.

Chapter 4

The parking lot for fifteen hundred and seventy-nine cars at Hewitt's Cove in the Hingham Shipyard seemed full, and Lauren Parker was lucky to find a spot at the far end, about a three-minute walk from the commuter boat pier. She stepped into the office to get out of the chilly air and to purchase a one-month pass for $136, which she paid with the same credit card her husband had attempted to use that very morning.

While she was waiting for the eight forty-five boat, Lauren noticed on the wall behind a flat oak bench several pictures of ferries that – until the early 1950's – had once crossed Boston Harbor from Lewis Wharf along Atlantic Ave. to Marginal Street in East Boston. The one in the center, the *John H. Sullivan*, caught her attention because of the story Kevin Sweeney had told her and the children about it.

Lauren and the children were enchanted by the story and had pressed for more details. "The ferry carried thirty five cars at five cents per car – one way – and numerous passengers for a penny each – per trip – and made four crossings an hour. Today, it would cost about five dollars per person.

"My uncle told me that the ferry had boilers, two very large iron beasts that consumed three and a half tons of coal every eight hours and belched lots and lots of thick black smoke into the air!"

"What's coal?" Steven had asked.

"You burn it, stupid," Danielle retorted.

"Now, now, children. Let's not." Sweeney continued, "My uncle was a fireman, which meant that the captain, pilot, engineer, and oiler were all above him, but the two deckhands were below."

"Where are the ferries now?" Brianna inquired.

"They're all gone. They stopped running before the Callahan Tunnel under the harbor was opened. I think it was in 1951 or 1952."

"Oh, that's sad. I like the ferries better. I wish we had one," Danielle mumbled.

"Kevin, how did the cars get on?" Steven wanted to know.

"They drove over a ramp straight through to the end of a gate. The first cars in were the first ones off. The ferry didn't have to turn around."

"Why not?" And so it went, with the children always asking Sweeney questions about the ferry every time he went to their house. Lauren admired his patience and ability to add one – just one more detail he had forgotten – to fire the children's imaginations.

Smiling, Lauren turned away from the picture and noticed that the passengers inside the terminal were headed out the door. She had not heard the boat's horn and quickly left to board, carefully descending the steeply angled gangplank to the commuter pier.

Lauren boarded the sleek, catamaran hulled boat that seated three hundred and forty-nine passengers and was much faster than a smaller craft with almost half the capacity. When this newer boat came into service, many passengers complained about its speed – twenty-seven knots – because they preferred the longer ride of the slower boat.

She headed for a starboard seat near a window, which was her usual spot. Always starboard, always in the middle, a chance to see both views coming or going. After settling in, she took a small, spiral bound notebook out of her valise and began writing down her to do list with the commemorative pen Kevin Sweeney had given her.

The boat left the pier exactly on time, headed slowly out into the Weymouth Back River, and rounded Webb State Park on the left before picking up speed and turning north towards Boston where it would be in twenty-five minutes.

From the corner of her eye, Lauren noticed a man walking past her towards the rear of the boat where refreshments or alcohol were served. She recognized his face because he was a regular on the eight o'clock run. Lauren casually smiled at him as he went by, saying nothing because she did not know his name.

Several minutes later, she heard a male voice behind her say, "I see you have one of those, too." Looking up, she saw the same man again, this time holding a cup of coffee and smiling at her.

"Oh, the pen? Yes. Yes, I do. A contractor gave it to me when we were having some work done on our house. Do you have one?"

"I most certainly do, and probably from the same contractor, Kevin Sweeney."

"Yes, that's right, Kevin Sweeney – from Weymouth, I think. Did he do any work for you?"

"Did he ever. A very large second story addition. We finished it about a year ago. I don't know how it went for you, but he was great with us. The workmanship was marvelous. Just marvelous."

"I think I know your house. Kevin said he was doing a second story project at Crow's Point over by the yacht club. Are you up on the hill?"

"Yes, the first right just as you turn the corner. We're on the left."

"The house with the porch and deck in front? My husband and I have driven by there many times. The view of the harbor is incredible."

THE INDEPENDENT CONTRACTOR

"I must say they were Kevin's idea. He thought we should have a 'gracious' porch and an open deck tied into the master bedroom suite on the second floor. The extra height gave us the view and probably paid for itself. Perchance, he gave you my name as a reference."

"I don't remember. Well, I hope you enjoy your house as much as we do ours. It's been nice talking to you," Lauren said abruptly, wanting to continue the conversation but needing to catch up on some work.

"Same here. By the way, my name is Graham Barrows."

"And I'm Lauren," she said with a lovely smile.

Before returning to her work in earnest, Lauren pondered the chance encounter with Graham. He was older than she by at least ten years and betrayed a distinctively British intonation, which she liked and thought was more cultured than the famous Boston accent.

He had a full head of wavy hair, which was recently cut, parted on the right, and a mixture of light brown and gray. His hazel eyes were warm and gently fixed on hers while they were talking.

Graham's darker moustache was neatly trimmed and accentuated his beautiful, soft white teeth, which could be seen through an engaging smile. As he drank his coffee, Lauren noticed his firm hands and long fingers with manicured nails.

That Graham took good care of himself was obvious in the way he looked and dressed, the careful attention to detail. His whole demeanor was that of a man of considerable charm, quite confidence, and effusive energy.

Graham returned to his up front, portside seat very pleased with himself. He had seen Lauren many times on the boat and had always wondered why she stayed so much to herself.

She wasn't unsociable at all. Maybe she was aloof or – most likely – a bit shy, but Lauren certainly was not another stuffy or aggressive American woman.

No matter. Graham Barrows liked her and secretly hoped that she would talk to him again. He then sat back to enjoy his coffee and the beautiful view of Quincy Bay, the catalyst for the clean up of Boston Harbor.

****

"Hey, Daz, got any receipts for me?" the bookkeeper called out to the tow truck driver as he passed the office counter around mid morning.

"A few," he said, putting his cigarette in his mouth while searching his pockets, Columbo – like. He then placed three credit card receipts on top of some papers on the desk of the bookkeeper, a formidable, seriously overweight woman by the name of Marion.

"How did you make out with Mr. Arrogant in Hingham?"

"He was Ok. Paid in cash."

"I thought he wanted to use a card."

"Me, too."

"So where's the money, Sweetheart?"

"Hold on. Hold on. I'm getting it." Dazzie then slowly counted out three ten-dollar bills and one five and gave them to Marion.

"Any cash receipts?"

"Nope. Had none with me."

Marion put the cash in a strongbox for deposit later that day. She wasn't sure about Dazzie Clarke but couldn't say much because he gave her the correct amount of money. There was something about that guy she didn't like.

He was only a part-timer, so Marion didn't have to deal with him every day. Clarke had told her that he wanted to get into construction and was now working part-time for an excavating contractor in Braintree. The money was real good, he claimed.

The extra ten dollars Dazzie, of course, kept for himself. He had taken a chance that the Hingham guy had extra cash in his wallet. "Screw him," he rationalized. "These people have plenty of money and don't give a fuck about the little guy. They'll never miss it."

****

"I can't believe you would do this to me. I simply can't. Tell me, Jay, what is it? Jealousy? Afraid of the competition?" Andrea charged as she closed behind her the door to Jay's office.

"You're taking all this too personal, Andrea. It was a business decision, and a good one."

"I'm taking it personal! I'm taking it personal? Why is it that every time a woman has a legitimate point to make with a guy and is emotional he accuses her of taking it personal? Of course it's personal, and you know it. Give me a break."

"Well, you have your women's intuition."

"Women's intuition? What the hell's that supposed to mean? Don't play those mind games with me, Jay. I deserve better," Andrea said, wanting to smack him.

"You know, men have their edge. Women have theirs."

"Women have their what? Ways? Is that what you mean? We're getting nowhere, and I think – no, I demand that you give me an explanation. I am really, really angry," Andrea said as she began pacing the area in front of Jay's desk.

"Look, calm down. Calm down, and let me explain," Jay said as he peered through the glassed walls of his office to see if any one was watching.

"This is one I want to hear. Well? Let's have it, straight from the hip," Andrea said as she turned away from Jay, leaned against the front of his desk, and ran her fingers through her straight, shoulder length, light brown hair parted in the middle.

She was shorter than Jay's wife, Lauren, a few years younger, and also wore overly large, light green eye glasses that he thought made her appear feminine, classy, and intelligent.

Andrea needed no prop; she had each aplenty.

"You've hinted to me several times that you always wanted to work in London. I knew there was an opening in the U.K. office, so I told Eleanor that I thought you were right for the job over there. It's a good career move for you, and the company benefits, too."

"What if I've changed my mind? What if I would prefer to be asked first, then decide? Did that ever occur to you?" Andrea fumed.

"I don't get it. First you let on that you would like to go to international, but now you don't. Is that what I'm hearing here?"

"No, it's not what you're hearing. It's what you're thinking. If you were listening, really listening, you would have known what I meant. I told you I would like to make a move, but I didn't tell you I want to go right now. I can't just pack up and leave, you know."

It was true; she couldn't, not unless her live-in boyfriend, a software and hardware computer whiz that was now out on his own, could find a new place to live somewhere else on the South Shore.

"This whole conversation is impossible. I'm supposed to read your mind. If I do, there are benefits. If I don't, I'm screwed and insensitive. It's the marriage feast all over."

"What are you talking about? The marriage feast? You sometimes make no sense to me at all," Andrea said, utterly baffled by Jay's remark.

"The wedding feast at Canaan in the New Testament where Mary, the Mother of God, says to Jesus, 'Lord, they have no wine'."

"Yeah. So what?"

"And he says, 'What will you have me do?'"

Frowning scornfully and moving her head slowly back and forth, Andrea said, "Now I'm the one that doesn't get it."

"Exactly, and neither does any guy. Why don't you women just come right out and say what you want? Everything's implied."

"So what does all this prove? What we already know? Men and women are different? How does that give you the right to screw me?"

"It proves that God himself couldn't solve the problem. If Mary had told Jesus, 'Lord, without wine this party is over, and these people have run out. I would like to stay, so can you make them some?' he would have known what to do without wondering what Mary wanted, done it, and you and I would not be standing here having this ridiculous conversation."

Andrea put her hand over her mouth and stared for a moment at the floor, tapping her toe. Looking back up, she smiled grudgingly. "I could kill you. You're really frustrating me. You come off like the good guy, and I'm the goofy bitch."

"Andrea, no one's calling you a goofy bitch or is out to screw you," Jay said softly. "No one. You've done a lot for me, and I thought it was my turn to help you. It's a great opportunity with a hefty salary increase and other benefits, and you can always come back if it doesn't work out."

"I'm more confused now than when I first came in the door," Andrea admitted, letting down her guard. "No one is out to screw me. I know that. I've done a really good job here, so it just wouldn't make any sense. This is The Big Break staring me in the face, and I'm feeling like shit. You should have come to me first, and none of this would have happened."

"You do have a point, but I was trying to feel out Eleanor before I came to you. If I had gone to you initially and she did not back me up, I'd look like the idiot," Jay concluded.

"Then why did you send me the memo?"

"I didn't send you the memo, or, a least I don't think I sent it to you deliberately. I could have clicked on the wrong name when I uploaded it and not realized. Besides, the memo was only a follow up of my previous discussion with Eleanor."

"Are you saying you were thinking of me, like, subconsciously?" Andrea asked with some hesitation in her voice.

"It's possible. Maybe that's it. Hey! I don't know."

"I'll have to think about all this, Jay, and we still have to go over the presentation one more time. Incidentally, there's no way – assuming that I go – that I'm coming back if things don't work out. They either work out or I'm a failure. I have to make it happen."

"I know how you can make things happen."

Andrea froze. "That's not fair."

"Meaning, you won't talk to me online tonight?"
"Meaning, you'll just have to wait and see."

****

"Hey there, Kevin, what's up?" Walter Nash of Walter Nash & Son Carpentry asked Sweeney as he cautiously walked up the makeshift gangplank to his client's house in Weymouth Heights.

"Not much. How was your weekend? Did you make it to Vermont?"

"Yeah. My wife and I closed the place down for the winter. It's so quiet and peaceful up there. No one around for miles and miles. No one up your ass. I'll miss it," Walter said over the loud hum of the pneumatic hammer generator and pounding beat on the radio.

"Then again, you'll have something to look forward to in the spring. How are you coming along here?" Sweeney inquired.

"Everything's fine. I just have to get my soffit and fascia on, and I can start my roof. I covered both roofs – the shed and flat one – with the water and ice dam preventer, so they're tight. You can bring in your plumbing and electrical anytime."

"Great. Exactly what I was hoping to hear," Kevin said, always bemused that the contractors referred to everything as 'my.' He loved the smell of the freshly cut wood. "Are the owners around?"

"I think the husband's downstairs. I did see him earlier, so he's probably still here."

"Where's Allen?"

"On the other side of this wall, in the bathroom, getting that floor ready."

Kevin walked around the wall and saw Allen on his knees pulling up the inlaid linoleum and plywood under it in the bathroom. "Hi Allen. How was the game the other night?"

"Hi, Kev. It sucked," he said, not looking up and continuing to pull up the floor with a pry bar and hammer. "They lost in the last minute on a fluke the Bruins' goalie never saw. I never should have taken my son. All he wanted to do was eat and buy stuff, and he couldn't sit still all the time. He had fun, I think, but didn't see much of the game."

"That's what being a dad's all about, Allen. I just talked to your father, by the way, and he said you're all set. Looks good."

"Yep. Moving right along."

Kevin wandered around the rear kitchen extension he was adding to a classic, Dutch Colonial house that had been built many years ago by an Italian immigrant as a surprise for his new wife who was coming to America.

All the interior finish – moldings, doors, casings, mantle, china cabinets, trim, and the like – were imported, hand rubbed mahogany that had a beautiful patina.

The present owners had the oak floors redone before moving in a few months after the new work had started, and Kevin was now busy making this beautiful home more functional without sacrificing its original character.

This part of his work Kevin loved, being on site, talking to the guys, joking, telling stories, teasing, thinking ahead, seeing it all happen. Like most contractors, he found the office work to be dull and tedious. On site, he could really learn something and have a lot of fun.

Sweeney systematically checked with the men first before surveying the job. The talk was deliberately small, away from the work, until he had taken the subcontractors' temperatures.

He watched for the slightest clue that hinted at a future problem – a comment a guy might make about his wife in a way that Sweeney had not heard before. Problems at home showed up almost instantly on the job, and Kevin always wanted early warning.

The signs were there, he said, if you knew where to look, like Walter's comment about missing his cottage in Vermont. He was past sixty-three – ancient for this business – officially retired, and now working for his son, Allen, whose wife had been on him about spending more time with her and the children.

Over the summer, Walter had gone to Florida for a few days with a friend who lived in a seaside trailer home park that came complete with a shop full of fine woodworking tools. The friend wanted Walter to come to live at the park and service all the retired or elderly owners whose stairs needed to be fixed, or a door, window, maybe an awning, or anything else that might come up.

"They will love you," the friend would say, and each time he did, Walter moved closer to deciding. "There's enough work here to keep you busy as much as you want. The beach is only a few hundred feet from your door. Don't feel like working? Take the day off; nobody's going to say anything. You can make enough on the side to keep yourself busy without the worries and winter on your back."

The vision of being the park's in demand handyman with a tool shop waiting for him was very appealing, and Walter was on the fence. His daughter was getting divorced – "She's partly at fault, too, even though she's my daughter." – and had already moved with her two school age children into her parents' home.

"She can pay the mortgage – it's piddling – be here to take care of the place when we're not, and I can earn enough to be comfortable the way I want. It's perfect, I'm telling you."

What about the cottage in Vermont? "I can always sell it."

Kevin was startled by this disclosure because Walter truly loved his cottage; the dump he tenderly fixed up over the years for the kids and the grandchildren, using left over or salvaged building materials from his jobs. No question about it, Walter was getting ready to move, and Kevin would be heartsick.

You weren't supposed to become friends with the subs, but Kevin usually did, and it had hurt him more than once. He realized that problems on the job were generally easier to solve than the ones at home, and the men frequently confided in him.

Sweeney's projects were known for their even pace, organization, neatness, and cleanliness. He insisted that plastic be used to seal openings between the new work and the rest of the house to prevent the migration of dust, the implacable enemy of every homeowner who is remodeling.

If Kevin was taking up an old floor to get down to a sub-floor of boards over a basement, he covered the ceiling. Then the washer and dryer, sink, boxes, storage area, toys, or whatever would not get covered with sawdust or particles of horsehair plaster or gypsum board.

He made sure that articles in the attic were covered completely by plastic if a roof was being stripped and redone. Sawdust and granules from the shingles could make just as much of a mess and were usually not noticed until well after the contractor was gone.

Organization, neatness, and cleanliness, Sweeney believed, sent a subtle message to the homeowners: I care about your house, time, and personal comfort. He genuinely did, but there was another reason: the impression that everything was under control. The contractors got paid for taking these precautions.

Kevin had learned these virtues from his mother who had raised him and his older sister after their alcoholic father abandoned the family a short time after Sweeney was born. Their third floor, South Boston apartment was so clean, in fact, that his uncle joked that a dust mite would starve searching for a meal there.

Sweeney recognized that a subtle shift in his relationship with the homeowners would always take place once the construction was underway: we want you to care more about our house than you do about us personally.

He would tell his wife, Marie, many times over that "building and remodeling are not solely about construction. They're about relationships and decision making." He did not tell her that a neat home made him feel safe and secure, but, then again, he did not have to. They had been married for more than thirty years.

After his brief but informative exchange with Allen, Sweeney went downstairs to the basement to find the homeowner, George Matthews. He saw a light turned on in the far right corner, heard some rustling of boxes, and figured that George was trying to clean up the area.

"Hi, George. How's the settling in coming along?"

"Kevin! How've you been? I never get to see you that much anymore."

"I'm doing well, George. I just wanted to check in, you know, get your thoughts on the progress of the work."

"Kathy and I are thrilled with the way things are going. Walter and Allen are fantastic. Really, really nice guys. I can't believe their work. Everything is just so. They're really old school.

"I didn't think you'd mind if I asked Walter to do a little side job for me in the garage under the living room. We need some storage there, and he's going to install some shelving."

"I don't mind at all, and thank you for telling me."

Kevin knew that Walter and Allen would welcome such work since it was usually paid for in cash. All the contractors who worked with him were eager to do little side jobs, and Sweeney never objected as long as the work did not interfere with the schedule.

Sweeney also thought it was unwise for the contractors to accept cash or personal checks from the homeowners. "If the work is off the contract, it may be legally regarded as personal. Then you are – in my opinion – exposing all your personal assets to a lawsuit if one should ever develop," Kevin would say, making sure that he was not giving legal advice.

Although what Sweeney said was true, all the contractors ignored him and the chances of an IRS audit. Oddly enough, these side jobs seemed to be in direct conflict with another business strategy of the contractors, the freebie, which the homeowners loved.

Many subs, Walter Nash included, found it difficult to charge for the little things they did that were not expressly in the contract. "I don't want to nickel dime them to death. It keeps everyone happy," Walter would say. Oftentimes this work involved helping the other subcontractors, such as opening a chase in a wall for the plumbing, heating, or electrical work to be installed or repairing something they had done.

"What's the value of anything you do for free?" Kevin would ask the contractors. "If you are not going to charge the homeowner, you should show what you did for free on the bill. It has value, especially if there's a misunderstanding over a charge for an extra. It all adds up."

THE INDEPENDENT CONTRACTOR

This idea was a good one, the guys thought, and they began using it. "There's nothing wrong with a pleasant reminder during an unpleasant conversation," Sweeney said. He was now taking the temperature of his client and was very interested in what George Matthews had to say.

"Overall, we're very happy. I think we may even be ahead of schedule," George noted.

"I do, too, but have to warn you. It's sometimes two steps forward and one step back. I do have an important matter for you and Kathy. You have not resolved the kitchen cabinet design, and I can't install the rough plumbing, electrical, or heating without that plan."

"I know. I know. I've been after her to get it done, but it just hasn't happened. She can't decide whether to go with the custom guy or get a nice, higher end stock cabinet. If it were up to me, I would just say, 'Screw it,' and get the custom cabinets. When do you need to know?"

"Well, I need to know within the next two days or we will have a scheduling problem. The subs can't wait for you to decide. They have other projects to look after, and those homeowners have already started pressuring them to start now."

"I understand. You'll have your answer tonight."

"Either way, you have to realize that this kitchen's not going to be ready for Christmas. The custom guy is saying he will put the cabinets in production as soon as he gets a commitment from you. I'm not knocking him, but I do think his schedule is a bit optimistic. We're getting into the holiday season, which, as you have heard me say more than once, is a time of national paralysis."

George laughed at the last remark. "Listen, Kevin. It's not your fault. It's ours, and we're going to have to live with it. Oh, by the way. Did you get that check that I left for you on the dining room table a couple of days ago?"

"I did, but there's a problem. It didn't clear."

George appeared wounded. "It didn't clear? I don't understand. Why didn't you tell me before now? We set up that account just for the remodeling. I'm terribly sorry, Kevin. Let me check into it immediately. I can't see why there would be a problem."

"I wasn't worried. Besides, I'm telling you now. We trust each other. Why don't you check with the bank and let me know? Meantime, I have work to do for you, so I have to head out. Tell Kathy I said, 'Hello'."

Kevin knew George was telling the truth because he was not defensive, seemed genuinely surprised, and was quick to pay him in the past. They were nice people who would be more embarrassed by the incident than Kevin would be inconvenienced.

"Hey! I almost forgot. How's the cat?" Kevin asked.

"She's fine. You do know that she took off for three weeks. I think she hated the construction and was mad at us for moving. She had lost of lot of weight and must have decided that an upset house was better than sniffing around for a meal. They're funny."

"Well, I'm glad she's back, but I think it's more out of opportunity than gratitude."

"You're probably right, and I thought she missed us."

"Here's one. My mother has a cat and said that if a dog sleeps in your bed it's because the dog loves you. If a cat sleeps there, it's because the cat loves the bed."

Kevin thought his client's pets were fascinating although he did not have one himself. All his life he had been afraid of dogs but had come to like and admire them after watching on public television dog trainer, Marty Margolis, who advised viewers to treat their dogs with love, praise, and affection.

It wasn't a bad strategy, Kevin thought, and might even work on kids and contractors. He was working to overcome his past reaction to dogs'– which was like Dracula to the cross – and simply couldn't resist when a client's dog would nose him for attention.

Marie Sweeney watched the program with her husband and learned a great deal, too. Their son, Mark, was soon thereafter overheard saying to his sister, Lisa, "Mom's treating Dad like a dog." "What? She's what?"

"Yeah. Really. Every time he does something she likes, Mom says to him in a high-pitched voice, 'Marie's proud,' just like the guy on TV. She's really funny, and Dad even laughed the first few times."

He didn't laugh very much when an excavator brought his three-month-old Doberman puppy to the job site every day several years ago. By the end of the project six months later, the puppy had become a "vicious predator," according to Kevin.

The other subs were also nervous and relieved when Sweeney asked the excavator to leave the powerful beast at home. "I could turn Ole Yeller into an attack dog," Kevin lamented to anyone who would listen.

Having no other business with George, Sweeney then did a final walk through of the new work, which consisted of a complete gutting of the present kitchen, opening up the back wall, an eating area addition to the kitchen, a half-bathroom, pantry, and stairs to a lower walkway.

His eyes moved constantly as he searched for anything new or old that was not perfectly level, true, or plumb. Is there a belly in the second floor joists that will prevent the upper wall cabinets from going all the way to the ceiling? Are the new and old floors exactly in plane? Do the old walls and new meet each other square?

From his long experience in residential construction, Sweeney knew that the maxim, "They don't build them the way they use to," was a positive thing, not the criticism intended. Builders of yesteryear cut their corners, too, and put their money into materials, which were more expensive at the time than labor.

Most owners of older homes did not realize that the non-bearing interior partitions were two-by-threes, which were cheaper than two-by-fours, or that the oak flooring in the upstairs bedrooms could be all the short pieces, many with knots. If a kitchen had wood flooring, the material was likely to be fir not oak, which was more expensive. Pipes could be lead or threaded brass, not copper; the insulation in the walls, missing, in the ceiling, seaweed, and in the old furnace box, asbestos; the electrical system, a firetrap.

It was also not uncommon for an older home to have floor and ceiling joists and roof rafters that were over spanned, undersized, and failing, the most obvious evidence's being cracked walls or ceilings. The builders of the past – the real craftsmen of romance – were not much different from their counterparts today. They worked with what they had and knew.

Any number of guys could cut corners now, but Kevin had never met one clever enough to turn a cube into a ball. Homeowners who wanted everything done right bought the marketing jingle and wrongfully assumed that there was only one way to do something.

The downstream consequences of the conditions Kevin saw in this house, well built sixty years ago, could be major. Better check now. Take the time, he reminded himself.

Satisfied that all was in order, Sweeney said his good-byes to Walter and Allen and headed for the door. He suddenly stopped, turned around, and went back to where Allen and Walter were measuring and cutting the primed, exterior pine boards.

"Walter, I have a joke for you," Kevin yelled over the noise from the compressor and radio.

"Work? I don't need any more goddamned work. I've got all I can handle now. Where am I supposed to get the time to do more work?"

"He didn't say 'work,' you asshole," Allen sneered at his father. "He said he had a joke for you."

"A joke? Oh, a joke! Yeah. Ok, what is it?" Walter asked somewhat embarrassed by his other wisecrack.

"I heard it from my wife the other day. It's really funny."

"Alright. Alright. So what's the joke?"

"It's about this very old couple that has been married for more than sixty years, and the husband's dying."

"Heard it already."

"Fair enough. I'll take off then," Sweeney said.

The gabbing over, Kevin again headed for the door. The guys are slipping, he thought. No one had kidded him about not bringing the coffee, but then again no one kidded Walter about his worsening hearing loss.

****

Sweeney had no sooner arrived at his office than the phone rang. Kevin picked it up immediately, as he did any incoming call because he would rather deal with it then than later.

"Hi, Kevin. Ono. I think I might have something interesting for you. Remember those people over there in World's End, Hingham? We went to look at the heating a couple of months ago."

"Sure do. The Carlisles. Why?"

"Word has it that they're pulling their own building permit and are talking to all your subs about doing the work. Mr. Carlisle hasn't called me yet, but I know for a fact he did talk to Eddie, Mike, Butch, and a few more of the guys. I knew you would want to know."

When Kevin hung up the phone, he stood by his desk for a minute or two. He was not happy about the news he had heard from Ono. Sweeney had spent a lot of unbilled time on the plans and specifications for the Carlisle project, and now they wanted to cut him out.

It was a chance Sweeney had taken, and he wasn't all that surprised. "These people love what I do but do not respect me for it," he concluded one day. "They think all they have to do to get what I provide is hire the contractors involved with my business and buy where I do. I wish it were that simple."

Kevin was right, or course. Nate and Carol Carlisle had no past experience with the subcontractors, no history with them, and no understanding of their strengths, weaknesses, or idiosyncrasies. They would not know how to encourage one while avoiding the other.

It would never have occurred to them that the contractors would increase their prices because the Carlisles were a one shot deal with no experience in construction. The subs were not going to let the homeowners use them or waste their time.

Nate Carlisle and his wife, Carol, were two people Kevin did not like from the beginning. They acted as though they had a lot of money, important jobs, and connections in the town. They seldom had much time for him, and when they did, the children or an endless stream of phone calls, which they always answered with no hesitation or apology, always distracted them.

He felt used. Loyalty was to the dollar in big business or small.

Kevin wandered upstairs to the kitchen and found himself in front of the refrigerator. He had no idea as to how he got there or what he had been doing before. It was almost automatic: he was hungry, and his body took over. Most likely, an emotional trigger was pulled.

Working at home required discipline, and there were days when Sweeney had it more than others. Today was not one of them, and he had no clue as to why. His weight fluctuated up and down by a few pounds, and he had long since abandoned the hope that the beautiful clothes hanging in the upstairs closet would ever fit him again.

Kevin loved to eat and often joked that he never met a cookie he didn't like. Or a box of them, so it appeared.

Kevin returned to his basement office, which was his sanctuary and battlefield all at once. When he was laid off from his high tech job nearly twelve years ago, Sweeney did over his basement as a means of keeping himself productive and emotionally stable. Kevin deliberately chose contrasting colors and materials: the lower portion of the walls was rough sawn pine, stained a warm, medium brown, the upper walls, sheetrock painted light cream, textured carpeting on the floor, and acoustic tiles for the suspended ceiling.

Sweeney built the bookcases and cabinets with raised panels and all the passage doors. He wanted to take things at the opposite end of the scale – hard and soft; smooth and rough; light and dark – and combine them in such a way that the basement space would be beautiful, relaxing, and harmonious.

The final effect was exactly what Kevin wanted, and only he knew that the simplicity of it all took a lot of work and planning. The basement, which was converted into an office a short time after he finished it for his children, was a metaphor for his life at the time: out of contradiction and chaos came creativity and calm.

It was all very satisfying and a source of great pride for Kevin. He could easily understand why men, in particular, loved construction. There was the smell of the wood, the measurable results every day, the steady hum of the machines, and, above all else, the camaraderie.

Seeing children playing with scraps of wood the men saved for them was also a delight for him. Their expensive toys frequently stayed in the closet as the children found new and interesting ways to experiment and create with the irregular wood shapes.

Kevin's work transformed for the better the lives of many people, yet it did little for himself. Sweeney was torn then as now between so many conflicts. "So what if no one wants a white, educated male over forty," he thought then. His life would go on, but much more differently than ever before. He was now over fifty.

He was somehow in the middle of all the extremes he had seen in his life and had found a safe harbor. Holding to a steady course would be much more difficult than Kevin would ever have thought possible, and more than one ship would pass him by along the way.

****

"Yes. Good morning. May I speak to Lauren Parker, please?"

"Sure, Jay. This is Paula. Let me get her for you."

"Hi. It's me." Lauren said. "What's the matter? I've only got a few minutes before a meeting with some investors."

"Nothing much. I just thought I would call to see how you're doing. I was going to e-mail you, but thought I would call instead."

"I'm fine, and I registered the children in the enrichment program. Brianna and Danielle both wanted to take drama but were worried that they would have to share a part because they're twins. The drama coach said she would find different roles for each one, so they're registered and all excited. They're so cute. Steven's in the art course, and he's pretty excited, too."

"Sounds great. I would rather have them involved in something productive than sitting around watching TV. By the way, did you pay off the family credit card? I had a problem with it this morning."

"Of course. I paid that bill with all the others. I don't know why you would have had a problem with it because I didn't."

"What do you mean?"

"I used it this morning to pay for my boat pass."

"I don't know. Something's screwed up. Would you mind checking into it?" Jay then added, "You handle all the bills."

"No, I don't mind checking into it," Lauren sighed. "I'm just really, really busy with work and everything else." Carly Simon knew something: "Baby sneezes; mommy pleases; daddy breezes in," Lauren thought to herself.

"I know, and I appreciate it. I'm pretty busy, too."

"When's your presentation?" Lauren inquired.

"That's another thing. I uploaded it to Eleanor this morning, and she never got it. I also sent her a memo about Andrea, and she didn't get it either. Andrea did."

"Whoops!"

"Yeah. Right. Something's weird. I'm not off to my best start today. I'm ok with the presentation. There were only minor changes. I just want it to come off very professional, very well done."

"Who's the client again?"

"Are you on a cell phone?"

"No. I'm in my office, my little cubby. You're getting paranoid."

"I better not say, but it's a state, a whole state pension plan. It's big time for sure."

"I'm impressed. What did Andrea have to say?"

"At first she was very angry, but I explained the whole thing to her. We left everything up in the air, but I think we'll get it all worked out. She and I went over the presentation together, and it was as smooth as silk. I'm excited. We're meeting the clients actually in a couple of hours. Two o'clock to be exact."

"It sounds like you've got everything under control. You'll do fine. By the way, did you remember that I am going to the Monet Exhibition at the Museum of Fine Arts tonight? Maureen's going to stay with the kids for an extra few hours, so that end's taken care of."

"Surprise, surprise. I did remember. I saved your e-mail. Have fun. You'll enjoy it. Oh, did I tell you about the note?"

"No, you didn't tell me about the note."

"As I said, something's weird. I get this handwritten note on a pink memo slip, and it says, 'Have you had your salami today?' No one in the office knows where it came from or what it means."

"Someone's playing a joke on you. Listen, I've got to go. I'll talk to you later. I'm not sure what time I'll be home, but I should see you sometime tonight."

"Fine. Don't tell those investors too much."

Lauren laughed. "Don't worry. Only what I have to."

She wasn't kidding. Lauren was the CFO for a software start up in South Boston and frequently discussed the company's future with investment bankers and venture capitalists that sought her out.

She had developed an excellent reputation for her ability to take public software start up companies that became huge successes. The money involved was enormous, and the smart money was now betting heavily on Lauren.

With a CPA and three successes already under her belt – and stock in the most recent start up and two earlier ventures – she had become a valuable asset herself. When she cashed in some of the stock from the last initial public offering, Lauren used the money to finance the remodeling of her and Jay's lovely home in Hingham and purchase their two automobiles. She was in the fast lane.

Their house was not the only beneficiary of her successful career. Jay was, too, and the leads she gave him – not outright, but hinted – were passed on to knowledgeable people at his investment company. It was all very incestuous, he knew, and all very legal. Of course husbands and wives talk.

Jay's fast rise at the firm – from marketing specialist to vice president of marketing – some thought was his just reward for having targeted for investment three companies that paid off richly. There were times when Jay thought so, too, and he was in the market for a really impressive success to call his own.

Bringing in a whole state's pension plan would rank right up there, and Jay was a man who recognized when The Big Break was staring him right in the eyes. He was a man who wouldn't be denied his place in the sun and knew how to make the most of an opportunity.

Chapter 5

Kevin Sweeney was having a late lunch in the family room, listening to the news about President Clinton's sexual travails, and reading the newspaper. He seldom prepared a sensible meal from the four groups and usually ate whatever he could scab up from the refrigerator, breadbox, lazy susan, table, or cake dish.

While he was having lunch, a caller from Cape Cod Building Supplies left a message on Kevin's answering device. The special order, out-swinging door for the Matthews job was in, and it would be delivered to the house along with the double mullion window unit and another steel door for the back entrance. Both doors were keyed the same and had deadbolt locks.

Kevin immediately called Walter Nash and left a recorded message about the delivery, which would be early the next day, a Tuesday. Sweeney had no intention of driving to the site to tell Walter in person and was headed, instead, for a popular gym down the street, just off the Southeast Expressway.

He was a little bit early for his workout – about an hour – and was hoping he could get in and out of the gym without encountering the guys he usually saw at his regular time. There was no guarantee that he would not run into someone who would slow him down, or vice versa, but the chances were better if he went before three o'clock.

Kevin never thought about going to the gym; he simply showed up or he would have otherwise not gone at all. He hated the workouts but loved the results.

Two and a half years after he started, Sweeney felt and looked great, except for the tire around his waist. Only diet and aerobic exercise would cure that problem, and Kevin had the will for neither.

He had suffered no injuries, and his energy now was greater than it had been at any point in the last twenty years. Kevin also learned that a little bit at a time added up to a lot of progress in the end. Sweeney was keenly aware that he couldn't avoid getting older, but he did not have to accept being unhealthy or unfit.

When Kevin was done with his regimen, he could always leave the facility knowing that he had made a good faith effort. He showered at home, although the gym was well equipped and had a sauna.

In addition to the physical benefits, the social aspects of the gym greatly appealed to Sweeney because he was a naturally sociable person, although the isolation of his basement office – The Bunker – was an additional factor. He got to know the regulars, guys who were at the gym sometimes every day and some who were there not as often, and talked to men and women of all ages and backgrounds.

The gym was an especially democratic scene – except for the loud, contemporary music – and the very place where Sweeney had met Lauren Parker who became his client almost a year and a half ago.

****

"Hi, how did it go?" Lauren Parker asked her husband on the phone.

"Not as well as I had hoped. For some reason, the computer wasn't working properly, and I had to improvise a couple of times," Jay answered. "Everything was on PowerPoint, and sometimes you forget how you have it set up. Some things happen automatically; others are timed, and then you can click."

"I'm sorry to hear that. I know how much you were counting on everything going perfectly. You probably did better than you thought. No one thinks better on his feet than you do."

"Thanks. I know. It's just so strange. It worked perfectly before in the run through, but you're right. Only Andrea and I know that it didn't go off exactly as planned. She was great and played off me very well. On the one hand, I'm hopeful, but still disappointed."

"Maureen said she'll have supper ready for you. She's really great that way."

"Yeah, she definitely is. I don't know. Today has just been so weird. The whole Andrea – Eleanor mix up, the flat tire, credit card screw up, the laptop computer bug, that thing about salami. It's just weird. I haven't had so much get fucked up in one day, Lauren, since I was living with my parents."

"Jay, don't get down. Sometimes things happen with no explanation. Think of all the things you've got going for you. It's a long way from Pittsburgh," Lauren said with encouragement.

"The best thing I've got going for me is you and the kids. Without my family, I'd have nothing. Absolutely nothing."

"We'd have nothing without you, either, Jay. Come on. Snap out of it. Talk to Andrea and Eleanor. They probably picked up on some things you didn't. You'll feel a lot better if you do." Lauren always had good advice to offer Jay and most of the time he listened.

"Getting back to the credit card. I called a garage to fix the flat and change the spare rather than drive home on it. The card didn't go through, so

I had to pay in cash. Good thing I took enough at the ATM this morning. I must have had a premonition."

"I haven't had a chance to check out the card, but I'm certain it's ok. Go home, have something to eat, play with the kids, and read them a story. You love doing that, and they do, too."

"Yeah. I will. Thanks. Talk to you tonight. I love you."

****

Graham Barrows left his client's office to catch a subway ride across town, turning up his collar as he stepped into the cool, moist late autumn air thick with the smell of the ocean. He walked up State Street and past the Old State House, which had been duplicated in Weymouth as the Town Hall.

At the intersection of State and Washington, Barrows turned left, crossed, walked up School Street to Tremont Street where the Parker House and King's Chapel stood opposite each other, crossed again, and headed towards Boston Common.

A half block down Tremont, he passed the Old Granary Burial Grounds, where three signatories to the Declaration of Independence – John Hancock, Samuel Adams, and Robert Treat Paine – were buried. Everywhere in the city there were past reminders of how his native country screwed things up with his adopted home, which he loved for its vitality and excitement. Barrows ducked into the Park Street subway to take the Green Line trolley.

The Green Line in Boston was slow and noisy because of its many turns that followed, roughly, the streets above. The trolley exited the tunnel in the middle of Huntington Avenue and let off and boarded several passengers at the station for Northeastern University. Barrows got off at the next one, Museum Station, walked across the street, and quickly made his way to the Museum of Fine Arts.

****

Kevin Sweeney got back to his house around four, just in time, he hoped, to prepare a special dinner for Marie who would be coming home from work around five-thirty. Marie was a health educator who became an administrator several years ago. When she was teaching, her schedule was predictable, but the new job brought more work, responsibility, and very long days.

Before Kevin went shopping for groceries, he checked on a job he was doing at Crow's Point in Hingham. The carpenters, Dana and Dan of Twodie's Carpentry and Remodeling, were about to remove a heavy, cast iron tub from the demolished second floor bathroom. "I see the girly man has shown up just on time. Ya. With all his new muscles, you know. Ya. Maybe the girly man can help us, but I don't tink so," Dana fired at Kevin.

"Jesus Christ. I come down here to see what's up, and all I get is Hans and Franz. What bra size are you up to for that flabby chest, you dumb, Arian brute?" Kevin shot back in the same mock German. "There's no girly man here, you know." The three men laughed and aped the muscle bound pose popularized by Dana Carvey and Kevin Nealon on *Saturday Night Live*.

Although three stooges could handle the job, it would be a struggle and dangerous going down the stairs. Clearly, a plan was needed, and Dana was the first to offer one.

"I say we put it in the shoot and drop it into the dumpster."

"The shoot is not reinforced, and it will come apart," Dan countered.

"I think the shoot will hold up, but fall out of the window," Kevin said. "If the tub falls off, it will go right through the roof of the enclosed porch below. Any other ideas?"

"I think we should go for it," Dana urged the other two. "It's going to work."

Kevin offered a compromise. "Why don't we move the tub to the window, lift it into the shoot, check things out, then decide?"

The three blokes moved the dead weight tub across the floor, raised it onto the window, balanced it, and held their collective breath.

"What are we going to do now?"

"Well, we've come this far."

"Hey! It's not my call."

Looking at each other, they spontaneously pushed the tub into the shoot and watched as it flew down and into the dumpster, which it hit with a loud clunk and without shattering. The shoot fell out of the window and broke apart. Two women who were watching the incident from across the street seemed shocked.

The men were all right and laughing their asses off. It was almost fun enough to do over again.

"Dana, do you know any masons?" Kevin asked abruptly.

"Sure. A few. Why?"

"One of the guys I was talking to at the gym said a commercial contractor he knows couldn't get any masons from the union hall. All those guys are working in the city, and there's a real labor shortage developing."

"I hate them union bastards," Dana responded. "As soon as Boston's over, they'll be coming down here to take our jobs away. You know how it is. Working on the side while collecting."

"I thought I would ask. The money's supposed to be excellent. I've got to go," Kevin said. "I'm thinking of working up a nice supper for Marie."

"Ya. The girly man's got to go just when the hard work has to be done, you know, and the fun is over. See you later, girly man. We tink you are looking for love, you know," Dana kidded.

"I don't tink I want to see you again, but a good German man always says, 'Aufweidersehen,' Dummstimmer."

Kevin stopped by Shaw's Supermarket in Weymouth, where he bought some meat, vegetables, and other odds and ends.

Once at home, he pulled out his cookbooks and set them up on the counter and table with Post-Its placed in certain pages. The preparation always took the most time, and tonight he was having chicken breasts stuffed with cheese and spinach and simmered in dry white wine, asparagus in Dijon mustard sauce, diced potatoes in roasted garlic, and caramelized carrots.

He quickly sliced some cheese, placed it on a serving dish with fresh grapes and a few slices of bread, covered the plate, and put it in the refrigerator to keep until Marie came in. "This will hold her off," he said to himself. "Better get her wine ready, too."

When Marie came home, Kevin had her appetizer and wine all set up in the living room, the afternoon newspaper on the cocktail table, and the stereo playing her very favorite singer, Frank Sinatra.

"What's this? Ooh. Everything smells so good. Dinner all ready for me? How lovely."

"Not quite, but you sit and relax until everything's prepared. Can't talk. Have to turn over the chicken."

Kevin returned to the kitchen frantic that he would not have all the food ready and hot on the table at the same time. He had the timer going and was trying to clean up as he went along.

Ten minutes later, Kevin called Marie for supper in the dining room, which was dimly lit. He had properly set the table with their best china, candles, and flowers from Shaws. "I love this," Marie said.

"I know you do, and I should really try to cook more often. I just don't get around to it, or I'm off doing something else."

"I really appreciate it. What are we having?"

"Right now, supper," Kevin answered. "Later, it's up to you."

****

Lauren Parker rushed uptown from her South Boston office on the waterfront to South Station to take the subway to the Museum of Fine Arts by way of the Red Line to Park Street, then the Green Line to Museum Station. It was quitting time for most companies in the city, and the streets were filling with workers eager to get home or about their business.

Lauren arrived at the MFA around five-thirty and used the side entrance of the building. She hung up her coat in the room to the left of the lobby, walked over to the end of the line for the Monet Exhibition, and casually waited to enter.

The line soon shortened, and Lauren handed the attendant her ticket, then walked through several exhibits on the first floor – to the front entrance – and up the stairs to the Gund Gallery where the exhibit was being held. Lauren had been given the ticket by one of her professional associates, a banker who could not make it. She would have loved to go with Jay, but he was more interested in sports than art or museums.

As she was standing in line to rent a headphone to listen to a recording that explained much about the life of Monet and several specific paintings, Lauren saw near the front a man she thought she knew. When the man turned to put on his headset, she could see his face and recognized Graham Barrows immediately.

She tried to get his attention before he entered the exhibit and stepped out of line to greet him. "Hi there, Graham. Fancy seeing you here tonight."

"Why, hello, Lauren. Yes, it 'tis. I can assume safely that you came here to see Monet and not me."

Lauren laughed. "Yes. Yes, I did. Are you with anyone else?"

"No, I'm really on my own. I got a chance ticket from a client, and here I am. What about yourself?"

"I'm alone, too. Perhaps we can see the exhibit together, if you don't mind," she suggested.

"Not at all. I can't see any reason why not. Do you have a headset?"

"I will in a minute."

Lauren stepped back into the line to get her headset and then walked back to Graham. "Do you know how to use these?" she asked him about the headset.

"I've used one before. It's really quite simple. Just turn it on and listen to the directions. You'll get the hang of it quickly."

Graham and Lauren moved towards the large entrance of the exhibit as the tape instructed and turned to view the extensive display of lily pond pads on the right front wall. Next to one of the paintings was a disclaimer from the MFA regarding the rightful ownership of the work.

"Did you read that notice?" Graham asked Lauren.

"Yes, I did, and it's chilling. You don't think of the Holocaust and the

Nazis stealing artwork from the Jews when you come to an exhibit like this. Of all the lily pond paintings on that wall, it's the most beautiful one, I think."

"Yes, I quite agree, on all counts. I didn't know that the exhibit was devoted exclusively to the period of his life from 1900 until his death. Did you?"

"No, I didn't either. I guess we won't be seeing the haystacks or his work during the Franco – Prussian War. That's ok. I'm not disappointed. The paintings here will be a treat. I still can't believe that he did four hundred and fifty during this period and reinvented himself."

The pair wandered about the first room, stopping, viewing, and then continuing with the help of the tape. "I love that one, there," Lauren said, "the garden scene with Monet's house barely visible. Are you supposed to get only the impression of the house, you know, the sense of it, or look deeper?"

"I think you can do both. In some of the other paintings, there's more of the house. I don't think Impressionism is superficial, that you only get to see what's on the surface. It's mysterious in a way."

"Interesting. Makes me wonder more about his house, what's going on inside there."

They soon came to a much smaller and narrower room than the first, and the paintings – with Venice as the subject – were on the left sidewall. Graham and Lauren lingered there awhile before heading for the next room.

"What did you think of the three paintings of the same Venetian palace at the far end of the room?" Graham asked.

"I thought they were very different. According to the tape, they were painted after Monet lost his wife. You could really see the emotional shift in his work. I would say they were more real, less impressionistic."

"Absolutely. I don't know if I would have noticed the difference unless I had seen them side-by-side. I like art, mind you, but I'm not much of a student."

"You don't have to be a student to appreciate it. You're learning now, aren't you?"

"Yes, most definitely I am. I'm having fun, too."

"And so am I," Lauren said with a beautiful smile.

Lauren and Graham strolled about the exhibit, sometimes stopping to gaze at a particular painting, other times moving by slowly, rewinding the tape, or commenting in between. Soon they came to the last room where Monet's enormous murals were being shown in public for the very first time.

"Did you notice that you could see the murals on the far wall perfectly if you were standing a distance from them? Once you got up close, you could see all the details but not the picture. It's absolutely amazing," Graham observed.

"It sure is. I can't help but wonder how he painted them. What technique he used. It really is amazing. They're so large and beautiful. I've never seen anything like them before. All this beauty overwhelms you.

"I think we've come to the end of the exhibit. Is there anything else you would like to see?"

"No, not really. Actually, I'm a bit hungry. There's a quite lovely café downstairs. Would you care to join me?" Graham inquired.

"Sure. I'm getting hungry myself. I could even go for a glass of wine."

Their tour of the exhibit over, Graham and Lauren went downstairs to the café outside the museum art store. While they were waiting, they talked more about the exhibit and their reactions to it. Soon they were shown a table under a tall plant, and Graham pulled out Lauren's chair to seat her before taking his own.

Graham ordered soup, a Rueben sandwich, and a glass of Riessling, Lauren, cabernet sauvignon and a cheese board with large grapes.

"So, tell me, Lauren, what line of work are you in?"

"I'm a CPA, certified public accountant. Right now I'm working for a start up software company that's developing a product for Internet security. They're hoping to go public sometime next year, and my job is to get them ready."

"Really? It all sounds very exciting. I'm involved with software. Are you at liberty to say what yours does?"

"Yes, I am, but I really do not understand it, so I'd better not say. I'm the numbers person who makes sure we're on plan. We're not profitable yet, but we didn't plan to be for the first two years. Next year will be a turning point, and I feel pretty good about where we are headed. What exactly do you do?"

The waitress interrupted their conversation when she brought their orders and set them down on the small table. Graham then lifted his glass towards Lauren. "Cheers."

She lifted hers, tipped his glass, and repeated, "Cheers."

"What do I do? I'm a systems programmer, now consultant in my own business. I started my career many years ago in England developing operating systems. I have background in FORTRAN and COBOL, and Y2K problems. I moved around a bit, until I took a position with a new company that sold dedicated, networked hardware and software systems to the newspaper and graphic arts industry. That's where I met Kevin Sweeney. We've stayed in touch ever since."

"Really. I was wondering how you met him. How long have you been here?"

"Oh, I came out to the States, let's see, almost fourteen years ago. The kids are still in England with their mom but like visiting. My father stayed with us for a few weeks over the summer, and he had difficulty going back home. He and Kevin got along quite well."

"By the way, I love your accent," Lauren said, moving away from the subject of Kevin Sweeney for the second time.

"Thank you. Very British. Very proper, they think here, you know. It sounds Cockney in London."

"Cockney?"

"Yes, a dialect. Something like the New Jersey accent here. I noticed from your accent that you're not from this area either."

"No, I'm not. Both my husband and I are from Pittsburgh, but that's another story," Lauren said, her eyes turning away from Graham's.

"Pittsburgh? I've been to the newspaper down there. Didn't get to see very much. We usually worked very long hours, hit the bar at the hotel, then the sack. It was exhausting for days on end, but lot's of fun."

"The city's come a long way, but it's nothing like Boston. We really love it here. There's so much to see and do. The ocean's nearby, and, if you like the mountains, they're only two and a half hours away, maybe three."

"Have you traveled abroad much?"

"Not as much as I would like, although I did get to Sweden, Denmark, Frankfurt, and Paris. All business, in and out. How about you?"

"In the beginning, I traveled so much it destroyed my first marriage. I still travel some, but after awhile, it gets tiresome. My wife actually couldn't believe I was working and was very resentful. Everything sounded so exotic. South America, Africa, Italy, Germany, France, the States, and so on. I miss it, but I wouldn't want to do it again," Graham candidly admitted.

"Africa? Really? What's it like?"

"It's a most remarkable place, nearly impossible to describe. Did you see the movie, *Out of Africa*, with Meryl Streep and Robert Redford?"

"Yes, I did, with Jay a long time ago. B.C., as we now say. Before children. I loved it. He didn't care for the ending."

"I can understand why. Well, Africa is a lot like that movie. It has an almost fatal beauty to it. My wife's grandfather was a friend of the man played by Redford."

"You're kidding. Really? Tell me about it. I'm dying to hear."

"No. I'm not kidding you. They were the only white people there and were extremely isolated from the rest of the world, as they knew it. I'm not sure if this story is true, but my wife heard it from her father. Because there was so little to do, the whites made up games to amuse themselves," Graham said with a slight smile.

"Really? What kind of games?"

"Well, every now and then they would place over a line some sheets with several holes in them. The men would then stand hidden behind the sheets while their wives identified them by their private parts, you see."

Lauren was wide eyed, placed her hand over her mouth, and rocked with laughter. "God, that's really funny. What if the husbands' heights were different? Wouldn't that be a giveaway?"

"Yes, I should think it would be. Maybe they had little steps to equal things out."

They both laughed together. "Did they ever try it with their wives?" Lauren asked smiling.

"I can't say as they ever did. You Americans and your equal opportunity ideas!"

"Well, why not?"

"Why not indeed," Graham said convincingly.

"Do you ever wonder how people would get a game like that one going in the first place? You know, how would someone have the nerve to propose it? I mean I just can't see me and my friends up and doing something like that out of the clear blue."

"Perhaps loneliness, boredom, and some good Scotch would play a role, I should think, but I really don't know. I hadn't given it much thought. You're right, though. It's curious the way these things happen. Probably it's spontaneous or they dance around it."

"Where did you go in Africa?" Lauren asked, sipping on her wine.

"Mostly South Africa. Because of all my traveling I had run up quite a few frequent flyer points, which I used to take my wife, son, and daughter on a trip to Victoria Falls in Zimbabwe."

"It sounds so outlandish, but strange and exciting. I've read about Victoria Falls. What's it like to really be there?"

"My soup's getting cold. Sorry for doing all the talking."

"No. Not at all. I love it. You're so very interesting," Lauren said as she leaned forward onto the table and folded her arms under her breasts. She was sitting with her legs crossed but pulled in close enough to avoid tripping a passing patron.

Graham noticed he had her rapt attention and was enjoying every moment of it. He was taking in her beautiful, natural, shiny black hair, full at the top, close at the sides and back and the deep-set brown eyes with long lashes. Her high cheeks had perfectly applied makeup; her coloring; the radiant smile; long, lovely neck; the pearl necklace and matching earrings; long fingers and manicured nails; everything.

She's electric, intelligent, very sweet, and pretty, too, he mused to himself. Sexy as hell and doesn't even know it.

"Victoria Falls is such a fantastic place. It's in a massive national park with rivers, lakes, streams, and jungle. We were almost killed by a large hippo that nearly tipped over our boat as we were crossing a lake. It was quite frightening, really. Later that night, a lion left his calling card just outside our tent. We practically had to step over it the next morning."

"His calling card?" Lauren asked, an eyebrow raised.

"Oh, yes. We were right out there in the wild."

"How did you know the lion was a male?" she asked mischievously.

"I didn't, of course. I just assumed that a lady wouldn't do that sort of a thing," Graham rejoined with a smile.

Lauren laughed and thought to herself as she listened to Graham: so he's been married twice, has been everywhere, drinks, and likes a good time. He's absolutely charming, funny, and handsome and has European manners. Probably older children. What the hell am I thinking?

"Would you believe it's getting onto eight-thirty? We've missed our boat ride back to Hingham," Graham said.

"Eight-thirty? I can't believe it. I've been having such a wonderful time. The time really flew. Will your wife be wondering where you are?"

"No, I don't think so. She's used to my strange schedule by now."

"I wouldn't want her worrying. I know what it's like, the waiting, thinking something's happened."

"She's probably home watching the telly."

"I talked to Jay, my husband, earlier, so he knew I would be late. He's probably playing with the kids or reading to them. He's really great that way and loves having special time with them."

"It may not appear so to you now, but they're not children for very long. In a flash, they're taller than you or can look you in the eye. I swear it happens overnight," Graham shared with Lauren.

"I really cherish this time of the children's lives. Others have told me the same thing, my mother especially," she responded.

Just as the two were finished eating, Graham placed his right hand over Lauren's left and asked earnestly, "May I offer you a lift home? It's been so marvelous talking to you that I won't mind if the evening doesn't end just yet. All very proper, of course."

"Of course. I was thinking exactly the same thing. And, yes. I would love it."

The hand. He had touched her. It was warm and firm, but she felt a sudden surge of heat radiate up her arm and who knows where else. For a brief moment, she allowed herself to experience a harmless pleasure, and she felt like an elegant woman in the hands of very strong, sensitive, cultured, experienced, and caring man.

When the waiter returned to their table with the bill, Graham insisted on paying, but Lauren resisted. "There you go again, being a perfect, liberated American woman," Graham teased. "Let's settle it with you paying the tip."

"Deal. I can handle that."

Chapter 6

It was seven by the time Jay Parker got home from work, and the traffic on the Southeast Expressway was especially brutal. It had started to rain lightly, and the temperature had dropped into the low thirties, thereby creating an especially hazardous condition. Cars were skidding all over the place, but there were no accidents.

All in all, he had made good time, even after having stopped in a bookstore on Washington Street.

Although he was tired, Jay's face brightened when he came into the mudroom and saw the children all busy working at the kitchen island. "How are my Gemini?" he said to the twins who rushed forward to hug and kiss him. "Where's my big dog? Ah, there he is. How's my little buddy?"

Brianna took Jay's brief case and put it down on the built in desk while Danielle held onto his arm with two hands and slowed him down. He leaned over to Steven and kissed him on the top of his head before messing up his hair.

"Hey, what's that?" Jay asked, pointing to something on his son's shirt. When Stephen looked down and saw nothing, Jay nosed him with his index finger. "Gotcha! You have to stay on your toes, big guy. That's twice since yesterday."

"You always get me. Dad, look at what I'm doing," Stephen said, trying to draw his father's attention to the Lego® space station he was building.

"No, he's supposed to look at what I'm doing first," Danielle whined.

"Dad, you didn't see what I did," Brianna pitched in. "Look. It's neat."

The girls were almost finished assembling their Playmobil® café, which was similar to the one their mother took them to in Hingham Center. The café was a module of the larger city house set, which could be converted into a police headquarters or bike shop. Naturally, the children had all four and loved them.

Mom and Dad Parker loved them just as much, but for a different reason: both the girls and Steven played with them equally. Jay and Lauren had oftentimes felt that their battle against sexism was uphill, and the toy manufacturers weren't much help.

"Okay, kids. Come on. Let your father have some room there and his supper. He's tired from work and can look at your things once he's had something to eat," Maureen, the Parker's domestic helper, urged as she took Jay's supper from the microwave. Jay had called ahead his ETA.

"Hi, Maureen. Thanks for looking after the kids. How were they?" Jay asked as he started eating his heated supper.

"Oh, they've been fine, Jay. They always are. They were just sitting there nice and peaceful until you came in. I guess you have a way of getting them going," Maureen said pleasantly.

"If you want to stay awhile, Maureen, it's up to you. Don't worry about the clean up. I can do it. I'm sure you've had a long day, too."

"No problem. I didn't want to leave a mess. There's not much. You take your time. I think the kids want you to read them a story before they go to bed."

"I'm sure they do, and for that, I picked up something special."

"What?"

"What, Dad?"

"Where is it?"

"In my briefcase. Brianna, where'd you put my briefcase?"

"I'll get it," Brianna said, as she quickly retrieved the briefcase and brought it to her father.

"You're never going to eat," Maureen said.

"That's ok. I'd rather do this," Jay said as he opened his briefcase and took out a flat, shiny brown paper bag with a book inside.

"Looks like you're all set," Maureen said to Jay from the mudroom. "I think I'll be heading home."

"Thanks, Maureen. Lauren and I really appreciate it," Jay called out to her while turning towards the children.

"Tada," Jay said, holding the book up for the children to see. "Another Arthur."

"Oh, I love Arthur," Danielle said.

"Will you read it now?" Stephen and Brianna were just as eager.

"No. Not now. Bedtime."

"When's bedtime?" Danielle asked coyly.

"In about another hour," her dad answered.

"I'm sleepy," she said, acting and dragging it out.

"Me, too."

"So am I."

"I said, 'No,' and I mean it. Bedtime only."

Usually Jay was a soft touch for the children, but tonight, sensing he meant it, they backed off and returned to their sets. He was absolutely crazy about them, and didn't realize that he was staring so intently at Stephen. "What? What, Dad?" Stephen finally asked, feeling his father's eyes on him.

"Oh. Oh, nothing. I was just looking at you. I love watching everyone having fun and getting along. That's all."

Jay finished his supper and left the children in the kitchen to go upstairs to the master bedroom suite. He changed out of his work clothes into jeans, a faded cotton shirt, and very old slippers, and made sure that everything was hung in the closet or put away as Lauren would like. He then cleaned up in the master bathroom, which had been remodeled by the previous owner.

When Jay came downstairs, the children were still busy at play, and he stopped to see what they were doing and collect another hug, or kiss, or two before sitting on the couch in the family room. Maureen had left the evening paper there for him to read, and he headed right for the sports section to see how the Steelers had done the day before. He would hang up his coat and hat later.

"Dad, is it time yet?" one of the children called out.

"No, not yet. I don't think so," he said more than once. Finally, around eight o'clock, Jay told the children it was time, and they scooted to his side.

"Is everything all put away on the counter?" he asked. No, it wasn't. "No story until you do."

"Do we have to? You didn't," Brianna noted.

"I know, and I will. Yes, you do. Come on now."

The children quickly gathered up their sets and put – actually stuffed – them into their individual cabinets in the mudroom. They then took their usual places on the couch with their dad: the twins on each side, and Stephen sitting between his father's legs. Danielle had taken out of her cabinet several extra books, just in case.

With everyone seated for all to see and hear, Jay read the title of the book, *Arthur Lost And Found*, by Marc Brown, a Hingham author and artist of twenty four books in the Arthur Adventure group and co-developer of the Arthur PBS television series.

Jay began reading the story, slowly, using one of the many voices he could come up with to act out each character. He always stopped to let the children look at the illustrations and point out things they liked and wanted to talk about. He got more mileage out of the story that way and some insight into the children's tastes and concerns.

Sometimes the children would take a part, but mostly they liked to hear their father read the story. He liked the Arthur series because the author was respectful of his readers and didn't use baby words in a mature but simple story. Ever the marketer, Jay wondered if Brown knew his audience the same way as the baby food producers did: make it taste good for the parents. No matter, the books were wonderful.

Arthur Lost And Found was short, and the type size large, but Jay stretched the story out to fifteen minutes. As Danielle had suspected, there was still a little time left before bedtime, yet Jay did not want to get into another story, which was unusual for him. Instead, he went upstairs with them while they got ready for bed.

"Daddy, where's Mom?" Brianna asked.

"She went to the museum in Boston. She should be home soon. Don't worry."

The house had five bedrooms, including the master suite, and two full bathrooms on the second floor. Jay did not mind the children using the master bathroom, but Lauren preferred that they stick to their own. Once they were all showered, teeth brushed, pajamas on, and settled down, Jay gently ushered them off to their bedrooms.

"Goodnight, Dad," they would all say, and to each he answered, "Goodnight, Sweetheart." He then tucked them in and listened to a last request.

"Can I read a little longer?"

"Can I have pancakes with blueberries tomorrow?"

There was one rule that Jay strictly enforced at bedtime: no fighting. He liked that time to be quiet, restful, and the children complied. It was a long way from Pittsburgh, but they would never know.

Jay then went downstairs to the kitchen and turned on his PC at the built in desk. When the computer booted up, he logged onto America On Line® and went fishing in a chat room for the over thirty set.

The talk was drivel. Anyone from LA? Age and sex check.

Minutes later, he received an instant message from someone he knew, someone he was hoping to talk to that night:

Andrea: Hi, there. Got time for me?
Jay: Sure. Always have time for you. I didn't think you would be on.
Andrea: Were you hoping?
Jay: Yes. What did you think of today?
Andrea: What part? A lot happened.
Jay: The presentation.
Andrea: I thought it went well. A few glitches.
Jay: I didn't want well.
Andrea: What did you want?
Jay: Perfect.
Andrea: Ain't much that's perfect.
Jay: Think we'll get it.
Andrea: Don't know. It's tough to say. We did our best.

Jay: True. I'm hopeful.
Andrea: Lots of hopeful tonight.
Jay: I was hoping we could continue the story.
Andrea: I was hoping you would ask. Where were we?
Jay: In Newport. Would the lady like to know the scene?
Andrea: Yes, she would.
Jay: Have to sign off. Be right back.

While Andrea waited, Jay signed off, then back on again, this time with a different screen name, as he had done several times before during other sessions with her. Andrea thought it was his special screen name just for her.

Andrea: Where'd you go?
Jay: Just had to check on something.
Andrea: What is the weather like?
Jay: Weather? Autumn day. Warm, but not burning. They are holding hands on the Cliff Walk.
Andrea: They were not holding hands before in town.
Jay: Now they are. Does the woman like this?
Andrea: Yes, she does.
Jay: He does, too. He likes looking at her.
Andrea: Why?
Jay: She's very pretty and feminine. He likes the color and length of her hair. The lipstick she is wearing. Her nails. Her large eyes showing through her glasses.
Andrea:
Jay: Still there?
Andrea: Yes, what else does he like.
Jay: Everything, but she does not know.
Andrea: Why not
Jay: He has not told her.

Because every word was typed, sometimes with errors, the on line conversation took a lot of time and had to be abbreviated. There were some standards, like LOL, which meant laughing out loud, or RITA for rolling in the aisles. Also, characters could be used to express one's thoughts, such as ;) for a smile with surprise or :(for a frown. Such things were supposed to be simple and amusing.

Jay loved being online. It was a lot of fun and more. He was talking about Newport, Rhode Island, once the preferred destination of wealthy New Yorkers or moneyed gentry at the turn of the 20th century.

Andrea: When does he tell her?
Jay: Tonight. Would she like that?

Andrea: Yes. For certain. It's supposed to be day.

Jay: They stop at the Breakers and look through the fence. Standing close together. She feels him against her side, hears the ocean pounding the rocks below.

Andrea: She would like his arm around her. Her heart is pounding.

Jay: He knows. He turns towards her and puts his hand on her face near her left ear. She stares into his eyes.

Andrea:

Jay: U there?

Andrea: Yes. She is staring. Would say she definitely is.

Jay: He then kisses her, gently. Only their lips touch. Nothing else. Only seconds.

Andrea: She would cover his hand with hers.

Jay: They part, his arm brushes her front.

Andrea: In a way a man touches a woman?

Jay: He doesn't let her know. She is uncertain.

Andrea: No. She is going crazy.

Jay: No one is around. The Cliff Walk is deserted. Only the wind, warm sun, and ocean. Some seagulls. They walk again, hand in hand, to a very private place on the cliff

Andrea: Past the Breakers?

Jay: Yes. Does she know The Great Gatsby was filmed there?

Andrea: She does. She toured The Breakers once during a Christmas vacation. True Lies was filmed at Rosecliffe.

Jay: Really? The man didn't know.

Andrea: Maybe he will discover more.

Jay: Hmm. He steps down. She is above. Sun is behind her. He can see everything under her long dress. Would she mind.

Andrea: Probably not, if she knew he enjoyed it.

Jay: He does, very much. She's with him. Another kiss, longer, sensuous. She feels his… against her. Very sensitive areas

Andrea: Probably not.

Jay: What?

Andrea: Typo. Sorry. Yes, she does. Very sensitive!

Jay and Andrea were exploring new territory in their on line fantasies. The story was becoming more erotic and seductive. Neither had ever had such an experience before, but both were eager to follow it through.

Jay: Does the lady enjoy the cliff experience?

Andrea: More than she can say

Jay: Good. The man does, too. He sits on a flat rock. His back against a boulder. She is still standing.
Andrea: She wants to be with him.
Jay: She sits between his legs, her head on his chest. Arms wrapped around her legs. He holds her. Does she feel safe in his arms?
Andrea: She feels more than that with him
Jay: What does she feel?
Andrea: Very, very close.
Jay: They look out over ocean, hear waves crashing on rocks. There is mist, but they are warm.
Andrea: No, she's hot.
Jay: Inside?
Andrea: Yes.
Jay: Is she wet from more than spray?
Andrea: Yes, for sure.
Jay: He reaches under her long dress, rests his hand between her legs.
Andrea: She doesn't want him to.
Jay: He moves his hand away.
Andrea: No. Rest his hand.
Jay: He finds her under her lace panties.
Andrea:
Jay planned to finish his graphic frolic with Andrea but was getting nervous about the time. It was almost nine-thirty, and Lauren would soon be home. He and Andrea were both very aroused.
Jay: have to go.
Andrea: Wish not, but understand. Last time was The Dance. What is tonight called? Unbelievable?
Jay: Love on the Rocks.
Parker was no fool and realized that his fantasy with Andrea could be explosive for the both of them. He was particularly leery of sexual harassment charges between a worker and superior, especially a woman and a man, and had been well trained on the subject by his employer.
Even though the whole idea of what a sexual experience is had been thrown into question by the Clinton inquiry, Jay and most people – unlike the President – did not need a definition of sex to know that they had had it. Still, Parker's cyber encounter was extremely erotic and exciting, but did it constitute infidelity? It was tough for him to say. Maybe the sophists would know. He didn't actually do anything physical, at least not yet.
It was Parker's idea to use a third party – a man, the lady; he, him; she, her – which was a clever way for each to let the other know how he or she

felt while, literally, remaining detached. It was easy to talk about someone else who was in a story rather than yourself. Everything was nice and safe, and the erotic objective was accomplished.

Why he had become involved with Andrea in this way, Jay was unsure and didn't want to think about it. They just seemed to connect. There were many women on line who would enjoy a similar escapade, but doing it with a person Jay knew was more exciting to him. Besides, everyone on line had screen names that guaranteed anonymity.

"They're all wearing a mask," Jay thought to himself, "and I could be talking to a man I think is a woman. He could be a fag. Who knows?" Donning a mask didn't bother him; he wore any number on a given day: father, husband, friend, boss, worker, neighbor, son, whatever. No one is ever completely open with someone else, and we all wear masks for protection. No one would survive otherwise, he reasoned.

Parker concluded that even if Andrea saved the whole conversation in a file on her computer, she would have a hard time proving that it was he with whom she corresponded. He hated the idea of not being able to trust her completely, especially after they had shared such intimacy. There was always a but. Did she feel the same?

Anything on a computer, Parker knew, was untrustworthy because the information could be changed or manipulated. Computers weren't repositories of truth; they were what you wanted them to be. Tonight it was just another tool for a man and woman to find yet another way to do what men and women has always done. It was far easier, to be sure, or at least he thought so.

What could be done for people who were either on line or telephone sexually dysfunctional? Find a psychologist who specialized in such an area. If one didn't exist, it was only a matter of time. The marketing possibilities were out there, Jay thought.

Lauren would probably be home at any minute now. As he always did, Jay went upstairs to check on the children. He loved to see them sleeping in their beds and holding onto their favorite toy: Arthur at Bedtime, Arthur at School, and plain old Arthur.

He gently kissed them on the forehead and pulled up the covers before quietly leaving the room. They were everything to him, even when asleep. There was nothing Jay would not do for them, including finding for Christmas, which was nearly eight weeks away, a toy ferryboat that carried cars.

Parker was no sooner settled in the family room watching the Monday night football game and pouring himself a beer, when he heard the garage door open. He knew it was Lauren, of course, because she had a remote and always left her car inside instead of out, like himself. She came into the house by opening the unlocked door from the garage to the adjacent mudroom, where she hung up her coat in the closet. Jay went to greet her.

"Hi. How was the exhibit?"

"It was wonderful. I had a really nice time. How was your day?"

"Aside from being bizarre, all in all, not bad."

"How are the children? Did everything go ok?"

"They're fine. I read them a story and tucked them in. We had a great time. I picked up a new Arthur book for them."

"See? All's well that ends well. I knew you would have fun with them. A better dad there never was." As she passed by Jay, she put her hand on his chest and kissed him lightly. "Anything to eat? I'm a little hungry."

"Didn't you have supper?"

"No, not really. I'll find something in the fridge." Lauren poked around in the refrigerator and came up with some chicken breast from the night before. She put it on a plate, picked up the saltshaker, and went into the family room with Jay. Between bites, she looked at her husband, drew a deep breath, and said, "Jay, can you tell me exactly what did go on between you and Kevin Sweeney?"

"Kevin Sweeney? What's with Kevin Sweeney? First the kids, now you."

"The kids?"

"Yes, they want a car-carrying ferry boat toy for Christmas. They said Kevin told them about one. I've been looking around and can't find any such thing. No one makes it."

"God, aren't they sweet? They were telling you about a real ferry, not a toy. Kevin's uncle took him on a Boston ferry as a little boy. One day he told us all about it. You know how much he loved to tell the children stories. He'd exaggerate, and always come up with some other detail. The children loved that story."

"Well, I never heard about it until just now. Why are you asking me about Kevin?"

"I'm asking you because I had several reminders today. There's an actual picture of the ferry he talked about hanging on the wall at the commuter boat office. I saw it today. Then I met someone who knows him. You still haven't answered my question."

"Nothing happened between me and Kevin. I thought he was a great guy. Real straight and up front. We paid him in full. The asshole I'm upset with is the excavator. He tore up all the outside lighting and ruined the brick patio and still wanted to get paid."

"Jay, I was standing there when that happened. He told me it would and asked my permission. I agreed because there was no other way to dig the foundation for the family room. If anyone is at fault, it's me, not him. He refused to go over the septic system."

"I made it clear to Kevin that I did not want heavy equipment coming into the back yard from the left. I told him to use the right side between our house and the neighbor's."

"Jay, there was no other way to get into the yard. He did what he had to do. What else did you expect?"

"I expected him to let me know about the problem before he tore the place up. That's what. I didn't expect him to cut down the crab apple tree and ruin the patio. He should have known better."

"I made the decision about the tree. If he came in the other way, we would have had to cut down the spruce tree your father gave us when we moved in. Your beloved tree, Jay. Is that what I should have done? You weren't here, and it was costing us $125 an hour for an operator, helper, and a machine.

"They didn't want to wait around for us to have a conference. I tried calling you at work, but you were busy. I approved everything they did. We had nothing to put on the patio except some plastic covering, which they did. They tried."

Their voices were rising.

"Lauren, listen. I don't want to argue with you over Kevin Sweeney. What's done is done. It's only common sense that you take care of the property, you know; protect the patio when you're working. Put down plywood. You don't just tear everything up and expect the homeowner to pay for it. That's incompetence."

"I don't want to argue with you either, Jay, but I really like Kevin, and the children are crazy about him. He did a beautiful job for us, advised us well on how to handle the excavator, and was always professional and finished on time. It's embarrassing.

"All the extra charges were our doing, not his, and no one took advantage of the situation. He made sure everyone was fair. If you ever meet a man more honest than him, let me know because I think you're going to be looking for a very long time."

Growing impatient, Jay said, "I've got no argument with Sweeney. It was a matter of principle, so I didn't pay the excavator. We had to pay the electrician and mason extra to repair the damage."

"Jay, you're not getting it. The specifications Kevin developed mentioned – as a possibility – the very thing that happened. You were informed. You just never read the specs."

"Lauren, I have no more to say about it. I still think it's the principle of the thing. That's it. What more do you want me to say?"

"I don't agree with you, and I think you were wrong. I still don't like the way everything ended. The children would love to see Kevin, but he would probably feel uncomfortable here. It's all wrong."

Having said her piece, Lauren finished eating in silence, and noticed Jay was drinking a beer. She said nothing to him, but he felt her disapproval anyway.

"Don't," Jay said firmly. "I'm just having a goddamn beer like millions of other guys tonight. I'm ok."

"Well, I don't like it, and neither do the kids."

"Stay out of this, Lauren. I'm a big boy. I don't need another mother telling me what to do."

"I'm going to bed," Lauren said disgustedly, as she left the room, leaving Jay speaking to her from a distance as she headed towards the stairs. She hoped the doors to the children's rooms were closed.

"I hate it when you do that. You know what I feel like now? Like some little puppy just shit on my front porch, and I have to clean it up. You get everything off your chest, just get up and walk away, but I'm left to deal with it on my own. It's not the way things are supposed to be, Lauren."

It wasn't, but it would soon become more and more so. To make matters worse, the holidays were coming up, and there was no darker time of the year for Jay than then.

His father would probably want to visit.

****

Before calling it a day at seven-thirty that night, Kevin went downstairs to the bunker office to answer several calls that had come in while he and Marie were having their romantic supper.

Much had been made in the media of the advantages of working from a home office, but Kevin had another story to tell.

There was no way for him to his escape his work, weekends and holidays included. Before making any phone calls, Sweeney sorted his business mail into three piles: bills, correspondence, and trash.

Kevin was quick to pay his bills because he hated having them, but very slow to do his accounting, which was computerized and very easy to use. If he had bank statements to balance, he would scan them to make sure that his deposits had cleared and generally knew how much money he had to work with. It was another bad habit he had yet to overcome.

Sweeney immediately threw out any unsolicited mail and catalogues, which he seemed to get every day. You would think that with all the technology available someone would know that he was not ordering from a catalogue and stop sending it. Not so, there was always hope, he supposed.

He did keep the catalogue from the University of Massachusetts, Boston Campus, which was a short distance from the Kennedy Library. Kevin was thinking of going back to school for a Master's Degree in Instructional Design, and he knew UMASS would be a perfect place for him because most of its students were older.

One carefully typed business envelope caught his attention because Kevin was hoping for a response to a letter he had sent to the company, which was searching for a computer trainer. Every now and then, Sweeney would scan the classified advertising section of *The Boston Sunday Globe* for positions that interested him and for which he appeared qualified. There was always the hope, but not this time. It was another form letter saying "No Thanks."

Of the hundreds of well paying jobs Sweeney had applied for over a ten-year period, including the time during a recent labor shortage, he had been hired only once, and that position was part time.

Yet, he loved it. Kevin got the marketing consultant job in the early 1990's for a Commonwealth of Massachusetts sponsored program that helped unemployed people start their own businesses. His previous unemployment was actually a qualification. The idea behind the sixteen-week program was that self-employment could be a remedy for unemployment under the proper guidance, direction, and training. It was six months of pure joy.

By the time the first program, the pilot, was completed Sweeney had had his doubts. There was a major difference between creating a business that became a saleable asset and having a job in that enterprise. Once the euphoria of wearing every hat and making every decision about the business wore off, all that was left was a job to do.

What most people created was a job, not a business, and it was one they would eventually come to hate.

On the other hand, entrepreneurs created successful businesses and hired people to do the job of running them. The real satisfaction came from the result, not the process.

Sweeney would know because he was in a job – and situation – of his own making, and it was unimaginably difficult for him. The worry, strain, uncertainty, physical and emotional stress, and countless hours took their toll, and Marie could see it in his face every day and felt helpless to do anything about it.

Kevin never once complained nor was he bitter. The jury was still out on his idea: the economy was not right, the volume was still not there, it takes time to build a business – good arguments all which did little to change the reality of his life. Sweeney was getting older, the business was providing a marginal livelihood; the longer he stayed in it, the more difficult it would be to get out.

The consulting position offered him the first real hope for change, but when the program was expanded to Southeastern Massachusetts, he was deliberately overlooked for the well paying position of director. In fact, despite his inspirational instruction and leadership, he got only a thank you, a chocolate watch, he used to say. Local politicians controlled those jobs in the extended program, and none of them were going to anyone who did not vote in their district.

At home, the sound of the phone was sometimes enough to make him tense because it rang often and was disruptive and intrusive. He could turn off the business phone on the first floor, of course, but then he ran the risk of missing an important call.

Kevin picked up two messages from his answering device and wrote down the names of the callers but not their telephone numbers. The calls were from two subcontractors, an electrician and a plumber. He decided to call the electrician but would let the other call go until the next morning.

Sweeney turned to his computer and opened a program he used to record all his appointments, telephone calls, or correspondence. It was a powerful database Kevin used to streamline his company's business and a means by which he could record important information without resorting to his memory or a scrap of paper. Both calls were expected because each had been tracked.

"Steve, it's Kevin. How are you doing?"

"Hey, Kevin. Did you get my message?"

"Yes, I did, what's up?"

"I'm just checking in. What's up with Matthews and Bailey?"

"We're moving right along at Matthews. Walter has most of the framing done, and he'll be roofing within a day. I'll probably need you the beginning of next week. I still don't have the kitchen layout yet, but George tells me it's imminent.

"Bailey's been slow, but it's a huge project anyway. Dana and Dan have just about gutted the second floor completely, and they'll be taking off the roof within a day or two. I had a lot of fun with them today getting rid of the cast iron tub," Kevin said without elaborating.

Steve would find out about the stooge act on his own. "All right," he said, "so there's only the demo there for me to do until they get started with the framing. With Matthews, are we still looking at the first floor addition in back and the kitchen? What about the second floor addition?"

"That's it. They're not doing the second story addition. I don't blame them. With only three people in the house, they did not need an extra bedroom. Once we added everything up, it became obvious what to take out."

"Always does. It wasn't that much work for me anyways. So what do you think? Monday ok? I can start upstairs rewiring the old boxes and putting in the paddle fans they added. Will the sidewall be finished by then?" Stevie asked.

"Pretty close. Weymouth's not like Hingham. The inspector doesn't care if the siding is on or not before we start the mechanicals. He's not a permit Nazi. It would be great if all those guys were on the same page."

"Every town's different, Kevin. I've seen wiring inspectors disagree with each other in the same town. It's like going to confession in the old days. You hope you get a good guy and a couple of Hail Marys."

"A couple of Hail Marys? When the hell did you ever get a couple of Hail Marys? I thought you got eternal penance," Kevin said.

"It's been a long time since I got a few Hail Marys. Every now and then. From what I hear, you were no saint either." Neither one of them knew at the time that Steve would soon need more than a few Hail Marys.

"Forget all that. The altar boy stuff and my twelve years of parochial school at Gatie count big time. Too bad I didn't know to buy some property in Southie to fix up. Prices are going through the roof, you know. My mother's house is worth a small fortune. It's amazing. People who had nothing most of their lives and had to struggle to get by are now worth a lot of money."

"That's the way it goes these days," Bonnano responded to Sweeney's comments about change in his old neighborhood. "Hey! When we going back into the city, Kev? I miss the South End. Remember that great little restaurant we used to go to for lunch? The one owned by the fags?"

"My buddies? They were great guys, and you couldn't beat the food or prices. I might have something coming up. A guy called me who bought a building on Dartmouth Street and wants to put in an office and have the second and third floors combined into a single apartment. I'm going in to meet him this Wednesday."

"I'll never forget the time we went to lunch at that other little restaurant on Tremont Street. You know, the one you liked so much."

"That little place on the corner? It was great. I love that place."

"Well, I think the waiter loved you. That's why the fag sat us down at the booth with the ass on the wall. You should have seen the look on your face. You were very indignant, you know. I would have kept the booth, but, no, you couldn't sit there with some guy's naked ass staring down at you."

"I do have my reasons, you know. A woman's ass. That's another matter." Kevin did have his reasons, but Bonnano did not know them.

"How do you know that ass wasn't a woman's?" Stevie B. laughed, not pushing the subject any further.

Steve Bonnano and Kevin were more than business associates. They had become friends and broken the cardinal rule against such a relationship. Bonnano was Kevin's eyes and ears when he was not on site and a direct pipeline to him at all other times. Sweeney dubbed him, Stevie Bananas, because the electrician was a lot of fun and a part time wild and crazy guy.

Bonnano was tall, dark, and handsome, for sure, with light blue eyes, but badly overweight and a heavy smoker. Kevin's eating patterns weren't much help to Stevie, and the two never went to restaurants together where they served yogurt or cottage cheese.

Sweeney thought Bonnano was two different people, the first rate, funny, loyal friend and business associate and the other guy everyone else saw. Even Bonnano's wife, Annie, noticed the difference. "I don't know what it is, but when Steve's with you, Kevin, he's not the same. You seem to bring out the best in him. I wish I could." He did, but then again, Kevin often had that effect on a lot of people.

"Let me know about that one. I hear what some guys are charging, and I don't know how they do it. I can understand something extra for the down time just trying to find a parking spot, moving the truck half a dozen times to let someone out, or parking tickets. You know, Big Dig bullshit."

"I guess the people don't care what they pay as long as they're getting the quality and service."

"They care, all right. They just don't know the difference. Don't forget, there's a real labor shortage in Boston. You got anything else for me, Banana Man?"

"Banana Man! I'm going to whack you. Don't let those fags hear you saying that. I'll be fucked."

"I wouldn't go that far, unless you really wanted to."

"You asshole. And you're supposed to be my friend," Steve said with gentle humor.

Every time Steve called he had something interesting and fun to say. Kevin loved the tidbits and could always tell that Steve had no intention of ending the conversation. It was something like an Irish Goodbye, except that

Bonnano was proudly Italian. "I'll talk to you later," he finally said, which was his trademark sign off.

Kevin laughed before saying goodbye and hanging up the phone. He knew that by the end of next week, Stevie would have all the electrical work done and inspected and a complete profile on the Matthews.

Kathy and George Matthews would tell Steve their whole life's story, effortlessly and without reservation, and wouldn't even know it. Bonnano had a way of uncovering such things – and much more – and these people, like every one of Kevin's clients before them, would accept Steve like a long lost member of their family.

Their son, Jonathan, would not be the first to cry when Steve left the job a few months down the road. There was nothing malicious or calculated in what Bonnano did. He simply liked people, took an interest in them, and loved to talk.

Immediately after that conversation, Sweeney entered a few notes into Bonnano's follow up phone call form, scheduled his own work for the next day, and quit the database. Before opening Microsoft Word, Kevin paused and took a deep breath.

He was suddenly overcome with emotion and knew that he could no longer put off writing a poem that had been welling up inside him.

Sweeney already had the title, *My Two-Bye Guy*, and loved the rhyming possibilities of the word, guy, and the play on words of "two bye" for someone in construction.

The poem would be about his son, Mark, who had gone off to Vermont – almost six months ago – for a new job as an art director. Kevin had been lost ever since and could not bring himself to change a single thing that Mark had left in his messy studio right next to his bunker office.

Marie was amazed – Mark and Kevin had argued many times about the studio's condition – but never said anything to her husband. One day she cleaned up the area herself. Kevin noticed the change, of course, but managed to say only, "Thank you," out of relief not gratitude.

That day early last spring, Kevin saw Mark load up his sporty new car with his clothes, stereo, mountain bike, some personal effects, and not much else. There was much he left behind.

Kevin told himself over and over, "He's not moving out; he's moving on," but the rationalization didn't help a whole lot. Sweeney watched Mark from the large picture window in the living room and made sure that his son did not notice him looking on.

Mark came back into the house to get something else, hugged his father, and said, "Bye," as he went out the door. Within seconds he was back, this time annoyed that he didn't have his keys. "Dad, do you know where my keys are?" No, he didn't.

"Do you have your wallet?" He did, and then he found his keys. Once again, Mark headed out the door, and for the second time said "bye" to his father, who said nothing. Tears were streaming down Kevin's face, and he turned away from the window as Mark backed his car down the long driveway.

"Can't burden him with my emotions," he thought to himself. "He needs the emotional freedom to be on his own." Kevin then went into the kitchen to get a tissue and struggled with himself.

He stood by the back door, which he would forget to close before leaving the house in the warm months, and gazed out at his brick patio and the birds streaming into and out of the feeder. He may have stayed there ten minutes or more.

Mark never left the house without forgetting something and being annoyed that he did, and that early spring day was no different. One happy "bye" was always followed by an impatient one. He was his father's Two-Bye Guy. Deep down inside, Kevin thought he would die.

Chapter 7

We know from the Bible that God placed in the Garden of Eden the Tree of Life and the Tree of Knowledge of Good and Evil.
What you say is true.
We also know that Eve ate the fruit of the Tree of Knowledge of Good and Evil.
Yes, the Old Testament tells us so.
At that moment did not Eve become aware of good and evil and her own mortality?
Such an understanding seems correct.
I ask you then. When Eve gave Adam the fruit to eat was she committing homicide?
No, that conclusion would be false.
Why say you so?
She did not kill him. She made him her equal. She broke the laws of God, not man.
Agreed, but then your argument that man is the measure of all things cannot be so.

****

"…And you think you're having another heart attack, like the one yesterday? Ah, huh. And you'd like to see the doctor? Sure. Ah, huh. Then why don't you come in? I understand. No. Not at all.

"Is your niece there to drive you to the office? She is. That'll be fine. Yes, the doctor will be happy to see you, Mr. Ambrose. I'll let him know you're coming.

"Right. Sure. No, that's ok. It's better to be safe. I'll be watching for you. Bye now," the receptionist said as she continued writing down the information she was gathering from Arthur Ambrose, the eighty three year old, long standing patient of Dr. Adam Pierce.

She spoke slowly, distinctly, and respectfully without shouting.

"What was that all about?" Stephanie Lahey, the pretty young nurse standing nearby, asked Rebecca Solberg, the office receptionist.

"That was Mr. Ambrose again. He thinks he's having another heart attack. He's so sweet, the poor man. He didn't want to impose on the doctor. It must be awfully difficult for him. He hates to rely on anyone for anything, especially his niece."

Neither Stephanie nor Rebecca seemed worried about the condition of Mr. Ambrose who was suffering more from depression than a heart ailment. Since the time two years ago when he fell getting out of his car and broke his wrist, life was becoming increasingly more difficult and complicated for him.

Though alone – his wife had died of heart disease years ago – Ambrose would not leave his modest, well kept home. "They'll take me out feet first and with my shoes on," he frequently said.

His health was definitely failing and, Rebecca thought, his spirits were, too. "Mr. Ambrose's niece will be driving him in. I think you've met her before."

"Oh, yes, I have. She's really very nice to help her uncle out the way she does. Do you know if she works?" Stephanie asked.

"I'm not too sure about what she does. What I do know is that she's his only surviving relative around here. Most of his family has died off or moved away a long time ago. He's very isolated, which is not good. And I don't think he's been eating very well."

"There's nothing about him that Dr. Pierce can't tell you. He knows the whole story from day one."

He certainly did, as completely as he knew the whole story about all his patients, most of who had been with him for almost thirty years. Dr. Pierce knew not only the medical condition of each patient but all the minute, seemingly unrelated details, things like the larger family history, where relatives worked and lived, names of their children, where they went to school, what they majored in, how many children they had, what awards they won in school, their age, their interests, ad infinitum.

Most amazing of all, Dr. Pierce remembered everything he was told.

Medicine wasn't all science, and there was nothing like the warm, human touch he demonstrated with all his patients. Dr. Pierce always had time for them and, it seemed, infinite patience. Visiting him was like going to see a close friend.

Mr. Ambrose – Arthur to the doctor – would not be going to a modern clinic to meet Dr. Pierce; he would, instead, visit the doctor at his home office, which had been completely done over less than a year ago. The home, located in Cohasset near the picturesque harbor, was a large, modern colonial with five bedrooms, three and one-half baths, gourmet kitchen, and a dining room that stepped down to a family room with glass walls on two sides and a large, atrium like skylight in the center.

Its main feature was a stunning living room that had an open, wooden staircase leading to the second floor where there was a narrow balcony at the top and left sides. The ceiling was cathedral, and had several stacked skylights and many sloped, recessed lights. On the two outside walls, joined casement windows ran from floor to ceiling and were spaced apart every eight feet on center.

The overall impression was of a great formal hall or library, and the distinctive furnishings and spacious, modern paintings added to that effect. The only thing missing was a coat of arms.

The new office area was large, bright, airy, cheerful, tastefully decorated, and connected to the main house by an enclosed breezeway. Based on the patients' reactions, they loved the difference from the old office, which had been in the basement of the main house but was easily accessible from a side door.

"It's so quiet and peaceful here," he would often hear them say, which was testimony to the effectiveness of the sound deadening techniques and materials used in the project. Everything that could be done to accommodate Dr. Pierce's elderly clientele had been.

He had hired an architect with expertise in medical facilities to design the building and worked with an interior designer to coordinate colors, textures, carpeting, and window treatments. The two professionals cooperated very well with each other and openly shared their ideas.

To avoid a ramp, the addition was built at near ground level, which was a nice feature that also eliminated the need for railings and other safety requirements.

Much attention had been paid to the waiting room, which had a receptionist's desk near the elegant, solid oak front door. A play area stood in the corner for the "tots," as Dr. Pierce liked to call them.

The wallpaper consisted of large, colorful flowers, which was appropriate for the scale of the room. The floral theme was picked up in the large, comfortable – but firm – sofa that sat three people. Completing the seating arrangement were several individual chairs, also upholstered, and several more that looked like dining room chairs but with cushioned seats.

All were grouped around one large, circular table that was centered on an elegant, gas log fireplace. On the table were plenty of magazines, all of them current.

The children especially liked the window seats built into the bay windows on either side of the fireplace and enjoyed looking at the fully landscaped garden outside with its brick walkway, beautiful trees, and bird feeders and bath.

There were no fluorescent or recessed lights in the waiting room, only table lamps with bulbs that had been light corrected to 3600K, which made one's skin color appear more natural, neither too much to the red or blue.

A contrasting, level loop carpet – a better and safer choice than cut pile – covered all the floors of the new facility except, of course, the bathroom, which was handicap accessible and equipped with a toilet that was higher than normal for patients who had arthritic joints or difficulty sitting.

All the colors – floors, walls, ceiling, furniture, and curtains – were soft and friendly, the perfect look for someone who wanted you to feel as though you were enjoying the comfort of his living room. Blue was not used anywhere because most elderly people had trouble seeing that color.

The pictures hanging on the walls were mostly beautiful, recognizable, New England land and seascapes.

The receptionist's cherry wood desk – really a writing desk – had curvilinear legs and two small center drawers and held the office computer, which was shared by Stephanie, Rebecca, and Dr. Pierce. Behind the desk were the file cabinets and a customized, built-in, cherry bookcase with adjustable shelves, raised panels, and solid brass hardware.

The doctor's office also had a desk – a large, traditional one made of maple – and several nice, comfortable chairs, which he preferred to use when talking with a patient. Behind the desk were his diplomas from Harvard University and John Hopkins School of Medicine, and other framed citations and certificates.

Pierce had a pedigree and was the son and grandson of fine family physicians. His practice catered to the elderly, most of who were on Medicare.

His two assistants had not been with him very long. Stephanie, who was twenty-four and recently engaged, had joined him fresh out of nursing school. Dr. Pierce hired her because she appeared to have a genuine love and affection for older people.

Rebecca Solberg had been with him for less than a year and had found out about the job through her niece's husband, Auggie, who was a foundation subcontractor associated with Kevin Sweeney whom Dr. Pierce had hired for the construction of his project. Nancy and Auggie were expecting their first child, which was due in four months.

There had been something about the need to blast ledge to install the foundation, but that work – which was very expensive – was not in Auggie's contract. If it had been a problem, Dr. Pierce showed no evidence of it to Rebecca when she interviewed for the job.

At fifty-five years of age, she was just getting her life back together after having lost her husband, mother, and stepfather to various diseases over a period of fifty-one months. A year ago, Rebecca had sold her waterfront home on the bay side of Hull and moved into a condominium complex on a cliff overlooking Nantasket Beach. The money she had inherited from her parents' estate as their only child and the sale of her own house left Rebecca with no bills, solid savings, and extra money she could put towards retirement.

Rebecca knew something about sickness, pain, loss, and sacrifice, but she never allowed or sought pity from anyone. She went about her life with dignity and purpose and accepted the fact that she would probably be alone – without a man – for the remaining years of her life.

Being around other couples was difficult for her, and the world she knew was a very coupled place. Nine months ago, a female friend succeeded in pressuring Rebecca into going to a wedding with her so that she herself would not be alone or feel out of place. It turned out to be a fortuitous decision because Rebecca met a man, Barry Sobilof, who soon became romantically significant in her life.

Rebecca had lived in Hull most of her life and knew many, many people, including Tony Romano, who had become something of a local legend for his amazing financial success. In fact, teachers who knew Romano urged their students to work hard, ala Romano, if someday they wanted to be like him.

Romano's parents were patients of Dr. Pierce, and Rebecca had spoken to Mrs. Romano when she came in for a checkup, accompanied by her son and husband. She hadn't been feeling all that well, but couldn't quite say what was bothering her. Dr. Pierce had ordered some tests, but the results were inconclusive.

He scheduled an appointment for Mrs. Romano for three months after her visit, but insisted that she call him if there was the slightest change in her condition. The chances were good he would call her before that time, regardless.

Pierce thought Rebecca was a godsend. There was almost nothing around the office she couldn't or wouldn't do, given that she was really an experienced medical secretary with excellent interpersonal skills. Overnight it seemed, all Dr. Pierce's patients loved her and delighted in talking to her. Some kept secret tabs on her blossoming romance.

"How's everything going with your gentleman friend?" they would ask. A few advised her, "Don't get married. Move in like the young kids. It's better for Social Security. All my grandkids did."

It was a perfect arrangement. Rebecca freed Dr. Pierce to practice medicine, and he gave her the freedom to run his practice. Rebecca did everything from scheduling to bookkeeping – everything, that is, except balance the bank statement. That disagreeable task, the doctor reserved for himself, even though he knew he could trust her with such sensitive information.

Exactly why Dr. Pierce would have gone through such an expense for his new office addition was something of a mystery. The doctor was, after all, sixty-four years old, already into his second family, nearing retirement age, and in the autumn of his life.

There wasn't that much risk involved in the $145,000 improvements he had made to the house. With a much smaller, additional investment, the office could be converted into an in-law apartment prior to the sale of the home, which was by far much more than a family of four needed.

The doctor had been divorced from his first wife, Ellen, for nearly twenty years and had two children by her, a boy and a girl. The marriage just didn't work out, but she managed to exact an onerous settlement for putting him through medical school, raising their family, and sacrificing her career for his.

She had maintained custody of the children, and he kept his practice, which had once belonged to Ellen's father. Those times were rosy and full of expectation, but the subsequent divorce had left Dr. Pierce heavily in debt, bitter, and disillusioned.

He thought he had been doing everything right by working seven days a week for more than five straight years before taking off a single day. He was earning over $100,000 back then during the late sixties and had it all: a fabulous career in a highly respected profession, a wife, children, house, summer cottage, sailboat, memberships in all the right clubs, including the South Shore Country Club, and a wide, wealthy, influential circle of friends.

Adam Pierce had played by all the rules and done what was expected of him. He had provided for his family by working hard, very hard, and in the end, it all meant nothing.

Dr. Pierce was resolved not to make the same mistake with his second wife, a petite, warm, understanding, and friendly nurse he met at the hospital in Boston. He wasn't divorced when they met, but he just as well might have been. Judy was an irresistible attraction to him, and their impassioned affair became the subject of much delicious gossip amongst their colleagues.

She was younger than he by almost twenty years, a fact that fueled even more the speculation about the esteemed Dr. Pierce. He was not sold on the male mid-life crises crap and had refused marital counseling by arguing that psychology was philosophy not science. Things just didn't work out, and they never would. To hell with what anyone else thought. Time to move on.

His relationship to his children remained distant, but he never forgot his financial obligations to them and had paid for their expensive Ivy League, college education. They were adults now and, much to his relief, on their own, and very successful. Neither had married.

Although he privately wanted to see his son follow the family footsteps into medicine, Dr. Pierce was equally relieved that the son did not. Medicine was changing. There were HMO's, Medicare, Medicaid, and insurance companies to deal with all the time.

It was hard to tell who was in charge, the doctor or the insurers.

The quality of care, Pierce believed, depended on the decision of some clerk, and more and more time was being spent on bookwork than casework. Medicine was a business, and Pierce hated that reality.

The paperwork involved in running the business was voluminous and enough to be demoralizing. Like most doctors, Pierce hated the business side of medicine and was, as a result, not a very good businessman. Ironically, he was like many contractors who love to do the work but hate working on the books.

Ever the nonconformist, Pierce continued on his own as a solo practitioner, which was becoming increasingly rare and bucking the trend in the medical profession. He was not about to join an HMO that would pay him a salary and limit his income.

HMO's, he thought, were an evil business that did not work well for either doctor or patient. Pierce had e-mailed colleagues about the gag rule some HMO's required of their physicians. "Can you imagine being in a position where your employer will fire or sue you if you tell a patient she needs an MRI because the HMO doesn't want to pay for it?

"The HMO trade association says its members don't have gag rules. If it wasn't a problem, why did thirteen states pass anti-gag legislation? The once sacrosanct, doctor – patient relationship has gone out the window. Double pane, I might add," he wrote, expecting them to get the pun.

He had hopes of someday selling his practice, believing that, as the population was already rapidly aging, gerontology would be a good place for a younger physician to start his or her career. The old, venerable pro would get out with his honor and principles intact.

Pierce's wife, Judy, was not so sure of the future and had taken steps many years ago to ensure her career. She had earned a master's degree in hospital administration, which paid well but took her away from home on frequent consulting assignments.

All in all, the couple was doing well, financially, but new strains on their finances were on the horizon. They had two teenage daughters, one a senior in high school, and the other a junior. Both had big plans for college, were academically near the top of their respective classes, and wanted to go to an Ivy League school.

Scholarship money was unlikely despite the girls' academic standing; loans, a possibility; but major help from their parents almost a certainty.

Mom and Dad had been able to put them through private schools – starting with first grade – at the expense of savings and retirement funds. The family's expensive vacations would be next and then other resources, like the adjoining lot they owned.

There was, however, a problem with the lot that left in doubt its status as buildable. It would certainly perk ok for a septic system, but the small, abandoned pool that the previous owners had installed many years ago was now being considered by the conservation department as an inland body of water. As such, locating a house a proper distance from the man made, overgrown pond would be impossible, and a variance was out of the question.

Pierce had once hired a lawyer to look into the matter, but the attorney was not able to settle the problem. "You may never get it resolved," she told him.

New cars would have to wait, but then again, the old Mercedes was becoming a classic and was still in great shape. All the tires had been recently replaced – they needed it – especially since one had been badly damaged by a roofing nail left over, most likely, from the new construction. Judy's 1994 BMW still had plenty of mileage left on it.

Pierce felt he could do no less for his daughters than he had for his other two children. Somehow, it would all work out, and somehow he would continue practicing medicine until the financial pressure was off, and then decide what to do next. He still had his options, and, to the outside world, everything would appear normal.

The teenage girls knew nothing about the family's finances, but their father worried about money almost as much as he did his patients. Pierce was angry at the state of medicine throughout the country and blamed greed for it.

"There was a time when the doctor was revered by his patients," he had e-mailed a friend, "and he was respected in the community. The care and treatment of his patients came above all else. I thought what I was doing was noble. Can you think of anything that's more meaningful or important than helping people? You know that saying in real estate about what's most important? Location, location, location. In medicine it used to be Patients, Patients, Patients. Now it's Money, Money, Money!"

Pierce was sick of arguing with Medicare over what he felt was proper reimbursement for services rendered and terribly frustrated that someone else – a bureaucrat – could be in control of his earnings.

"I should just bill them an extra ten to fifteen percent to get back what they're already taking away from me anyway," Pierce said early one morning to his wife, Judy. "Medicare figures you're charging too much anyway, so they cut you down almost automatically. Unilaterally, like or leave it. If you think about it, I should treat them the way they treat me.

"It's a principled thing to do," Pierce pressed on. "I can understand why other doctors overcompensate. It's the only way they can get what they deserve. The system forces you to do things you don't want to do but gives you no other choice. My patients would never question the Medicare bill. It would be unseemly to them."

It would be, if they even remembered to look at all. Besides being occasionally forgetful and confused, older patients held their doctors in awe and were completely dependent on them. Given the large number of elderly patients he cared for, it would not be difficult for Pierce to spread around the overcharge. There would be no pattern, nothing obvious to draw further scrutiny.

No one in the office would question him. Judy gave no response. Given her background, she could see both sides of the issue. Maybe there was no answer. "I just don't think I can take anymore," Pierce said bitterly. "The whole damn system is wrong and unfair."

What Dr. Pierce did not know was that his receptionist, Rebecca Solberg, had come in early that day and had unintentionally overheard this disturbing conversation. She felt sick at heart that a man of such principle and stature in the community and medicine would even think of doing something so foolish.

She was so despondent for the rest of the day that even the doctor noticed. "You don't seem your self today, Rebecca. Anything I can help you with?" he asked with great concern.

"No. Not really. I just have something on my mind. It will pass. Every now and then, I get like this. I'll be ok," she said reassuringly.

He had been so good to her and everyone else. She couldn't let him do it. She wouldn't let him do it.

Rebecca would watch for signs of over billing, such things as blood or lab tests that had not been performed or visits to nursing homes where the patients were asleep or hospitals where they were unconscious after coming out of surgery.

Solberg knew where to look, and now the government web site that Dr.

Pierce had book marked made more sense to her. She had checked it out and knew it identified many fraudulent schemes that had already been tried and failed.

Or did it? What if Dr. Pierce was providing this information to his patients to prevent them from becoming victims? Many of them required medical devices and supplies used in the home, things like oxygen equipment, wheelchairs, artificial limbs, braces, and hospital beds, all of which were covered under Medicare and had been scammed.

Besides, the site also provided information about choosing a nursing home – a decision many of his patients might have to face someday.

She had heard chilling rumors that temporary medical help agencies were placing personnel in offices where the doctors were suspected of Medicare fraud. The federal government was supposedly paying the agency to establish the theft. The amount paid was at least thirty percent of what was billed fraudulently and all other penalties and fines.

There was no way Dr. Pierce could possibly think she was a mole, but he must have heard the stories. He knew she had returned to work by temping at first. He was the nicest and most understanding employer she had ever known and gave her a lot of freedom in her job.

No, Dr. Pierce could not have given his patients the information or else Rebecca would have known. Besides, he wasn't that great on the computer – other than using e-mail, which he loved – and had trouble doing simple things like printing.

Rebecca would look after Dr. Pierce and see to it that no trouble came his way. She'd get the proof then protect him from himself. It would be easy because she kept the books and could double check with Stephanie regarding the nature of various visits made to the doctor or his whereabouts.

There could be a patient confidentiality problem if Rebecca talked to Stephanie in too much detail, but she would find a way around it. Maybe Stephanie herself was providing the information about nursing homes. It would have been her job, but Rebecca seldom saw Stephanie on the computer.

DAP – Dr. Adam Pierce – was the mnemonic name of the Quicken accounting file on the office computer. She would keep two sets of electronic books, DAP1 and DAP2. Rebecca would send them to herself via e-mail as attachments she could open up on her personal computer at home. She now had her own e-mail account set up on the office computer. Before then, everyone used the same account.

Dr. Pierce had given Rebecca permission to do the bookkeeping at home. He didn't care how or when it got done, as long as it did. If anyone asked about DAP2, which was highly unlikely, she would say it was backup for DAP1. Some things had to be worked out, but she could do it. She wasn't sure how, but she would try.

Mrs. Rebecca Solberg would do the wrong thing for the right reasons, just like Doctor Adam Pierce himself.

Chapter 8

"And what would you like, sir?" the sweet, attractive, thirty-plus waitress with a tight jersey top and black slacks asked. She had already announced that she was "Chris, and I'll be your waitress."

"Me? I think I'll start with an appetizer. How about an order of shrimp and a Sam Adams?"

"Sure," she said, writing down the order while moving on to the next person.

"And you, sir? Can I interest you in an appetizer?" As soon as she said it, the waitress knew she was in trouble with this crowd, a bunch of contractors who were having lunch with Kevin Sweeney at the Venetian in Jackson Square, Weymouth. Kevin was picking up the tab because it was the day before Thanksgiving and he wanted to show the guys his appreciation for all the work they had done for his clients during the past year.

"You leave her alone now, and behave yourself," Kevin said playfully to the contractor sitting on his right.

The waitress laughed, and it was clear that she was enjoying herself and the attention from the guys.

"No. No appetizer for me, but I would like a beer, if my friend here doesn't mind."

"Fine. Draft or bottle?" the waitress asked.

His friend, Kevin Sweeney, did not mind but also had not had a drink in more than fifteen years.

Each knew why and respected him for it. Sweeney had told the guys about his father and grandfather on his mother's side, both of whom were alcoholics long since in their graves.

"There's so much alcoholism in my family on both sides, I figured I was at risk. No matter how much I drank, an ounce or a quart, it was always the same. The next day I would be so depressed that I felt as though someone had taken a scalpel to my soul," he had said.

Kevin was not your typical reformer and never said a thing about drinking to the men, unless he suspected it on the job. Then, he would immediately sever his relationship with the contractor and never gave him a second chance.

Sweeney was in a great mood and loved Thanksgiving. "My favorite holiday is the Fourth of July, followed by Thanksgiving, then Memorial Day.

I hate Christmas, which is a commercial feeding frenzy masquerading as a religious holiday," he said.

Assembled around the table were highly skilled contractors and friends who could build anything. Although they did not all get along together, each man did respect the abilities of the other. Kevin called them his motley cast of characters and seemed attracted to them for the very reason someone else might not. Their personalities were all very different from his own.

Sitting on his right was Steve Bonnano, the electrician who liked to think of himself as Sweeney's right hand man. Beside him was Dan O'Neil, the carpenter working at Crow's Point, Hingham, his partner, Dana, Ono Cazeault, the HVAC sub, Bruce Lacey, a plumber, Lacey's friend, the quirky and flinty Dan McPhee, a flooring subcontractor, the father and son team, Walter and Allen Nash, and Eddie Matros, the excavator, on Kevin's left.

While the waitress was finishing up the orders, the guys were talking amongst themselves or checking her out. Bruce Lacey who was sitting opposite Kevin was deeply religious, a born again guy, a bit effeminate, divorced, intelligent, and sensitive in a way that a woman would like. Some of the guys called him, "Spacey Lacey" or "The Lace," and took exception to the fact that he never used foul language or told racist, sexist, or ethnic jokes.

He was an easy target for Steve Bonnano. "Hey, Bruce, I have something for you. The other day, I was thinking of Jesus, and something came up I wanted to ask you about."

"You? About Jesus? Is this a joke?" Bruce asked skeptically.

"No. No. It's no joke. I can think about Jesus, too, you know. Here's what I was wondering. Jesus was supposed to be a carpenter like his step-father, Joseph, right?"

"Well, we don't really know, but I think we can safely assume he was," Bruce said guardedly and looking around at the others for support. "I don't think of Joseph as Jesus' step father."

"Ok, whatever. We also know that Jesus was poor."

"Yeah, he was probably poor, although archeologists now believe that Nazareth was not a poor town and may have been a suburb of a wealthy city." All the guys were listening, wondering where things were headed.

"Really? I didn't know that. Something like Hingham and Abington? Anyway, he's also God and knows everything."

"I believe that he was the Son of God, the Second Person of the Trinity," Bruce asserted sincerely, not wanting to give up any ground.

"Here's the thing. Jesus is God, a carpenter, and poor. If Jesus knew everything, then why was he always the low bidder? I mean, wasn't one crucifixion enough?" Naturally, all the guys started to laugh, and even Bruce gave in, graciously going along with everyone else.

"Another thing," Steve continued. "Jesus is thirty years old and living with his mother. Sounds like a modern guy to me." Stevie Bear was right where he wanted to be: the center of attention getting all the laughs.

"You're just setting me up," Bruce said, fully aware of what was going on. "I should have known better."

"No, I'm not setting you up. These are questions that have been bothering me. So, then Jesus goes out and recruits all these guys to follow him and stir things up. Takes them right from their homes. What do you think they would call the Twelve Apostles today? Saints?"

"I have no idea, Steve," Bruce said coolly. "I'm sure you do. Why don't you tell us all?"

"Dead beat Dads," Steve said, which was followed by more laughter.

It was too much for Lacey. "Come on, Steve. You have to show some respect here. I mean, it's funny and all, but it's my faith you're knocking, and I take it seriously. You just can't do that."

"Oh, come on, Brucie boy, lighten up. I'm just busting your balls."

He sure was, and busting balls or its variant, busting chops, was a well-accepted sport all the men played. It wasn't hard. All you had to do was know or probe for a guy's weak spot, hit it, and get a good laugh from the audience or a bad reaction from the target.

Kevin loved these mental duels and was very, very good at it. They reminded him of his high school days when he and his buddies would hang out on the corner in Southie and rank each other all day long.

The game required that you not lose your cool, which would invite endless ridicule, if you did. You had to make your opponent feel lower than you did, always trumping him. "I'll rank you so low that…." was the opener. Everything and anything from your father, mother, sister, brother, religion, looks, habits, clothes, brains, masculinity – even your dog – were fair game. Nothing was sacred.

It was a pastime that only men could play because they took no offense to what was said, and the process was more important than the outcome. Women would take such remarks as a personal attack or insult they would harbor with deep resentment forever.

Kevin once shut up one tormentor and had his friends talking about it for days afterwards. "I'll rank you so low that when you look up you'll still see down," he had countered.

The Lace couldn't let it go. "Kevin, you're a well educated guy. You grew up a Catholic in Southie. I've never asked you before, but don't you believe in the Bible?"

"Do I believe in it? Can't say as I do, Bruce. It's an interesting book that teaches a lot of good lessons. I don't take it literally," Kevin said. The guys at the table weren't interested in this side bar and were back to talking amongst themselves.

"I do take it literally," Bruce said. "To me, it's the inspired Word of God. What do you think it is?"

"I think it was the DNA evidence of its time," Kevin answered without hesitation.

"The DNA evidence of its time? What do you mean?"

"The incontrovertible truth. There were only a few people in the ancient world that could read or write at the time. They were the elite. What would people in those societies admire most? The written word, I would say, just as we admire science and technology. Idolatry in both cases, if you ask me," Kevin explained. "Not much has changed."

The Lace stared at Sweeney but could think of nothing to say. He would run it over in his mind, ask around at his church, and come back to Kevin later with a counter argument.

The waitress returned with the appetizers and drinks and then waited to take the men's orders. There was a lot of good-natured teasing underway, especially by Steve who seemed to have the waitress' attention most. He loved flirting and could say things that would make the other men cringe, but the women appeared to like it.

"Hey, Kev. What ever happened to Jesse? You seen him around lately?" Ono asked.

Before Kevin could answer, Allen Nash jumped in. "That asshole. I hear he's lost his business and is smacking his wife around. Do you know how old he is? Would you believe twenty-eight? No shit, that guy looks like he's in his forties."

"What happened?" Kevin wanted to know.

"I heard it was coke. His wife finally threw him out. She was the one with all the money, you know, had it tied up in some kind of trust set up by her parents. I feel bad for his kids. They're all screwed up," Allen explained.

"Really, that bad," Kevin said. "I thought he was off the booze and drugs."

"Only when he was around you, Kevin," Allen said seriously. "Too bad he wasn't around you long enough." It was too bad, and it was just as bad that Jesse's personal life had become so chaotic that the guys were now calling him "Talk Show."

"I've got one for you, you won't believe," Eddie Matros said. "All you guys worked on the Auto Dude's house in Cohasset, right? You remember that short, fat bastard with the beard and the long hair tied in back? The homeowner's pal?

"Well, he comes to me and asks me if I need any help. So I ask him what he can do, and he says he has a Class A license. I could have used a guy to move my equipment around, but this guy gives me the fucking creeps. He's a real sleaze. So, I said, real serious like, 'Ya, sure, you got a resume?'"

All the guys howled. "You asked him for a resume?" Dan O'Neil, the framer, asked in disbelief through a laugh. "What'd the little asshole say?"

"He didn't say nothing and just walked away. Anyway, I hear that Buddy Roper in Braintree puts the guy on. He's got some very impressive – very expensive – equipment, his own yard enclosed with chain link, and a couple of Dobermans he leaves out.

"Six months after Buddy hires Sleaze, his Komatsu disappears."

"Disappears? What do you mean disappears? Where the Christ do you hide an excavator?" Walter asked.

"Yeah, were do you hide an excavator?" Kevin demanded.

"Kevin, come on, figure it out. You can be so naïve for such a smart-ass. You think everybody's a nice guy and only does good.

"Here's the deal. Sleaze has a Class A license, so he loads and unloads equipment, drives it around. He's not an operator," Eddie said. "It's gone, man, out of here, Saudi Arabia, and Sleaze ball had something to do with it. He probably wasted the dogs, too."

This news was not new to most men in construction. Word had it that lots of construction equipment – especially in Boston where the Big Dig was underway – was disappearing and being shipped overseas.

"What makes you think so?" Dan McPhee joined in. "I met that guy at Romano's, and he had a big, foul mouth. Telling me crap about his Harley and the guys he hangs out with at Nantasket. Said he was getting more ass than the toilet."

Eddie looked around at the guys and leaned forward on the table. "Right. More ass than the toilet. The only ass he gets is his own and Stevie boy's over there," Eddie said, not passing up the chance to get a shot in at Bonnano.

"I heard that, Matros," Steve said immediately. "I'm keeping score." The kidding between Steve and Eddie was all in good fun but they really did not like each other. Matros looked him off.

"Remember Patrick, the Irish plasterer?" Eddie continued. "He worked in

Southie when he was just starting out about ten years ago, and you'll never guess who he worked for," Matros continued.

With all eyes on him, Eddie knew how to build tension into a story. "Romano," he said, "and he paid all the guys in cash. Every last one of them, says Patrick. You tell me, where does a guy in his late twenties get that kind of money, unless he's Talk Show?"

"Ok Columbo, what else do you know?" Allen interjected.

"I know that Romano and Sleaze are tight. I know that a lot of cars disappeared around here back then and were never found. Not the slightest trace. Gonzo.

"This Sleaze is so dumb he wouldn't know how to piss in the snow, and the Auto Dude's not the brightest bulb in the pack, either.

"Sleaze ball tows cars now, legally has tools to break into them. We're talking minimum wage here with less than minimum smarts, and then he shows up with a brand new Harley after Buddy's Komatsu evaporates," Eddie said. "Two shitheads with all that money.

"My daughter's boyfriend works at Romano's place. He's a mechanic there and says some weird shit's been happening lately. Orders for cars have been wrong, customers complaining, that kind of stuff. It shouldn't be happening, he says, because the Auto Dude's got the latest and greatest in computers.

"Now get this. A very, very expensive, special order truck shows up about a week ago, and nobody can figure out how it got there. From what I hear, Romano had to pay for it up front because it's a special. It's tying up his cash.

"The truck's now sitting out on the back lot, which is how my daughter's boyfriend found out about it. He fell in love with the goddamn thing and started to ask around. He says the truck would never have come in without a buyer already lined up and a heavy deposit taken.

"How much do you want to bet the super truck disappears?"

The guys were riveted because they all knew that Matros was no bullshitter. He invariably shot straight from the hip, which made him something of a confidante to Sweeney. Eddie always seemed to be in the know about the dark side, which Kevin found fascinating.

"Kevin, how the fuck did you ever get involved with the Auto Dude anyway?" Matros asked.

All eyes turned to Sweeney. "Christ!" Kevin said, "I had no idea what this guy was up to. He had a ton of money, but I had no delicate way of asking him where it all came from. He never paid me in cash, always by check because I insisted. Patrick never said a thing."

"That's Patrick for you. He probably didn't want to bum you out," Eddie said. "Whatever happened to the carpenter who worked on that house? Didn't you tell me that Romano fucked him over, too?"

"You could say that," Kevin said. "Romano stiffed him for about five grand, and the guy had just bought a small house in Rockland for himself and his wife. She was trying to get pregnant. Really screwed up his life. I felt very bad about it."

"What happened?" Walter asked.

"It's a very long story, but not for today," Kevin said, but then added, "Another time."

"I was just thinking about that long driveway at Auto Dude's house, and it reminded me of something," McPhee cut in. "It was one of your projects, Kevin, in Duxbury, and you had some other guy, not Eddie, doing the site work.

"Nice guy we all called, Mr. Clean, because he looked like the steroid guy on the bottle. He's the one with the Doberman puppy.

"I'm trying to lay my flooring, and the power keeps going out. I got real pissed and asked Steve to do something about it. Remember?"

"Yeah, yeah, I remember," Bonnano said. "Mr. Clean kept ripping up the underground service because he was trying to get the water line in. His final payment depended on it, but the ground froze solid, about four feet down. He did it three times – three times – and I almost killed him.

"So he tells me he needs to get paid and get out of there, and I tell him he'll have to wait because I ain't going to let him near my lines again. So you know what he wants to do? He wants to set charges and blast the thing in. And he was serious," Steve said, still laughing and sounding incredulous.

The Lace had something to offer. "Those people called me a long time ago to do some work on the first house they had been living in, the one next to the rental that was once an office.

"You talk about money. They were renting the house, the office, and the apartment over it.

"So, anyways, I'm talking to the husband there, and he tells me how much he and the wife loved the house you did for them, Kevin, and how they got in over their heads."

"You don't have to tell me," Kevin said. "I know all about it. They filed for bankruptcy."

"Bankruptcy? How could they file for bankruptcy and still have all that property?" Bruce asked.

"Beats me, but here's something else you don't know. They owned all this land right next to the new house and were planning to subdivide and sell it to pay for that work. Only the real estate market collapsed right around the time they were building, and they were stuck with the land. They were using credit cards to pay for the construction.

"It was a real mess, and they kept everything but the bills."

"Mess, my ass. Those two knew exactly what they were doing," Ono said sarcastically. "They told me the same story because I've been servicing their system all these years. Didn't stop them from sending their kids to Ivy League schools. Probably helped them get loans because they could say they were bankrupt."

"Whoa, nasty, nasty you," Sweeney said. "What's up?"

"Nothing's up," Ono said. "I got kids in school, too, you know; and we can't get any money. How do they do it?"

"I don't know, Kev. You've had some beauts over the years. I mean, most of your clients have been super, especially to me, but, Jesus, you've had some real winners," Steve said.

"Ever hear from the Cock Doc in Cohasset or that mega bucks couple in the Historic District in Hingham? Them two were a real pair," Bonnano added dryly about the Parkers. "I thought she was ok, like she didn't think her shit was ice cream. She had a very, very sexy voice over the phone."

"You know, I actually liked that couple. No one handed them their money, and I know because I got pretty close to them. They worked for it and just hit it big. You guys should have taken Lauren more seriously. She knows something about IPO's, you know, initial public offerings of stock," Kevin answered.

Sweeney continued. "I loved the kids and miss them. I baby-sat for them a couple of times while Lauren went out. They had all sorts of books and loved being read to or would ask me to tell them stories. They were a good family, but the guy wasn't wrapped too tight, if you ask me. Eddie can tell you more about him."

"You bet your ass I can," Eddie said taking up the subject quickly. "The bastard stiffed me for over $2,500 and didn't even have the balls to talk to me directly about the problem. He left his wife to do it. She said she was sorry, and I think she really meant it.

"I'll give her credit though. She admitted he was at fault. Most wives would never do that. She was acting like they would get divorced or something if she ever crossed him. So I'm right in the middle.

"For all their money and fat ass jobs, I wouldn't want to live in that house."

Walter pressed. "What was the problem? I thought that job turned out fantastic. I know the carpentry was because I did it."

"It did, but I'm still pissed off about it," Eddie said. "It's a real sore spot with me because I got screwed, and they got that beautiful house. That's my money they're enjoying. I'll tell you another time all the gory details."

Stevie Bear saw an opportunity to dump on Matros. "They treated me pretty good, paid me right up front, no problem. I've been back there a couple of times to add some outlets. The husband bought himself a flashy BMW and was bragging to me that he paid cash. Told me to tell you thanks for the sound system."

"Fuck you, asshole," Matros said instantly and meaning it.

"Why didn't you just put a lien on the house or take them to small claims?" McPhee asked Matros.

"Are you shitting me? Small claims court? Not on your life. I've been there, and the judges think that all contractors are lying and stealing thieves. The homeowners lie through their teeth, and the judge sympathizes with their fucking sob stories.

"It's not justice. It's a screwing," Eddie said, the anger obvious in his voice. "I didn't lien them because they were one of Kevin's clients. Up until then, I had never had a problem on one of his jobs, and it's been at least eight or nine years.

"The specs covered problem resolution, and we were supposed to go to arbitration. It could have put Kevin in the middle."

Walter Nash had a similar story. "So I figured I'd take the guy to small claims because he did not want to pay me for some extras. It wasn't much, I think about $280. The guy tells the judge he never ordered the extras, which is why he hadn't signed for them, that I just did them on my own. Hands the judge my change order unsigned."

"No way," Dana said. "What's the judge think, that you're just a nice guy giving away the store?"

"I don't know," Walter said, "but here's what I think. The judge figures I'm screwing this guy anyway because, you know, I'm just a fucking contractor, and that's what contractors do. So in the judge's mind, the homeowner's getting back what I stole from him in the first place. I swear to God that's how they think. You're out to bleed the homeowner or nickel dime them to death.

"So, I lost. I'll tell you one thing. I'll never, never go back to small claims court again. It's all a big joke, and I'm the one they're laughing at," Walter said bitterly.

Walter and Matros were telling the truth, and all the other contractors could attest to it. Taking the homeowner to small claims was a waste of time, which no one could afford to take away from a job. The limit in the Commonwealth was $2,000.

Suing the homeowner meant that the lawyer would get all your money. The cost of bringing the suit could easily be more than what you would collect; the emotional wear and tear while the case dragged out even greater. Most of the contractors just walked away figuring the cards were stacked against them.

"Try being honest in this business," they would say. The guys Kevin was associated with were honest and principled men who simply wanted to get paid for the work they did, but all of them had battle scars.

Walter wasn't finished. "I've been in my own business now about thirty-five years. Most of the people I did work for were really very nice, but you get a few," Walter said trying to show some balance.

"I think the worst ones are the ones with money, and I don't mean only Hingham and Cohasset either. The ones who never cancel the cleaning lady or the guys doing the landscaping. The ones who still go out to nice restaurants while the job's being done. They still take their nice, big, fancy vacations and come back and tell you all about it.

"Then they want to argue with you over the bill for some small goddamn thing. The people who really get me are the elderly, and I've got nothing against them. I mean, I'm getting up there, too." The guys laughed and kidded him about being an old man.

"You get these senior citizens, and the first thing they say is, 'I'm on a fixed income.' Well guess what, lady? So am I. You start the job, and you won't believe what they leave hanging around the house. One woman had five or six savings bank books she left right out on the counter. I figure it's my money for all her grandchildren.

"It's a tough, tough business that wears you out, and the public doesn't see it or care. That's why I want to get out."

For a moment, there was dead silence.

"Hey! I thought we were all here to have some fun," Kevin interjected. "How's the food?"

"Great."

"This chicken parm's excellent. I haven't had it in a long time."

"The fish was very, very good. More than enough."

"Walter, what's up with the Skipper?" Dan asked. "You still using him, that scrawny little shit?"

"Nah, I haven't used him for roofing for a few years. I think he gave my customers the creeps, especially the women. Allen saw him a few months back. He still looks the same."

THE INDEPENDENT CONTRACTOR

The Skipper would give anyone the creeps. He was a short, very thin man with jet-black hair, deep set black eyes, a heavy, fifty-grit beard, and wiry arms, a forty-eight year-old chain smoker who lit only one match in a day. Despite his physical appearance, Skippy was a very clean man and always wore a fresh set of work clothes each day.

Walter and Skippy had worked together for years but parted company for reasons neither man discussed. Allen had told Kevin that Walter had had enough when Skippy installed a roof upside down. The shingles weren't upside down, Skippy was.

He started nailing with his feet towards the ridge and worked his way up the roof – backwards – because he was too lazy to set up staging.

"He would just show up at their house," Walter said. "I got a call from a customer, and he tells me that Skippy just showed up in the living room with a can of beer in his hand. No one knows how he got in the house or how long he was there. He scared the shit out of them. Did it more than once."

All the guys were listening. "He wouldn't harm a flea, but they didn't know. I got somebody else. I couldn't have guys just showing up like that out of nowhere," Walter said solemnly.

Chris, the waitress, came by to check on her table and brought with her the dessert menu. "I'm not going to say what this is, so I'll just put it on the table," she said, smartly avoiding the obvious "Would anyone like some dessert." The guys got a big kick out of her – she knew how to handle them and herself – and a few of them ordered.

"So, Kevin, when do we start the depot?" Allen asked.

"No depot," Kevin said tersely.

"No depot? What happened? I thought this was going to be your new office with a nice big sign commuters would see twice a day," The Lace said.

The depot was a wooden railroad station on Pond Street, Weymouth that the Massachusetts Bay Transportation Authority –The T – was selling off as surplus real estate. Kevin loved the look of the building, which was in a state of serious decay and disrepair. He figured that with his resources, he could restore the depot and use it as an office.

"So did I," Sweeney said. "I got the RFP from the MBTA, and this one you won't believe. The RFP says that the successful bidder must restore the building according to federal guidelines for historic buildings and the Weymouth Historical Society's requirements.

"Bear in mind that the depot's not an historic building but that these guys would like it to be and want me to pay for it to please them.

"It also said that I would have to move the building away from the tracks, which is what I had intended to do anyway because it's sitting on a granite footing with a crawl space. I would wind up with extra space in the basement.

"But here's the kicker. I must agree to – and I quote – 'embrace the principles of affirmative action and hire minorities and women to restore the building' whenever possible.

"All of which means that you guys could be out even though you have made the most positive contribution to my business over the years."

"Come off it," Steve said. "They can't make you do that."

"Want to bet?" Kevin said. "Let me ask you this. Suppose I want to sell my house and included as part of the sales contract the condition that whoever buys it must change his religion to mine. How about your political affiliation? I mean, why not change it, too?

"This is the most offensive thing I can ever remember, and it's all very legal. The government gets me to carry out its social policy or agenda – and pay for the privilege – but says I can't carry out my own. I'd be sued for violating someone's civil rights, but to hell with mine. I still can't get over it. The arrogance of those bastards."

"Jesus, Kevin, you're really pissed. I haven't seen you like this in a long time. And you think we're a bunch of bigots. Prejudice works both ways, you know," Steve said.

"Look. I love this country to the core of my being, but I never thought it would call on me to screw my friends to get ahead. If separate but equal is wrong and unconstitutional, how can special but equal be right and legal?" No one offered an answer.

"Hey Walter! What was that thing you were whispering before about Kevin and the phantom shitter?" Dan asked. "Did I hear that one right? You just blew right by it."

"Yeah. Yeah, that's right, the Phantom Shitter. Steve knows about it. He can tell you," Walter said.

"What's this? Kill the host day? I'm taking this all back. You guys are bastards," Kevin said plaintively, which only egged them on more.

Stevie would handle this one, a story about Kevin's time in the Coast Guard. "Well, one day I'm sitting there having lunch with Walter and Allen, and Kevin here is trying to make this big impression with us real men," Bonnano began in jest.

"And he tells us he doesn't swear because he heard it all in the Coasties. And we're eating, mind you, when he tells us about this radar chief he knows who was out at sea – the North Atlantic – on a cutter for thirty days at a time. Its six weeks in; six weeks out.

"The radar chief says that after the first two weeks there's nothing else to read or do, and the guys go nuts from boredom. All of a sudden, the crew hears about some guy who has taken a shit on the table of the wardroom, but no one knows who it is, including the captain. The whole crew's spooked and upset."

The guys liked this one, too, and Stevie knew how to work the crowd and tell a good story.

"Then the guy shits in a few more strategic places, and there's all sorts of scuttlebutt – I got that one right – as to who the guy is. Some of the crew wants a special watch to track down the guy who becomes known as the Phantom Shitter, but no one will volunteer.

"Kevin, how am I doing so far?"

"I don't want to talk to you." All the guys laughed.

"The radar chief says that another chief, a quartermaster who is in the navigation shack, has a very weak stomach, but the two of them work together. So this radar chief decides to take advantage of the situation and goes down into the galley and gets some peanut butter and olive oil."

"Peanut butter and olive oil? What for?" Eddie asked.

"Wait a minute. You'll see. Be patient," Steve said slowing down the pace. "The chief then goes back up to the radar shack and spoons the peanut butter onto the floor with some of the olive oil. I should have said, 'deck.'

"He pipes the quartermaster chief – notice that nautical stuff, pipes? – to the radar shack and tells him he thinks that the Phantom Shitter has struck again. So the second chief comes running up to the radar shack, and the first chief shows him what's in the middle of the deck. He's starting to get a little pale because of his weak stomach.

"The radar chief gets down on his hands and knees near the pile and sniffs it. 'Smells like shit,' he says, and he sees the guy getting a little worse. Then the first chief scoops some on his finger and sticks it in his mouth and says, 'Tastes like shit, too.'"

The guys let go on that one and were cracking up.

Ono managed to ask, "So what happened to the second chief?"

"Him? He wound up on the rail puking his guts out! The Phantom Shitter had struck again."

All the guys laughed wildly. "How'd I do Kev," Steve asked innocently, as only he could.

"I'm screwed," Kevin answered. "You guys better watch where you step from now on." Sweeney was not the Phantom Shitter, but no one would believe otherwise.

After a few stories and a lot of laughs about Kevin and his wild adolescence growing up in Southie, some of the guys got up to take a piss.

All the contractors were having the best time, and Kevin's appreciation of them showed.

For the moment, Steve Bonnano could set aside his fears about his wife who had been treated for breast cancer, and Bruce did not have to think about when he would see his children next, especially around the holidays. His wife had custody, and he could only hope they would understand. The divorce nearly broke him four years ago.

Walter Nash's hearing problem and arthritic joints were not evident, either. Nor was McPhee's back problem from laying all that flooring all these years. If Ono coughed, no one heard him or asked about his asbestosis, which reduced his lung capacity by thirty percent and was terminal.

None of the physical or mental health problems that the building and remodeling trades could induce were noticed around the table. If the men were lucky, their wives had medical insurance policies at their workplaces. Some had no insurance at all, and to the man, they all had families to support. A few of them smoked and, despite the physical work they did, most of the subs were out of shape.

The tools of their trade included whatever was needed to get the job done, and the contractors kept them in perfect running condition or safe and secure. To steal a man's tools was the same as taking away his livelihood, and anyone suspected of doing so would find himself bumped off a staging or harmed in some subtle way. Accidents on the job were not always accidental.

The contractors loved gadgets like pagers, cell phones, and fax machines, but the one tool they needed most – a personal computer – few, if any, had. For the most part the men were technophobes who loved sports, but none of them were joiners or belonged to expensive clubs. You wouldn't be meeting them at the local builder's association anytime soon either.

You also would not see them glued to their TV's watching building or remodeling programs. They knew an infomercial when they saw one.

All came from families with strong traditions in the trades. If you asked, they would tell you they were contractors or small businessmen. No one would ever say entrepreneur.

You could find them in the phone book, but not under their company name because they all used a home phone instead to keep overhead down. The competition amongst contractors was so fierce that no one could afford an office outside the home.

Their wives were not a part of the business in a real sense, although most of them answered the phone calls from frustrated, rude, or angry customers and frequently bore the brunt of such ill-mannered behavior.

Without exception, the men ran businesses that could not be sold. Their companies, in fact, were little more than a job, not an asset they could sell before retiring. The minute they stopped working, their businesses were gone, unless, like Walter Nash, a son would take it over.

Sweeney himself had abandoned the hope that his unique approach to building or remodeling could be franchised. "I must have been delusional," he later said.

The men's ages ranged from thirty-eight to forty-two, still prime, but headed towards the downside. Residential construction was very much a young man's game and easy to get into or out of, which may have been the problem. Their bodies usually broke before their spirits.

The nation that depended on contractors for its new homes, repairs, and remodeling would be surprised to know that the billions of dollars it spent supported what was still very much a cottage industry.

The men were having a wonderful time with Kevin just being themselves, and perfectly willing to linger. The waitress kept them well lubricated throughout the nearly two, fast hours they spent at the restaurant.

There was, however, one more piece of unsettled business: the Cock Doc, as Steve Bonnano liked to call him. What had happened there? Kevin laid it all out.

"You're living in Cohasset where the term, 'Cohasset basement,' is well understood by everyone. You build around the ledge or you leave a huge boulder in the basement. In Cohasset they do it all the time.

"Not The Doc. He wants to hang Auggie out to dry because we'll have to blast the ledge to get the foundation in. Didn't like the idea of a boulder in the basement. No Plymouth Rock for him.

"Do you remember the big bear softy, Monk Morris who used to do some site work on the side? Well, he's an underwater demolitions expert, the guy who helped get that ship off the rocks outside the Cape Cod Canal about ten years ago."

"An underwater demolitions expert? Big, fat Monk? No way," Allen said.

"You underestimated him, Allen. He's also a helicopter pilot, a very interesting guy in my book. He's been in Boston working on The Big Dig and the harbor tunnel, and he comes down to help out Auggie. The bill's almost three grand, but The Doc then says he won't pay. It's not in the specifications, says he, but it is, as an extra with no amount shown because we had no way of knowing beforehand.

"Rather than argue with him because the job was a big one and I needed the work, I paid for the blasting," Kevin told the men. "Monk and I worked it out."

"You know, The Doc just got me thinking. Anyone see that knee operation on cable the other night?" Dana asked around.

Tim, Steve, and Allen had. "I'm sitting there watching this thing, and the doctor says he wants a saw, then a drill. Next comes a rasp with a hammer and chisel to clip away the bone. And he's got this jig all made up to get the exact articulation – you like that one? – of the knee joint." Dana was a well-read man careful not to use big words around the guys. They could be sensitive that way.

"Is it me, or what? I have all that shit in my toolbox, and no one pays me that kind of money. These guys are nothing but carpenters with degrees." Everyone laughed, especially because Dana usually didn't have much to say.

He wasn't far off the mark. The hand-eye coordination that carpentry and surgery required was very similar. Kevin had worked for many doctors, and they loved woodworking. It was very satisfying.

"So, Kevin, what's in the pipe? Anything interesting?" Ono asked.

"Are you interested in going back into the South End?" Kevin asked him and anyone within hearing range.

"The South End? When? Soon I hope?" Steve asked. He loved the South End.

"Pretty soon, but it's a fast track project, which, as you know makes me very, very nervous. I'm letting you know now because we may not have time to develop the specifications per usual."

The others indicated that they, too, were interested in the South End, despite the Big Dig. There was good money in there and something different to do. All of them grew up in the suburbs and thought the city was an exciting, adventurous place.

Kevin loved the city, of course, but had reservations that went beyond the fast track approach he was going to take with the project. The last time he worked in the South End, Sweeney would get off the Southeast Expressway at the East Berkley Street Exit, take a left at the end of the ramp, go under the Expressway, pass the Pine Street Inn, and find his way to lower Dartmouth Street.

The area by the expressway, especially the Pine Street Inn, was painful for Sweeney who unconsciously thought of his father every time he passed by the homeless, hopeless, and alcoholic men and women that inhabited that drab section of the South End.

His own father lost the Battle of the Bottle and died homeless and nameless. Had it not been for the social security number that was tattooed on his arm, the family would never have know that Patrick Sweeney had died at all that March in 1957.

THE INDEPENDENT CONTRACTOR

Kevin saw his father for the very first time lying in his coffin. He was only eleven years old at the time and would never forget his first encounter with grief. To please his mother, Kevin asked to serve at the Low Mass held in the basement of the Gate of Heaven Church.

He could easily recall leaving the sacristy with the Monsignor and the other altar boy to meet his father's coffin, behind which his family was gathered. Sweeney was carrying the thurible, a long chained, golden vessel that contained burning incense with a pungent smell he liked.

His grandmother, still speaking with an Irish brogue, and mother were dressed in black and wearing veils, hands clenched around their rosary beads, their faces wracked with pain.

Although there was a very large gathering of family and friends, Sweeney could remember no one else, especially his older sister to whom he was so close – then as now – or his mother's two beloved brothers who were such a positive force in his life. He did remember the organist playing the traditional and frightening, *Dies Irae*, or Days of Wrath.

Kevin's only other memory of the time was when he started to cry in the sacristy after the Mass was over.

"What's the matter?" the other altar boy had asked. "It was my father," Kevin said. The Monsignor gathered Kevin under his long black, woolen tunic and walked him down the side aisle and out of the church to the limo that was waiting outside with his family.

The long wait to go to Fenway Park with his father, to play catch, to wrestle, to tease, to go fishing, to get help with his homework, to learn how to ride a bike or skate was over. However, loving and caring relatives and neighbors would see to it that Kevin would not go without.

Years later, Sweeney would tell them that he had the happiest childhood anyone could ever want. He would bristle if you ever told him he came from a broken home.

It was a long time ago, and the one story about himself that Kevin had told to no one, not even his wife, Marie. Yes, there were some things about which Sweeney could not be entirely open, things that he needed to keep to himself.

The lads at the table in the restaurant were getting restless and looking to beat the traffic to get home to their families. All said their thanks to Kevin and their goodbyes to each other. Questions about where each was planning to spend Thanksgiving were asked and answered. Stevie Bear gave Kevin a towering hug and several slaps on the back.

Sweeney paid the bill and gave a twenty percent tip to the waitress. Each of the guys left a dollar or two for her on their own. "You can always count on the people who have the least amount of money to pay the best tip," the waitress said later. She had guessed correctly what the men did for a living.

****

Graham Barrows parked his car in the Passenger Drop Off spot in the parking lot of the Harbor Express in Quincy. He then took his wife's luggage out of the trunk and headed for the ramp leading to the ferryboat, which had not yet arrived.

His wife went into the Harbor Express office to purchase a single one-way ticket to Logan Airport, where she would soon disembark for England. She was going home – America was never her home – to care for her sickly father who was now on pension after many distinguished years in the British Foreign Office.

The couple met outside the office and stood by the rail looking at the water, the heavy cruiser, U. S. S. Salem, which was moored at a dock next to the Harbor Express, a defunct but soon to be rebuilt power station across the river in Weymouth, and everything else except each other.

Barrows drew a deep breath and spoke first. "I wish things had worked out differently for us. I still love you, you know."

His wife said nothing and stared out at nothing.

The two were separating. The house they had remodeled together with the help of Kevin Sweeney was not the marriage builder they thought it would be. No, it only brought to the surface tensions that had been buried for so long.

They had gone over all the reasons countless times.

It was late in the day and getting dark.

"I know," she finally sighed. "I know. And I love you, too. That's what so sad. But I think it's best this way. Best for everybody."

There wasn't much else to be said, and small talk seemed inappropriate. A few minutes later, the ferry pulled in. More passengers got off the ferry than would be getting on.

Graham's wife looked at him, stared into his eyes, lovingly ran her fingers through his hair, and kissed him goodbye. "Sorry," she said.

"There's nothing to be sorry for. We tried. I really think we did. Call me when you get there so I'll know you arrived safely. Please give my warm regards to your father."

"I will. Cheers." They embraced for the last time, and then they parted. Graham watched her leave, and never once did she look back.

Chapter 9

So, there I am, standing in the doorway, naked.
And there's these two guys staring at me. One is a sheriff, but I can't quite make out whom the second person is.
This other guy is waving a piece of paper in my face – wildly – and he rages, 'You see this document? You signed it – ok? – and legally I can take your fucking house away.'
The sheriff says, 'Sorry. I'm here to enforce the law.'
Then I recognize the maniac. He's the contractor who screwed up our house. 'So you better pay up, or I'll kick you the fuck out. I want my money, NOW, in cash or else.'
I then gave him this really evil stare, and the guy drops dead.
'I think you did the right thing,' the sheriff says, 'but you still have to pay.'
That's when the alarm went off.

****

The Time of National Paralysis, Kevin Sweeney's holiday season, was in full swing, and only two weeks remained before Christmas.

Jay Parker was busy working on the computer at the built in desk in the kitchen and had deliberately gotten out of bed much earlier than Lauren and the children. Weekends at the house were usually a lazy time and a relief from the hustle and bustle of the workweek.

Parker had poured himself a cup of coffee, which was getting cold, and had made sure that there would be plenty for Lauren when she finally did come down to the kitchen for breakfast. Neither was a big eater in the morning and usually preferred something light.

He did not hear her coming downstairs, but when Jay saw Lauren in her terry cloth bathrobe reaching for the coffee, he immediately quit Netscape and got up to greet her. It was eight o'clock.

"Good morning. How'd you sleep?" Jay asked.

"I slept fine. The children are still out, but they should be stirring in a few minutes. I didn't hear you get up. What are you doing?"

"Oh, I was just working on some things," Jay answered evasively. Lauren was not fully awake, so she did not notice. "Would you like some toast?"

"Sure. Thanks. You're in a good mood," Lauren said.

"Well, why not? I slept well. It's the weekend. I've already had my second cup of coffee, so I'm all set," Parker said.

Jay started Lauren's toast but then said he had something else to do in the basement. Lauren watched him leave the room while she sipped on her coffee, holding it with both hands.

"What's gotten into him lately?" Lauren asked herself as she started to come around.

She didn't have too many answers, and there weren't many questions either. Aside from a credit card problem, which was intermittent and justified his somber mood, he appeared to be up and down during the last few months.

Jay opened several other credit card accounts and used them to pay for service on his car at Tony Romano's dealership or purchases he made for Christmas. Initially, they went through fine, but then they, too, maxed out inexplicably. Curious, he tried his old card, which had been paid up but was refused, and it went through fine.

Although the e-mail problem disappeared, Lauren knew that the system manager where Jay worked was checking into it periodically as a precaution. The decision on the state pension plan would come sometime in January, so the effect from that one was still on the horizon.

More amusing and puzzling was the salami note. Someone at work must have known Jay hated salami and was teasing him about it, but no one there could figure out who the person doing it was. He would probably get a gift package of all the things he hated and everyone would laugh Lauren thought.

Recently, Jay had locked the door to the basement area under the new family room – a space the family did not need or care about – and refused to explain why. Although not asked, he would also have refused to explain why he logged off the computer anytime Lauren or the children came into the room.

That book order-slip from the Boston Public Library that Lauren found on the kitchen counter along with Jay's keys and some other things made no sense either. He wasn't a reader, and what would he be doing at the BPL? Lauren had said nothing because she did not want to get into another argument with him about his leaving his things around.

Not one single thing Jay did seemed all that peculiar, but added together, Lauren could see a pattern of secrecy emerging.

Why? What was going on? What did he have to hide? Was his father's Christmas visit too much for Jay to handle? Yes, maybe that's it. Nothing else makes any sense, she persuaded herself.

On the surface, Jay always appeared calm, but she knew her man better. Underneath, he could be a crosscurrent of emotion.

A short time later, Jay returned to the kitchen. "What are you doing down there?" Lauren asked.

"Nothing. I'm just working on something. I'm asking you, just this one time, forget about the basement. It's nothing. Really."

Parker could be very persuasive, but Lauren just shrugged and waved her hand innocently, letting him know she was perplexed but would say nothing else. Maybe he was hiding Christmas gifts for her and the children and didn't want them to see.

"How are you coming with the Christmas shopping?" Jay asked.

"Other than the fact that I could use your help, not too bad. My mother and father are all set, but I haven't done anything about your father. I could use a few suggestions."

Lauren said nothing about Jay's sister because they did not exchange gifts with her and her third husband. Jay rarely heard from his sister, and when he did, it was usually trouble.

Jay and Lauren did, however, exchange gifts with her sister and brother, and made sure that her nieces and nephews always had something special for them under the tree. Lauren put a lot of thought into what she bought for them, and they were always delighted by what she and Jay sent.

"You don't have to worry about my father. He's all set. I took care of that myself."

"You did?" Lauren said completely surprised. "When?"

"Actually, this morning."

Intrigued, Lauren wanted more details. "What did you get him? You never shop for your father. If it wasn't for me and the children, he would probably never get anything from you," she said gently.

"I know. I know, and you're right," Jay sighed. "I can't tell you."

"Fine." She understood that her husband was being playful, liked building up the suspense, and could keep a secret. No harm. She'd back off. "Will you be getting the tree today with the children?"

"I'm not sure. I may have some work to do," Parker replied.

"Couldn't it wait? You told them earlier you'd be getting the tree today. If you're not going to do it, why did you tell them you were?" Lauren asked.

"I didn't tell them I was. I said I thought we could get the tree today, but I didn't promise them I would. Can't I change my mind?"

"I think if you say you are going to do something, you should do it. It sounded to me as though you were planning to get the tree today. They're going to be disappointed. You also said you would help me put up the wreaths, so I guess you're not going to do that either," Lauren said showing her frustration.

"What is this? You've been up only fifteen minutes, and now you're planning my day. You know, I don't work for you. I'm not on your clock; I'm on my own. I was thinking out loud. There's always tomorrow, so what's the big deal?" Jay said, his frustration also showing.

"There is no big deal, but I might like to do something tomorrow. I was planning on getting the wreaths up today, not tomorrow. So, as usual, I'll rearrange my schedule to suit yours," Lauren said, not pleased.

Jay was not about to let things go. "Lauren, what are you doing tomorrow that you can't do today? Why are you always such a hard ass? Why is it that everything I say you take literally, but if you want to change your own mind, I have to adjust? I'm getting a little tired of this."

"And I'm getting tired of arguing with you all the time. That's all we seem to do lately, is argue. I hate it, and I don't like it when you talk to me like that."

Fortunately, the doors to the children's rooms were closed, and they were still asleep.

"If you don't want to get the tree today, Jay, fine. We'll get it tomorrow. Whatever you say is fine. I'll just be the passive wife and say nothing. You can tell the children."

Jay had come to his flash point. Hearing the door to one of the children's rooms opening, he looked towards the stairs then Lauren and said nothing. She could feel his rage but turned away from him to read the paper and finish her coffee.

"Goddamn, son of a bitch," Jay muttered to himself – not for Lauren – in bewilderment. "If she only knew."

****

Marie and Kevin Sweeney were in the dining room having their own breakfast, which, like the Parker's, was also light. On the weekends, Marie always got up a few minutes earlier than Kevin to put on the coffee.

Whenever they were having breakfast, Marie would say to Kevin, "While you are up, would you mind getting me some coffee?"

"But I'm not up," he would protest.

"You looked like you were getting up," she would counter while handing him her empty mug. Kevin would look at her then slowly get up and get her some coffee. It was a small price he paid for not getting up earlier to make the coffee.

The pair had a weekend tradition of reading the paper over breakfast and sharing something of interest. Marie loved the weekend edition of *The*

Patriot Ledger and read it first while Kevin checked out his beloved *Boston Globe*. Sometimes Kevin would breeze through the paper, and then ask for a section from Marie.

He also loved reading to Marie articles he found interesting. It was a wonderful tradition, and they never failed to follow it. Most importantly to Kevin, he learned things he might never have known otherwise and firmly believed that we only read what we like.

"If you think about it," he said to Marie, "we only read what reinforces our prejudices or view of the world. It's difficult to read something with which we strongly disagree. It's dangerous, really."

Shortly after eight-thirty, which was early for a Saturday morning in the Sweeney residence, the house phone rang. Kevin got up to answer it just as he got up for everything else.

"Hi, Kevin, this is Annie," Steve Bonnano's wife said.

"Hi, Annie. What can I do for you this morning?" Kevin answered cheerfully. She was a sweetheart, but why didn't she use the business line? Kevin was thinking.

"I'm not sure, Kevin, but I just wanted you to know that Steve suffered a massive heart attack last night, and he may not make it. He wanted me to call you to let you know. You and two other people," Annie said. "He didn't want me calling anyone else."

"What? Oh, God! Is he ok? Are you ok?" Kevin asked.

Marie heard the exchange and wandered into the kitchen to listen. She knew from the sound of Kevin's voice that something serious had happened.

"We don't know. The priest gave him Last Rites, and we're really scared. The doctors won't say. They can't say really, but I can tell from the way they're acting that they don't think he will make it."

"Is there anything I can do? What hospital is he in?" Kevin asked, rapidly, his mind racing.

"He's at the Brigham," Annie said not needing to add "and Women's Hospital." "They flew him in from the Jordan. His heart stopped on the way, but they were able to revive him. I can't talk much now, so I'll have to talk to you later. You can call the hospital to see about visiting hours, but they may not let you in. Only family."

"I feel sick at heart for you and the children, Annie. You go take care of your business. I'll take care of things on my end."

"Ok. This will probably sound silly, Kevin, but the one thing Steve is worried about is that he has let you down."

"Let me down? Oh, Annie. How could he ever, ever think of such a thing? You tell him I'm mad that he said so," Kevin said.

Sweeney wasn't mad, of course, he was distraught. Unlike most men in the residential construction business, Kevin felt that his relationships would continue once the work had stopped.

Immediately, Kevin told Marie what had happened to Steve, and she was just as shocked as he. "I hope they have insurance," Marie said anxiously. "I really hope they do."

A few moments later, the business phone rang, and Kevin went into the living room to answer it while Marie went back into the dining room.

"Eddie! Glad you called. I just heard from Stevie's wife, and she said he just suffered a massive heart attack last night and might not make it. I know you guys have had your differences, but I also know you wouldn't want anything like this to happen to him," Kevin said.

"You got that right," Eddie said. "I wouldn't want to see that happen to anyone. I know you have been on him about the smoking and weight, but he always said he was a big boy. How's his wife and kids doing?"

"Annie sounded really frightened. The children? You never know. Sometimes they can be more resilient than you think. Other times, they just can't take it. There's no easy way to know.

"I'm going to try to get in to see him either today or tomorrow. Sorry to lay that on you so early in the morning."

"No, no problem. I understand. I was calling you about something else," Eddie said.

"Sure. What's up?"

"Are you ready for a little more shocking news?"

"How shocking?"

"Not shocking to me, but shocking to you."

"Alright. Alright. What's up?" Kevin asked again apprehensively.

"Auto Dude. Remember that mega truck I told you about sitting out on the back lot?"

"Sure do. I think I know what you're going to say."

"That's right, pal. Gone, just like I said it would be. Someone cut right through the chain link fence."

Sweeney did not have to wonder about Eddie's source. He knew Eddie's daughter's boyfriend was. The mechanic at Romano's was a nice kid whose father was on the Massachusetts State Police, Norwell Barracks.

"When did all this happen?"

"Just the other day. I knew it would. I just knew it. That guy's bad news, Kevin."

"What do you mean? What makes you so sure he did it? I mean, why would he steal from himself? It makes no sense."

"To guys like you and me it makes no sense, but to guys like him and that sleaze ball he hangs around with, it makes a lot of sense. It'll be an insurance claim, and the Auto Dude's cash won't be tied up in something that's not moving. I say he makes money on the deal. I thought maybe you'd seen something in the paper."

"I guess it takes all kinds," Kevin said weakly. "And, no, there was nothing in the paper."

His business finished after some more small talk, each man said his goodbye.

Kevin joined Marie in the dining room to resume his breakfast and reading. He had no sooner sat down than the business phone rang again.

"Kevin. Ono. How you doing?"

"I'm not so sure, Ono," Kevin said. Knowing Ono was not aware of what happened to Steve, Kevin filled him in. He also told Ono about the truck theft at Auto Dude's dealership. Ono did not seem all that surprised by the news of either event, but he was worried for Steve and his family.

"I just wanted to let you know," Ono said, "that I'll be at Crow's Point on Monday. Dan's got most of the framing done from what I can see, and it really looks amazing. That octagon room with the tower in the front of the house is unbelievable. You just don't see that kind of craftsmanship anymore. Those two guys are something else. A truly outstanding job."

"I'll see you there Monday morning sometime around nine," Kevin said. "I have nothing to tell you about Matthews. We're just waiting. They went with the custom cabinet guy, and, just as I thought, he can't finish anytime before Christmas.

"I think Kathy planned it that way," Kevin continued. "She told me she wouldn't have to cook for the holidays. I'm sure she meant it!"

"Now there's a smart lady!" Ono said.

"You bet! It's too soon to involve you with the Evans project because we just started the designs. I think the whole heating system will go, and I think there may be some asbestos," Kevin said. "I will need you next week for the South End. We're just about finished with the demo, and will be starting the rough framing soon."

"That was fast. I've heard of fast track, but that's ridiculous. You were only talking about it a few weeks ago," Ono said registering his surprise over the speed with which the South End project had started.

"I know, and I'm uneasy about it. Walter and Allen were able to slot the time to get in there. One of their own projects got delayed, so they were happy to keep things going with me. In case you haven't heard, the guys who own the South End house are gay," Kevin said.

"I have no problem with that," Ono quickly responded. "Their money's green, isn't it?"

"Well said."

"I don't mind going over to Evans there to check the firebox for asbestos. Depending on the timing, Kevin, we may have to take that system out and replace it the same day. Could be late winter, early spring, you know."

"I know, but we've done it before. That's why I have you around. That's it. That's all I've got on this end."

"What about Hingham, that sheep shed thing you had talked about?" Ono asked.

"Oh, yeah! The sheep shed. The foundation's just sitting there, and I can't do anything until Dan's finished at Crow's Point.

"The weather has been pretty good, and I was hoping to pour the basement floor, but without the deck on I'm asking for trouble. I'm betting Dan's got another three to four weeks over there before I can get him to the sheep shed.

"I'll send you a fax summarizing the status of everything. And don't forget, no contract with the homeowner, no work. I'll attach your numbers to my specifications. You use your own contract, and you should be all set. Make sure your payment schedule is all spelled out and adds up to the numbers you gave me."

"I know the drill."

After hanging up the phone, Kevin wrote a note to himself about the plumbing lines at Crow's Point. Best not to forget them, especially now that the cold weather season was here, he thought.

Later he would put this information into his contact organizer on his computer and notify the subs and his clients of the upcoming schedules for all the projects. Like the subcontractors, Sweeney worked directly for the client, and it was his responsibility to see to it that men and material were on the job in a timely fashion and that the work was being done in accordance with the plans and specifications.

He also tracked changes to the specifications that resulted in a price increase or decrease, and adjusted the contract balances and payments to reflect their current standing.

The contractor, homeowner, and Kevin were all on the same page.

Sweeney did not pay the contractors or suppliers directly, the homeowner did. The system avoided the problem of large payments of a third or more to a general contractor who would then use the money as a means to control the homeowner. "Make smaller payments more often," he urged the home owners, "and use money as a means to build up trust not power."

THE INDEPENDENT CONTRACTOR

"If you don't like the attitude of the contractor," he advised the women, "make sure you are the one that writes the check, not your husband." It was very savvy advice.

Kevin received a percentage of the total amount of money spent. He was the Project Coordinator, the oil that kept the machinery moving smoothly. In nine out of ten cases, it worked exactly as planned, but ninety percent was not enough for Sweeney. "Aim for perfection; settle for excellence" was his company's motto.

With the homeowners' acting as the general contractor and the weight of Sweeney's company, knowledge, and experience behind them, his projects usually came in on time, within budget, and without the endless problems that typically plague residential building and remodeling.

It was a remarkable system that required everyone to be open and share information. In order to succeed, all parties must be willing to trust each other. Trust was the essential ingredient, and Sweeney got it implicitly from his clients, the contractors, related professionals, and suppliers.

The whole idea was the exact opposite of what one could expect in the residential construction industry, but typical for Sweeney.

****

It happened again, and Tony Romano was on the phone screaming at the person listening on the other end.

"I don't give a fuck what you have to do, I want this problem solved. There's something wrong, and it's been going on for too long.

"I don't want a new release. I don't want a patch. I don't want more documentation. I don't want to go to a Web site.

"I want a goddamn, fucking body here to fix this, and I want him now.

"I paid a lot of money for this system, and it still isn't working.

"If I sold cars the way you bastards sell software, I would be out of business. There are bugs in that system, and you better get your fucking ass up here and fix them.

"You're looking at a major lawsuit, pal, and I may just drop the whole fucking line. Sign on with one of your competitors. You know what I'm saying?" Romano screamed nonstop. "Have I made myself clear?"

Gayle Armstrong certainly thought so, and she was sitting in her office next to Tony's. A woman who worked in the service department was going over an invoice with Gayle, and she heard the outburst, too.

"What's going on?" Heather asked Gayle.

"Oh, the computer system is all screwed up. We've had some misplaced orders, cars coming in with the wrong accessories, inventory all screwed up, all sorts of stuff. Tony's called before, and all he's been getting is the run around.

"They even told him the problem was on our end, that we weren't following proper procedures, you know, and Tony went ballistic.

"He's got everyone all upset and nervous that they'll make some kind of a mistake and get fired," Gayle explained.

"I remember that thing with the special order truck, the one that got stolen last week. Was that a computer screw up, too?" Heather asked.

"Don't say nothing, like, that I told you. They said Tony placed the order himself."

Heather's jaw dropped. "No way! He must be going crazy."

"You just saw. I've never seen him get like this until recently. He's like a madman. It's really scary. I'm afraid he's going to drop dead of a heart attack if he keeps it up."

"They" had a point. Security at the dealership was incredibly lax, and anyone could use somebody else's computer. No one logged off or on, and most left their computer unattended while they went out for lunch or about their business.

The system was left up and running most of the time. Whenever there was a general problem, Tony relied on a local software and hardware company located in Braintree to fix things and get them running again. The company that originally developed it supported the application specific to the dealership.

No one really appeared to be in charge, and the system was left to run itself. Romano knew how to use technology for his own purposes, but how it worked was a total mystery to him.

In the beginning, everything seemed to run fine, and the dealership was lulled into complacency. All transactions were electronic followed by paper backup. There was even an audit trail to track changes.

Tony's attitude was blasé. "No one knows more about this business than me, and no one is going to steal a dime that I don't already know about or do something that I haven't already done myself," he confided to Dazzie Clarke. His past experiences with his former employer were strong evidence that Romano was not simply bragging. He had indeed done it all.

Yet, it had happened again. A second, heavily loaded truck identical to the first special order had just come in, and Tony was threatening the manufacturer and demanding that the vehicle be returned. Tony should have known it's easier to change people than policy. He would simply not accept the possibility that someone at the dealership had screwed up. No one could be that stupid.

Romano then did something at work that he had never done before. He checked on the balances of all his bogus businesses, the ones into which he was funneling all that money.

Nothing was out of order. "I must be losing it," he thought to himself. It wasn't quite time for a monthly withdrawal, and Tony had plenty of cash on hand. He could handle the minor cash flow problem produced by the theft of the first truck and the delivery of the second. Insurance would take care of the first, and he might be able to sell off the second quickly after the holidays.

Romano would want some cash for the final payment on the engagement ring he ordered for Liz. She would be surprised, as would all of Tony's relatives, friends, and associates since the two did not live together, officially. Weekends only didn't count. Tony's parents would be happy, especially his mother whose medical condition was not improving.

Dr. Pierce was unable to tell her why.

****

Christmas Day in the Parker home started early, as it does in any household where there are small children.

Brianna, Danielle, and Stephen still believed in Santa Claus and were wild with excitement. Each showed their parents and grandfather what Santa brought and invited them to play.

Jay's father jumped right in and sat down on the floor to share this magical moment. "Grampa, look at this," was followed by "Grampa, this is for you. I made it," or "Grampa, when you were a little boy, what did Santa bring you?" It was, "Grampa this" or "Grampa that" and Jay watched the unfolding scene in amazement.

Grampa was a major hit with his grandchildren whom he barely knew. Lauren wisely signaled Jay to help with breakfast and to leave Grampa alone with the children. "I can't believe what I'm seeing," Jay said to Lauren.

"Let him enjoy them," Lauren said. "Let them have their grandfather. It's good for all of them. It's Christmas."

It certainly was, but Jay felt like he was meeting his father for the very first time. "Like last night," he said to Lauren as though she were listening to his inner conversation. "My father and I sat there talking, actually talking. I had no idea he was a machinist at the mill. I always thought he worked in the mines."

"I just loved seeing the two of you sitting there, Jay. He really seems to be trying to, you know," Lauren said without finishing her sentence.

"I know. I know. It's just been so long. So many bad memories are hard to forget. I don't know if I'm happy or sad."

"I love my Christmas presents," Lauren said while adroitly changing the subject. "Very artsy. Even the package, the little house, they came in is cute. Where did you get them?"

"I got them at a store that sells things done by artists from all over New England. It's up by Queen Ann's Corner on Route 53. We should go in together sometime."

Lauren raised an eyebrow. Jay hated to shop, but his gifts for her were quite lovely. Gemstone earrings, matching necklace and bracelet. Delicate and colorful. Was he just saying it?

While Jay, Lauren, and his father were sitting watching the children, Jay suddenly got up and reached into the Christmas tree. "What's this?" he said, taking a large envelope from the center of the tree. The children immediately wanted to know, and Lauren and Jay's father seemed just as curious.

"I think it's a letter from Santa," Jay said as he opened the envelope. "Yes, it definitely is," he said.

The children could not contain themselves. "A letter from Santa? From Santa? What's it say?" they asked almost in unison.

"If you gather around, I'll read it to you," Jay said. Instantly they were at his feet, jockeying for position.

Jay then read the letter.

"Dear Brianna, Danielle, and Stephen,

"I got your e-mail asking for a car-carrying ferry boat. It's been many years since the Elves and I made such a toy, ho, ho, ho!"

The children laughed.

"My senior elf is retired now, and only he knew how to make one."

Jay looked at the children before continuing, and they seemed disappointed.

"So I had another idea, one I think you will like very much. It's an adventure for the whole family. Ho! Ho! Ho!"

The children laughed again, and their faces brightened.

"If you go to the Boston Archives in the City of Boston, you will learn everything about your favorite ferry, the John H. Sullivan. They have the entire history of the ferry service and can tell you all about it.

"Everything you need to make a model of the ferry is not under the Christmas tree. It's in the basement under the family room.

"Your friend and the friend of every little girl and boy, Santa."

The children shot out of the family room and headed for the basement. Lauren just stared at Jay. Her eyes filled.

"That's the sweetest thing you've ever done in your life," she said. "How did you ever think of it?"

"I'll tell you later," Jay said. "Let's catch up to the children."

Jay had left open the locked door to the basement under the family room. The children were looking at a four-foot by six foot, blown up, black and white picture of the *John H. Sullivan*. On a carefully prepared plywood table sitting on saw horses were several model making tools, paints, glue, brushes, clear plastic, sand paper, balsa wood, wood model making books, and other paraphernalia like wood files.

The space under the family room was a shop in readiness, and the children couldn't wait to get started.

All of a sudden, Jay's secrecy and odd behavior made sense to Lauren. He must have been researching the ferry through the Internet or the Boston Public Library. "That's why he wanted the Drummel set and all the tools," she thought. "I must have had it all wrong."

****

Christmas at Kevin Sweeney's house was always guaranteed to be a good time. Although he hated the commercialization of the day, Kevin did love the time Christmas afforded family and friends to get together.

Even if his heart wasn't in it, Sweeney invariably did what was expected of him, but Marie always felt cheated. Kevin was respectful, but it wasn't enough.

This Christmas, everyone would be at the Sweeney home. Mark had come down from Vermont, Lisa and her boyfriend were there, as were Kevin's mother and sister. Graham Barrows would be stopping by for dinner, which was sumptuous and carefully prepared by Kevin and Marie. Everyone would be taking home a goody bag.

No one would be asking why Graham was spending Christmas with them because he had done so previously. They would, however, ask about his wife and be told that she had gone back to England to look after her father. They were sensitive and sensible enough to ask no further.

Pictures of this Christmas Day would be taken, and old stories told and retold, including this year's haggling over the tree story. Years ago, the purchasing of the tree had fallen to Kevin, and each year he and the children would head out into the cold in search of one, usually a few days before Christmas.

Although Mark would not be there to help, Lisa was, and she was getting better at it than her father. "We could have gotten another five percent, Dad, but, no, you were getting cold and had to get home to warm your feet. I was willing to wait," she had said in her inimitable way before blabbing the faux pas to her mother.

Father, not Mark this time, would lay out the lights and hang them on the tree, which would be cut down to fit in the living room. Marie and Lisa would tell him how to fix the lights just so, their being the experts on such matters.

The decorations would be hung by all, and each would comment on one of the many special ornaments that had been given by their grandmother and aunt to Mark and Lisa at Christmas time.

The ornaments were still in their original boxes and dated. They gave the Christmas tree a family history, which Kevin eventually came to appreciate. The Christmas music would play in the background, and there would be plenty of goodies to eat and good wine to drink.

Although Kevin didn't drink alcohol, he was well read on wine and didn't mind spending an extra few dollars to get a nice bottle of cabernet sauvignon or merlot. A real character at the liquor store a short distance from the house made excellent recommendations and soon became known to the household as The Wine God.

Marie made sure Kevin had his juice or sparkling water. She had also made sure that the holidays bore her special stamp. The traditional Christmas Eve dinner with Mark and Lisa always consisted of fish, lobster, and shrimp, just as it did in her grandfather's home in Southie.

At the Christmas dinner table in the dining room, new stories would be introduced, and everyone would later step out into the cold night air feeling warm inside. A meaningful tradition would be honored, the family concept preserved.

In another week or so, the holiday season would be over. Christmas, Kevin admitted, might not be that bad after all. It could, indeed, be what you make it, and he chose to make it memorable.

Lisa would make it her last Christmas at home.

Chapter 10

The Time of National Paralysis, 1998, was history, and the nation was slowly getting back to business again. Although some Christian sects, most notably the Greek Orthodox, celebrated the Epiphany as Christmas on January 6, the two most important – Protestant and Catholic – recognized the day as the minor holy day, Little Christmas.

The Epiphany fell on a Wednesday that year, a day that doctors traditionally take as time off. Dr. Pierce was very much a traditional doctor, and the office was closed except for the help, meaning Rebecca Solberg and Stephanie Lahey were working.

"Well, how did your holidays go?" Rebecca asked the nurse, who had taken off several days before Rebecca took a few or her own. They hadn't seen each other in over a week.

"Pretty well," she answered.

Dr. Pierce had balanced his checkbook and had asked Rebecca to subtract the bank charges from the cash account. He had also asked her to close out the last quarter of 1998 and provide him with a print out of the employee records for that same tax period, all of which she did.

This information was reviewed by Pierce and would be given to his accountant who was a CPA. Everything appeared to be in order. "I can just e-mail him the information, if you want, Doctor," she told Pierce.

"All this computer technology! Sure. Why not?" he had answered.

Rebecca was still worried sick about the overheard conversation regarding additional billing as "a matter of principle." She had been looking closely at all the billing that had crossed her desk but found little hard evidence that Pierce was over-billing Medicare.

One good lead, an elderly couple at a nursing home in Braintree, dried up when she realized that the floor nurse would carefully check all billing before agreeing to process it.

The Romano case was more promising because no diagnosis of her condition had yet been made. What additional tests would be ordered and how many of them would be necessary?

Rebecca would be vigilant. She continued to e-mail DAP1 and DAP2 to herself through America OnLine. She kept DAP1 on the hard drive of the office computer and DAP2 on a zip disk she kept in the drawer.

She would keep looking.

****

It was now more than a month since the Parker exploration of the ferry, the *John H. Sullivan*, had begun.

The children were becoming very disappointed, but Jay Parker and Grampa told them that the ferry was a mystery that they would have to help unravel. Besides, it was a fabulous history lesson they would never forget. The girls had already noticed that all the ferries were named after men. They picked up on it before Lauren.

Since Christmas, Jay and Lauren seemed to be getting along better, and she put aside her suspicions about his odd behavior. Jay did tell Lauren where he got the idea for the building of the model ferry. It came from Kevin Sweeney whom Jay had run into at the South Shore Mall while he was trying to shop for his father or find a car-carrying ferry toy for the children. That revelation was a big surprise, and Jay told her that Kevin was real nice to him.

Lauren did, however, regret an ugly incident between her and her husband when Jay was trying to set up the tree. No matter where he put it, Lauren kept saying it didn't look right. Each change meant rearranging all the furniture in the new family room, which he patiently did the first two or three times.

"I think it looks fine on the wall opposite the fireplace," Jay said perturbed at the way things were going. "What's all this business about it doesn't look right? What do you expect? The It Doesn't Look Right Police to show up and fine us $500 for having bad taste? I can just see a SWAT team of women busting in here and pointing at me. 'You have bad taste. How dare you!'"

Lauren didn't think the remark was funny, although it was intended to be, and the children were confused. Stephen later asked her if police were coming to the house. "No, Stephen. No one's coming to the house," Lauren had reassured him.

For the time being, Jay was under more pressure at work because the decision on the state pension plan was being delayed for another month. It was eerily quiet on that front, and Jay, Andrea, and their team were getting concerned.

Like all companies, they had an inside source providing them with information, but that person had little to say lately. It was an ominous sign, and everyone from Eleanor on down was worried.

Jay was headed into work this day and listening to the radio when something frightening flashed into his mind. What if the e-mail and credit card problems he was having were somehow related? What if someone's reading his e-mail, or worse, the confidential files on his computer? What if that someone was a competitor for the pension fund, a local one from Boston?

In mid-November, he had been reassured by the system manager at work that there was no e-mail problem on that end. "As best as I can tell, there's no problem here," she told him. There was always a caveat, "as best as I can tell." Technical types were invariably that way, usually covering their asses.

She had suggested the possibility of a corrupted address book in Netscape, which could account for the incorrect routing. He might be able to fix it by making a small edit to each entry, which would probably re-write the data correctly to a new location on the disk or running diagnostics. "You can make the fix on your PC at home, then copy it to your laptop. Why don't you just use Outlook, which is what we have here?" she asked.

"No real reason," Jay responded. "It's what came with the system, and I've gotten used to it."

"Otherwise, you might have to re-create your address book. You could upgrade Netscape," she advised him. "Like all upgrades, there can be some unexpected results, but it might be an easier way to clean out any existing problems."

Parker had followed her advice to the letter on the laptop and PC at home. Everything appeared to run perfectly, and he liked working on the systems and knowing more about them.

Jay was in a near panic when he reached the office. For The Eye In The Center Of The Storm to show fear would certainly catch the eye of everyone there. He quickly went to his office, closed the door, and called Lauren at work.

"Lauren, this is Jay. I need your help," he began directly.

"Are you all right?" she asked immediately, sensing the tension in his voice.

"Yes. Yes. I'm all right, but I could be in big, big trouble."

"Trouble? What kind of trouble?"

"Remember that problem we were having with the credit cards? How sometimes they would go through, and sometimes they would not?"

"Sure I do, but we haven't had that problem in nearly a month, and it only happened a few times. Everything seems to be straightened out. I paid all the bills, and we're current. Has it happened again?"

"No. It hasn't happened again. But think about it. I was the only one having the problem. Your credit cards always went through. I just passed it off as some Y2K crap, like you hear all the time. Nothing was ever charged improperly to any of the cards, and the credit card companies came up empty when I asked them what was happening," Parker explained.

"Ok, so why are you in trouble? I don't understand."

"I don't want to get ahead of myself. Remember the thing with Andrea and the e-mail a couple of months ago? I thought I had sent it to her accidentally because I was in a hurry that morning. What if it was no accident? What if I didn't do it accidentally?"

"Yeah," Lauren said slowly. "What are you saying?"

"I think what I'm saying is that maybe there's a connection between the credit cards and my e-mail because I'm the only one having the problem. Don't you see what I'm getting at?

"I'm the one that bought all the model making stuff, and I used a credit card for some of it over the Internet. My father didn't get his Christmas gift from us, and I had ordered it over the Internet using a credit card.

"I e-mail over the Internet. What if a hacker's getting into my credit cards and e-mail? What if my files have been hacked? What if someone's broken in?"

What if indeed.

"Jay, hold on a minute," Laura said firmly. "I think you're jumping to a hasty conclusion. Have you talked to anybody at work yet?"

"Talk to anybody at work? Who can I talk to, Lauren? What am I going to say? 'Oh, by the way, I think someone's hacked into the system and is reading my files on the state pension plan. It's been going on almost three months.' I'd look like an idiot. How could I explain it? It would seem so obvious, common sense, and I didn't see it."

"Maybe there's nothing to explain. Maybe there's nothing there at all. I don't want to hurt your feelings, but you've been up and down over the last few months. I thought it had something to do with your father."

Jay said nothing, but Lauren could hear him taking a deep breath.

"I didn't tell you this before, but I'm having a really, really tough time with something. You'll never believe what my father said to me when we dropped him off at the Harbor Express to go home. He said he..." Jay was struggling.

"Are you alright?"

"No. I'm not alright," Jay answered.

"It's alright. You can tell me later. I understand."

"No. I'll tell you now. I need to tell you now. He said, he said, well, he said he was proud of me," Jay labored to get out. "Then he said, 'Build the boat or you're the goat.' It was a silly little rhyme, just like I do with the kids."

Lauren now understood why her husband's moods had been swinging. His father had told Jay he was proud of him, and the words had brought on an emotional crisis. He also rhymed like his father. She knew that Jay rarely spoke of his Dad, had basically walled him out and locked the door. Christmas had been wonderful for the two of them, and now cracks were developing and starting to show.

"Jay, I don't know what to tell you. I don't think he was being manipulative. I think he really meant it. He should be proud of you."

"It was the worst thing he could have ever said. Now what do I do?"

"Well, like this other thing, maybe the best thing to do is nothing. Give it a rest. I'm relieved that you told me because I was just at a loss about everything and didn't know what to do myself. Even the children were wondering about you."

"I'm sorry. I really am. The kids don't deserve this. Everything seems to be happening all at once. I'll be alright," Jay said, already trying to steel himself. "There is something you can do though. I remember that computer guy you told me about. Maybe I can talk to him. Maybe he would know something. Do you know how I can get a hold of him?"

"Sure, I have his number right here."

"You do? Can you give him a call for me?"

"Yes, he gave me his card when I first met him. He said he was in the computer business," Lauren answered, seamlessly covering for herself. She had not told Jay that she and Graham Barrows accidentally met at the Museum of Fine Arts or had been to lunch together several times at a quiet and cozy restaurant off Hanover St. in the North End. Nor did she tell him they had talked on the telephone and exchanged e-mail. Yes, she would call Barrows for Jay and did so.

As an Englishman, Barrows was typically reserved and reluctant to talk about his personal business with anyone, but he was a very good listener. He had hinted to Lauren that all was not happiness at home but did not elaborate. She did not press.

It was all very innocent, and appearances didn't matter. Lauren had lunch with many different men, and no one would think anything of it. She and Graham had by this time talked about a lot of things, some of them personal on her part, and he would know not to mention that he was already a paid consultant at Jay's company.

If that fact ever slipped out, Graham would only say that he and Lauren had never discussed it. Jay would interpret the lack of such details as an indication of a very casual relationship.

****

Life at Tony Romano's dealership was vastly improved, and the warm body sent to solve the computer problems did so splendidly. Tony never got an exact answer as to the true nature of the problem and, for the most part, he didn't care. It was over his head.

The technical support rep ran hardware and software diagnostic tests on all the desktop computers in the dealership, including the server, to make sure they were functioning properly. A few anomalies showed up, but they were not particularly serious and were corrected by the diagnostics. The rep wrote a report of his findings and made several important recommendations regarding security.

Each user of a computer would automatically be logged off if the monitor were not being used for a given period of time, which could vary from one department to another. Passwords were changed for everyone, including Tony, and virus protection installed.

A person was designated the part-time system manager and given a daily and weekly maintenance schedule to follow. "You probably think, Mr. Romano, that your business is the cars you sell, but it's not. It's the computer system. Without it, you're dead in the water," the tech rep had warned him.

Romano was in a very spirited mood because things at the dealership had been fixed with room to spare for the main event of the automobile selling season, Presidents Day in February. Some guy walked in off the street and bought the special order mega truck and seemed to like the idea that he could afford to pay so much. Romano had given him a good deal.

Tony's monthly cash withdrawal was uneventful.

Liz loved her engagement ring, and the whole dealership was abuzz – "Did you see the size of that rock?" – about what it meant for Tony.

Big changes were coming up in his life.

****

Kevin Sweeney had started graduate school and was beginning to feel like a different person. "I can't believe how much I missed learning something new and unusual," he told Marie after the first week of classes, which started in mid-January.

No one associated with his business, including Stevie Bear, knew Sweeney was taking classes. Such information could be ruinous to his company if the contractors and potential clients thought he was interested in doing something else. Kevin was protecting himself from an inevitable recession, which, like the night follows the day, was bound to come. It was his insurance policy against a downturn in the economy.

The previous October, Kevin took the Commonwealth's controversial Literacy and Communication Test for Teacher Certification. He also had applied for Alternative Certification through the Department of Education and was waiting to appear before the Review Board.

He was not interested in teaching but thought he should look into anything for which his background and interests qualified him. Kevin was especially encouraged about education because most people in the field were his own age. Although he thought it could never happen, age discrimination had become a major factor in his life.

Sweeney's business was doing well, and he had received since the holidays several calls that, if they panned out, would provide him with enough projects to last him for more than a year. Most importantly, the size of each project was substantial, which meant that he would earn more money while doing fewer projects. He could give each additional attention.

The Matthews project would be winding down soon now that the cabinets and counters were in. George and Kathy immediately filled them with all the things that were stored in the cardboard boxes in the front dining room. The cabinets were white with a greenish – gray granite top, and had a double bowl, stainless steel sink, and several upper units with leaded glass, which was lit from inside.

All the lighting, heating, and plumbing were in and functioning, which was a real morale booster for the couple.

Wild man Dan McPhee laid the random width and length red oak floor, and bunged the butted boards with walnut caps. Kevin had warned Kathy and George about McPhee and told them to stay out of the house when Dan was around.

McPhee was an arch loner who listened to his radio while he stacked against the walls each piece of flooring of the same width and height. His nailing technique was so steady that it produced a rhythm of its own, which was frequently interrupted by the sudden hum of the nail gun compressor. Sweeney loved to watch him work, but enjoyed even more the wonderful smell of the oak floors.

Dan was fussy to a fault, and the homeowners loved it. "This guy really cares about his work," they would say to Kevin.

Next up would be the painters who covered the newly finished floors with moisture proof tarps. They would lightly hand sand the newly installed, veneer plaster walls before priming. A second, and then a third would follow the first coat.

The work was now being scheduled according to the availability of labor not a project plan. Kevin would have preferred painting the Matthew's kitchen before the cabinets and floor went in, but the painters were on another job. Sweeney always felt that touching up was easier than cutting in and would save both time and money in the long run.

"No one will ever see it," was the standard line.

Dana and Dan were nearly finished at Crow's Point and would be headed to the Sheep Shed project sometime next week. Before driving into the South End, Sweeney had been to see them that morning to check out how things were coming along. All that remained was a small amount of siding on the left side of the house, which was very cold because it was exposed to Hingham Bay.

Just as Sweeney headed up the driveway on the right side of the house to the door at the rear, the six-foot-two-inch tall next-door neighbor came bounding out of his house heading straight towards him.

The man was in a rage, and his face was about a shingle's course worth away from Kevin's. "Didn't I tell you that I did not want that dumpster in the driveway? Didn't you promise me that it wouldn't be left there? I own half that driveway, and it says right on the fucking deed that you cannot block my access to it."

Sweeney knew what was coming next and braced himself to be hit. All his new muscles wouldn't save him now, he thought, because this guy is out of control. The neighbor continued to scream, but Kevin didn't hear him. Instead, he turned his body at a right angle to the neighbor's to give him less of a target.

"He gets one shot, but I get the next, and he won't be getting up," Sweeney thought to himself. "Next stop is the police station to swear out a warrant for his arrest."

What then happened was astonishing. Kevin looked the neighbor in the eye and said in a very low and soft voice, "Am I being rude or impolite to you? Am I being anything less than professional and respectful? Why are you swearing at me? Am I swearing at you?"

The neighbor looked dumbfounded and began to crouch down while holding one raised finger in the air. He was shaking, actually trembling, but stood up again to face Sweeney.

"No," he stammered, "and I owe you an apology."

"Done," Sweeney said, "but now let's get down to business."

Kevin then explained why the dumpster was left in the driveway: the homeowner's car in the front of the house where the dumpster was supposed to be placed was stuck in the mud that froze the night before. "As soon as the weather warms, we'll have the car and dumpster out of here."

Appeased, the man accepted the explanation but said no more. As the neighbor left, Kevin called to him. "The only thing you just proved is how much of an asshole you are," Sweeney said. It was mean, a deliberate kick in the teeth when the man was down. It was also very satisfying, and Kevin made sure the neighbor knew who had won the real battle.

Two days later, it rained, and the car and dumpster were removed.

Sweeney would be glad when this one was over although the homeowners had been wonderful. The project was a massive remodeling of a summer cottage into a magnificent Victorian home.

All projects, Kevin noticed over the years, had three distinct phases: the initial excitement, reality setting in, and eagerness to be finished. Unlike a typical contractor's payment schedule of a third, a third, and a third, the emotional phase percentages were not so easily ascertained. Every project and client was different.

His attention was turning to the South End and the drawings that were nearly completed for the Evans project in Hingham. Stewart and Michelle were very pleased with the prints, which were now being finalized and fine-tuned.

Kevin would then start the specifications, one of the most important functions he performed for his company and easily the most boring. Oh, well. He could still listen to his classical music.

****

The meeting between Jay Parker and Graham Barrows was quickly arranged for the next day at the Union Oyster House near the Quincy Market section of Downtown Boston. While Parker was waiting, he noticed on the wall behind the legendary oyster bar on the first floor a plaque to Daniel Webster.

Curious, he read that Webster was a frequent patron at the oldest, continuously in use restaurant in the city. The plaque said that Webster would drink one pint of a rum–water mixture between each of the six rashers of oysters he ate for lunch. No wonder the streets of Boston were so crooked back then.

Each man had a general description of the other, and Jay had no difficulty recognizing Graham when he entered the restaurant. Parker had asked for a booth on the first floor where it was fun and noisy, and the two were seated almost immediately.

After pleasantries were exchanged and the menu gone over, Graham and Jay ordered. While waiting for their meals to be served, the two got straight to the point.

"I'm worried sick that there has been a major breech of security where I work and that someone may be reading my e-mail and other files on my computer. Did Lauren tell you about it?" Parker began, dropping his usual "cooler than you" demeanor.

"No. No she didn't. She simply said that you needed to talk to someone about a computer problem you were having at work. She said nothing about eavesdropping. What makes you think so?"

Parker then told Graham pretty much everything he had told Lauren the previous day. Barrows was intrigued.

"I can't say that these things don't happen, but I also can't say for sure that it's happened to you. One instance is not exactly a trend, you see," Barrows said. "If you don't mind, I'd like to ask you some questions. Everything is confidential, of course."

"Of course. I just want to be sure of one thing. Is this something you feel you're qualified to handle?" Parker asked urgently.

"If you mean system security, I understand the concepts, but I'm not a security expert. There are people who specialize in just this sort of thing. I can probably direct you to some people I know."

"I would prefer to start with you before I escalate the problem. Correct me if I'm wrong, but I thought that a secured site on the Internet used encryption. I keep reading in the paper that the federal government does not want Microsoft and some other software companies to sell encryption software with their systems, that it's just about impossible to crack," Jay said.

Barrows stared at him. "Some of what you say is true, more or less. Encryption software is powerful but not failsafe. If the software companies sell encryption with their packages, they'll only make it more difficult for governments to break, but break it they will. For the everyday user without the resources of a government, it's about as safe as you can get. Do you encrypt files at work?"

"I have to tell you, no, I never do because I never thought of it. It's probably too late now," Parker said. "Would they be safe?"

"Before I answer, let me ask you a question. Have you ever heard of Bletchley Park?"

"No. What is it? A theme park or something?" Jay was clearly puzzled.

"No. It's not a theme park. Actually, it was an intelligence center during World War II and something of a museum now."

"I'm not getting your point," Jay said.

THE INDEPENDENT CONTRACTOR

"Before the war broke out, the Germans had created a prototype computer that they used to encode all their diplomatic and military traffic. One of the machines fell into the hands of a Pole, I think, and was then passed along to the British. It used three cylinders and a typewriter and was called The Enigma Machine."

At that point in the discussion, the waitress came to the booth with Jay and Graham's orders. Both were having a bowl of clam chowder and a sandwich.

"That's pretty interesting," Jay said. "Are you into World War II? I know a lot of guys who are, and I'm thinking about reading up on it myself. It was an incredible time in world history."

"No, I don't read much about World War II. Actually, Kevin Sweeney told me the story when he was visiting our U.K. office. He and I worked together in high tech for a time, you know. Bletchley was only a few miles away from the office, and I had never heard of it before.

"So there he was, an American, telling me all about this top secret British project during the war," Graham explained. "It was called The Enigma Machine because no one could figure out how it worked. Supposedly, German mathematicians had calculated that the odds of figuring out just one letter in a message would be in the tens of millions. So they felt safe that the code could not be cracked even though they were pretty sure the British had the machine."

"That's amazing. So what happened?" Jay asked enjoying the distraction from his real problem.

"The British Government recruited to Bletchley mathematicians, musicians, mystics, logicians, philosophers, card players, chess players, scientists, anyone and everyone who might know something about numbers and logic, got them to work together on the problem, and solved it," Barrows said. "Sorry. My chowder is getting cold."

"No problem. The chowder here is excellent."

"I find myself saying my lunch or dinner are getting cold a lot lately," Graham said apologetically.

"Hey! I don't mind. You're a consultant. You talk, Graham; people listen. I know I'm always saying 'It all adds up.' Lauren tells me all the time that I like to talk. I think what she means – but doesn't say – is that I tend to dominate the conversation, but I don't think that I do. Anyway, that's fascinating about the code. How long did it take to break it?"

"I don't really know. According to Kevin, the code was cracked only a few weeks before the war started. Sometimes it would take hours to decode, and the information would be useless because it was time sensitive. Kevin said that as the war progressed, the British sometimes knew what was happening before Hitler's generals did.

"There's some evidence that the Battle of the Bulge almost succeeded because Hitler was not using Enigma to communicate with his military, so the Allies did not know what to expect. Some people think that the Germans knew the code had been cracked because the Germans themselves had cracked the British code. It goes on and on.

"Then there's the American's breaking of the Japanese code, which was even more difficult because of the character set. My point is that given the right resources, any lock can be picked, and you have to watch out for arrogance. It's what did in the Titanic."

"Now I see what you mean," Jay said solemnly. "What do you think I should do?"

"On the basis of what you have told me so far, if you don't mind my saying, I think that you've got a case of the nerves. The credit cards seemed to have been a problem for a short time and now no longer are. No cash advances or improper charges were ever made. It sounds as though the problem was more aggravating than serious and worked itself out. Could there be anything else?"

Parker sat back in the booth. "Yes, there is something else, something that was more strange than anything. Lauren thought someone was playing a joke on me at work. I got a couple of pink memos with the question, 'Have you had your salami today?' I have no idea who left them, and I haven't seen one since around Christmas."

Barrows looked at Jay carefully, folded his arms on the table, and said, "This could be trouble."

"What do you mean? It was probably nothing more than a joke. It's dumb. Lauren thought I would get one of those dead jokes from people in the office, things like dead flowers, salami, which I hate, stuff like that. It never happened," Jay responded.

"Obviously, you don't know anything about this, but someone could be setting you up for more than a joke," Graham said grimly.

"How? I don't get it."

"Let me just finish my sandwich and I'll explain. You better eat up, too. You're going to need it."

Jay seemed to blink at what he considered Graham's conspiratorial theatrics. "What the hell could it be?" he asked himself while waiting for an answer from Barrows.

"Sorry, but there's another little history lesson I'll have to give you here," Barrows began. "Sometime in either the late seventies or early eighties a programmer got caught stealing money from a financial institution. He got caught because some customer's accountant couldn't find a penny in his company's bank balance. It was nothing more than a penny in interest, and the programmer got caught."

"Over a penny? Why bother? Come on, that's ridiculous."

"Not if you know anything about programming it isn't. You're not getting it, are you?" Graham asked.

"I'm definitely not, and I don't think I'm ever going to. A penny? Really," Jay said, sounding indignant.

"I think you will. Do you know anything about rounding up a number? For example, if you bought something here for ninety-nine cents and paid a five percent sales tax, what would the total amount be?"

"This is silly. It's obvious. You'd pay $1.04. That's only common sense. I still don't see it."

"Technically – or mathematically, I should say – the correct amount is $1.0395. After the point zero, the three nine five is rounded up to four. That's why you pay $1.04 because you do not have coins that represent mills. Theoretically, a computer can calculate as much to the right of the decimal point as it does to the left. It wouldn't matter."

Jay was listening.

"So, let's say that I write a program where there is no rounding up, that all the values from the third position to the right of the decimal point are captured and placed in a special account I set up for myself. How many interest calculations does a large, international financial institution do in a year?" Barrows asked rhetorically.

"It would be in the multi-millions," he continued, "and each calculation would slice an infinitesimally small amount from each account. The technique is called, Salami Programming, and no one has ever proven that it hasn't or can't be done."

Jay looked away from Barrows and saw the waitress. "I'll have a Sam Adams," he said.

"Are you getting it now?" Barrows asked politely.

"Oooh! I think I am," Parker said slowly. "You don't steal the entire loaf all at once. You take unnoticeable slices until you have the whole thing. Very, very clever, I must say."

"I think you've got it," Barrows said firmly but quietly. "Are you familiar with the Brink's Robbery in the early fifties? It happened not very far from where we're sitting," Graham said.

"Yeah, I've heard of it. There was a movie with Peter Faulk as the main Italian guy who planned it. What about it?"

"I read a book written by two of the men who committed the crime, and it was something of a tell all. One of them had a colorful name, Jazz Maffee, I think. Did you know that the robbers had been stealing money from the Brink's trucks long before they hit the facility in the North End?"

"I can't say I remember it from the movie, but, ok. I'll take your word for it," Jay said.

"The amazing thing about it was that the thieves had keys to all the trucks. The thefts were never reported because Brinks did not want its customers to know. It would have been bad for business, and Brinks covered its own losses. The robbers also had keys to the North End facility and went in and out of there at will. Some of the men took their girl friends there to see inside the place before the robbery. They were really bold and confident that they would not get caught."

"Wow, that really is amazing. I'd call that having a lot of balls," Jay said.

"I would agree. What's most interesting to me about the story is that authorities at first thought it was an inside job and ruined the lives of some of the employees whom they suspected of being involved. It was quite a caper, and most of the money was never found. They got caught a short time before the statue of limitations ran out because Specs O'Keefe broke. He was going to be murdered."

"Maybe I should read the book," Jay said impassively.

"There's a lesson in it, I think," Barrows said. "Security is relative, and there are people out there with the resources and imagination to break into almost anything."

"Ok. So what does all this mean to me? I haven't done anything, and I don't know of anyone who would want to do anything to me. It's a fascinating story, the whole thing about the salami programming, I'll grant you that, but I don't see where I fit into it."

Barrows thought for a minute. "Let me ask you. Have you made any large purchases lately?"

"Sure. Of course. Lauren and I remodeled our house. We used some of the money she got from stock she had in her company when it went public. That would be easy to prove. We paid the capital gains tax and filed our state and federal taxes properly. It was a ton of money, but that's what we did. We didn't want to wait, and we didn't want to be in debt," Jay told Barrows.

"Anything else?" Graham pressed.

"I don't know. Sure. My BMW. The Land Rover, which we bought at a dealership on Route 3A in Weymouth."

"How did you pay for them?"

"We got a bank check for the Land Rover but paid cash for the BMW.

Lauren thought I was nuts. We went to the bank and got almost seven hundred, one hundred-dollar bills for the BMW. I just wanted to see what $70,000 in cash looked like. She was a nervous wreck, and we got into a big argument about it. I just wanted to make everything seem real to me. I mean, all this money, and it doesn't seem real, you know what I mean?"

Barrows answered, "Yes. I do know what you mean. It all seems so unreal at times, almost as though it can't be money at all. That's why casinos use plastic chips. But here's the problem. If someone is playing around with you, the cash purchase of the BMW might not look good. There could be questions about where the money came from. Doubts could come up. It could appear like an impropriety to someone."

"Who? There's nothing illegal about paying cash for a car. The dealer in Hingham told me people do it all the time," Jay argued. "Incidentally, there's just one thing I wanted to ask you. If that guy at the bank got caught, why wouldn't your theoretical person get caught, too?"

"The real guy got caught because he was keeping the money for himself. The short answer is greed. If someone was taking the money and putting it in an account for you, that would be a different story. You would be the one who would have to get caught. You see everything has to do with appearances. In this case, you might appear to have too much money on your hands and paid cash for the car to launder it. People do that all the time, too," Graham countered.

"If this person was really smart," Barrows continued, "you wouldn't even know he was around. He or she would come in the back door or window, do his dirty business, and leave. Then he would suddenly reappear and do it again, and so on. Show up out of nowhere, just like that," Barrows said, snapping his fingers, "and then vanish. There's always that window of opportunity, as you like to say here."

Parker interrupted, "You mean someone could hack into the system, turn off the round up or whatever, put the money in an account for me, disappear, then do it again whenever? Why? What would be the motive? Obviously, I don't have the skill or background to do all this, so how can I be suspect?"

"That would be easy," Barrows replied. "You could be working with someone on the inside or someone else wants to settle a score with you, a subordinate, let's say, to whom you gave a bad performance evaluation. Perhaps, there's someone who is resentful about not getting a promotion. It could be anyone for any reason. Sometimes the person you least expect of turning against you does. I would take nothing for granted," he advised.

Jay appeared worried. "If all this is possible, why can't we just check the system to see if anyone has been screwing with it?"

"What you say seems sensible enough, but is not so easy to do. The program, Jay, could be buried so deep in the operating system that no one could find it. Some of these systems have millions of lines of compiled code. Finding the exact routine in all that code would be like the proverbial needle in a haystack."

"Yeah," Jay said slowly. "So what?"

"Companies don't throw out this software investment even when something new comes along," Graham said. "Don't forget, all the software developers or technical people over the past thirty or more years probably had easy access to your company's computer system and did not use conventional methods to get into it. That's a lot of people, and who knows where they might be today?"

"So, if it's happening at all, it could be anyone," Jay asserted.

"Yes, it could be anyone. In a way, it's a custom entry system, one set up especially for the programmer or technical support. The technique is called quite simply, back door, and all their passwords or keys to the system are probably still there. And people move around all the time in this business going from one company to another."

Jay was thinking. "These people aren't hackers in the true sense, right?"

"Exactly. You wouldn't need a hacker at all. It's much easier to get into a system and do damage than you think. You can safely assume that no one comes in the front door with an extra key you don't know about and may or may not get discovered," Barrows clarified. "You can't exactly set a trap."

"I understand what you're saying, Graham, but what I really want to know is, am I in trouble? Is it possible that I'm a victim here, and, if so, what can be done about it?"

"Sure, you could be a victim, but it would be very hard to prove and prosecute. It's also very hard for any company to know whom to trust. I'll give you an example told to me by Kevin.

"When he was in charge of the training staff at our company, a vice president called him about a special project and asked that he swear to secrecy. Kevin was told to train a customer system manager from New York, but the training had to take place over the coming weekend at our company's headquarters in Bedford, and it was now Friday afternoon. Kevin had to make up the training on the fly, make it appear special.

"That Monday, the vice president called Kevin to tell him what had happened. The system manager had been arrested by the FBI the instant he got off the plane from Boston."

"Why? What did he do?"

"The system manager had access to everything on the system, meaning every file, and used what he knew to tip off his friends about companies that were being acquired or going public. The system manager worked for a law firm that handled their business. He had insider knowledge, and he used it to his advantage, which is illegal."

"How did he get caught?"

"That part of the story Kevin never told me. I'm not sure he knew himself. So you see, many people in a position of trust with authority and access to the system can be compromised. Usually, they're good people who get a little greedy. They try it one time and get drawn in."

"Anyone who does that is an asshole. I think we have firewalls at work to prevent security problems and unauthorized access," Jay offered.

"You probably do, but the entire system is only as good as the people running it. I don't want to alarm you, but I did want to make you aware of some of the possibilities. Programmers can use their tools to create havoc, you know. Have you ever heard of a time bomb in computing?"

"A time bomb?" Jay asked. "What's a time bomb in a computer?"

"It's a program that will go off if the programmer ever gets fired or let go. The time bomb could wipe out an entire database, and nothing could be recovered off the disk. If a certain condition is not met, like the programmer logging onto the system for a month or more, then the bomb goes off automatically. The mere threat of such a thing could hold the employer hostage."

"Wouldn't the employer prosecute the employee for destroying property? Wouldn't it be a crime?" Jay asked in quick succession.

"Practically speaking, it would make no sense. The employer would cut a deal with the programmer to stop the clock. It would probably cost a lot less than going to court and trying to reconstruct a destroyed database, even if there was backup. The bomb could be built into the database so no matter what precautions you take you can't get around it. The back up copy would also destruct.

"The company, especially a financial institution, would not want this information to become public. It's too sensitive, and the public would not understand. And, yes, it is a crime," Graham said earnestly.

"So the guy gets off and it's almost impossible to prove a crime has or would have taken place," Jay observed.

"It's not the clean and respectful business you think it is, I'm sorry to say. Now getting back to the salami programming. The programmer could also set a clock, which is to say, as soon as a certain condition is met, the program executes," Graham continued. "It comes and goes."

"I'm not following you," Jay said.

"Here's another misconception about computers. Do you think it's possible to generate a completely random number on a computer?"

Jay looked puzzled but said, "Sure, I suppose so. Why not?"

"I'll tell you why not. Logic is used to generate a number, even if you multiply any number in a given list by the value of pi. The computer would have to know which number in the list to use and when. It's all part of a structured program. It's all logic, which is the key."

"The key to what?" Parker asked.

"It's the key to understanding how computers work. To be fair, you are right that a completely random number can be generated but only when an event is completely random."

"I'm not following you."

"Let's say that three people are using a computer. Each logs onto the system at different times and on different days. The time stamps to record that event are stored in the computer. The time stamps could be added up when all three are entered, and a completely random number would be generated each time.

"The dilemma is, that in order to record the random event, a routine – a logical operation – would have to be created to handle it. So you would be right back to where you started. Encryption programs have the same problem. They can't be absolutely random."

"Where are you headed with all this? It's getting late," Jay said, showing his impatience.

"It's how the salami programming could be invoked in a practically random way. It's how a phantom could get into the system, take care of business, and get out by vanishing into thin air. Someone and something like that would be very, very difficult to discover," Barrows said while checking his watch. "Sorry, you're right. It is getting late, and I have some work to finish up before I go home. Let me think about everything, and I'll get back to you."

"Jesus, you've got my head spinning, Graham, with all this techno-babble. I still can't figure out whom or why anyone would do this to me unless it's some kind of weird joke. It makes no sense. The e-mail thing, if it happened at all, I can see, but this one is ridiculous."

"It may sound ridiculous, Jay, but you never know. Reading e-mail is no big deal. It's called packet sniffing. Oh. One final point. Remember what I said earlier about breaking the German code?"

"Yeah. Are we back to that? I have to get going."

"Right. Well, the technology may have been fail-safe but the human system was not. Some of the operators forgot to turn the tumblers before

THE INDEPENDENT CONTRACTOR

sending a message. The cryptographers noticed a pattern, which gave them great insight. It was a procedural error, not a technical one that contributed to the breakthrough."

"It's all very interesting, Graham. Do we split the bill?"

Jay had said nothing about Andrea Wilson or the fact that her boyfriend was highly skilled in computer technology. Could she have said something to the boyfriend about the transfer to England? Did the two figure out a way to guarantee that Andrea would be coming back to Boston well rewarded for her work in England – if she took the job, which was still unfilled and waiting for her?

Had the boyfriend used Andrea as a way of getting to Jay? Was he working for the competition? The two of them hadn't been together all that long, maybe the last six or seven months.

What about Parker and Wilson's on line frolics? Jay felt he was safe there because he had never read anything that confirmed that AOL chat rooms or instant messaging had been compromised by hackers.

He never went on line from work; it was always at home.

Everyone usually connected directly through a modem to AOL's computers and from there went out on the Internet. AOL was where Jay and Andrea connected to each other.

****

It was nearly five-thirty in the afternoon on the same day when Parker and Barrows met that Lauren left the conference room at work and softly closed the door behind her. She was exhausted and had been in protracted talks with several venture capitalists and bankers all day long. Her company had made great strides in the Internet security software it was developing, and had recently beta tested it. The pressure was on to complete the software and release the product to the marketplace. Hopes and excitement were high, as were the stakes. If all went well, the company could go public a year before it had planned. There was much speculation as to when it would be.

Lauren decided to try Jay at his office to find out how his meeting with Graham had gone. She didn't look it, but Lauren was nervous.

"Jay? Hi. It's me," she said. "How did things go with Mr. Barrows today?"

"Hi, Lauren. How did things go? They went pretty good, actually. He thinks I'm just nervous about a lot of things, mainly the delay in the state pension plan decision. He's a very interesting guy, I'll tell you that much. My head was spinning after talking to him."

"Your head was spinning? Why?" Lauren asked.

"I think he felt it was his responsibility to lay out certain possibilities to me in layman's language. Some of it, like absolute randomness, sounded like techno-babble to me. He did tell me some pretty interesting things about the computer business that I didn't know."

"It sounds as though your meeting went well. Where did you go?"

"We went to the Union Oyster House near Quincy Market. It's a great place that has this ancient horseshoe shaped bar where people sit and eat raw oysters. You should see it. Some guy named, Daniel Webster, used to eat there all the time and drank six pints of beer for lunch. It must have been a record or something because they have a plaque about him on the wall."

"Sounds like you're really getting into Boston," Lauren commented. "What else did you and Mr. Barrows talk about?"

"Well, he told me some interesting stories. One thing that really, really seems strange to me is how Kevin Sweeney keeps on coming up. Barrows worked with him in high tech. Did you know that?"

"I think so. He told me that Kevin did work at his house just before he was at ours. We drove by the house at Crow's Point several times. Do you remember it?"

"Yeah. I remember it near the Hingham Yacht Club. It's a beautiful spot out there. I guess he and Sweeney are pretty good friends from the way he was talking. Anyway, Barrows thinks that salami note I told you about might not be a joke. It's a programming technique that has to do with rounding up numbers and stealing money."

"That's pretty interesting. What else did he say about it?"

"A lot of what he said was theoretical stuff, things like how someone might be trying to make me not look good. It's pretty complicated, so I better tell you later. I'd like to get out of here sometime tonight."

"Do you feel any better after talking to him?"

"You know, Lauren, I've been wondering the same thing myself. I don't know. He said he would get back to me about it. I mean if there is something serious happening, yeah, it could be trouble. I just don't know, and he doesn't either. We'll just have to wait to see how things play out. As I said it's complicated, weird."

"Maybe you and I can get away for a few days, go down the Cape or something. We seem frayed around the edges."

"It sounds great to me, as long as Maureen is willing to stay with the kids for a few days. They should be all right. We haven't done it very much over the years, if you think about it."

"A nice little inn down the Cape, maybe in Harwich on the beach, a fireplace, some nice wine. Moonlight. Just the two of us," she said as her voice faded.

"Are you hitting on me, Mrs. Parker?"

"You'll have to figure that out for yourself."

"I wish I could figure out what's going on. Graham's a pretty interesting chap, I should say. Very British. Very proper," Jay said trying to imitate Graham's accent. "I liked him. We got along. He passed along a story from Kevin when he was training in high tech. He helped some system manager in New York get caught by the FBI for sharing information with his friends on companies that were being acquired or going public. It was interesting. So when do you want to go to the Cape?"

"He did what?"

"Who did what?"

"Kevin Sweeney. What did he do?"

"I thought we were talking about the Cape."

"Jay, listen to me. What did Kevin Sweeney do?"

"I just told you. He helped the FBI catch some guy for insider trading."

"Oh, God, no! Now you've got me on the edge."

"Why? What did I do?"

"You didn't do anything. Jay, you're not thinking. My company may be going public anytime soon. There's a real possibility this company will be acquired by another software company. Do you know what that means?"

"Well, yeah. It means your job will be done, and you'll be out of there with all that stock and a chance to do it all over again. It sounds great to me."

"You're still not thinking. Suppose all this stuff with the credit cards, the e-mail, that spaghetti thing, all those screw-ups were meant only as a distraction, and the real target's me or my company.

"Jay?"

"I'm thinking, Lauren. I'm thinking. This is crazy. I can feel a headache coming on. I need a break. It's too much for one day. Let's pick it up when I get home."

"Fine with me. We can talk once the children are in bed. Now I'm starting to feel nervous."

"Lauren, we've been through some tough times before, and we'll get through this one, too. We're in the dark. It's all speculation at this point. We'll drive ourselves nuts, if we keep it up."

It was a long day, and Jay and Lauren were both very tired. They felt as though they were under assault, and nothing binds people together faster than a common fear.

Chapter 11

It was President's Day, and Kevin Sweeney was headed out to make his rounds. "Would you like to go with me, Marie," he called to his wife who was on school vacation that week. "No," she answered. "You'll be talking business, and all I'll be doing is sitting around."

Sweeney had four clients he planned to visit on President' Day, beginning with the Sheep Shed in Hingham.

The project was not about the building of a shed, of course, it was about its removal and replacement with a two story addition consisting of a family room, two offices, and a huge master bedroom suite with dual walk in closets on the second floor, a seating area, and bathroom with a Jacuzzi, separate shower, two sinks, and 1.6 gallon flush toilet. Kevin's company had handled the design and specifications and was now coordinating the work.

The Matthew's project had been completed, turned out just as planned, and came in on time and within budget. They were very happy with everyone and the workmanship done on their home. Kevin put them on his reference list.

Dan and Dana had finished their work at the Crow's Point project and were now working at the Sheep Shed. Despite some inclement weather, they had made a lot of progress over the last month. The ice storm that hit transformed plants and trees into bejeweled spectacles of nature and the construction site into a dangerous place.

The floors and walls were done, and all that remained was the framing of the roof. Today the pair worked outside but would go inside to button up all the odds and ends, things like installing the blocking or non-bearing interior partitions or strapping the ceilings, when the weather turned foul. They knew how to make good use of their time and keep the work going.

The idea that the homeowner could save money by having the work done during the winter was good marketing but a come on. A project could cost more at that time of the year because the weather could always be a problem – the foundation or utilities could not be installed – and the men, especially the carpenters, had to wear heavy clothes that restricted their movement, which cost time. Snow had to be shoveled from the deck.

Dana was in the yard cutting out the roof rafters from a pattern.

As a result of all the coffee he drank as he drove from one project to the next, Kevin usually had to use the bathroom a lot. He noticed that his clients' bathrooms in the construction area were generally kept clean when the project started but eventually became filthy. It was almost as though they thought that the frequent use of the bathrooms by the contractors contaminated them in some way.

Any guy would piss in a toilet, but few would take a shit. Someone had a bowel problem and left ass flak all around the bowl. It was pretty disgusting and something that neither the homeowners nor the contractors ever discussed. Eventually, someone cleaned the toilet.

Sweeney left Dan and Dana to themselves and drove to the Evans house near Hingham's Historic District. All the plans had been completed, and Kevin was now presenting to Stewart and Michelle the first draft of the specifications.

Both were extremely pleased and had a lot of questions. "How long from the time the specifications are done until the bids are back will it be?" Michelle asked. "Much longer than I would prefer," Kevin answered, "but the worst ever was almost two months. The market is very busy right now, so I suggest you prepare yourself for a long wait."

"We're really anxious to get going, Kevin," Stewart said. "Everything has moved along so smoothly to this point, I'm surprised about the delay. As you say, the guys must be really busy."

"I understand completely. I would love to turn the bids over in less than a month. I couldn't pay the contractors to get them back to me faster. Incidentally, the two-month period I mentioned was in the early nineties during the recession. I think the guys were depressed. I would rather prepare you for the worst than be overly optimistic. I am anyway, but it's come back to haunt me."

"I guess we'll have to be patient. I'm willing to wait, if that's what it takes. Let's say it's two months. How long after that will it be before we are under construction?" Michelle asked.

"That time can take two to four weeks. Usually what happens is this. The homeowners nearly pass out when I give them the figures. You'll be getting somewhere around twenty pages of line items. Once you know exactly what something is going to cost, you can make a decision. It's no extra effort for me to remove things and reduce the project by half, if necessary," Kevin explained.

"By half? That's a lot," Stewart said.

"It sure is, but it can be done because we have identified all the labor and materials for each section of the house. It's a modular approach and really works well. Once we're underway, the delay won't seem to matter," Kevin said with some encouragement. "The good news is that while you're waiting, you won't be inconvenienced. With the plans, specifications, and pictures, the contractors have little reason to come here."

"That really is amazing," Stewart said. "I've told some people at work about you, and they couldn't believe it. I've told them so far so good. You've delivered on everything you said you would and when."

"Thanks for the complement," Kevin said. "Once you're over the shock of the bids, get ready for another," Kevin said smiling.

"Another shock? What kind of a shock?" Michelle asked.

"Hiring all the subcontractors," Kevin replied. "It's like getting married without a courtship. Not much different from living together as they do these days, but at least with a contractor you have a contract."

"Well, that's a different way of looking at it," Michelle said with a smile. "That's why we hired you, Kevin. To help us through those decisions. I think it's great. Maybe there's another business opportunity there for you."

"No thanks," Kevin said. "Solving the problems with the residential construction industry is complicated enough. I've been in it a long time now, and I'm still learning. Anyway, if you have nothing else for me, I would like to conclude our meeting. Is that ok with you?"

"I have nothing else, unless you do, Stewart. We'll just keep our fingers crossed." Michelle then gave Kevin a check to pay for the work he had done to date. He thanked them and headed for his project at Crow's Point, after which Kevin took the Southeast Expressway to the South End. The Big Dig was nearing the halfway point.

****

"I'm really, really sorry to hear that, Jay. I know you worked very, very hard to bring the pension plan in. I can't imagine how disappointed you must feel," Lauren Parker said to her husband who had just called with the bad news. The state pension plan had gone to a competitor, a local company in Boston's Financial District. Both she and Jay were working on President's Day.

"Thanks, Lauren, but here's how I'm trying to look at it. The company's still doing well and growing, and there will be other opportunities," Parker said, sounding philosophical. "It's not the end of the world. I just can't help but wonder if I did anything wrong, something I should have known, anything, that I didn't. I still think it's possible the system was hacked, but I have no way to prove it."

"Wasn't Graham able to help?" Lauren asked.

"Other than that first conversation we had, I don't think he did much. All it did was get you thinking about your own situation. I think you did the right thing by telling the owners that they needed to tighten up security. Did they ever do anything about it?" Jay asked.

"They sure did. One of the owners said it was ironic that we would be developing software for Internet security while ignoring what's happening inside our own company. So, maybe some good came out of it. How did Andrea take the news?" Lauren asked.

"She took the news pretty well. After all, she's going to the U.K. and everything worked out fine for her. Eleanor was amazing, full of praise for all the work we did, trying to keep the staff up. She took it very well, but I can't imagine how it will play in the boardroom."

"Well, like me, Jay, I guess it's on to the next one."

"Yeah, Lauren," Jay sighed, "I guess it is. You know, I didn't tell you, but I've been having some pretty weird dreams lately."

"Weird dreams? No, you haven't said anything about weird dreams, but I wouldn't be surprised. You've been really stressed out."

"Normally, I don't remember my dreams, which are always in color, and I never dream about you or the children. It's strange, sort of. I never dream of anyone I know."

"I think dreams are fun, and I don't put much stock in them. I think like you do that Freud could have used time on his own couch. What kind of dreams have you been having?"

"It's pretty funny, I guess, but I'm almost embarrassed to tell you. In one of the dreams, I'm a prosecutor with a slam-dunk case, and I lose. The defendant uses The Remodeling Insanity Defense. In another, I'm a Greek philosopher arguing about morality," Jay said while laughing.

"It sounds like fun to me. You'd make a good prosecutor. You think well on your feet. And you're pretty persuasive, too. The Remodeling Insanity Defense. That's pretty funny. Any more?" Lauren asked.

"Oh, yeah, there was one more. This one you'll laugh at, I'm sure. I killed a contractor!"

"You killed a contractor? Was it when we were having our house done?"

"No. No. I don't think so. It was some time after. Don't you want to hear how I did it?"

"Sure."

"I gave him the Evil Eye, and he dropped dead."

"That is pretty funny, too. You do have a crazy imagination. It's probably a dream a lot of people have had or wouldn't mind having."

****

THE INDEPENDENT CONTRACTOR

Tony Romano was having a ball, doing what he liked best, taking care of business. The dealership had a lot of foot traffic on this President's Day afternoon, and sold seven, very expensive, foreign imports. The domestic car line was doing well also.

With a full showroom and plenty of leads and sales, it looked like the week would be a very good one for Romano, and the day was still young.

The only downside in his life was the condition of his mother. Dr. Pierce suspected leukemia, which would account for her lethargy, and was having her tested. The results would be back in a day or two.

Tony's father was very worried about his wife. "At this point in my life, I really have nothing but you and your mother," he told Tony a few weeks ago when they went for dinner to the Hingham Bay Club at Hewitt's Cove in Hingham.

"She's in good hands," Tony said. "Let Dr. Pierce do his job, and we'll take what comes after. She's going to be ok, Dad. Medicine's not like it used to be fifty years ago, and a lot of cures have been found. If there's anything she needs, you just let me know, and it'll get done. Money's no problem, so stop worrying."

"I know, I know, but I can't help it. I just keep thinking something's going to happen to her. Why don't we change the subject? Have you and Liz set a date yet? That's on my mind, too, along with everything else," Romano's father said.

"Not yet, Dad. We still have to see what's going on with Mom, then we can decide. I don't want to be thinking about a wedding if Mom's having a problem."

Tony will still very much the good boy and devoted son. The wedding could wait but not his mother.

****

When Sweeney returned to his house later that same day, he picked up his mail, drove up the long driveway, turned off the car, and went through the mail he held in his lap. The one letter he was looking for from the Department of Education had arrived.

Kevin's heart started beating faster. He quickly went into the house and opened the letter in the kitchen. The first sentence said it all: the Review Panel had rejected him for Alternative Certification.

He went numb, and then got angry. All the management experience and training he had had in high tech and running his own business meant nothing at face value. Kevin wasn't getting into the club.

Marie came home just as Kevin finished reading his letter. "I didn't get my certification," Kevin said. Marie seemed not to hear him, so Kevin repeated himself. "I know. I heard you the first time. You can't be serious," she said.

"Oh, I'm serious alright," he said. "It's the final insult. It's over for me. There's no point of my looking at anything else because, obviously, I'm not getting anywhere. No one wants me, and it's as simple as that. All this bullshit about a labor shortage, companies not being able to find good people, not enough administrators in schools is nonsense.

"These people ought to be ashamed of themselves. I'm not saying that I deserve anything, but I met the very criterion they established. I doubt they even read it. All that time and energy for nothing."

Marie never disagreed with educators or challenged them. "Even I'm shocked," she finally said. "It just seems so unfair. You spent months responding to the Department of Education's criteria for that certification and answered every one in detail. Your background is better than mine, and I have the same certification you applied for. This is awful."

"I'm going to the gym," Kevin said. "At least everything I do there benefits me."

Marie heard him leave and was heartbroken for him. No matter how high up her husband dared to look, he still saw down.

****

Lisa popped home shortly before supper at five-thirty. Marie was not expecting her, but offered to share her supper anyway. "There's plenty for two or more," she said. Marie then told Lisa what had happened to her father earlier that day.

"He needs to believe he can have the life he wants," Lisa told her mother. "He just needs to get out there and do it."

"Lisa, he's been trying for a very, very long time, and even I have to admit he's getting nowhere. He thinks no one wants him, and there's nothing you or I can do to change his mind. Graduate school's going great, and he's meeting a lot of new people. Maybe it will lead to something else," Marie said.

"To what, Mom? Does Dad really know what he wants to do? I mean, it's great running a business and all, but if you're not happy doing it, why bother? He's doing pretty well now, but what about next year or the year after? I think that's his problem. He's so worried about the future that he forgets about today."

"It's a lot more complicated than that. If you see him, talk to him. He listens to you sometimes more than he does to me."

"Mom, I have to go into school tonight, and I may stay at David's instead of driving all the way home. I have to do some research in the library. There were no classes because of the holiday. We'll see. What's cooking?"

****

Two days later, Lauren Parker was standing over her desk at work going through her mail, which had just arrived, and she was sorting it all out before going home. A large, handwritten manila envelope caught her eye, so Lauren opened it first.

Inside were several typewritten pages that made no sense as she perused them. Suddenly, Lauren felt the blood leaving her face and the rest of her body. She thought she was standing in a pool of it and slowly sat down in her chair.

Lauren was seized simultaneously by shock and fear the instant she understood what the papers contained. They were an erotic and graphic, online exchange between two people, and one of them had to be her husband. His name was not on the papers, of course; it was some screen name used in a chat room or for instant messaging.

Although she could not discern the woman involved, Lauren did recognize the settings – Newport's Cliff Walk, where she and Jay spent several memorable afternoons, Minot Light Beach, Cohasset Harbor, and Marginal Way in Ogonquit, Maine – all the places by the ocean where the two strolled, walking and talking, the children tagging along. It would be too much of a coincidence for the man not to be Jay.

On the commuter boat ride home later that night Lauren would have something else to sort out: whether she should confront Jay or let matters go. Maybe it was just a lark, maybe not. Jay had been right; someone had been reading his e-mail, after all, and most likely his files at work. She had advised him to do nothing, and Jay may have lost the state pension account because of it.

She had also downplayed the salami programming scheme, but maybe now that bad joke would be coming back again, too. Whoever was trying to distract Jay certainly had done a good job.

Lauren had set aside her instincts, and she was now in a quandary. Her initial fear that she could be the real target of all the antics against Jay returned. Who was behind it all and why? She had few, if any, real friends in the area, and she was not used to getting on the phone with them or her family to discuss problems at home or work. The only person she really talked to was Jay, which she was not about to do.

For the moment, the only friend she seemed to have, the one person who would listen to her and understand all that she was going through was Graham Barrows. He had taken the commuter boat to work that morning, and the two had chatted briefly. They were careful not to be seen together too much because such things on the commuter boat were noticed.

Appearances there made a very big difference.

When Lauren saw Graham later after work waiting for the commuter boat at the pier behind the Boston Harbor Hotel complex, she immediately approached him. "Are you heading straight home tonight?" she asked him not so innocently.

"Well, yes, I had been planning on it. With my wife back in England now, eating out alone most nights has become quite boring. I'm actually getting fairly good at preparing a nice meal for myself, you know," Barrows said. "What about you?"

"I was wondering if you might have time for a cup of coffee. There's something important I need to talk to you about. Would I be imposing?" Lauren asked. She had known about Graham's situation for a while now.

"Imposing? No. Not at all. I'd be delighted. There's a coffee shop on Route 3A near the old police station. Shall I meet you there?"

"Yes, that sounds fine. I know where it is. I'll see you there."

Lauren then used her cell phone to call home and ask Maureen to stay with the kids an additional hour or until Jay came home. "Just let him know I'll be a bit late," she said. "Thanks, Maureen. You're a doll."

While boarding the boat, Lauren thought to herself, "This is silly. We're adults, and we're acting like we shouldn't be seen together." Once she was inside the cabin, Lauren turned to Graham and said, "There are two seats together over there. Why don't we just take them? I don't think anyone will be using them."

As the boat left the pier and its passengers were settling in, Graham asked Lauren what was going on. "I hope it's nothing with Jay," he said showing his concern.

"Actually, there is something going on with Jay, but not what you think," Lauren said. "It's not work, but then again it could be. At this point, I'm so confused I don't know what to say."

Graham and Lauren then discussed her fears that she was the real target of a computer hacker, not Jay. "It doesn't make much sense to me," Graham admitted. "If someone was out to get information about your company, why not just go for you straightaway? There would be no reason for any diversionary tactic, if my understanding of the situation is correct."

"We thought of that, too, and talked about it. My company took steps to make sure that security has not been breached. Important correspondence is either encrypted or kept on a separate computer in a locked room. Only three people have the key to the door, the two owners and myself. You can't use the computer without a password, it's connected only to a printer – nothing else – and there's a shredder sitting right next to it. Any important documentation is locked up, too. The copying machine is right outside the more senior owner's office.

"We hate the idea that someone inside the company can't be trusted because it's such a small operation with a wonderful spirit and belief in the future. We have no choice but to take precautions," Lauren explained.

"It sounds to me as though you're doing all the right things. All companies should take precautions, not just yours. It's only good business practice," Graham said. "The irony is that the more dependent we become on technology, the more vulnerable we are. Other than being over-confident, I don't think you have too much to worry about."

"Oh, but I do," Lauren said immediately. "There is something else, but I would rather discuss it in private than here."

"Certainly. I understand. I don't want to seem forward, but we can always go to my place, if you would like." Graham said directly. Watching her reaction to his offer and not wanting to offend her, he then quickly added, "There's just myself, and I'm pretty good at putting coffee on. There's not a whole lot in the refrigerator, but there's plenty for two."

"The coffee sounds great," Lauren said pleasantly. "I really don't think I can eat anything right now. My stomach's a bit upset."

As soon as the commuter boat reached the pier in Hewitt's Cove, Hingham, all the passengers disembarked and quickly found their cars in the huge parking lot across the street from the facility. Lauren would meet Graham at his house on the hill at the tip of Crow's Point.

Barrows had just arrived when Lauren pulled up behind him. "I never thought I would get to see your house this way," she said. "I always thought it would be from a distance, you know, driving by. This front porch must be wonderful in the warm months. Is there a view of the water from here?"

"No. Not from here. Well, actually, I should say there are glimpses between the trees and the houses across the street. The real view is from the master bedroom. Too bad it's so dark, or I would show you around the outside. We English are fond of our gardens, you know. Here. Come on in," Barrows offered as he opened the door and turned on the lights.

"This is really beautiful, Graham. The open staircase is stunning, and there's so much room in the hallway. Very elegant. And the floors, too, with that dark wood in them," she said as she gave her coat to Graham to hang up in the closet.

"It's really the thing that sold us on the house, and everything's been refinished. All the flooring is maple. The thin strips of dark wood around the edge of the room are walnut, and the technique is called stringing. Kevin's floor chap did a wonderful job on all the floors. We were very pleased with him. Bit of an odd man, I would say."

Lauren laughed. "A bit? Kevin said he was quirky and flinty. We just stayed out of his way, and everything went fine."

"Can I get you something? Coffee? Maybe a bite to eat?"

"You know, if you have a nice red wine, I would prefer that instead of the coffee. I really should eat something. Any crackers and cheese to go with it?"

"I always have plenty of wine and cheese in the house. It's not as much fun when I'm by myself. Let me show you the kitchen."

Graham ushered Lauren in the general direction of the kitchen, which was off the front hallway and in the rear of the house. She was also impressed with the work done in the kitchen. "This is really beautiful. Was the whole house done over?" she asked.

"Pretty much. The kitchen is new, of course, but the rest of the first floor was fix up and repair. It was starting to look a little tired."

Barrows took the cheese out of the refrigerator and began slicing it. "Let me do that," Lauren said. "You take care of the wine." Graham located and uncorked a nice bottle of cabernet sauvignon from Argentina and poured it into two large, pear-shaped glasses he had taken from an upper cabinet. He knew cabernet was her favorite.

"Cheers," he said, lifting his glass to Lauren's.

"Cheers," she returned.

"Do you have a plate for the cheese?" Lauren asked.

"Yes, or you could use the cheese board. Whichever you prefer."

"I like a nice plate. Any crackers to go with it?"

"Crackers? Ah, right. I call them biscuits. Right over there in the lazy susan you should find a box." She found them easily.

Lauren then finished slicing the cheese, which she arranged with the crackers around the edge of the dish.

"A woman's touch, I see," Graham said as he reached for a cracker and slice of cheese. He quickly sipped his wine, put the glass down again, and sampled the cheese on the cracker.

"Women like things to look nice, Graham. It makes a much prettier presentation, don't you think?"

"Yes, it does. When I'm here alone, I just pull the biscuits out of the box and slice up the cheese as I go along. I like your way better."

Lauren smiled. She liked the way he talked. Biscuits and chaps.

"I have some nice vegetables I can cook up with some other odds and ends. Care to try it?" Graham asked as he was looking in the refrigerator.

"Sure, but please don't go through any trouble for me. Can I help?"

"It's no trouble at all. Here, why don't you sit at the island while I get things ready? I can talk and work too, you know."

Lauren smiled as she sipped on her wine. "I'm sure you can," she said while watching Graham washing and cutting up the vegetables. "Can't I at least set the table?"

"Sure, but I thought we could sit right here at the island. I kind of like it. The dishes, Lauren, are in the upper cabinet to the right of the refrigerator, and the knives and forks are in the draw under it. There should be matching place settings and napkins in the middle draw."

Barrows set up a large, non-stick skillet, poured into the pan enough green colored virgin olive oil to cover the bottom, added some garlic, and began to sauté it on a medium high heat. He then tossed in several chopped shallots, poured in a small touch of a sauvignon blanc, about one-third of a cup, added the mushrooms, and mixed everything together with several flicks of the wrist.

"Hey, pretty fancy there," Lauren said. "It's starting to smell good already." She had everything all set out on the island and was enjoying the wine and cheese. "Can I help with anything else?"

"Sure. In the draw under the stove are the pans. I'll need one that can hold about four quarts of water. In the lazy susan, you'll find a box of angel hair pasta. Just take it out, and we can cook up the whole box. It's too much for two people, but I can always reheat it later."

Lauren found everything just where Graham said it would be and started to prepare the pasta. Graham had added to the mix zucchini, broccoli, some green and red peppers, several crowns of cauliflower, a little celery, some asparagus, and yellow beans. He carefully measured and added one-quarter teaspoonful of sea salt and the same amount of crushed black pepper.

The smell of the steaming food and wine soon filled the kitchen. Lauren stood next to Graham and breathed in the aroma. "This is going to be wonderful. Everything smells so good. I'm getting really hungry already." She had brought the water to a boil and was about to add the pasta when Graham suggested, "Lauren, could you please break the pasta in half and stir it in the pan? We should be done in another eight or nine minutes." He flicked his wrist again to stir the vegetables, and turned down the heat to medium.

Just when everything was almost ready, Graham speared several of the vegetables and asked Lauren to sample them. He cupped his hand under her mouth, while she took the food off the fork. "This is delicious," she said. "Perfect." She seemed to be having fun and delighting in the experience.

"Jay never cooks with me," she said. "You know, it's really great fun. This is great, and it all seems so simple. You're pretty good."

"I'm glad you're enjoying yourself. It's a treat for me, too. How's the pasta coming? There should be a colander where I keep the pans. If you add a touch of olive oil now, it should keep the pasta from sticking," he said. "I like to get everything on the table all hot at the same time. This is my variation on a pasta primavera. Let me get some rolls. Here, sit down." Graham then got some rolls, which he put in a basket covered with a white linen napkin and placed them in front of Lauren.

Barrows picked up the colander with the angel hair pasta, mixed it in with the vegetables, took Lauren's plate and filled it, then his own.

"Everything looks so good, and it's so colorful. I can't wait to get started," Lauren said.

"Care for some more wine?" Graham asked.

"Yes, not a full glass, though, just a bit. Bon apetit!"

"Bon apetit! Eat! Enjoy! Try the rolls. They're from a small bakery in Weymouth." Graham filled his glass and Lauren's, placed his napkin on his lap, and began eating. "Not bad," he said. "Maybe it could use a touch more salt."

For the next half-hour, Lauren and Graham dined and talked. If a candle had been added, both would have admitted that the meal was not only tasty but also romantic. Lauren now seemed to be very much at ease and having a good time.

Every now and then, she came back to Jay.

"He had a terrible childhood because of his father," Lauren told Graham. "There's a lot he won't tell me, and I can't get him to open up about it. His sister did one day tell me that Jay slept in a tool shed when they were growing up because of their father. We have a two-car garage, and he parks his car in front of his side.

"All the tools, you know, the lawn mower, snow blower, rakes, spreader, all the yard things are on his side of the garage. Oh! And his golf clubs, too. That's why he parks his car in front of it. He won't buy a tool shed."

Graham understood immediately. "It sounds as though his father liked his tea too much. I saw some heavy drinking at the pub when I was a lad. A lot of people excused it because it was the pub, unlike what you have here. The pub was a neighborhood social setting, and you could eat there, too. No one ever talked about when everyone went home after being there all night. It's quite a shame, really."

"It sure is, and Jay has the scars to show it. His father's not drinking now, and he spent the holidays with us. The children really took to him, and I think he's realized his mistake and is trying to make things right. I don't know if Jay can ever trust him again," Lauren said.

"Everything was so good, and it's still early. Good thing I called home. Would you like help with the clean up, Graham?"

"Sure. It won't take long. I hate having a dirty kitchen. I think that if the kitchen is dirty, the whole house seems so. Would you agree?"

"I would because I feel the same way. I like everything in its place. It's just as easy to put something away as it is to leave it out. I'm having a great time, by the way. This was a very good idea."

After cleaning up, Graham asked Lauren if she would like to see around the rest of the house. She had also freshened up.

"I'd love to," she said. "This kitchen is really beautiful. It's so nice and open, and I love the oak cabinets with the maple floor. It's a beautiful contrast. The Corian counter and molded sink. You still have room for the table and chairs."

"Yes, it is a good size. We also have a pantry, which my wife really loved. It's a bit of an old fashioned idea that's coming back I'm told."

Barrows and Lauren then wandered throughout the first floor of the house, their unfinished wine in hand, stopping at various points for additional discussion much as they had when they met at the Museum of Fine Arts in early November.

"Would you like to see the upstairs? That's where we really expanded, made all the rooms larger, added the gables. It's quite lovely. Here, let me show you."

As Lauren ascended the stairs, she did so slowly and admired the craftsmanship. "Is it my imagination or are these stairs easier to walk up than normal?" she asked.

"It's not your imagination at all," Graham responded. "They are a perfect step, meaning six inches high and twelve inches deep. Multiply the two numbers and you get seventy-two. Most stairs today are seven and one-half by ten inches, which is close at seventy-five but not perfect. The higher the riser and the more shallow the tread, the steeper the stairs feel."

"Very interesting. And just where did you learn so much about steps?" Lauren asked playfully.

"Kevin, of course. He gave me a wonderful magazine to read, and there was an article about steps in it. The first step of this staircase with the curves on each end is called the starting step. The curved part of the rail, the post, and the balusters make up the birdcage. It's a classic design that adds charm and character to the house."

Graham then showed Lauren the rest of the second floor, including the master bedroom suite, which had its own bathroom, dressing and seating areas, and French doors to a roof deck with an ocean view. All the furnishings were contemporary with lots of oak, brass, and glass. Barrows opened the doors and invited Lauren outside.

"It's a bit cold and dark out here, I'm afraid, but on a clear night, you can see all the way up the North Shore. See those little lights all lined up? They are planes heading into Logan Airport. Over there where the light is glowing in the sky is Boston. Right in front of us is outer Hingham Bay, and Hull is over there where all the small lights are," Graham said as he pointed to them.

"How beautiful!" Lauren said, as she drew together the lapels of her jacket and stood behind Graham.

"Are you cold?"

"A little bit. You can block the wind. You can get a whole different perspective of everything out here. I didn't realize how close to the city Hull is. Even the North Shore doesn't look that far away. Everything, really, is so close together. What's over there?" Lauren asked pointing southward.

"Over there you have Hingham Harbor. The whole area is quite beautiful. My wife and I used to sit out here and read. Sometimes at night, we would have a late supper up here. It's one of Kevin's best ideas yet," Graham said. "I'm getting chilly. Perhaps we better pop inside," he said thoughtfully.

"Everything in the house is just beautiful and so tastefully decorated. It must be wonderful to have a house like this." Lauren did not ask why it was that Graham seemed to own the house without his wife or whether it might be part of her divorce settlement.

"It is wonderful, but not when you're here by yourself all the time. Now that my wife's gone, I'm not sure what I'm going to do. Perhaps I'll just do nothing and see how things work out. I'm not in any hurry."

The pair returned to the kitchen, but then wandered into the living room. Graham set the wine and cheese on the right side of the large, glass table in front of the oversize, flowered sofa with multicolored pillows, and gestured for Lauren to join him. Before settling into a comfortable, overstuffed chair next to the sofa, Graham started the gas log fireplace. "It's a bit cool in the house. I keep the temperature low during the day. The fireplace will add some heat, and it's nice to look at," Graham said.

"That's beautiful," Lauren said. "You can feel the heat right away."

"I like it. I'm not one for a woodpile. Some people really get into it, cut and split their own logs. It's too much work, and I don't have the time," Graham said. "Would you like me to put on a CD? I don't have too many. Do you like Natalie Cole? I've got one of hers and a Sinatra. *Duets* it's called."

"I love Natalie Cole, and Sinatra is Jay's favorite," Lauren replied.

Barrows knew the moment for Lauren to discuss what was on her mind was now at hand, so he moved the conversation in that direction. Cole's rendition of her late father's, *The Very Thought of You*, played softly in the background. "Are you comfortable?" he asked. "Would you like some more wine?"

"Yes, I am," she said. "Just a little bit more. It's very good. I'm having the best time. I wish it were under different circumstances. Would you mind if I put my feet up?" Lauren then took off her shoes and folded her gorgeous legs on the sofa while she rested on the arm.

"Certainly. No problem. So, Lauren, what's really going on? You said there was something else you would rather discuss in private. Nothing too serious, I hope."

"I hope so, too," she began, "but I really don't know. That's why I asked if you and I could talk. Are you familiar with America On Line?"

"Oh, sure. I was on it myself for a while, but I found it boring. I'm around computers all day, and it was like a busman's holiday."

"A busman's holiday? What's that?"

"It's a company paid vacation on a bus for a bus driver," he said with a smile.

"Oh, I get it. Cute. Anyway, you must be familiar with the chat rooms and instant messaging."

"Yes. I am. If you're curious about what teens in America are up to after school, check out the teen chat rooms. There must be thousands of them. I went into a few to see what they were like, and you wouldn't believe the language and talk. It was quite shocking, really," Graham said.

"I can only imagine. Our two girls still believe in Santa – this will probably be their last year – so we're still a few years away from that one. More to the point, I got something in the mail today that knocked me off my feet. It was three or four conversations, I guess you would call them, between a man and a woman. They were using screen names and talking about things."

"What kind of things?" Graham asked, seeing that Lauren was taking her time telling him.

"This is not easy, so I'll come right out with it. They were conversations men and women who are intimate with each other might have. They were very erotic and sexual."

"Really? Why were they sent to you?"

"That's the big question. I am certain from some of the details that the man, at least, was my husband, Jay. There. I said it. That's it. That's what's upsetting me. I feel hurt and angry all at the same time."

"Of course you feel hurt and angry. Do you think he's involved with this woman? Is that the real problem?"

"I don't know if he is or not. I didn't read through all of them. It was easy to get the gist of the conversations. He's been acting so weird lately, and I thought it was because of this big account he was working on and his father. They don't see much of each other, and there's a lot of hostility there on Jay's part. I figured that must be it, but maybe it wasn't," Lauren explained.

"Are you planning to talk to him about it? Maybe the person you should be talking to is him, not me. I don't mind helping you, of course," Barrows quickly added.

"That's the problem, Graham. I want to talk to him, but I can't. I think it's obvious that someone has been watching what he does on his computer, just like he suspected all along. He was probably right, and I advised him it was nothing to worry about," Lauren said, looking away from Graham and sipping her wine, which was nearly gone.

Barrows corrected her. "You're not the only one who advised him not to worry. I did the same thing. Any reasonable person would have. I have to assume that the woman in the conversations did not save them in a file and send all of them to you herself, especially if you knew her."

"I have a suspicion, but it's only a suspicion. There's a very attractive woman he works with in the Boston office who just took an assignment in the U.K. Jay had advised his boss that the woman be transferred and sent her a confirming e-mail, but it wound up in the hands of the woman."

"Ah, I see. Was it a transfer or a promotion?"

"Jay thinks for some reason the woman thought he was trying to get rid of her, but he wasn't. He was trying to help her career. He said they worked it out, but I don't know. Jay said it was a promotion."

Graham looked at Lauren and said softly. "Lauren, that simply makes no sense. If she took the position, she must have done so willingly. Why be angry about it and try to hurt Jay through you?"

"I thought of that, too, Graham. The only other thing that makes any sense is her boyfriend, because he's not going to England with her. Maybe he was angry and took it out on Jay. I've met him once before at a company party, and he's something of a computer nerd. I don't know what to think, and my head's really not too clear at the moment." Lauren was now staring at the glass table.

"So how do you feel about this fantasy thing, Lauren? You must be pretty upset."

"I am upset. I go from feeling hurt to angry, then back again. Especially because all the places he talked about are special to us. That's how I knew he was involved and that someone had not just made it all up. I mean it was so stupid of him. So unimaginative."

"Do you think they were involved with each other outside work or just in the chat room?"

"Supposedly, the last one to know about an affair is the wife, but I can't accuse him of that. It would be just like Jay to experiment until he got bored with it. He's the kind of guy that requires a lot of stimulation. That's why he loves his job so much. I think it gives him everything he wants, and he's satisfied."

"If you don't mind my asking, Lauren, how are things between you?"

"For awhile, Graham, things were awful, but they got better over Christmas. It's been up and down ever since. If you're asking, well, how's our sex life, it's the same. One minute he seems there with me, and the next he's remote and distant.

"You know, when I said earlier that Jay would never cook with me, I should have added he would rather watch a game on TV. Later, he'll want to have sex, but it just doesn't work for me. I just go along," Lauren said without holding back. "May I have a bit more wine?"

Graham poured more wine into Lauren's glass and twisted the bottle to avoid spilling a drop. "I wasn't asking about your sex life. Sorry."

"No problem. I would tell you. I think Jay thinks I'm trying to control him," Lauren continued. "He says things like he doesn't work for me when I ask him to help me with something around the house. It sounds so stupid because I'm not trying to control him. Then he's says I'm always criticizing him, but sometimes he does such ridiculous things. I can't tell when he's being playful or a jerk, which I know must sound terrible."

She paused, looked at Graham, and then continued. "Jay can be really very sweet and thoughtful, but he doesn't always follow through, which drives me crazy. He promised the kids to research and build a ferry as a family project but hasn't done much about it since Christmas. I'm sure the children are disappointed. I know I am."

"Lauren, it sounds like there's an awful lot happening between you two. Have you ever had a chance to just slip away and air things out? Sometimes a change of scenery helps," Graham offered sympathetically.

"No, we don't get away much because of the children. When we do go away, we take them with us. We do everything as a family. It's just that there's so little time for us to talk, and when there is Jay does not want to. We go around and around.

"I wanted to get away to the Cape for a weekend, but he hasn't taken me up on it yet except to ask about the golf courses down there. That makes a lot of sense because I don't golf. He's big on it and is a member at the South Shore Country Club right down the street from us. It was one of the reasons we bought the house.

"Anyway, I really feel lost, like I don't know where I am. We just go around and around, and there's no way to break out of the cycle."

"Understandably so, Lauren," Graham said as he wiped his hands over his face and rubbed his eyes. He then took her hand in his and said, "There's a lot that needs to be sorted out here, and I don't think we're going to be able to do it all this evening.

"Let me give this one some thought, and we can talk later. In the meantime, I think you should say nothing to Jay. I think you're caught in your own anger and pain and the possibility in your mind that you let him down. Naturally, Lauren, you're confused. Who wouldn't be?"

"That's just it, Graham. What do I do next? If I say anything to Jay, I may set him off. He could turn on me, and then what? I get all the blame for what he did. We have three small children, and I want to look after my family."

"Believe me, Lauren, I understand. I've gone through one divorce, and I'm about to go through another. It doesn't get any easier."

"I'm sorry to hear that, Graham. At least this time there are no children involved. That's when it really gets complicated, as you know."

"Excuse me for a minute, Lauren. I don't mean to seem insensitive, but I have to let the cat out."

Lauren looked at Graham and smiled. As he got up to leave, she held his hand tightly and gently put it against her face. Looking up at him, she said, "I'm really glad I had the chance to talk to you. Thank you for everything. It's just wonderful to have someone I can talk to."

"That's quite all right. That's what friends are for," he said while fixing his eyes on hers. Graham felt Lauren pull his hand towards her as though she wanted to give him a hug. He knew instantly her eyes said something else, and he bent down to accept her kiss.

He responded long and tenderly enough to seem more like a friend than a lover. Drawing back slowly to stand up, he felt Lauren move towards him, so he put his hands on her shoulders and gently pushed her back. "We best be careful, here," Graham said quietly but firmly.

"Yes, I agree. We need to be careful," Lauren said as she moved towards him again. There was no doubt about the second kiss or of how much each wanted the other. It was longer than the first. The smoldering sexual tensions that existed between them since the night they met at the MFA started to come to the surface.

Even so, Graham left her to attend to the cat. When he returned, Lauren was sipping her wine and watching the flickering flame of the gas log fireplace.

"It's very pretty, the flame, but there's no snapping like in a real fire. We thought of a gas log, too, but I like the real thing. I suppose this is easier to keep?" Lauren asked.

"Yes, it's a lot easier, which is why we installed it. Like you, I prefer the real thing. It's beautiful and more romantic."

Lauren turned to Graham as he sat down in his chair beside her. "Now that you've heard the whole story, what do you think I should do?" she asked while extending her hand to his. Graham took her hand again and held it while looking in her eyes, as he had done before.

"I don't have an answer for you tonight, Lauren," he said kindly. "At some point, you're going to have to decide what you want. I don't think it's good for the children to see their parents up and down all the time or unhappy with each other. You do have to think of them as well as yourself. Maybe after a good night's sleep, you'll be able to think more clearly. There's seems to be lot of uncertainty in your life."

Lauren said nothing, but stared back at Graham. Once again, she pulled him towards her, and once again they kissed; he from his chair; she from the sofa. Their tongues touched, and they lingered. "Sit here next to me," Lauren said.

Graham did, and he then put his arm around Lauren and drew her to him so that she could lay her head and hand on his chest. They both put their feet up on the glass table and sat that way for several minutes while watching the dancing flames of the gas log fire.

"What are you thinking?" Graham finally asked.

"I'm trying to think about nothing," Lauren answered.

"Then what are you feeling?"

"I'm feeling warm inside being with you. I'm feeling relaxed, comfortable, a little nervous."

"Why would you feel nervous?"

"I'm feeling nervous because of what you might be thinking of me."

"I wish I could tell you everything I'm thinking about you, Lauren. How much I admire you. How much I respect you. Right now, I wish I could say everything, but I might make a fool of myself."

Laura sat upright and looked Graham straight in the eyes. "A fool of yourself? You've got to be kidding." This time, she held nothing back and let her passion show in an ardent kiss. Reading her right, Graham began touching her face, neck, side, and legs.

Her lack of resistance encouraged more exploration, and he started unbuttoning her blouse to undo her bra. Before he could get that far, Lauren stretched out on the couch, and Graham held her in his arms. "Are you sure you want to do this?" he said, and Lauren answered with another kiss, this one more sexual and combustible than all the other others. She let him know how aroused she was and began kissing him everywhere.

Graham was soon on top of her, and Lauren's skirt was up around her waist. Their lower bodies were pressed against each other, and they could feel the intense heat there.

"It may be more comfortable upstairs," Graham suggested. He tried to get up, but Lauren pulled him down. "Come on," he said resisting, "Let's go upstairs."

Graham then took Lauren by the hand and led her towards the central entrance staircase. About midway up the stairs, she stopped and looked at him. "What's the matter, Lauren? Are you ok?"

"No, I'm not ok, Graham, and what we're doing is not ok either. Believe me, there's nothing I want to do more than go into that bedroom with you and make love. As right as it feels, it would be wrong. I can't. At least not now. That teen chat room flashed into my mind. We're no better than the kids."

Graham then embraced her, but did not attempt a kiss. "I understand. There's probably too much happening just now. Maybe now's not the time. I wouldn't do this if it weren't right for you. I wouldn't want to do anything to hurt you or have you do anything you were not comfortable with. Let's go down stairs. Maybe it's best that you get going."

"I'm so sorry. I never should have started this," Lauren said.

"There's nothing to be sorry for. We just better be careful, that's all. These things can happen. I don't think we were looking for it."

"I don't know if I agree with you there," Lauren said with a curious smile. The two of them then turned around, walked down the stairs, rearranged their clothes, and went into the kitchen.

Shortly thereafter, Lauren said she had to leave, and Graham saw her to the front door. "Before you leave, there's just one thing," he said.

THE INDEPENDENT CONTRACTOR

He then took her in his arms and kissed her warm and tenderly.

"Remember me that way tonight," he said as he opened the door and kissed her hand while looking into her eyes. She searched his face. "Are you going to be alright?" he asked.

"Yes. I'll be fine."

"Are you sure?"

"Yes. I'm sure. Don't worry. I'll see you tomorrow on the boat. I think we can sit together now."

"Fine. Cheers."

"Cheers. It was a wonderful, wonderful evening," Lauren said. She then walked to the driveway. A moment later, she drove off.

Graham thought he could hear the waves washing over the rocks at the base of the bluff across the street. "It must be close to high tide," he thought to himself. He turned off all the lights downstairs and headed for bed.

He and Lauren would have trouble sleeping that night. The CD played Natalie and her father singing together the tender song, *Unforgettable*.

****

Bruce Lacy called Kevin Sweeney later that same night to check up on the status of the Crow's Point, South End, and two Hingham projects. Sweeney had picked up the business phone in his living room. "Hey, Kevin, how you doing?"

"Bruce! Not bad, buddy, not bad. What's up?"

"Well, I was wondering where you might need me next. I'm trying to plan my schedule, and everyone wants me all at the same time."

"I know the feeling. You can't be in more than one place at a time. Besides, in this weather you've got a lot of emergency work to do, I assume," Kevin said off handedly.

"Yeah, you do. You get your calls for heating systems that are down, water heaters gone. That sort of thing. Pipes burst. If it's really bad out there, it's pretty good for me that way.

"You know, I meant to tell you, Kevin, that George and Kathy there in Weymouth, boy, what nice people. You've done some super jobs over the years, but that one really, really looks great. And they seem very pleased."

"Thanks, Bruce. It's nice to hear from the people who really know. Yeah, I think it went well, too. I've been trying real hard lately to prepare the client for the construction phase of the project. Key them in on what to expect. I worked up a sheet they can refer to throughout the project. The first time I used it was with George and Kathy. I think it made a difference."

"You never stop trying to improve your business, do you?" Lacey said. "I really admire you for it. Some guys wouldn't care. I have to tell you, from where I'm sitting, it's as good as it gets. The way you handle everything. The organization. It means a lot to me, and I'm sure the rest of the guys also."

Sweeney could always count on Bruce to be encouraging to him.

"Well, thanks again," Kevin said, enjoying the unsolicited praise. He did not doubt Bruce's sincerity. "Remember, you don't owe me a thing. All I ask is that you perform, and you always do. I think it's why we have something special. When I was a general contractor a number of years ago, it was awful, something like hand-to-hand combat. I got screwed for being honest with the homeowners and subs."

"I know what you mean. I just thought you should know that the guys and myself appreciate what you're trying to do. I just hope you're getting something out of it," Bruce said earnestly.

"I'm getting by. I can pay my bills, but it's only a good business in a good economy. Right now, things are great, but who knows?"

"I knew there was something else," Lacey said. "I had a great time at the restaurant on Thanksgiving. Steve was a bit much, but it was a lot of fun. You were something of a devil as a kid, so much the opposite of what you are now. That apartment thing and the Coast Guard stuff. It was very, very funny. How's Steve doing by the way?"

"I had a great time, too. It's just fun to be out with the guys and swapping stories. Steve? He's doing fairly well, but it will be a long recovery. It was a good thing he had Donnie working for him, or there would have been no money coming in. Annie doesn't work. I'm really worried about him and his family, but there's not much I can do beyond being a good friend."

"Is he still smoking? Some of the guys said he was. I haven't seen him, but I thought I could smell it at Matthews."

"I hope not. Whenever I ask him, he says, no, but he could be too embarrassed to tell me the truth. What are you going to do? He's a big boy. No matter."

"I'm going to have to get going," Lacey said. "So, getting back to my original question, will you be needing me anytime soon."

"Yes, definitely. Let me look at my schedule tomorrow and fax you a countdown on all the projects. That way, you can plan your time. Hey! I loved our little conversation. It's always fun talking to you."

"Same here, Kevin. I'll catch you later."

Chapter 12

The six-man crew dredging Cohasset Harbor during the last week of February 1999 was an interesting, colorful, hard living and hard driving group who worked for a marine contractor on the North Shore. One more night shift after this one and they would finally be off for the weekend. It was a Thursday night.

Smart laborers on the crew wore layers of clothing and dressed warmly and sensibly for the weather and work that they did. A guy might wear overalls that were quilted and heavily lined on the inside, a sweater over his shirt, and a float coat or other life preserver over both.

The coat was really a short, navy blue jacket with heavy nylon on the outside and foam insulation on the inside. It was extremely warm and comfortable and looked like a motorcycle jacket.

He would also have on green rain gear pants, a yellow rubber coat to break the wind, and high rubber boots. Although he was not required to wear a hard hat, he would have on a Goat Roper, which came in three different colored pastels, was made of fleece, and provided ear protection. It was a goofy looking getup that kept him warm, but he was lucky in a rainstorm if the water did not run down his neck.

It was not raining this night, and the deck hands were busy working away. Their rig consisted of a fifty-foot by one hundred-foot spud barge on top of which sat a 375 Cat excavator. Alongside the barge was a five-pocket dump scow capable of holding fifteen hundred cubic yards of the material – mostly course sand, mud, and mud clay – they were removing from the channel that night. A second scow that could hold seven hundred cubic yards was also being used on the job, but was kept off to the side.

Five deck hands ran lines, operated the spud, maneuvered the scows, looked after refueling, and repaired the equipment.

An operator ran the CAT, which hummed along steadily as its arm dug into the channel, came up, turned, and deposited the dredged material in the dump scow. To help him see what he was doing, lights were trained on the general area where the operator was working.

The Army Corps of Engineers had finally gotten around to dredging the harbor, which had been heavily silted over for years. It was getting nearly impossible to move around the harbor at low tide, and the commercial fisherman welcomed the operation. By contract, the dredging had to be completed by the end of March, weather notwithstanding.

Once done, the new depth of the channel would be eight feet below the mean low tide or the average depth of the water at low tide during any time of the year. The operator in the heated cabin was dressed differently from the other men because he was protected from the elements. After scraping the bottom of the channel, the operator started to bring the bucket up when he stopped and was heard saying, "Jesus H. Christ. What the fuck is that?" Something was flashing in the light.

Given that the crew had seen just about everything come up from the bottom – debris, anchors, mooring boxes, and the like – they weren't surprised much by what they saw, but this time it would be different. "Hey, Tommy! Get a light over here," the operator said.

Tommy did, and the other guys started to work their way towards the excavator bucket, which had just broken the surface of the water. "What is it?" the operator asked no one in particular. "It looks like some chain link fencing, but we can't really tell," one of them said. "Take it up a bit. Not too much."

The operator took the bucket up a couple feet, and most of the water drained out. "Ok, hold it," a voice said. One of the men then called to the operator, "You better take a look for yourself, Big Guy. There's more here than a little fencing."

The operator stopped the machine's arm, put on his float coat, and jumped out of the cabin to where the men were standing. Although the light trained on the bucket was helpful, the operator used a flashlight for a better look. "I don't know what the fuck this is. It looks like a bunch of chain link fencing with license plates attached to it. What do you think?"

Before any of the men could answer, one said. "Have you ever seen a fence that walks? This one's got two feet; all bone, no meat."

The operator pointed his flashlight to the left end of the rolled fence and discovered two feet sticking out from the center. All the men just huddled around and looked at each other. Clearly the situation called for a pow-wow.

"Anybody got any ideas?"

"Yeah. I got one. I say we drop it in the scow. Who the fuck will know the difference?"

"We report this, and the authorities will shut down the rig. Like whoever the fuck he is, we're dead in the water."

"I don't think we should walk away from this."

"You feel like coming all the way down here in a couple of weeks? I don't. It's no work, no pay, you know."

"Come on. It's nighttime. We've got perfect cover."

After much discussion about the economic hardships associated with reporting an obvious homicide, the crane operator finally said, "I can't do it. What if it's some woman? Some family is out there looking for a loved one. It wouldn't be right not to report it."

Some of the guys grumbled, but the operator got his way. Although the Big Guy had a two-way radio inside the cabin, by instinct and training he knew not to use it. Someone was dispatched to the Cohasset Police Station, which was located almost in sight of the rig.

Within the hour, serene and picturesque Cohasset Harbor would be alive with activity and flashing lights. All the newspaper and television heavies from Boston would weigh in. Helicopters would shine bright spotlights on the water showing the rig and crew. Interviews with the Big Guy would be conducted. If all went well, the murder would make the eleven o'clock news and carry over into the weekend.

Frequent updates of the alleged crime would be given throughout the night. Because of the unusual disposition of the body, which was wrapped in chain link fence and license plates, the suspected homicide would be dubbed the Tortoise Shell Murder and become a sensation.

By early morning, everyone would know the victim was Dazzie Clarke. Only six people would know how close the murder victim came to being involved in a perfect crime because his feet were all bone and no meat.

The dredging company, thank God, would get an extension on its contract.

****

The two Massachusetts State Police investigators assigned to the Clarke murder by the Norfolk Country District Attorney's office were seasoned professionals with almost forty-seven years of law enforcement experience between them. Knowing that the first twenty-four hours of a homicide investigation are crucial, they were prepared for a long night and arrived at the scene of the crime a short time after the report first came in.

The investigators immediately took control, secured the crime scene, and interviewed the Big Guy and his crew, but they had little to offer beyond their discovery of the body and the time when it was first reported. There appeared to be a discrepancy between the two – anywhere from one to four minutes – but the difference seemed immaterial. It was around nine that evening.

Photographs and video of the scene and the body in the bucket were taken immediately. Crime scene technicians then carefully removed the body – still wrapped in the chain link with the license plates attached – to a van for transportation to the medical examiner's office in Boston.

Working together, the crime scene technicians and the doctor in the medical examiner's office gathered trace evidence and took the victim's fingerprints, which was possible because his arms had been positioned tightly alongside the body. Drowning caused his death, and his body had been in the water for approximately one week, according to the best estimates of the medical examiner's staff.

While the exposed areas of the feet and head and other soft tissue had been consumed by marine life, the torso was still fairly intact. The wallet in his pocket made Clarke's identification easy but not conclusive. The picture on his license was no help.

The chain link fence, which was both rusted and painted in several areas, was held as evidence along with the license plates, which revealed several patent – meaning visible – fingerprints that were immediately photographed and scanned into a computer. The plates also held other patent prints but they lacked sufficient detail to be useful to the investigation.

The investigators got very lucky on the fingerprints because they were made from grease or mud and not destroyed by the salt water or erased by the movement of the current in the channel of Cohasset Harbor or its white water inlet nearby.

Either of the two substances could have been on the plates themselves or the hands of the individuals who mounted or removed them from the cars. Otherwise, there would have been little chance that any fingerprints – visible or not – could have been obtained at all.

Additional prints were identified as the victim's while the others were being compared by the Automated Fingerprint Identification System – AFIS database – on the State Police computer. The victim's prints were also input for comparison.

Although AFIS developed a list of candidates that had similar prints, an investigator did the actual confirmation manually. The database held the owner's first and last name, address at the time the prints were taken, social security number, date of birth, physical description, charges, if any, or other relevant information.

AFIS produced a match between its database and the patent fingerprints of the victim. Although Dazzie Clarke had no criminal record, he had once been fingerprinted as a suspect in the vandalizing of Hull High School when he was a sophomore there. No charges had ever been filed, and the most likely explanation for the fingerprinting was that someone had wanted to teach Dazzie Clarke a serious lesson.

Apparently, someone was equally interested in teaching Tony Romano the same lesson because his fingerprints were also matched by AFIS. He had no criminal record either.

The license plate numbers with the patent fingerprints had been run first, and it was determined that they all belonged to vehicles that had been stolen but not recovered in the late eighties. Several plates were more recent and from commercial vehicles, including one that had been reported stolen by a Braintree contractor the previous November. The remaining license plates would be run later that night.

The cell phone found on the victim had quickly corroded in the salt water but still might be helpful to the case. After drying, it could be tested for fingerprints, and its telephone records would be obtained from the phone company. If Dazzie was like most cell phone users, he undoubtedly would have left the cell phone on, thereby making it possible to trace his whereabouts.

The unpleasant job of notifying Clarke's next of kin was the investigators' responsibility and necessary for them to ascertain pertinent facts of the case. Around twelve-thirty in the morning, McCarthy and Symolon left the crime scene and drove to the small, winterized cottage in Hull that was the home of Dazzie's parents.

Roused from their sleep by the ringing of the doorbell and the sound of knocking on the door, both went to see whom it was. Dazzie's father turned on the outside light and saw two men he did not know standing on the front stairs. He carefully opened the front door but left the storm door closed.

"Are you Mr. Clarke?" the father heard one of the men say.

"Yes, I am. Who are you?"

The investigators then identified themselves and asked to be let inside the house where they delivered the bad news. Although visibly shaken, Dazzie's parents were able to answer several sensitive questions asked by McCarthy and Symolon.

Their son still had a small room there, they said, but he was more likely to stay with friends than with them. They very seldom saw him, and when they did, he breezed in and breezed out.

The last time they saw their son, Mr. and Mrs. Clarke were certain, was last Friday night. He had come by to visit them sometime around seven that evening, but they were going out to see some friends. Dazzie was still there when they left at seven-thirty but was gone by the time they came back around ten thirty. "He would have been up watching TV and drinking beer, if he was staying here. He was himself, quiet. Nothing about him seemed out of the ordinary."

With the permission of Dazzie's parents, investigators McCarthy and Symolon had searched his room but found nothing of any significance. In the small garage in the back yard, Symolon discovered Dazzie's Harley, which was fairly new and had low mileage.

"It was not like him to leave his bike in the garage for more than a week because he used it to get back and forth," Mrs. Clarke told the investigators. "He would hitch rides in the real bad weather. If a few more days had gone by, then we would have wondered."

"Did you talk to your son very often?" McCarthy asked.

"He wasn't much of a caller, and, you know, as a parent you like to have your children call you. We were never sure of where to reach him. It's just the way it was," Mrs. Clarke said matter of factly.

"I was just thinking of something," Mr. Clarke interjected. "There was something funny about that night. It was the Harley. We found it outside the garage the next morning, so I put it inside. Dazzie would never have left it outside if he wasn't going to use it."

"That's right," Mrs. Clarke affirmed. "We didn't think much of it at the time, but now maybe it means something."

Symolon and McCarthy looked at each other. "I'm afraid we'll have to get a warrant to search the garage, and it will take at least three to four hours to execute. I'll have someone from the Hull Police Department come here to secure the area in the meantime," McCarthy said to the couple.

Discovering nothing else, the investigators left the Clarke residence with a list of Dazzie's friends, acquaintances, employers, and other miscellaneous information and promised to keep them informed on the progress of the investigation.

By six-thirty Friday morning, their son's body was released to a funeral home in Hingham where the wake would be held the following Monday from seven to nine. A Funeral Mass would be said the next day, Tuesday morning at ten in St. Ann's Catholic Church in Hull.

Friday morning – when it was safe to do so at first light – an underwater search for additional evidence in the area where the body was found was conducted, but the State Police divers discovered nothing else to go on. Additional pictures and video of the scene were taken.

The investigators had learned from Clarke's parents that the victim worked part-time for a towing company now and previously an excavating contractor in Braintree. Since the registration of the stolen commercial vehicle and the name of Clarke's former employer were the same, the detectives decided to pay Buddy Roper a visit at two that morning. When the

THE INDEPENDENT CONTRACTOR

pair arrived, they immediately noticed the painted chain link fence around the entire property.

"Hi, Mr. Roper. I'm Dick McCarthy, and this is Wes Symolon of the Mass. State Police," the older of the two men began while showing his badge. "May we come inside? We have some questions we would like to ask you."

Roper immediately let the investigators inside his construction trailer, which was located within the yard surrounded by chain link fencing. He was completely surprised and puzzled by the visit.

"Sure. Anything. Come on in. Want some coffee? I can put on a fresh pot," Roper suggested.

"No, thank you," McCarthy said. "I'm all set for now. The investigator then got right down to business and began the interview. "For starters, Mr. Roper, we would like to know when you employed a Dazzie Clarke of Hull and for how long."

"Dazzie Clarke? Sure. I remember him. That's easy. He came here just before May of last year and left about two weeks after my Komatsu disappeared in early November. What's that? Five or six months, maybe?"

"Right. Was he a good employee? How'd he get along with the other workers?"

"Dazzie was ok. Nothing special. The other guys thought he was funny. I guess he had some pretty good stories to tell. For the most part, he minded his business and did what I asked him to."

"You mentioned a Komatsu," McCarthy said. "Was it stolen? What can you tell us about it?"

"I can tell you that Clarke had a license to move construction equipment around and that I had him working for me part-time. I do both residential and commercial work, mainly commercial, and every now and then I get a call from a contractor working on the Big Dig to come and give him a hand. So, I do, and the money's great," Roper explained.

"So, I hired Clarke to move my excavator into Boston whenever the guy called, just so I could have it there. If he weren't driving to Boston or other sites, I'd have him doing odd jobs. Sometimes the guy in Boston had his own operator, and sometimes I provided him one. I give him the option. So there was nothing special about my equipment being moved around day or night."

The detectives were listening and taking notes.

"Are you moving equipment tonight?" Symolon asked.

"No. I got nothing going tonight. I'm not usually here this late, but I had a bunch of stuff I needed to get done, some paperwork, and I'm trying to catch up before I head out again at seven. Like it or not, you have to make the money when it's there, and who besides the owner would be crazy enough to work these hours?"

"So what happened with the Komatsu?" McCarthy asked.

"One morning I come into the yard early, five or so, the gates are closed but not locked, and the machine's gone, and the dogs don't come, even when I call them. I knew Dazzie didn't move it, so I can't figure what the fuck's up. I page Dazzie, of course, but he doesn't know anything from nothing. I had heard rumors about equipment disappearing and being shipped overseas, but I thought with the Dobermans I'd be safe. I mean, who's going to walk in on a couple of Dobermans?" Roper explained.

"I'll tell you who," he said answering his own question. "Someone who knows the dogs are dead. Whoever did it poisoned them, and the funny thing is, those dogs were practically harmless. I think I felt worse about the mutts than I did about the machine. All the guys kidded me about them, and they were just good dogs, friendly as hell. Strong, but friendly.

"Anyway, I report the theft, and the insurance company settles, but I didn't get nowhere near the value of the machine. And I had a lot of jobs I couldn't do without it. You just don't have a rental clause in your insurance policy for a loss like that the way you would a car. So it cost me, big time. Oh yeah! They found my low bed and cabin on some empty lot in Roxbury a few days later. It had been vandalized, and the plates were gone, but the registration was in the glove compartment."

McCarthy asked Roper, "Did you file a report with the Braintree Police?"

"Yes. Yes, I did. Basically, it says pretty much what I just told you. I don't know if I mentioned Dazzie or not. Nothing came of the investigation."

The investigators were very careful not to give information in the phrasing of a question. McCarthy asked, "Other than the dogs, what other security did you have at the time?"

"Well, I had a chain on the gate, with a lock, the fence around the property, floods on the corners. That kind of thing."

"Who had the keys to the lock?"

"I kept them here in the trailer, and I kept that locked, too. I usually opened up because you never know who's going to show up for work. The chain was cut, and they just came in. I kept a key on my chain."

"Where in the trailer do you keep the keys?"

"Right over here. I'll show you."

Roper then showed the detectives a small cabinet hanging on the wall. Inside were all the keys for his equipment, each carefully marked, identified, and hanging on a separate hook.

"Do you mind if we have a look around?" Symolon asked.

"Sure. No problem. Whatever you want, just go ahead. Let me show you around."

"That's OK," McCarthy said, "Maybe you can locate Mr. Clarke's employee records for us." While Roper was searching for Clarke's records, the two detectives conferred. "I'll check outside," Symolon said. "You can keep him busy."

Using a flashlight, Symolon did a quick tour of the yard because he was not interested in Roper's machinery, but he did notice that the place was neat and practically spotless. Even the machinery was clean. "As you can see, I like to keep things ship shape," Roper said to Symolon when he returned to the trailer.

"I noticed the fence has been painted. How long ago was it done?" Symolon asked.

"I'm guessing, but sometime last September, early October. I had Dazzie do it. Here's those records you wanted," Roper said as he handed McCarthy the thin file on Dazzie Clarke.

"Any chance that you might have some of the paint hanging around?" Symolon asked.

"Yeah, there probably is. He did a suck job, by the way. Sprayed over everything, including some of my equipment. I think it's over in the shed."

Symolon then went outside again and found an old can of the silver paint used on the fence sitting on a shelf inside a small shed. He took it with him when he returned to the trailer a second time. McCarthy saw the can but said nothing to the other detective.

"You keep a neat yard. What do you do with any left over materials? I didn't see much around outside," Symolon said.

"It's like this. If I kept every single thing I got off a job and stored it, I'd have no place for my equipment. Some things you hang onto, but most of it I let the guys take if they can use it."

"Did Dazzie ever take anything?"

"It's hard to remember exactly, but I'm pretty sure he did. He asked me one time about some short lengths of rebar and some fence I had, said he could use them to reinforce a concrete patio he was building at his parents' house. I said sure. It wasn't much."

"Rebar? What's that?"

"You know, you've seen it. It's a round steel bar you find sticking out of forms they're doing on the new construction for the Big Dig. You use them in foundations, sometimes with landscape ties. Just bars."

"Ok Sure. I've seen them. Do you remember what kind of fencing it was?" Symolon asked.

"Yeah. It was a small section of chain link. I'm guessing six or eight feet or so. I had it hanging around for years. I think it was left over from the yard fence, but I never got around to doing anything with it. As I said, I try to keep the place clean. It wasn't much, so I probably didn't notice it."

"And you're fairly sure that Mr. Clarke took that section of fence?" McCarthy asked.

"Yeah. I think so. Yeah. That would have been it."

"How did he remove the fence? Truck, car, or what?" McCarthy probed further.

"He had a friend with a truck help him out, I think. With everything going on around here, it's hard to remember, you know, what happened when. He definitely did not put it in his car because he didn't have one. He was really into bikes and had a pretty nice Harley. I never thought to ask, but can you guys tell me what this is all about? Is Dazzie in some kind of trouble?"

"No," McCarthy answered. "He's not in any trouble. He was murdered, and we're investigating his homicide."

"You've got to be shitting me, right? Murdered? I can't believe it."

"I'm afraid it's true, Mr. Roper. We're in the early stages of the investigation. I want to thank you for being so helpful," McCarthy said, indicating that the interview was over.

"We will need a warrant, after all, to take a section of fence and the paint can. Until it's issued, I'm going to have a trooper stay here. I'll call it in right now," McCarthy told a now nervous Buddy Roper.

"Yeah, sure, but I have to get some sleep. Is it ok if I just crash on the sofa over there? That's what I planned to do anyway."

"I have no problem with that, just as long as we can serve the warrant and come onto the property. I don't know how much sleep you'll get," McCarthy said.

Roper then volunteered, "You know, there's one thing. I never entirely trusted that guy. There was just something about him I couldn't put my finger on. Here I am trying to help him out, you know, give him a job, some income, and he up and quits on me a couple weeks after the excavator is swiped. Didn't even stick around for the holidays. Said the place spooked him. And I was paying him decent money, too."

Symolon looked at his partner and then Roper. "Do you have any idea why someone would have murdered Mr. Clarke?"

"I'll tell you what I think," Roper said earnestly. "You know, this is a business where you feel lucky to have a warm body and a couple of hands. Good help is very, very hard to find, and, if the guy even shows up, you think you've got something. Guys come and go all the time. It's not a business where you check references, if you know what I mean.

"I have this feeling, and I've had if for quite some time, that he had something to do with the Komatsu. I had no way of proving it, of course, so what could I do? He acted all surprised and everything, and he didn't quit on the spot, but it left me thinking. If it were true, I'd want to kill the bastard myself. It cost me a lot of money."

McCarthy was still taking notes. Finished, he said, "Well, thank you for your time, Mr. Roper. You've been very helpful. If you remember anything else, you have my card."

The two investigators then left through the front gate of the contractor's yard, got in the car, and called for a trooper. "What do you think?" Symolon asked.

"I think he was straight with us, very forthcoming. I think he knows who stole the excavator, and he'd probably want to kill the bastard himself, just like he said. But I don't think he's involved."

"My take, too, but we'll have to see what shows up in the paint. Only a total idiot would wrap a body in a section of the same chain link that's around his property."

"Bad people don't always do stupid things anymore than good people always do smart things," McCarthy responded. "We're looking at his behavior, not his intelligence. It's a good thing stupidity isn't a felony or we'd all be in jail." Symolon laughed.

Roper came out to the car and tapped on the window. "I don't know if it means anything, but every now and then Dazzie slept on the couch in the trailer. I kind of felt bad for him, like he'd didn't have any place to go. That's it."

"Thanks," McCarthy responded and rolled up the window.

The investigation was shifting into gear, and the investigators still had a long night before them.

****

The phone rang at seven in the morning Friday in Kevin Sweeney's office. "It's early for the phone to be ringing," Sweeney thought to himself. He had a policy of encouraging clients to call him at seven-fifteen if they had a question or an emergency. Having no idea why a client would be calling him, Kevin picked up the phone.

"You watching TV?" the voice on the other end demanded.

"At seven in the morning?" Kevin answered his friend, Eddie Matros. "I never turn on the TV in the morning. I hate it. What's up?"

"Your buddy Romano. Remember him?"

"Of course I do. Something happen to him?"

"No. Nothing's happened to him," Eddie said, "but they just fished his sleaze ball pal out of Cohasset Harbor."

"Jesus! Really? What happened to him? Did he drown?"

"Didn't drown either, Kevin. It was no accident. He was sleeping with the fishes."

Kevin instantly recognized the saying from the movie, *The Godfather*. "Are you serious? He was murdered?"

"You got it! Check it out on TV and get back to me," Matros said.

Kevin immediately turned on the TV in the family room and clicked around to get the news on the murder. He stopped at Channel 5, his favorite, and listened as the reporter interviewed the Big Guy who now looked tired and washed out.

Reporters were already playing "the poor boy murdered in the rich town" angle of the story. Hull and Cohasset would be compared. To save time and the need for analysis, all the usual cliches would be rounded up, including "close knit," "tight lipped," "blue collar," "working class," "community," "mostly professional," "upscale," "sleepy," and "seaside village."

Film would reinforce the stereotypes, which would save even more time explaining the labels associated with them. The news would be repackaged as entertainment.

Speculation would overcome reason and sensibility, and the facts would not get in the way of a good story. The media would come into town, take care of business, and disappear. It was all very competitive. Reporters were always looking for a scoop, one bigger and better than the Big Guy's, and they might come back later on an anonymous tip.

No doubt about it. Dazzie Clarke had been sleeping with the fishes. Kevin then wondered what, if anything, would happen to Romano. "This could be interesting," he said to himself. "I better check *The Globe*."

****

When Lauren Parker boarded the commuter boat in Hingham at her regular time that Friday morning, she naturally looked for Graham Barrows. The previous day, they had traveled together to Boston and had had a chance to talk about the events of the night before.

They both admitted to each other that neither had slept very well that

Wednesday night. "I couldn't get you out of my mind," Lauren had told Graham. "It was the same for me," he had said to her. Although they had agreed to be careful, neither one sounded very convincing.

Graham boarded just as the boat was about to depart. He immediately spotted Lauren and took the seat she had saved for him next to her. "How are we this morning?" Graham asked cheerfully.

"Better," Lauren answered with her beautiful smile. "Much better."

When the two looked at each other this time, it was with a subtle familiarity only the keenest observer would notice. There was excitement and much being said without a word ever spoken.

Graham offered to get Lauren a cup of coffee, but she declined. When he returned to his seat, he seemed more formal to her.

"I've been thinking about that e-mail matter, Lauren, and I have a hunch that something may be up. It's just a hunch, mind you, but something I think I'll check out after I see another client. I doubt I'll see Jay, but, if I'm right, I may have an answer to his problem."

"Really? What kind of a hunch is it?"

"I think it's something of a game called, Find the Needle in the Haystack," Barrows teased.

"Ok, but how will you find it and where?"

"I don't know really. It's just a hunch. It has to do with the salami programming thing. I think someone is playing with Jay, a programmer who is saying 'Catch me, if you can.' This person is very confident he or she will not get caught. The risk of getting caught is what makes it fun and exciting."

"I'm not following you. Get caught doing what?" Lauren asked, her eyebrow raised.

"Setting off a time bomb, if you will. I think it has something to do with the fiscal year 2000, which starts on July 1, 1999, for the state and federal governments and many companies, too."

"I don't see what that has to do with setting anything off."

"It has to do with computer applications that use that date. All the federal programs, like Medicare and Social Security, start their fiscal year on July 1 and continue through June 31 of the following year. You're a CPA, so you would know."

"Graham, I certainly understand what a fiscal as opposed to a calendar year is, but I still don't get it. You're being very mysterious."

"Most people think that Y2K problems will start to show up on January 1, 2000, but they're wrong," Graham continued. "I think our joker is giving us until July 1 before he or she starts the clock on the round up. The needle

I have to find in the haystack is the program that will do it. The routine has to have a name, and I think it's called, Monet."

"What? Monet? How did you ever come up with that?"

"Who is more famous for haystacks than Monet? It's all very fanciful, I know, but I'm still going to check into it. No one denies that the needle isn't there. It's almost impossible to find, but it is there."

"Well, find it, I hope you do. And is this why you couldn't sleep the other night?" Lauren asked mischievously.

"No, it wasn't, but it came to me because I was thinking of you and the night we met at the Museum of Fine Arts. It was the Monet exhibit, and there were no haystacks on display."

"Oh, yes, there were, Graham. Oh, yes, there were."

"Really? I distinctly remember none," Barrows protested.

"They must have been there because I started to see things in a different light," Lauren replied playfully.

Graham looked at her, and they both smiled knowingly.

****

"Has anybody seen Tony?" Gayle Armstrong asked the crowd that had gathered around the service desk. "This is not like him. He's usually here by eight, and it's almost nine now. I need to talk to him about something. It's very, very important."

"Gayle, where've you been? Didn't you see the news this morning? His friend, Dazzie Clarke, was murdered, and the body was found last night," Heather said. "They fished him out of Cohasset Harbor."

"Oh my God! There were two men just here looking for Tony. That's why they must have been here. I saw it on the news, but I didn't think it had anything to do with Tony. I never heard of this Dazzie whatever. Did you say, 'murdered?' Did I hear you right?"

"You heard me right, Gayle. Everyone in the office is talking about it," Heather said. "It's all over the news. Tony's probably down there now or at the mother's trying to help out. If he didn't call in, he's probably not coming. Him and Dazzie were tight, you know. What did the two guys say?"

"They didn't say nothing, just that they wanted to talk to Tony. Heather, I have to get a hold of him. I also just got a call for Tony from his mother's doctor. He said it was urgent and wanted Tony to call back right away. I don't know what to do."

"I don't think there's anything you can do. You can try him at home or at his parents' house. I don't have that number, but I'll bet he has it on his phone upstairs. He probably put it on the first button," Heather suggested.

"Thanks, Heather, that's a good idea. I'll try it and see. I hope Tony's all right."

Romano was not all right. The TV news of the murder of his childhood friend was calamitous, and Tony went immediately to the house of Dazzie's parents. He was shocked to see black and yellow tape extending down the driveway to the garage in the back of the house and the police standing around.

As Tony was about to enter the house, he saw what he thought must have been police detectives coming out of the next-door neighbor's. He correctly figured that the people in Dazzie's back yard were photographing and collecting evidence.

Romano had no way of knowing that shoe prints, blood stains, and other trace elements had been found in the garage along with a small box containing several old license plates from the late eighties.

People were milling about or talking in small groups and looking on. The print and broadcast media were there, too, taking notes and conducting interviews of their own. The whole scene made Romano very anxious.

Beyond offering the Clarke's his condolences and help, there was little else Tony could do, so he left for the dealership. His appearance there caused quite a stir, but he went to his second floor office so quickly that no one had a chance to talk to him. Everyone just stared blankly at each other.

Gayle saw Tony enter his office, shut the door, and sit down heavily in the large, leather, swivel chair in front of his desk. Immediately she went to him to ask what had happened. Romano did not have much to tell her beyond what he learned from the news on television, although the tone of his voice alternated between calm and anger.

She then told him about the two men who had come to see him. "I think they said they were with the State Police. They left you this card and want you to call them as soon as possible."

Romano seemed disconcerted, so Armstrong waited until Tony had composed himself before she mentioned the call from Dr. Pierce.

"Tony, your mother's doctor called about twenty minutes ago, and he wants you to call him right back," she said without elaborating.

Romano looked up from his chair and stared at her. "Thank you," he said as he slowly reached for the phone. He knew the call must be important because Dr. Pierce had never called him before at the office, even when all the other tests on Tony's mother were being done.

"Dr. Pierce's Office," Rebecca Solberg answered. "May I help you?"

"Hi, Rebecca. Tony Romano here. Is Dr. Pierce in?"

"Hi, Tony. Yes, he is. He's with a patient right now, but I'll get him for you. Please hold a moment." Although Rebecca had heard the news – Cohasset Harbor was within a five-minute walk of the office – and knew Dazzie Clarke, she said nothing to Tony and went immediately to get Dr. Pierce.

Knocking softly on his office door, Rebecca let Pierce know that Tony was on the phone. "Thank you, Rebecca. Tell Tony I'll call him back in ten minutes or so," he said.

Rebecca then conveyed the message to Tony. "Does he have good or bad news about my mother?" Romano asked.

"I haven't seen the test results, Tony, and, even if I did, I would not be able to tell you. I'm sorry, but you'll have to talk to Dr. Pierce. He won't be that long. He's just finishing up now with a patient."

"Ok, Rebecca. Thanks. There's not much else I can do. I'm at work, and Dr. Pierce has the number." Romano then hung up.

At that moment, Stephanie approached Rebecca and asked if she had heard anything more about the murder in the harbor. "I heard from a patient that they've identified the body, and you'll never believe who it is."

"Someone I know?" Stephanie asked with astonishment.

"No, I don't think you know him, but Tony Romano sure does. They were best friends."

"Oh my God! No way! Are you sure?"

"Yes, I'm sure alright. I knew the murder victim myself. His name is Dazzie Clarke, and he and Tony went to school together and have been close friends for years. I was going to say something to Tony, but what could I say? He's got that on his mind, and now his mother, too."

"I know. I saw the test results," Stephanie said. "It's really too bad. He seems like such a nice guy. I mean, he's like, really devoted to his mother. How long have you known him?"

"I've known him since he was a little boy. He didn't live too far from where I grew up. His parents had a tough life, and Tony was determined, I guess, to make sure that they had it better. I think Dr. Pierce is calling him now," Rebecca said as she looked down at the telephone and saw the outside extension button light up.

"Tony. Hi. Dr. Pierce here. How are you?"

"Not too good, Dr. Pierce," Romano answered. "Did you hear about the murder in Cohasset Harbor?"

"Yes. Yes, I did, Tony. It's quite a tragedy. Did you know the victim?" Pierce asked wondering why Romano had mentioned the crime at all.

"Yeah, I knew him. Him and I have been friends since we were in first or second grade. I was at the parents' house this morning, and they're pretty shaken up about it. There wasn't much I could do, so I left," Romano said. Knowing that the doctor had not called to discuss the loss of his friend, Tony said, "I assume you're calling me about my mother. Are all the tests back?"

"They are, Tony, and I'm afraid the news isn't good."

Romano interrupted Pierce before he could finish. "What do you mean not good? What's that mean? Is she going to be ok?"

"Tony, I have no other way to tell you, but your mother is a very sick woman. The tests confirm that she has leukemia."

"Yeah. All right. So? You suspected leukemia and said it could be treated, right? So what do we do next? When do we get the treatments started?"

"Tony, it's not as simple as that or quite so fast. Yes, I did suspect leukemia, but it comes in several forms, and the type your mother has is, well, the very worst."

"The very worst? What does that mean? How bad is it?" Romano asked, the worry and fear now apparent in his voice.

"What it means, Tony is that the conventional ways of treating the disease don't work. We could put her through blood transfusions, chemotherapy, or radiation, but she's probably not going to get any better. If anything, she's going to get worse."

"Not get any better? Get worse? What are you saying, that she's going to die?"

"Based on what I know about your mother, Tony, her overall health, age, the progress of the disease at this point, I would have to say that, based on my best medical opinion, she is not likely to live much longer. I'm terribly, terribly sorry to be the one who has to tell you, Tony, but I've known you and your family for all these years, and I'm just sick about it."

"She's going to die. My mother's going to die, maybe soon. Is that what you're telling me?"

"Yes, Tony, that's what I'm telling you." Dr. Pierce waited for what seemed forever before asking Tony if he was ok. "Yeah, I'm ok, Dr. Pierce. It's just such a shock. I mean a few months ago, she seemed fine, a little tired, but fine. Now I'm finding out she wasn't fine and hasn't been. I just don't know what to say. I feel numb. I mean, what do we do now? Is there any hope, some other treatment, something experimental even, that we can try?"

"I don't want to get anyone's hopes up, Tony. There are alternative treatments, holistic approaches that can help in some cases but in my opinion, there is little real science to support them. None of them are covered by Medicare, so the cost would have to be borne by the family."

"That's no problem. Money's no problem here. You know that, Dr. Pierce. If it's going to help her, I say we go for it. Forget the money. Whatever she needs, she gets. It's that simple. Maybe we should try some other tests. Maybe the test results were wrong."

"It's understandable to think so, Tony, but the tests weren't wrong. I took a careful approach with your mother. We did a complete series of blood work, took x-rays, and even did a bone density test to rule out osteoporosis. The CAT scan was negative, so I did an MRI to rule out any other possibilities," Pierce explained in a calm voice.

"The bone marrow aspiration was conclusive, and there's no escaping the fact that your mother has leukemia, the worst kind possible. I wish for her sake and your family's that it wasn't so, Tony, but I'm afraid it is."

Pierce could hear Tony struggling with himself and breathing heavily. "Goddamn! I just don't know what to say. I don't even know what to do. What happens next? Is there any way to know how much time she has?"

"We don't know for certain, and every patient reacts differently. She probably has a range of three to six months. That's the best I can say. At this point, we need to get the whole family in here to discuss your mother's situation. If there's nothing else you have for me, I'd like you to go see your mother and father and talk to them. Call me later today, if you can, so that we can set up an appointment and take matters from there."

Romano agreed with Dr. Pierce's suggestion, but sat for several minutes twisting back and forth in his leather chair. "This can't be happening," he thought to himself. "This has to be a nightmare, and I'm going to wake up and walk away from it."

Chapter 13

Shortly after nine-fifteen, Wes Symolon and Dick McCarthy returned to Tony Romano's dealership on Route 53 in Hingham. Romano did not own the facility, which had previously been a dealership. The investigators immediately went upstairs and found him in his office, his head in his hands.

"Mr. Romano?" Symolon called to him.

"Yes. Can I help you?"

Symolon and McCarthy identified themselves, their reasons for the visit, stepped into Tony's office, and then closed the door. "I'm sorry to hear about your friend, Mr. Clarke," Symolon began. "We were wondering if we could talk to you about him."

"Sure. Anything I can do to help. What you got?"

"We've got some questions we would like to ask you," Symolon said.

"Go ahead. Shoot." Symolon asked all the questions in the beginning while McCarthy looked on and took notes.

"When was the last time you saw the victim and where?"

"I'd have to say a week to ten days ago at the bar at the Red Parrot on Nantasket Beach. He wasn't a guy that I saw all that much, but we were good friends, to say the least. Since first grade. He would, you know, show up, drop in, that kind of thing. He never called before he came around, but I didn't care. We both hang around in the same places, so sometimes I would just run into him."

"Is there any way you can say for sure it was a week ago or ten days?"

"Let me think. Yeah. I was planning on meeting Liz, my fiancée, later that night and going back to my place. So it must have been Friday."

"Ok. Would you know what time that would have been?"

"It would have been right after work. On a Friday night, I usually leave here around five. It takes maybe fifteen minutes to get there. So, between five-fifteen and five-thirty Friday night," Romano clarified.

"Did he seem to you as though he was in good spirits or something else?"

"He seemed fine. Dazzie was an even-tempered guy, minded his own business, had a lot of acquaintances but not many friends, I guess. He could be pretty funny at times. Always a joke or two, usually dirty or gross. He could be really gross when he wanted to and knew how to bust your balls."

"Would you know the time when you saw him last?"

"Yeah, sometime around seven. He said he was headed up the street to see his mother and father. You know, I want to tell you something. He was my close friend and all, but he wasn't very good about the way he treated his parents. He didn't call much, and he only visited them when he needed a place to stay. Sometimes not, but you know what I mean."

"Right. Do you know if he had any money problems?"

"None that he ever told me about. He didn't always have the greatest jobs in the world, but he seemed to get by. About the only thing he ever spent any money on was the Harley. If anything, he lived pretty simple."

"Did he ever come to you for work?"

"Once in awhile he would ask me if I had anything. I got a policy on that. If you look around, you won't see any of my relatives or friends working here. I just don't think it's good business. You can lose friends that way."

"Mr. Romano, did Clarke ever mention that anybody was threatening him or giving him a hard time?"

"He never said anything like that to me. He might have been short, but Dazzie was a pretty tough bastard. That biker group he hung around with was pretty tough, too. I don't think he was someone you could intimidate very easily," Romano offered.

"Do you know if he had a permanent address?"

"I think you'd have to say, technically, that he still lived with his parents, but he wasn't there very much. Mostly he'd stay with friends. He had one job there where he could sleep in a trailer. I'm pretty sure it was a contractor in Braintree."

"About the contractor in Braintree. Do you know how he and Mr. Clarke got along? Did Clarke ever talk about the contractor?"

"Yeah, Dazzie said he was a pretty nice guy. Treated the men pretty good. Let them scab up stuff from jobs. Ok, I guess."

"What kind of things did they scab up?"

"Stuff he couldn't use, I think. Extra stuff hanging around the yard. Scraps of wire. Bars. The guy did a couple of teardowns, Dazzie said, and he let the guys go into the houses and take whatever they wanted. It was all going to the landfill anyways."

"Do you know if your friend ever took anything?"

"It's hard to say because Dazzie didn't tell me much, just that the boss was a nice guy. Dazzie would only take something he could sell, believe me, and I'll bet there's not much of an after market for recycled houses," Romano said jokingly.

"Plus, he didn't have a truck, so it was more of a hassle then anything. I remember he did get some wire fence he was going to throw into a concrete patio he was building for his parents. That's about it."

"Did you ever see the fencing?"

"Yeah. I saw it at his parents' house, out by the garage. There were a few lengths of rebar. It was for the patio."

"Do you remember when you saw the fencing?"

"Sometime last year. I really don't remember exactly."

For the next several minutes, Symolon asked Tony innocuous, general questions about Dazzie Clarke to get more on his background. Suddenly, the strategy shifted. "Have you ever had anything stolen from your business, Mr. Romano?" McCarthy asked.

"Have I had anything stolen? Yeah. Once. Only once in five or six years, about a couple months ago. I had a special order truck taken right through the fence. It was never recovered, and I filed an insurance claim. That was it."

"Did you file a police report?"

"Sure I did. Of course."

"How much was the settlement?"

"The insurance covered the cost of what I paid for the vehicle. As I said, it was a special order with no mileage."

"Who was the buyer? Did you take a deposit?"

"That's just the thing. There was no buyer. I had to pay for it up front because it was a special. I got into a big beef with the manufacturer because I was certain we didn't order it. We were having problems with the computer system at the time and figured the two were related."

"What security did you have at the time?" Symolon inquired.

"I'm on a main road, and the place is lit up all night long. The building is alarmed, of course."

"Was there anyone here at night?"

"You mean a guard? No, there was no guard. Sometimes people would be here until ten or so, but that was probably the latest."

"Did they have keys?"

"Yeah, some of the people have keys. My sales manager, myself, of course, the service manager in the shop because he comes in early. Like it or not, you have to trust someone. We haven't had any problems."

"Did Dazzie Clarke ever talk to you about any equipment that was stolen from a contractor's yard in Braintree?" McCarthy inquired.

"Yeah. He told me about it."

"Well, what did he say?"

"He didn't say much, just that it was probably stolen. That was all."

"That was all? Just that the equipment was stolen?"

"Right."

"Right."

"Did he say anything about Dobermans?"

"He didn't say nothing about any Dobermans."

"We've got something of a problem here, Mr. Romano. Can you explain why your fingerprints were on some license plates found with the victim's body?"

"Can I what? License plates? What?"

"That's right. Your fingerprints were found on license plates with the victim. Can you tell us how they got there?"

"Hey! I'm in the automobile business, if you look around," Romano said sarcastically, his affable demeanor now disappearing. "I handle license plates all the time. It's what I do. What's so strange about that?"

"What's so strange? I'll tell you what's so strange. The license plates were taken from expensive domestic vehicles that were stolen but not recovered somewhere around ten years ago. One of the plates has the same four numbers as your social security number. That's what's so strange. How do you explain it?"

"What do you mean how do I explain it? What's there to explain? It could have been just a coincidence. Not everybody knows their social security number, you know," Romano said while looking away from the detectives.

"Just a coincidence? Do you own a lobster boat?" Symolon asked.

"Yeah. I do, but I haven't used it much in the last couple or three years."

"Who uses it?"

"My cousin."

"Where do you keep the boat?"

"In Cohasset Harbor."

"Year round?"

"Yeah. Except when I haul it out to get some work done on it at the boat yard. I keep it in good condition."

"Ok. So, you keep it in good condition even though you don't use it. You must know the Coast Guard regulations about identification of gear, right?"

"Yeah. I know them. I haven't read them lately, but I know them."

"Then you would know the number, 4622, on the boat and your buoy is the last four digits of your social security number, right?"

"If you say so."

"Well, what do you say, Mr. Romano?"

"I say that – if that's what you say – it must be so."

"Were you in the automobile business ten years ago, Mr. Romano?"

"Yeah. I was in the automobile business back then. I worked for a dealer on Route 3A in Cohasset. I've been in the business most of my adult life."

"What did you do for your former employer?" McCarthy asked.

"I did all sorts of things. It's where I learned the business. I worked on cars, delivered them, towed, sold for a while, worked in parts and service. Everything. Whatever needed to be done, I did it."

"When were you towing cars?"

"I towed them all the time, all year round, even stolen cars for the police. Cars break down, you fix flats. I opened and closed trunks all the time. I must have gotten my hands on more than a few plates. Then you have people lock themselves out with the engine running, so you help them get the door open."

"Did you tow for AAA?"

"Yeah. We were an AAA emergency road service contract facility. Towed for them all the time."

"Were any cars, inventory, or equipment ever stolen from the dealership?"

"Not in all the years I was there. No. Definitely not."

"How many years were you there?"

"I started working when I got out of high school with a small garage, so, I was eighteen or so then. I left there and went to the dealership about a year later. I got my own place early in 1993. Somewhere around fifteen or sixteen years."

"So, you've been here for about six years. How's business?"

"Business is excellent. We're having a good week. There's a lot of serious money in this area, especially Hingham, Cohasset, and Duxbury. I've got the right product for the market. Yeah. Definitely. Business is good."

"One last question, Mr. Romano. Do you have any idea of who may have killed your friend?" Symolon asked skeptically.

"No, but I wish I did know. I truly wish I did."

"Here's my card, Mr. Romano. Thanks for your cooperation. We may still have some more questions for you later."

McCarthy and Symolon left the dealership. As they were heading back to the office the two compared notes.

"Everything we just heard from Mr. Romano," Symolon began "about his stellar career seems to check out. Until his former employer told us this morning, I don't think that he had ever put together Mr. Romano's departure and the increase in inventory for the tires and batteries. I wonder what he thinks of his former most trusted employee now."

"That was interesting, alright. The guy even thought he was helping Romano by telling us about the truck theft. You know, Romano was the victim of a crime himself. Anyway, what's your impression of Mr. Romano?" McCarthy asked.

"Well, you've got a guy who just admitted that he was something of a hired hand, a jack of all trades at a dealership, and now he's the owner of one. His best friend's something of a low life with an appetite for Harleys and who just so happens to be familiar with two companies where construction equipment's stolen.

"One of the companies was the victim's employer; the other his friend. Romano's cover for the license plates is all bullshit. He's obviously lying about the theft at the other dealership. I'd say we have a suspect."

"I'd say we do, too."

****

As Kevin Sweeney drove up his long driveway after making his rounds that same Friday morning, he noticed his daughter's car parked under the hemlock tree, which was his usual parking space.

"What's she doing home at this time of day?" he thought to himself. Lisa was seldom home these days but could be found at graduate school, her part time job, or her boyfriend's. Kevin found her in the kitchen.

"Hey, Sweetie. What's up? I thought you had school," her father said as he hugged Lisa and kissed her on the cheek.

"I do, but the class was cancelled. I thought I would come home before going to work. How are you doing?" Lisa asked.

"I'm doing fine. I'm pretty busy. I've got a project going on in the South End, and two more in Hingham. We're getting ready for another Hingham project, but I have to get the bids back from the contractors. There's a lot happening," Kevin responded. "My buddy Stevie is back on the job, and he's lost so much weight you wouldn't recognize him. He really looks great."

"That's great news about Steve, Dad, but what's the story?" Lisa asked impatiently. "Every time I ask you how you are, you tell me about the projects you're working on. No offense, but I don't care about the damn projects. I was wondering about you. I want to know how you're doing. So, let's try it again. How are you?"

"Me? Oh. I'm sorry. I don't have too much to say, I guess. I'm fine. Really," Kevin responded.

"Really?" Lisa asked skeptically. "Mom told me about the certification thing and said you were really upset. I'm really sorry it didn't work out, Dad. I know how much you were counting on it."

"Yeah. I was pretty upset. I was really hoping to change direction. I don't see much point to continuing with graduate school after this semester. I don't know what I'm going to do. I feel kind of lost."

"You know, Dad, with your background and all the things you've done in your life, you should feel better about your future. I mean you could always go back to teaching. Mom said finding English teachers is really hard, and you're certified. Why don't you go teach?"

"Lisa, I tried it once before a very long time ago, and it just didn't work out. I don't think I would have the patience now or the energy. I saw what it did to your mother for all those years when she was in the classroom. I'm thinking about training in high tech, but those companies ignore my background and see me as a contractor. It's a laugh," Kevin explained to his daughter. "I've tried before, and I got nowhere. You should see all the rejection letters I have downstairs."

"Dad, you've said it yourself many times. Things change. If you give up, nothing will change. You'll feel even more frustrated than you do now. I don't like to see you this way, and Mom's really worried."

"There's no reason for either of you to worry. Let's not forget. I do have a successful business and the prospects for the future look good. I would like to see more financial reward for the worry and stress, but I manage to pay my bills. I've done my best, and that's about all I can say. Have you had lunch?"

"No. I haven't had lunch, and don't you go trying to change the subject, either. Don't forget, Dad, I know you better. I know all your tricks."

Returning to her main point, Lisa said to her father, "Dad, you have to decide what you want to do and go for it. If you wait around for something to drop into your lap, you'll be waiting for a long time. I think you should look into high tech again. There are more jobs there now than ever before. So what if you get a few rejections!"

"I know. I know, but it's so hard to do, Lisa. It takes so much energy, and I don't have it at times. And by the way, let's not forget that your mother hated it when I worked in high tech. My traveling as much as I did brought our marriage to its knees. The first thing she will want to know is how much traveling is involved. Then where am I?"

Sweeney did not have to remind his daughter of that difficult time when he traveled in his high tech job. Marie didn't just hate being alone with their children; she hated knowing that Kevin liked traveling and found it stimulating.

Lisa wanted to press her point. "Have you even talked to her, Dad? How do you know she hasn't changed her mind? Things are different now. There's practically just the two of you. I'm hardly here."

"I know," Kevin said, "and I really miss you. We used to have some great talks. I miss your not being around, and your mother does, too."

It was Lisa's turn to change the subject. "Hey, Dad. Did you see that thing in the paper today about the murder in Cohasset? Must have shaken up that pretty little town, wouldn't you say?" she said sarcastically.

"I saw it alright," Sweeney said. "And here's one for you. The victim was a close friend of a former client of mine."

"You're kidding, right?"

"No. I'm not."

"Is he a suspect or something?"

"I don't know. Something tells me he's not, but you never know. You think you know someone well, then you find out differently. He was a shady guy, but I certainly hope he's not mixed up in this. I can't imagine killing your best friend."

****

"Alright, everyone, listen up," a very tired Wes Symolon began as he addressed the four other investigators who were assembled in the meeting room at the Norfolk County District Attorney's Office in Dedham to discuss the Dazzie Clarke murder around eleven-thirty that same Friday morning, the 26th of February. He and Dick McCarthy had been on the case for nearly fifteen hours and were quite exhausted. It would be another two hours before they could go home and finally get some sleep, which they had not had for almost twenty-four hours.

"What I would like to do is kick around a few ideas, you know, confirm what we know, what we need to know more about, or discount and exclude. Dick, why don't you start? I can add to what you have to say as you go along, and we can take it from there."

"No problem. Be glad to. All right, here's what we have. We have a male Caucasian, Ronald Clarke, from Hull, age thirty-eight, heavy set, who was murdered most likely sometime around seven-thirty to ten-thirty Friday night of last week. What's that, the 19th? Right. It was the 19th.

"The victim went by the nickname, Dazzie. His body was found last night at nine, wrapped in chain link fencing with ten domestic car license plates attached to it with twisters, in Cohasset Harbor. The body was discovered by a contractor and his crew when they were dredging the harbor," McCarthy informed the team.

"We have positive identification of the victim from fingerprints we obtained from the body and matched with AFIS," he continued.

"We've interviewed the parents, and some of you have talked to their neighbors, which I'll come to in a moment. We've served a warrant for two locations, the garage belonging to Mr. Clarke's parents and a contractor's yard in Braintree," McCarthy said. "Russ, you with us?" McCarthy abruptly asked another detective seated at the table.

"Yeah, definitely," Russ answered, turning his attention to McCarthy and away from the woman sitting next to him but at the end of the table. The woman, Darlene Coakley, was a very professional and highly competent investigator who was well respected by the men but a lovely distraction to Russ who was wondering what she had on under her clothing. Darlene was focused on the meeting and taking notes.

McCarthy continued. "We have videotape and pictures from the site where the body was discovered around nine, but we think the crime scene's the garage at the parents' house. We found an additional thirty-six license plates there in the garage, the victim's fairly new Harley, numerous footprints, a nearly empty roll of duct tape, and some trace evidence we are still analyzing, including blood droplets. Other than the blood, there were no signs of a struggle.

"Wes and I think that the victim was knocked unconscious with a blunt instrument – probably a rebar, based on the marks left on the skull– in the garage, by someone or persons known to him, bound and gagged with duct tape, removed, wrapped in the chain link, and then – since his lungs were filled with water – dumped alive at night in the harbor. Matt, you have a question?"

"Yeah, I do. What about the contractor in Braintree? What's that all about?"

Symolon pitched in. "The contractor's the former employer of the victim and himself the victim of the theft of machinery we think Mr. Clarke was involved in stealing. Among the license plates attached to the chain link, we found several that were commercial. One of them belonged to the victim's former boss, the contractor, and he said he knew of rumors that construction equipment was being stolen for shipment overseas."

"Ok, got it," Matt said, "but what about the other plates?"

"All the license plates, we know," McCarthy said, "were taken from very expensive luxury cars that were stolen in the Boston area and the South Shore in the late eighties. None of the cars was ever recovered. I know I don't have to remind you that Massachusetts was then the car stealing capital of the country. I'm not sure where we stand today. We found patent prints – but none latent – on the plates and matched them with AFIS. The database turned up two names, Dazzie Clarke, the victim, and a Tony Romano who happens to be his best friend and lives in Cohasset."

Wes Symolon picked up on his partner's thought. "We think that it's reasonable to conclude at this point that Clarke and Romano were stealing cars back then and disposing of them. Exactly how, we're not sure, but we have some ideas. Darlene?"

"Thanks. Getting back to the Braintree contractor. Do you think he's involved?"

"As I said, we interviewed him and obtained evidence from his yard. He was very cooperative and straightforward. No. We don't think Mr. Roper was involved, but we are fairly certain that the painted chain link fence in which the victim's body was wrapped came from the contractor's yard. No rebar has been found, as of yet, even though it was seen near the garage by both Clarke's parents.

"The picture he paints of Mr. Clark is that he was an ok worker, nothing special, a drifter, not all that bright. Let me check on that. Yeah, it's right here in my notes. A 'dumb fuck' he called Mr. Clarke." Everyone laughed. "Roper also told us he suspected the victim was involved in the theft of his equipment. He actually said that if he could have proven it, he would have killed Clarke himself." Everyone in the room laughed again.

Not saying much but taking notes was Kent Costigan, a newcomer to the investigative team. "What were we able to find out from the parents? Anything significant?" he asked McCarthy.

"They were very helpful," he answered, "especially when we talked to them the second time this morning. They remember the fencing and rebar out in the back yard by the garage, but they could not remember when they first noticed it was missing. Mr. Clarke said he doesn't park his car in the garage, so he didn't go out there very much.

"They gave us a late photograph of their son and a lot of important background on Mr. Romano, their son's best friend.

"According to the victim's parents, Romano worked for an auto dealer in Cohasset and now has his own business in Hingham. Their son had taken them to see several properties that were being extensively renovated in South Boston in the early nineties, and they all belonged to Mr. Romano. They even saw the work that was being done on his fancy house in Cohasset."

Recalling what Mrs. Clarke had said about her son's failure to call her, Dick then added, "Romano's not without his qualities. He takes real good care of his parents and a cousin of his. The cousin took over Romano's side business in lobstering a few years back, and you'll never guess where he moors his boat."

Darlene guessed Cohasset correctly. "Bingo!" McCarthy said. "The Coast Guard tells us that Romano's lobstering license number is 4622, the same as the last four digits of his social security number, which he said he couldn't remember. One of the recovered license plates found with the victim has on it the number, 4622. We didn't find any prints on it."

"The boat's only a couple hundred yards away from where the body was discovered. You can clearly see its buoy with his colors and lobster license number. The harbor master confirmed that the boat belongs to Romano."

At that point in his explanation, an officer who gave him a slip of paper with some writing on it interrupted McCarthy. Dick then continued. "Romano and his fiancé have been in the Clarke house many times over the years. Yeah. The parents were very helpful."

"Russ, you and Darlene talked to the neighbors this morning, right? What did you come up with?" Wes inquired.

"Not much. Certainly no one noticed anything strange going on that Friday night in question. No one heard any strange noises, either. The neighbor on the right thinks that he saw a sporty, black BMW around the house late that evening, but he can't say for sure when. They all said the neighborhood was quiet, and they were pretty shocked by the news."

"A black BMW? Interesting. See if you can find out who might have been driving a black BMW down there that night. You may want to start with Mr. Romano. By the way, we've interviewed him and his former boss, and we think Mr. Romano's full of bullshit. When we asked him to explain how his fingerprints showed up on the plates, he gave us a lame excuse.

"He also denied that any theft had taken place at his old boss' place, but we think otherwise. We're fairly sure he had a side business going in stolen batteries and tires. Most importantly of all, Mr. Romano had a very expensive truck stolen from his dealership a couple of months ago. So what you have is the deceased knowing intimately two people who had something expensive stolen from their businesses. It's just too much of a coincidence."

"Dick, do you have any ideas on where the investigation's headed?"

"Most definitely we do. It's pretty obvious that Romano and Clarke were involved in stealing cars. It's likely that Romano arranged for the theft of the truck at his place because it was tying up his cash and he had no buyer. He blamed his computer system for the order.

"Romano came from nothing, and he's now a pretty wealthy man at a fairly young age. How did he get that far that fast? We don't know yet whether Romano murdered his best friend, but he's a likely suspect. We don't know whether Romano was involved in the theft of equipment from the Braintree contractor, either.

"We do think Clarke and Romano could have argued over money. Romano lost nothing on the truck theft because it was covered completely by insurance. Maybe he thought Clarke owed him a piece of the action. Maybe Clarke thought Romano was a paying customer. We just don't know yet, and we may never know. Either way, it looks like the two of them have had a lot of money on their hands over the years, and it all had to go someplace."

Symolon interjected, "From what we know to date about the victim – for a guy who may have had some money – he led a simple life. For that reason, Dick and I think that Romano and Clarke were not equal partners, which ties back into the money thing. Maybe one of them got greedy. They got into an argument. Things happen."

Dick McCarthy then added, "Before Wes and I head out, here's what we need to have done.

"Check Mr. Dazzie's cell phone records, and see if you can ascertain his whereabouts the night he was murdered. Maybe we can triangulate the calls from the cell phone. If he was like most people, he never turned it off. We want to know more about his friends, especially the gang he hung around with on Nantasket Beach. I'll want to know more about where the victim bought his Harley, when, and how he paid for it.

"I want to know a lot more about Mr. Romano. Kent, you've got some background in financial crimes, don't you?" McCarthy asked.

"Yes, I do," Costigan responded. He had recently transferred over from the Norfolk County District Attorney's Office to the homicide section.

"Great. Then why don't you check out the properties Romano renovated in South Boston on Third and B Street and Sixth and O and his house on Atlantic Avenue in Cohasset. Find out from the building departments who the general contractor was for each property. Get a handle on what was done to them, if you can, who holds the mortgages, the amount, and so on. Talk to the renters or some long-standing neighbors, especially Townies. We're going to take our time with Mr. Romano and be very procedural.

"Check with the Planning Board in Hingham on Romano's dealership on Route 53. There should be a record of when he went before the Board sometime in 1991 or 1992. The Cohasset Police will keep an eye on Romano's boat in the harbor until we execute the warrant. We don't think he's stupid enough to try anything with it, but you never know.

"If there's nothing else, you know where to find me."

"Dick, there's something else," Kent said. "These license plates. They make no sense."

"What do you mean?"

"First of all, why would Clarke even keep the plates in his garage?"

"It's a good question, but we don't know. Wes thinks the idiot kept them as trophies of his nefarious deeds." The "nefarious" comment got some laughs.

"Alright. Let's say Romano's involved," Kent pressed. "Why would he take the time to attach all the plates to the chain link? If there were some kind of message being sent here, wouldn't Romano know that it pointed back to himself? It sounds like 'return to sender' to me."

Symolon answered the question. "It's puzzling, I'll grant you that. Obviously, we have a lot more work to do. Romano probably had no way of knowing that his and Clarke's prints were on the plates. I'll bet that – even if he did – he thought the salt water would wash them off.

"The AFIS matching was a lucky break, and there's no way Romano knows that his prints are on file for a prank he may have pulled when he was in high school some twenty plus years ago. It looks like one of those things where someone was trying to teach him a lesson at the time. There were no charges filed, and his friend, Mr. Clarke, was involved with him then, too.

"They certainly seem to have a long and questionable history between them. It may boil down to the age-old story. Someone got greedy."

Costigan persisted. "Could Romano have been stupid enough to dump the body where he knew it would have been recovered? I mean the guy's got his own boat, so why not dump Clarke a few miles offshore where no one's ever going to find it? To me, it makes no sense.

"If I were in his situation, I might chance talking to the dredging crew. Romano's got a lot of money, and money talks. You never know what someone desperate will do."

"Not every murder makes sense," McCarthy responded to the newly assigned investigator working on his first homicide case. "It's not likely that Romano would want to involve anyone else. There could be something about lobstering at night. Maybe it's illegal and would draw attention. I like your line of reasoning, though. Check it out."

"This new kid's going to be alright," McCarthy thought to himself. "He has an open mind; takes nothing for granted. He could be good."

Darlene then asked McCarthy, "Dick, you didn't say anything about Mr. Clarke's present employer. Have you – or do we talk to him?"

"Oh! Thanks, Darlene. We got a bit sidetracked there for a minute. Wes and I have already spoken to the employer and some people in the office. It's a twenty-four hour a day, seven day a week towing and repair operation.

"They pretty much confirmed what we were hearing about Mr. Clarke. He was a steady worker, kept his nose clean, and did what he was told. The owner didn't seem all that surprised that Mr. Clarke didn't come to work for the past week. Said it happens all the time. He figured the guy just up and quit. According to him, people – good, bad, or otherwise – come and go all the time. Not too many give notices. The bookkeeper – the redoubtable one, Wes called her – said Mr. Clarke always made her uneasy. She didn't care for him but said he was a steady, reliable worker who told a lot of off color jokes."

The "redoubtable" description got another good laugh from the investigators for several reasons. They immediately understood that the bookkeeper was a sizeable woman built like a fortress and a person who took no shit from anyone. They also knew that Wes Symolon never used the word, redoubtable, or nefarious, for that matter.

McCarthy did on his own. He was a fun guy and serious reader who showed off his extensive vocabulary by blaming it on Wes. Otherwise, everyone would dump on him. "Use simple English," they would say.

Wes and Dick made for a very good team.

****

Although the door to Dr. Pierce's office was closed and he was seeing his last patient of the day, Rebecca and Stephanie knew who was inside. Tony Romano, his father and mother, and Dr. Pierce were discussing the crisis that now faced the family.

Suddenly, the door opened and family and physician slowly walked to the waiting area, their faces solemn and somber. "Dad, why don't you and Mom go sit in the car for a moment. I'd like to talk to Dr. Pierce about something. I'll only be about a minute or two," Tony said. "Here's the key. Turn the car on, and the heat will come right up."

Turning to Dr. Pierce he said, "I think we should look into this holistic thing, even if you're lukewarm about it. You did say that some patients benefit from it, that it can help the suffering in some way, and I want to help my mother any way I can. Is that alright with you?"

"Sure it is, Tony. I just wanted you to be aware of the costs and not get your hopes up. You can stop by the front desk, and Rebecca can give you the names of several agencies and some sole practitioners. I know it's a shock to everyone, but she's going to need your strength now more than ever before. If you have any questions, just give me a call."

"Understood," Tony responded.

Romano stopped at the front desk before leaving. "I'm terribly sorry to hear about your mother, Tony," Rebecca began, "We're all just heartsick for you and your family."

"Thank you, Rebecca. We're not done yet. Dr. Pierce told me you could give me the names of several people who do holistic medicine. If I can get the names now, that would be great. By the way, how are you doing? How are things between you and Barry?"

"Me? Oh, I'm doing fine. Things between Barry and me are moving along quite nicely. I feel like a kid again. Listen, I have a suggestion. Why don't I e-mail you the names so that you don't have to wait? You'll have them before you get home. Some of the agencies even have WEB sites you can link to, so you can check them out before calling. Makes it nice and easy."

"Ok. I'm something of a fumbler on a computer, but you know what they say. If you're not moving ahead, you're falling behind."

"There you go! That's a good attitude. I can't imagine what you're going through today, Tony, what with your mother and friend and all. How are you doing?"

"How am I doing? I have never had a worse day in my life, Rebecca. I keep thinking it's a nightmare, and I'm going to wake up, only I'm not. I'm trying to look on the bright side, at what I have, not what I'm losing. I'll get – we'll get through it somehow."

"You better get going. Give us a call if you need anything, and don't worry about putting us out. We're here to help, you know. It's what we do best. Really."

"I know, Rebecca," Romano said wearily. "I know."

Chapter 14

Early that next morning around seven-thirty, Kevin and Marie Sweeney were enjoying their traditional Saturday breakfast when they saw a car coming up the driveway. Not recognizing whose car it was, Kevin went to the door and opened it. He was certain the man and woman getting out of the car were not missionaries from some church, and he began to feel uneasy.

"Hi. Can I help you?" Sweeney asked them as they walked up the stairs and approached him.

"Yes, you can. Are you Kevin Sweeney?" the woman asked.

"Yes, I am," Kevin said, still not knowing what to expect.

The pair then identified themselves as Darlene Coakley and Kent Costigan of the Massachusetts State Police and asked to come inside. Kevin invited them in and ushered the detectives into the living room where they sat on a couch opposite him.

Sensing something unusual, Marie immediately joined them. "Is something the matter?" she asked very anxiously. "I'm sorry I'm not dressed," she added with embarrassment.

"No, ma'am," Costigan said. "We just wanted to ask your husband a few questions relating to an incident that happened Thursday night in Cohasset. Would you mind if we spoke to him privately?"

"No. No. I understand. Sure. Would you like some coffee? I can put some on."

"No, thank you. I'm all set. Darlene?"

"That's alright. I'm all set, too. We shouldn't be too long."

Marie then left the room, and decided to put on more coffee anyway. Actually, she didn't know what to do, so she went upstairs to get dressed, make the bed, or busy herself while the detectives were downstairs talking to Kevin.

As usual, one of the detectives took the lead while the other took notes before alternating. They were very practiced and seemed to know instinctively when to change interviewers. Coakley began.

"Mr. Sweeney, we're investigating the murder of Dazzie Clarke of Hull. Perchance, did you know the victim?"

"Did I know the victim? God, no. I mean, I know who he is, but I never met the man. I heard about the murder from the news. From what I hear he was a close friend of a client of mine from Cohasset."

"Can you tell us who that client might be?"

"Sure. His name's Tony Romano. He lives in Cohasset."

"And in what capacity did you know Mr. Romano?"

"Well, I knew him because he hired my company to remodel his house in Cohasset. We finished the project, I'm guessing, sometime around a year and a half or two years ago. I really haven't heard from him since. I do know that he has referred my company to a few other people, though."

"What is it that your company does, Mr. Sweeney? Are you a general contractor?"

"No, I'm not a general contractor. It's a bit complicated but, basically, my company sees to it that the homeowner doesn't get screwed by the residential construction industry."

The two detectives looked at each other. Costigan then asked, "And exactly how does that work?"

"Actually, it works pretty well."

"Can you be a little more specific?"

"Oh! Sure. Sorry. It works like this. I consult with the homeowners before the project starts and get them to do some research with the town or state agencies to make sure that the project is even feasible. Then I submit a proposal for the three basic services we offer."

"You say 'we.' Is there more than one person in the company?"

"Yes. I have part-time help I use for the electrical, plumbing, and heating specifications, the mechanicals, if you will. They are guys who have been with me almost since I started the company in 1988."

"Ok, so you're what? A consultant?"

"Yes. Exactly. I also help the homeowner with the designs, specifications, and then the actual coordination of the project. In a way, the service is an alternative to hiring a general contractor."

"What did you do for Mr. Romano?"

"I handled the designs, the specifications, which included competitive bidding and pricing materials, and coordinated the work. For the first two, I charged him hourly. For the construction phase, I charged him ten percent, based on the total amount of money he spent. The project was huge and very, very complicated."

"What if the project goes over budget? What do you do then?"

"We've never once had a client go over budget. We know in minute detail the cost of all the work according to each area of the house, the materials being used, and who is doing the work. We carry two and a half percent above that cost for contingencies."

"No one's ever gone over budget? That's amazing. Never heard of it. What do you do when you coordinate a project?"

"What do I do? I have several responsibilities. Mainly, I make sure guys are scheduled and materials delivered in a timely fashion, that the work's being done in accordance with the plans and specifications, track changes, and update the contracts.

"I'm at all my projects on a daily basis. I check up on them in the morning, come home, have lunch, make calls, hit the gym, and make more calls, sometimes until late at night. I also send a lot of faxes from my computer in the basement, which is where I keep my office."

"Mr. Sweeney," Darlene began, "How were you paid by Mr. Romano?"

"Like all my clients, he paid my company by check. I have a firm rule about that, and I never change it. It's probably no secret to you that a lot of guys in construction take personal checks or cash, but I never, never do. I think it's bad business."

"In Mr. Romano's case, who hired the contractors?"

"He did. He was acting as the general contractor with the help of my company. We worked as a team."

"Who took out the building permit?"

"He did, just like all my clients do. They sign a waiver voiding any claims against a guaranty fund the state has set up for contractors who default or do substandard work."

"Did Mr. Romano pay for the building permit?"

"I assume so, or he never would have gotten one."

"Do you know how much he paid for it?"

"No. Oddly enough, I don't. It's one of a handful of things I don't include in my project fee, so I don't track it. Every town's different in what it charges. I would not be surprised if he paid $2,000 to $3,000 for the permit."

"Would you be surprised if he paid a lot less?"

"No. I wouldn't be surprised at all. Most homeowners who are acting as the general contractor themselves deliberately understate the cost of the work because they resent paying the town a lot of money for a couple of twenty minute visits and the bullshit that goes with them. It's done all the time."

"How would you characterize his spending on the project? Careful about money, or what?

"Very seldom do I meet anyone who is not careful with money, regardless of how much he or she has. I can tell you this much, though. I knew he had a lot of money."

"How did you know? Did you do a credit check?"

"No. I never run credit checks of my clients. I don't know of a single contractor in the business that does. It's interesting in a way. We trust them to pay us, but they don't trust us."

"Ok. So how did you know Mr. Romano had a lot of money?"

"Well, I develop a cost projection sheet of nearly six or seven hundred individual line items. When I present this information to most clients, they practically hemorrhage, even though much of the cost is deliberate daydreaming. Not Mr. Romano. He looked at me and said, 'Let's do it.' I was pretty shocked."

"Do you know the total cost of Mr. Romano's renovations?"

"Yes, I do."

"Well? How much was it?"

"Including my fee, $415,000, give or take a few thousand."

"Who paid the contractors?

"Again, he did. He paid directly for all the materials and the subs. I kept track of the payments and adjusted the contracts accordingly."

"Do you know where he got the contractors?"

"I referred all the contractors to him. By contract with my company, he's supposed to give me the name of contractors I don't know as a way of protecting himself against overpricing, but he didn't bother. So, he used the guys who work on most of my projects."

"What about Workers' Compensation? Who paid for that?"

"Each subcontractor pays Workers Compensation on himself and his employees. We require the sub to have his insurance company mail to the homeowner his Certificate of Insurance. We don't accept a copy from the contractor."

"What if a contractor's not insured?"

"It happens, but the homeowner will know. I recommend that the client increase his homeowner's insurance policy to at least a million dollars or more. In the event of a serious injury, insured or not, the employee or contractor can sue the homeowner.

"That's the problem. You can't prevent someone from suing you. In this case, the homeowner's policy will respond and, at least, pay legal fees and, possibly, other damages."

"Would you know whether any of the contractors working on Mr. Romano's house were paid by personal check or cash?"

Kevin hesitated. "I checked frequently with the contractors to make sure they were being paid. Anytime money's a problem, I hear about it real fast."

"How do you know how much they have been paid? Do you just take their word for it or the homeowner's?" Costigan asked.

"In most cases, I have a form that I give to the homeowner to record the date, check number, contractor, reason, and amount of a payment."

"What did you do in Mr. Romano's case?"

"I gave him the form."

"Did he use it?"

Sweeney hesitated again. "For the most part, yes."

"What do you mean, 'For the most part?' Either he did or he didn't, right?"

"Right. What I mean is that he never gave me the check numbers, but he did give me everything else. I've had other clients do the same thing. You ask them for the check number, and they don't have it. Sometimes they're working from two or three checkbooks and moving money around in them. I asked him; he told me. No big deal as far as I was concerned."

"Ok, so going back to the original question, would you know whether any of the contractors working on Mr. Romano's house were paid by personal check or cash?"

"I would know."

"And the answer would be?" Darlene asked.

"The answer would be 'yes.' I knew that every contractor had been paid, the exact amount, and how. Every one of them was paid by check, of that much I am certain. Was the check made out to them personally or their companies? I don't know, and I probably did not want to know."

"Did these guys do any side jobs, you know, little jobs for the homeowner who paid them cash."

"Hey! Come on. Look. These guys are out there trying to make a living. There isn't a contractor in the universe who doesn't do side jobs for cash. There are some things about the business that I think it's best for me to overlook. I have to work with these guys, you know."

Costigan took over. "Look, Mr. Sweeney, we're not trying to bust your balls. We only want to know how Mr. Romano paid the men. If it helps, we're not interested in them. We want to know about Mr. Romano. Did everyone get paid in full? Were there any problems?"

Sweeney took a deep breath. "Yes, there was a problem, and, no, everyone did not get paid in full. Romano stiffed the framing contractor for about $5,000 for a leak in the roof, which turned out not to be a leak at all."

"Did the contractor take Mr. Romano to court?"

"No. He didn't."

"Do you know why not?"

"I have my suspicions."

"Do you care to tell us?"

"I suspected that Romano paid the framer in cash and knew he could stiff him because the framer would not be able to prove in court how much money he had been paid. He certainly would not have wanted the court to know that he took in all that cash, which probably went unreported."

"That's not what you were saying a moment ago. You said every guy was paid by check. Right?"

"I did. I should have been clearer. To me, a personal check is cash. You take it to the bank and cash it. That's the way I think. Seldom do you see anyone pay in actual cash as opposed to a personal check. Most people don't keep a lot of hard cash in the house. Usually, it's just money for the week. I'm sorry."

"That alright, now that we have the clarification." Costigan did not look pleased.

"How much money do you think Romano paid the framing contractor in total?"

"I know exactly how much he paid. $75,000."

"$75,000? In cash?"

"$75,000 in cash, more or less. I can give you my organizer for the Romano project, and it has in it all the names of the contractors, the retailers, who got paid what and when, and the total cost of the project, broken down by each sub and all the materials. Would you like me to go get it? I'll give you the disk, too."

"Sure, that would be great, very helpful. But before you do, just one thing. Why this guy? Why was the framer the only one of all the contractors to be paid in hard cash?"

"I have my suspicions."

"Do we have to do this again?"

"It's like this. All the bidding contractors knew the bids but not who submitted them. The framer was much lower than the next two bidders who were pretty close to each other in their bids.

"The framer told me he really, really needed the job and would take a look at the house and talk to the homeowner. I think they worked out a deal, which was to pay in cash. I don't know who suggested it, but $80,000 in cash, untaxed, is worth at least $100,000 or more to a legitimate business. He did it because he was the low bid."

Costigan and Coakley looked at each other without saying a word.

Kevin then went to his office to retrieve the project organizer. While he was there, he opened up his personal information manager, CAT, created a report of all the contractors who worked on the Romano project, and printed it out.

When he returned to the living room, the two detectives were standing and looking around. "Beautiful ship, you've got here," Darlene Coakley said, referring to a model frigate displayed in an antique case. The comment broke some of the tension Sweeney was feeling.

"Yes, it is," Kevin responded. "A real family heirloom that was handed down to me from my grandmother's brother. He had no children, and I was the only one who ever expressed any interest in it over the years. When he died, the ship went to my grandmother's sister. When she died, it came to me.

"My mother used to take my sister and me to visit my uncle every now and then. He kept the ship on a mantle over an unused fireplace and would lift me up to see it. When I saw it for the first time in more than forty years, I was surprised to see how small it was.

"I even have the bill of sale. My uncle paid $200 for the ship in either 1934 or 1935. We are not sure of the year because it was over struck."

"Really? That's pretty amazing. Any idea of what it's worth now?"

"Let me put it this way. During the Great Depression, $200 was approximately one third of an average worker's earnings. It's worth about the same today. Everything is relative, I suppose."

"Interesting. Were you able to find those materials?"

"Yes. I have them right here. I also printed out for you a list of all the contractors who worked on Romano's house. I've given you all their addresses, phone, pager, and fax numbers, and when and where they can be reached. I am assuming you will want to speak with them."

"You assumed very well," Coakley responded while taking the project organizer from Kevin then handing it to Costigan. "Do you keep this much information about all you clients?"

"Every single one of them. It's taken me over ten years to perfect the system, and there are still some improvements that can be made. The disk is in the side pocket of the binder. You should be able to open up most of the files because they were done on Microsoft Office."

Coakley nodded approvingly but wasn't finished. "Have you ever done any work in the South End of Boston?" she asked.

"The South End? Definitely. Several times. I even have a project going on in there right now. I'm originally from Southie, and I love going into the city for work. I wish I had a few more projects in the South End."

"Have you ever worked on any triple deckers in Southie?"

"You know, funny thing. Other than helping my mother occasionally with her three-family, I have never done a triple-decker. Most of my city experience has been on brownstones in the South End. They're tricky and very challenging," Sweeney volunteered.

"Would you be familiar with construction costs on a triple decker, say a complete rehab?"

"Somewhat. A three-story brownstone could be more expensive to restore than a triple-decker. It all depends on what you're doing. There are a lot of factors. Most of the work going on in Southie now is converting those three deckers into condos. A lot of guys are making some serious money doing that. I hear they are getting over $200 thousand for a first floor, five-room apartment. My mother paid much less than that when she bought her house in 1986 at the height of the real estate boom."

"Can you give me a for example, you know, a ball park when things weren't so good, say in 1991?"

"I hate the 'ball park' thing because it's so misleading. Here's what. I did a brownstone in the South End in 1992 or around then. A total gutting of the first floor, which was actually in the basement, and a fixing up of the second floor, which was really the first floor."

"Yeah. What did it cost?"

"Including my services, around $70,000 at the time."

"So, about $35,000 a floor, right?"

"No, not really. I would have to estimate that the homeowner spent only $15,000 on the second floor, and the rest was downstairs and on the courtyard in back. Take out the yard work and deck, and you would have about $40,000 for the first floor, which includes the kitchen, new heating system, electrical, insulation, the works."

"I see where you're going. So, a triple-decker could cost – what? – $35,000 to $45,000 give or take, per floor seven or eight years ago?"

"Yeah. That's fair. Sounds pretty good."

"If I were acting as my own general contractor I could get it done for even less, right?"

"No, not necessarily. The contractors could look at you as a one shot deal and not want to give you any breaks. If you don't have experience in the trades, you could even cost them. On the other hand, if times are tight like they were in the early nineties, you might do ok. Chances are, the contractors would be looking to make deals."

"Really? What kind of deals?"

"You could have guys who are collecting unemployment be willing to do the work for less as long as they were paid in cash, you know, work under the table."

"Would you have been willing to buy a triple decker in Southie in the Lower End in the early nineties, pay maybe $120,000 for it, then spend almost the same amount again fixing it up?"

"I don't know. I think it would take, if you'll pardon the expression, two balls – brass and crystal – for me to do it, and I don't have either. Some guys will, and that's how they make their money. You know, the bigger the risk, the bigger the reward. Are you looking to invest?"

"No, no. I'm not looking to invest. Just asking. Well, you've certainly been very helpful and cooperative, Mr. Sweeney," Coakley said. "If we have any other questions, we'll get back to you. In the meantime, you have my card."

While Darlene was talking to Sweeney, Costigan had been going over the Romano project organizer, which was opened on the coffee table in front of the couch. He had turned to the section on project costs and payments.

"Mr. Sweeney. I notice here that Mr. Romano made credit card payments totaling almost $60,000. Isn't that a lot of money to put on a credit card for a construction project? What was he using it for?"

"He's like a lot of people. Rather than open an account with the building materials supplier, he used a credit card. I'm assuming he did because he got frequent flier points with some airline. My clients do it all the time. It's something of a benefit they would not get with a general contractor," Sweeney explained.

"And he just told you how much he paid? How would you know?"

"It's easy. I would simply ask the supplier to bill him first, fax me the receipts, and then switch payment to the credit card. It was an extra step or two for them, but I'm a good customer because I bring in a lot of business."

"Alright. I got it." He then got up to join his partner who was headed for the door. "Thanks for your help, Mr. Sweeney," Costigan said as she was leaving.

The instant Kevin closed the door behind the two detectives, Marie flew down the stairs. "What was that all about?" she asked.

"They're investigating the murder in Cohasset they told me. Most of the questions they asked involved my business and what I did for Tony Romano, my client and the best friend of the murder victim.

"They were very, very interested in the method of payment to me and the contractors. I feel sick to my stomach."

"Why? They're not investigating you, are they? What could you have done?" Marie asked.

"I don't think they're investigating me. No, they can't be. They must be checking into Romano. I hope to hell he is not involved in this thing. I don't think he is, but something tells me the whole thing has something to do with money.

"You know me. I can account for every penny every client has paid me ever since I have been in business. I've got nothing to hide, I mean, it's all there. It has to be him. They're investigating Romano."

"What about the other guys who worked for Romano? I know Steve and Eddie did. Dan, the floor nut, too. All of them. What about them?"

"I don't know what's going to happen. They said they're not interested in the contractors, only how they got paid. Christ! You know this business, they all have their side jobs, and they all take cash. I gave up years ago telling them it was risky business. Exactly how risky, I had no idea. We'll just have to wait and see."

Marie stared at Kevin. Both were disbelieving of what had just happened. Their hearts were racing.

As Kent Costigan backed the car down Sweeney's long driveway, Coakley asked him his impression of Kevin. Before answering, Costigan thought for a moment, and then started up the street.

"Well, what do you think?" Darlene asked again.

"I think this guy has a very interesting business. This project organizer is very, very impressive. The only money he handles is what the homeowner pays him. He doesn't pay any of the subs, and he doesn't pay for any of the materials. He has no contracts with anyone except the client, and no or little overhead when he coordinates the project.

"The homeowner pays all the bills, including overruns, which he says they don't have, and Sweeney more or less knows about everything because that's what his fee is based on.

"Here's another thing," Costigan added. "This guy's very, very smart. You can tell by the way he speaks. He was very fast with his answers, except a couple of times when he was reluctant. And I can understand why. He was trying to protect his guys, and you can't fault him for that. I'll tell you something else. He really knows his shit."

"Ok. So we've got this very smart guy running a very clever business," Coakley said. "I wished I had know about him when I was doing over my house. My husband and I had all sorts of problems with our contractor, and I'm sure we paid more than we had to.

"But here's the thing. Did you notice how he said he had a policy about accepting checks made out only to his company?"

"Yeah. I picked up on that immediately."

"I think he's smart enough to have done it to cover his own ass, like he was above it all, couldn't have been like the other guys, even though he knew what was going on."

"If he ever wanted to, he could have a nearly perfect front for laundering money. I mean, think of it. He's got all these contractors out there, and not one of them is unwilling to work under the table. Then there's the union guys on the sly," Costigan suggested.

"My thought exactly, but there's just no way. Where we headed next?"

"To a beauty shop in Stoughton. Wes and Dick want us to interview Mr. Romano's fiancé. They plan to talk to him around nine-thirty and want us to see her then, too."

****

Unlike the first time when Wes Symolon and Dick McCarthy visited his dealership, Tony Romano was expecting them.

"What's the story?" he asked. "Why the warrant on my lobster boat? You're not going to find anything there because there's nothing to find."

"Like we told you, Tony," Dick McCarthy answered. "We're investigating the death of your friend, Dazzie Clarke, and we're looking into a lot of things. For example, do you have any idea why he would have called a Mr. Al Sanderson from his cell phone around seven-thirty the night he was murdered?" As the question was asked, Symolon and McCarthy very carefully watched Romano's reaction.

"No. I wouldn't. Why should I?"

"We didn't say you should, Tony. We're only asking. Do you know Al Sanderson?"

"Yeah. I know him."

"How do you know him?"

"I know him because he bought a car from me a couple of years ago. I gave him a real good deal."

"Beyond having bought a car from you, can you tell us anything else about Mr. Sanderson?"

"No. I really can't."

"Do you know where he lives?"

"No, I don't. We probably have it in our records somewhere."

"Could we take a look at those records?"

"Yeah. You can take a look. I don't have them in front of me right now. I can have my bookkeeper get them for you."

"Do you have them on your computer?"

"I don't know. She can tell you."

"You don't know what's on your computer?"

"Hey! What do you want me to say? I own the fucking business. I'm not involved in the day to day with customers, unless I'm selling a car, which I still like to do. What more do you want from me?"

Symolon stepped in. "What we want from you, Tony, is the truth. So, can you tell us where you were on the night your friend was murdered?"

"Yeah. I can tell you, but I also can tell you this. My attorney tells me I don't have to tell you squat. I'm going against his advice because I'm telling you straight out that I had nothing to do with this. Nothing."

"Ok. So are you going to tell us or not where you were when Dazzie was murdered?"

"Look! I got nothing to hide. I'll tell you. I was with him at the Red Parrot until he left around seven or so. I had a beer at the bar, and then I left to go see my parents who live nearby. When I get there, they're not home, which is a little unusual because my mother hasn't been feeling well lately, and I didn't expect them to be out."

"What time would that have been, Tony? From the time you got there until the time you left their house?"

"I don't know exactly. Shortly after seven-thirty to, maybe, eight forty-five or nine. So I wait around for them to come back because I have nothing else to do. I was supposed to meet my fiancé later at the Red Parrot."

"Alright, so you were there for about an hour and fifteen to thirty minutes. Is that correct?"

"Yeah. That's right. About an hour and fifteen to thirty minutes."

"What time did your parents come home, Tony?" McCarthy asked.

Romano hesitated and looked around his office. "What time, Tony?" he repeated firmly.

Tony shook his head and gestured with his hands. "I know this don't look too good, but I'm telling you the truth. They didn't come back, so I left. All right? They had gone to the Hingham Bay Club, which my mother loves, and it's jammed on a Friday night. So they didn't eat until late. I never saw them that night."

"Fair enough, Tony. Did any of the neighbors – someone you know – see you come or go?"

"No. There was no one around or people must have been out. I didn't run into nobody. I saw some lights on in the houses."

"Ok. So you waited around for your parents, and they didn't come home. Then what did you do?"

"I don't remember what I did then. I think I just went back to the Red Parrot to meet Liz."

"And what time would that have been, Tony?" Symolon asked.

"I'm guessing. She sometimes works late on a Friday night because she's a hairdresser. That must have been it. I'd say sometime after nine that night. Maybe nine-fifteen."

"You're sure about that?"

"I'm about as sure as I can be."

"And you went straight from your parents to the Red Parrot? Is that correct, Tony?"

Romano said nothing. He rolled his eyes around and turned away from the investigators. Looking again at Symolon, he said. "Not when you put it that way. No. It's not."

"Then how should I put it, Tony?"

"You have to understand something here. I'm talking to you because I had nothing to do with this thing. My lawyer doesn't even want me talking to you, but, like I said, I got nothing to hide."

"Do you want an attorney present now, Tony? It's your right, you know. Or, we can just leave right now."

"I know all about that. I just don't want you getting the wrong idea. I don't need no lawyer here."

"We're not going to get any wrong ideas, Tony, if you just tell us the truth. So far, so good. You left your parents and then did what? It doesn't take fifteen minutes to get to the Red Parrot from your parents' house."

"As I said, I'm talking to you without my lawyer, and I don't want you to have any wrong ideas here, you know what I'm saying? I'm looking to cooperate. So, anyway, I left my parents' house, and I had a few minutes, so I figured I'd run by Dazzie's to say hello to his parents. I haven't seen them in awhile, and I've known them all my life. They're good people. Real good people."

McCarthy and Symolon glanced at each other. "Yes, they are real good people, Tony, and they're pretty upset about the loss or their son. So, did you stop there or what?" Dick asked.

"I parked my car and rang the door, but no one answered. There were lights on in the house, but nobody around. I figured they were out, so I left."

"Did you look around outside the house?"

"No. Like I said. I rang the bell, waited, and no one answered. So I left. That's it, whether it looks good or not. I'm telling you the truth, just like it happened."

"Ok, Tony, I understand what you're saying. You've been very cooperative. One last question. What were you driving that night?"

"That night? What I always drive. My black BMW."

"Unless my partner here has any questions for you, Tony, I have all I need for now. If we have any further questions, we'll get back to you or, if you can think of anything that can help us, give us a call," McCarthy said.

"I've got nothing," Symolon further responded. "Thank you again, Tony, for your cooperation. I'm sure you'll understand the warrant we're getting for the car. A Hingham cop will be here until it's served."

****

Later that same morning, Kevin Sweeney went into his family room to watch a tape of a program on the Discovery Channel he had recorded several weeks previously. Marie was so upset by the visit of the State Police that she went shopping at the South Shore Mall in Braintree.

When the home phone in the kitchen rang, Kevin got up to answer it but was surprised to discover someone was calling about business.

"Is this Kevin?" the caller asked.

"Yes. Who's this?"

"Kevin, Andrew McKinnon here. Remember me? The framer at Tony Romano's house in Cohasset?"

"Yeah. Yeah. I remember you, Andrew. I haven't heard from you in a long time. How are you doing?"

"How am I doing? Are you shitting me? You know how the fuck I'm doing. Thanks to you, Kevin, the State Police showed up on my door an hour ago and interrogated me about the Romano project. They told me you gave them my fucking name, you fucking asshole."

For a moment, Kevin breathed deeply, said nothing, and let Andrew talk. "You just turned my fucking life upside down, you cock sucker. They think I had something to do with money laundering because Romano paid me in cash. Isn't that what you told them, you bastard? If I was there right now, I'd break your fucking neck."

Kevin said nothing again.

"Are you still there, Kevin? Are you there?" Andrew demanded. "Where are your balls now?"

"Yeah, I'm still here Andrew. I think you're mad at the wrong guy," Sweeney said softly.

"How the fuck can you say that? You told them Romano paid me in cash for the work I did on his house. You told them, right? Admit it, you gutless piece of shit."

"I never told them you were involved in money laundering. What I did tell them is that I had my suspicions."

"Suspicions about what? Exactly what suspicions did you have?"

"Andrew, what do you take me for, a complete idiot? Romano paid you in cash, and both you and I know it. You would never have taken that job otherwise because you were almost twenty-five percent lower than the other two guys who bid on the job. You saw the figures because I gave them to you, and you knew you were the low bid by a lot of money."

"So what's that supposed to mean?"

"It means that you cut a deal with the home owner and may have made a deal with the devil instead. You left $5,000 on the table that Romano owed you and never took him to court. Why not? You knew I would have backed you.

"I spent hours and hours of my own time researching that problem, and I came up with the answer. I had all the evidence, including video. How many times did we go over it? Does daily ring a bell?"

"That $5,000 is none of your fucking business."

"Right, it's none of my fucking business but it's ok for you to call me here and ream my ass out. You have a short memory, Andrew. I told you to be careful with that guy, and I told you more than once. The person you should be angry with is yourself, not me. You went into that job with your eyes wide open and your mouth shut."

Andrew was the one to say nothing now.

"I think I'm a nice guy, Andrew, and I always thought you were, too. I can only take so much, and I know you're upset. At least you had the balls to call me and tell me to my face. I can respect that. Do you have a lawyer?" Kevin asked.

"A lawyer? Fuck. You think I'm going to need a lawyer?"

"Andrew, listen to me. They're investigating a murder, and it's very possible Romano's involved. I'm sure that's why they came to my house this morning. He used me, too, you know.

"Those guys scared the shit out of me, and I wasn't about to lie to them. If I were you, I would find myself a good lawyer. You're going to have a lot of explaining to do."

"Kevin, I paid my guys and myself with the cash. What's going to happen to them? This fucking thing could go on and on. I could be in big trouble with the IRS."

"I don't think they're interested in your guys, or you for that matter. I think they are looking to prove that Romano was laundering money and used his house to do it. And I also think they want to show that money was somehow behind the murder.

"Some of the guys have told me some things about Romano that are pretty hard to believe. If there's anyone in deep shit, it's him."

Sensing that McKinnon was calming down, Kevin asked, "How's your little girl doing? One of the guys told me that you and your wife finally had a baby. I know you had been trying hard for a long time."

"She's great, Kevin. She's really great. I just feel like a fucking asshole right now. How could I have been so stupid? I thought I could really help my family get off to a good start. We were buying the house, you know, making plans to start a family. You want to know how this whole dumb ass thing came all about?"

"If there's one thing I don't want to know, Andrew, it's how the whole thing came all about. Right now, you have to think of yourself and your family. I am sorry for what's happened. I really am, but I wasn't going to lie for you and put myself on the line.

"As I said, think about getting a lawyer and just tell the truth. It's probably your best defense."

"Hey, Kevin, look, I'm sorry for blowing up at you. I hear what your saying, and I'm man enough to admit that I got myself into this fucking mess entirely on my own. And it's just at a time when my business is going great. What the fuck you going do? That's life, I guess."

****

After his confrontation with the framing contractor, Sweeney returned to the family room and continued watching the program from the point where the tape had been paused. Kevin found it hard to concentrate and began to wonder how many other phone calls like that one he had just had with Andrew he would be getting the rest of the day.

He would not have to wonder for very long because the business phone in the living room rang a short time thereafter.

"Kevin, how you doing?" the caller asked, dragging out each word.

"I don't know, Eddie. Tell me how I'm doing."

"You're doing fine. What the fuck's the problem?"

"Are you serious? You don't know?"

"I don't know about your strange visitors and mine? Is that what you mean?"

"Yeah. You know what I mean. What happened?"

"What happened? I'll tell you what happened. Nothing happened. Just that a couple of Staties came to my place of business and asked me a lot of questions about you, Mr. Romano, and some of the other contractors. It happens every day."

"Come on. Will you stop it? What happened?"

"I'm telling you. They asked me some questions, and I told them what I know. How did they put it? Yes, I was very forthcoming and helpful."

"You don't sound too upset."

"Why should I be upset? I'm upset for you, of course, but I shouldn't be. You didn't do nothing, and neither did I."

"What kind of questions did they ask you? What did they say?"

"Mainly, they just wanted to know how Mr. Romano paid me, by check or in cash. I told them by check. They then wanted to know whether the check was made out to me or my business, so I told them both."

"Both?"

"Yeah. Both. You know all that fill I hauled in there at Romano's to raise the grade?"

"Yeah. What about it?"

"I told them Romano gave me a personal check for some of it. Everything else was made out to my company. They really seemed to appreciate me being honest about it."

"What else did they ask you? Did you tell them that the guy whose yard you hauled the fill from paid you in cash?"

"No. They didn't ask me that, but I would have told them. They asked me about other jobs I had done with you and how I got paid on them, and any problems I might have had getting paid."

"Yeah?"

"I told them about the hotshot in Hingham, the guy who paid cash for his BMW at Romano's place. The Cock Doc who screwed you out of the money for blasting the ledge. Patrick Walsh, your plastering buddy from the old sod. That was it. I got along fine with them. They were good shits, very down to earth."

"Eddie, you told them about Parker paying cash for his car at Romano's dealership? Why did you do that?"

"Because, Kevin, I can put two and two together. They think Romano had something to do with the murder of his best friend. You could just tell by the questions they were asking that they know money has something to do with the motive. I was just helping them out, is all."

"Remind me to always keep you as my friend, Eddie. I would not want you for an enemy. That's pretty devious. So, what did they say about the doctor?"

"Nothing. They didn't seem to give a shit about him."

"So, you're cool with all this?"

"Yeah. Like I said. They asked me some questions, and I answered them. I think they got the big picture on Mr. Romano. I wouldn't worry about it, if I were you. We're nothing but little fish in this whole thing."

Chapter 15

Although it was only seven in the morning that Monday, the second day of March 1999, Nantasket Beach was not deserted. Regardless of the day, time, season, or weather, there was always someone walking, running, or admiring the beach. It was what people who live by the ocean do, and nothing could be more uplifting.

Tony Romano loved the beach, and walked its nearly three-mile length many times over the years. Today Tony would walk the beach alone hoping that he would not run into anyone he knew.

Romano wanted some time to himself in a place where peace and beauty seemed everywhere. The rhythm of the heavy waves pounding the beach and the effervescent sound they made receding reset his internal clock. The ocean had an inexplicable way of calming him down.

Thoughts of his mother flooded his mind, and he clung to the desperate hope that the alternative, holistic approach to her illness would produce positive results. Sure, the treatments would be very costly, but he had the money and wouldn't hesitate paying for them. Mrs. Romano would get the best care his money could provide.

In about another hour, Romano would attend the funeral of his best friend and be one of six pallbearers. Somehow, he would get through it. There wasn't much he could do to help Dazzie's parents through their grief, and they seemed to be in an emotional daze.

He had asked them about the funeral expenses and was told that they had on their son a small insurance policy they had been making payments on all these years. Romano figured the policy would not be enough and planned to withdraw money that morning from one of his bogus business accounts to help the Clarkes along.

It was the least he could do for the parents of his best friend, even though Tony knew they might gently protest. Mr. and Mrs. Clarke had pride and knew the difference between charity, which they would not accept, and kindness, which they would.

Plodding through the sand, Romano was alone with his thoughts, which were pierced occasionally by a screaming seagull announcing its presence and position. It was getting late, so Romano turned at a break in the seawall to retrace his steps. In the distance, he could barely see the waves breaking over the cliffs at the base of the condominium complex where Rebecca Solberg lived.

He knew what she had gone through several years ago, and was inspired now by her courage. "Rebecca did it, and I can, too," Tony said to himself as he headed up the beach and towards the parking lot. Romano turned up his collar and put his hands in his pocket.

Wanting to stay but knowing he had to go, Tony watched for a few minutes as the incoming, offshore fog moved quickly across the beach. There was nothing like the sight, sound, and smell of the ocean up close. The view from his house was magnificent, to be sure, but not quite the same as being on the beach where he felt more at home and comfortable.

Romano put his car into reverse and slowly headed out of the nearly empty parking lot. His next stop was the funeral home in Hingham, and the two detectives who were looking into his life were not going to prevent him from being with his friend for the last time.

He was certain the investigation of his boat and black BMW would turn up nothing.

****

As Lauren Parker was waiting to board the commuter boat and anxiously scanned the crowd to see if Graham Barrows was amongst the passengers, she repeated to herself, "Please. Please be here today, Graham. I need you, really, really need you." Not wanting to wait any longer, Lauren went to her regular seat, midships, starboard side. "He's usually one of the last passengers on. Please be here," she thought to herself.

With barely a minute to spare, Graham boarded the boat, found Lauren, and sat down beside her. One look at her told him something was very wrong.

"Hi. What's the matter?" he said. "You look – how shall I say? – dreadful, just dreadful. Are you alright?"

"No, Graham, I'm not alright. Something terrible happened over the weekend, and I'm really, really frightened."

"What is it?" Graham asked anxiously. "Has something happened at home?" he asked, sensing the source.

"You're not going to believe what happened," Lauren said, grabbing Graham's arm and holding it tightly. "Two detectives from the State Police came to the house and asked us a lot of questions about the BMW we bought last September. They even wanted to know our whereabouts a week ago last Thursday or Friday night," she said, practically whispering in Graham's ear.

"My son, Stephen was so frightened he started to cry, the poor little thing."

"Stephen? I'm not following you. What could he have to do with anything?"

"He doesn't, of course. It was a joke Jay made before Christmas. He said something about a SWAT team coming to the house and fining us for having bad taste on where we put the tree. It was funny at the time, but Stephen thought the police were coming to the house. He was pretty upset then, too."

Clearly puzzled, Graham just shook his head back and forth and frowned. "This is just baffling. I'm missing something here."

"I know. I can see from the expression on your face. I'll tell you what happened. Did you see anything in the news about the murder in Cohasset last Friday?"

"Yes. Yes, I did. I saw something in the paper, but I glanced right over it. I still don't understand."

"Well, the two detectives who came to the door are investigating that murder and wanted to know an awful lot about the man Jay bought his car from in Hingham. They especially wanted to know how we paid for it.

"Once Jay told them we paid in cash, their whole attitude changed, and they started asking some very pointed questions, like, whose idea was it to pay in cash, was it actually cash or a personal check. It was unbelievable. I almost felt like they were accusing us of something."

"I don't believe it. Jay and I discussed that very thing the time we met at the Union Oyster House. I was speaking theoretically about how something quite innocent can be made questionable and might not look good. We were talking about the salami programming scheme, and I was just giving him some hypothetical scenarios."

"Did he tell you how we paid?"

"He did. Yes, he told me all about it."

"Then he must have told you why."

"Well, yes, he did but, frankly, I would have been curious myself. Naturally, I would not have done it the way he did, but I did wonder. I even told him so."

"Really? I thought it was the stupidest thing I had ever heard. I was a nervous wreck, and we had a big argument over it. I thought it was just juvenile. It must be a guy thing."

"When Jay and I were talking," Graham said, "I never thought for a moment, Lauren, that any of it could come true. This whole thing is truly unbelievable. I don't know what to make of it."

"Well then, you can only imagine how Jay reacted once they left. But that's not all. They showed us a picture of the victim, and I recognized him immediately. I just blurted it out. The guy had been to our house sometime last fall to fix a flat on Jay's BMW."

"You can't be serious."

"Oh, I'm serious alright. And then the most unbelievable thing of all happened. The detectives took Jay to the Hingham Police station to have him fingerprinted. Can you believe it? Fingerprinted. I guess they're trying to rule out his fingerprints or something."

"Lauren, I'm absolutely flabbergasted. No, I simply can't believe it."

"Well, Jay's now in a total panic, and I'm talking about a man who never shows his fear. It's one of his qualities. He seems so confident and self assured all the time. It's one of the things about him that first attracted me. I wanted to call you over the weekend, but I didn't think I could with Jay around. Obviously, I wasn't going to e-mail you, either.

"Where were you Friday night? I was looking for you," Lauren said.

"Is that it on the police visit? Did you want to discuss it more? This is all very shocking, utterly shocking."

"No. There's nothing more about it to discuss beyond what I just told you. Now I have to pick up the pieces somehow, and I'm a wreck."

"I should say so. I have never heard of anything like this."

"So, now you can see what I'm going through. As I said, I was looking for you the other night at the commuter boat pier."

Graham drew a deep breath before answering Lauren. "I had a very busy day at one client's place, then I slipped over to Jay's company and stayed late. The system manager there and I have a very good relationship, and she lets me do pretty much what I want. I tried to locate in the system software, the source code, that needle in the haystack I told you about."

"You did?" Lauren asked, her face brightening and grip on Graham's arm tightening again. "Did you find anything?"

Graham shook his head. "No, Lauren. I didn't find anything, and I'm not even sure at this point that there's anything's there to find. I mean, I can still keep looking, if you like, but I don't think that the outcome will be any different. My idea about haystacks and Monet was more romantic and illusionary than real. Very dumb actually. It's a nearly impossible task."

Disappointed, Lauren slumped back into her seat. "Graham, what if it's not on the system? What if it's on the Internet?"

"I don't see your point, Lauren. The Internet? Why the Internet? I just don't see it. Of course, I suppose anything's possible, but," Graham said not completing his thought and shrugging his shoulders.

"Maybe you're looking in the wrong place. Maybe you should be looking on the Internet. At this point, I'm willing to pull out all the stops. If someone's setting up Jay, we need to know, especially since this latest development with the police."

Lauren paused before continuing. "And you better get ready for this. I confronted Jay Friday night about the on line stuff, and after what just happened over the weekend, I don't know what will happen next."

"You confronted him, Lauren? Are you joking? Why in God's name did you ever do that? This whole thing is spiraling out of control. I'm simply shocked, really. I thought you were not going to say anything."

"It's a long story, Graham, and I'll talk to you about it later. Right now, we have to do something and get to the bottom of this – of this thing – whatever this thing is."

"Lauren, I'm at a complete loss as to what to say or do. I thought I could help. I would want to help you any way I could. You know that. I'm surprised he didn't call me himself. Why don't you just tell him that I found the problem and got rid of it? Maybe it will calm him down."

"How can I do that? He doesn't even know you consult with his company. He's a man who lives by his instincts and would know I was lying. No, that would only complicate things. I certainly don't want him to know about us, even though, well, you know."

"Right. Right. Good point. Things are already complicated enough."

The commuter boat was passing under the Long Island Bridge and would soon pass Spectacle Island, the destination of much of the dirt being hauled from The Big Dig. Graham turned away from Lauren to get a better look at the work going on there. In another ten minutes, they would be pulling into Boston.

"Oh. By the way, Jay couldn't call you. I told him I left your number at work. Will you do something for me?" Lauren then asked, tugging on Graham's coat and something else.

"Of course, I will," Graham said as he turned towards Lauren. "You don't even have to ask."

"Ok. Then here's what I want you to do. As you know, my company has developed an Internet security product, and maybe it can help us find out what is going on. You could install it on Jay's system at work, do the analysis, and see if anything turns up. Nobody will even know the difference."

"I don't think so, Lauren. For one thing, I'll know. This is a very serious matter. It would be unprofessional – no, unethical – of me to install software on that system without telling my client. It's just not something you do. I don't think that this is an Internet problem. It's probably internal. I would be using my client, and I just don't think I can do it. You may be asking for too much."

"How would you be using them?" Lauren countered. "If you found something, you would be helping them, and – don't forget – me. What's the big deal?"

"Lauren, I'm surprised at you. Really. If my idea about Monet and haystacks was foolish, yours is simply preposterous. It's not the answer. Aren't you being hasty and losing sight of something?"

"Of what? No, I'm not, Graham. We have a chance to put this whole thing to rest once and for all, and I want to do it. Just like you would say, isolate the problem and eliminate all the possibilities. And I need some peace and harmony in my life. I just can't sit here and do nothing. Besides, you did say you would help."

"Yes. Yes, I did, Lauren, but not with something like this. I didn't mean it literally. I was just saying, you know, talking out loud. It's a manner of speaking."

"Now you're starting to sound like Jay. I ask him to help me do something, he says he will, and he doesn't follow through. If you say you're going to do something, I think you should."

"Lauren, this is quite unexpected from you. Really. I want to help. I do, but I don't want to jeopardize my career. What about your position at the company?

"Your company has not released that product to the public yet. I'm becoming, well, very uneasy about all this. To be perfectly honest with you, I really don't like it. It's a most unpleasant business, really."

"Graham, I'm trying to protect my family, and you won't help? Of all the people I thought I could count on, you, now you're telling me I can't? I am not putting my career or company at risk in any way. I own stock in the company, and when it goes public, I could be set for life. I have a vested interest in what happens to that company."

Graham sighed. "Lauren, I don't like it. As long as you can reassure me that the principals of your company are willing to let you borrow the software, I will see if I can't work out something on my end. I'm not making any promises, mind you. I'm willing to consider helping, if everything can be done properly. Otherwise, Lauren, I quite simply will have to say 'No.' There's too much at stake here."

Lauren thought for a moment. "Graham, I want you to trust me. You let me take care of my end, and you take care of yours. If it works, it works; if it doesn't, it doesn't. Will you be going home at the usual time tonight?"

"Yes. I should be."

"Great. I'll see you then," When the commuter boat pulled into Rowe's Wharf, Lauren turned to Graham and kissed him on the cheek. "I, ah, oh well," she heard herself say.

"What? You were about to say something."

"Never mind. Another time, maybe. Thanks. You're a real friend, Graham," she said. "And more."

Graham just looked at Lauren, staring into her beautiful, captivating eyes.

She put her arm on his again and smiled. "Can I plan on seeing you tonight?" she asked.

"Yes," Graham said trying to muster up some conviction. "You can plan on it."

****

Rebecca Solberg had just come into work and was preparing herself for the day ahead. "I just can't believe that it's already March 2," she said to herself as she turned the page on her desk calendar. "Where has all the time gone?"

One possibility was the trash bin. Her vigilance in keeping two sets of books for Dr. Pierce's own good proved to be a complete waste of time. He was, she finally concluded, exactly what he seemed, an old fashioned, principled, honorable man and caring physician who put his patients above all else.

Ok, some of the tests he had order for Christina Romano were questionable, but he practiced medicine to rule out questions. Although Pierce preferred certainty to any doubt or lingering questions, he recognized that medicine involves art as well as science.

She had never resolved in her mind what she would do if she found that Dr. Pierce was committing Medicare fraud. Simply switching the books during an investigation might not work. In fact, she had unwittingly put herself at risk because Pierce – if he was involved – could always claim that he had nothing to do with the bookkeeping. If mistakes were made, they must have originated with her.

It was a dumb idea in the first place, Rebecca concluded with some pain of conscience. "How could I ever have thought so poorly of this wonderful, loving man? Many people, myself included, have feelings they never act on," she deliberated with herself. "What's the point of continuing all this extra work?" she finally asked herself.

There was none, and she would now have even more time to enjoy a life that had really begun to flower once again. She had much to look forward to, especially the impending birth of a baby to her nephew, Auggie, and his wife. She was going to be a great aunt for the first time.

Rebecca then put into the drive the zip disk with the second set of books on it and relegated Dap2 to the trash.

****

Kevin Sweeney was making his rounds and had driven in early to his project on Clarendon Street in the South End of Boston. He and Steve Bonnano had gone out for coffee and were sitting at the table of a small café on Tremont Street. Walter and Allen Nash were hanging a solid core door in the first floor office, and Ono Cazeault was balancing the heating system. Neither of them had said anything to Kevin about the murder investigation.

A wrought iron fabricator was installing a deck on the second floor of the homeowner's apartment. That phase of the project had not gone so well, and Kevin was glad to see that the work was finally being done. It was a down side to fast tracking the project, and the delay in completing that work was putting a lot of pressure on Kevin.

"How was the traffic when you came in?" Steve asked.

"Not bad. Fuck the traffic. I want to know what happened," Kevin told Steve.

"Like I said, nothing much. Just a lot of questions about the Auto Dude, some about you, and a few more about me. I don't know why you're so upset about this," Bonnano said to his friend. "They're not investigating you. They're after that Romano guy."

"Stevie, twelve years of Catholic education does something to you. I am now, and always have been, deathly afraid of authority. If those two investigators had pulled me over and told me to step into oncoming traffic, I would have done it," Kevin said seriously.

"Well, that's what you get for going to Gatorade," Bonnano teased.

"It wasn't Gatorade, you idiot. It was Gate of Heaven. When I went to Florida and told them there where I went to school, they thought I said 'Gator Heaven.' I couldn't understand why they were all laughing. I found out later it was my accent, and that I talk too fast. I told you all that a long time ago."

"Yes, you did," Steve said. "I still like Gatorade better."

"Fine. Getting back to those two investigators. What did you tell them about me?"

"I told them the truth. That you're a real pain in the ass."

"A pain in the ass? Why would you tell them I'm a pain in the ass?"

"Because you are. I told them that you're a pain in the ass because you're always making sure that everyone is doing things above board, that you're as straight as a goddamn arrow. You are. You're a pain in the ass. You're like a watchdog. We know how much we can tell you."

"I'm sure you do. Ok. Then I take it as a compliment. So what else did they want to know?"

"They wanted to know how everyone got paid. I told them I was paid by check, made out to my business, just as you like. I also told them about the side job at Romano's parents' house where I put in a fan, a few new outlets, and a couple of circuits."

"Don't ask. Yes, Kevin, I told them he paid me cash for the extra work at his parents'."

"That's alright. I'm not upset. Eddie told them pretty much the same thing, only he didn't call me a pain in the ass."

"Knowing him, he probably called you something else."

"What is it with you two? You're always going at each other."

"Long story. Has he ever said anything to you about it?"

"No, he hasn't."

"Really? Then I won't say anything either. You know me. I can work with the guy because he's on your project. He can work with me, too. We're professionals."

"Listen. I have to get going. I have a lot to do today. When do you think you'll be getting an inspection?"

"Probably not for another few days. I still have to get the electrical permit."

Kevin just looked at Steve. "You'll never change, will you? And you call me a pain in the ass. I just better not find out that you're smoking again. Then there'll be hell to pay."

Sweeney was not all that bothered about the electrical permit. There was always some question anyway as to when one was required for the electrical work. If the electrician was only doing repair work, which Steve was that day in the homeowner's office on the first floor, technically, he did not need a permit.

If there was anyone who knew how to use the technicalities to his own advantage, no one could beat Stevie Bear.

****

Tony Romano had done it. He had gotten through Dazzie Clarke's funeral and committal service in Blue Hills Cemetery in Braintree. Liz was there with him; his mother and father were, too. They did not notice the tension between Tony and Liz Jensen, and they did not ask why he was driving a different car.

Before heading back to the Clarke house for the traditional gathering of relatives and friends, Tony stopped along the way at a small bank where he kept one of his bogus business checking accounts.

"It can't be a year since I was here last," he said to himself as he turned into the driveway to park his car. Earlier that morning – before he left the house for his solitary walk along the beach – Tony checked the balance of the account and knew he had over $8,500 in it.

He would not need that much. Anything over $4,500 would seem like charity to his friend's parents, he thought. Having made out the withdrawal check beforehand, he approached the teller and handed it to her along with his driver's license. "I'll be right with you," the teller said as she began punching keys on a keyboard. Tony waited patiently, assuming correctly that she was checking the balance of the account.

"I'm sorry, sir, but the amount of this check you gave me is greater than the balance in your account. Are you sure you wanted this amount?"

"Yes, of course, I'm sure," Tony answered. "Wait a minute. What are you talking about? I checked the balance before I came here. What's going on here?"

"I'm not sure of what you mean, sir. According to my records, you do not have enough money in your account to cover this check," she said politely.

Quickly recovering his senses, Tony realized that he probably made a mistake. With the present turmoil going on in his life, he must have checked the wrong account. No problem. He could always go home later that day, get the right checkbook, and then the money.

"Oh. That's all right. You're right. I must have thought I had more in that account than I really did. I keep several accounts at different banks. One's near work; another's near my house. I'm sorry. My mistake."

"No problem at all, sir. You know, you might want to look into an ATM that allows banking from several institutions. It might be more convenient for you that way. There is an amount limit, though."

"Right. That's a good idea. I'll look into it," he said as he turned towards the door. "Jesus. I have to keep my head on straight. A lot of people are relying on me. Maybe I'm not through it yet, after all."

Romano immediately returned to his car. "Did you get what you came for?" Liz asked. "No, I didn't, and I'm really mad at myself. I took the wrong checkbook. Mom, how are you doing back there? Is it warm enough in here?"

"We're doing fine," Tony's father answered. "I don't think it will take us too long to get to Dazzie's house. How are you doing on gas?"

"I'm ok. A little bit more than half a tank."

"I'm not so fine, Tony," his mother said. "I think it's terrible, just terrible that those two men came to our home to ask questions about you. What kind of people do they think we are?"

"Mom, listen. There's nothing for you to worry about. They're just doing their jobs. They have to check into everything." Tony did not tell his parents that the State Police had been to Liz's workplace.

"What could your lobster boat have to do with it?" Mrs. Romano asked. "You don't even use it any more. I can't imagine what the neighbors are saying. It's been all over the news."

Tony's father joined in. "You know, Tony, them newspaper and TV people have been up and down the neighborhood asking awful questions. They were even at the cemetery today. They have absolutely no respect for the dead or anyone's privacy. Now I can understand why so many people hate them."

Neither Tony nor Liz said anything.

"In fact, Tony, I think I would rather go home than back to the house," Mrs. Romano said. "I'm really not up to it, and I'm feeling very, very tired. I probably should not have come to the service, but I didn't want to let Joe and Eileen down."

"They'll understand, Mom. I'll give them your regards. Don't worry about it."

Although distracted, Tony waited for several cars to pass before he turned left out of the parking lot. He was disappointed and wanted to give the Clarkes the money when he got to their house. Now he would have to wait. "Fuck," he said to himself. "What are you going to do? No point in getting upset about it. I've had about all the stress I can stand lately. I keep this up, and I'll be lucky to make it to forty."

Tony's stress level was about to go up. He had led McCarthy and Symolon to believe that he had known Al Sanderson from the time Sanderson bought the car. Liz had told Darlene Coakley and Kent Costigan that Tony had introduced her to Sanderson more than ten years ago. She remembered him well because her girlfriend dated Sanderson for several years after their first encounter at Liz's house in Stoughton.

Liz also told them about Mrs. Romano's medical condition. There was very little – other than the car thefts and drug dealing, which she did not know – that Liz Jensen had not told the two detectives the previous Saturday morning. She had cooperated fully, believing Tony was completely innocent of any involvement in his best friend's murder.

They both knew that McCarthy and Symolon would not be going away and that this thing was far from over.

****

"Alright, let's listen up everyone," Wes Symolon began the second meeting of the investigative team that day around noon. "We've made some substantial progress on the Clarke case, and I would like to start this time by summarizing our meeting of this morning then move onto other matters. Is everyone with me?"

All the heads in the room nodded. "As you all know," Dick McCarthy pitched in, "we have two main suspects, Tony Romano of Cohasset and Al Sanderson of the North End. We are certain from the lab results that Sanderson was involved in the murder because we found some fingerprints belonging to him on the duct tape that was wrapped around the body.

"Stealing cars was nothing new to him, and he was caught and convicted for it some thirty years ago. He just got more clever and got out of stealing and into exporting them. Along with construction equipment, I might add, although I am speculating.

"We also know that the victim made a phone call to Al Sanderson on the night he was murdered, most likely to talk business at a prearranged site. In all likelihood, Clarke knew that his parents would be going out because they always do on a Friday night."

A hand went up. "Are we proceeding on the assumption that Sanderson was either the murderer himself or an accomplice, in other words, two people were involved?" Matt Henderson asked.

"Yes, we are, Matt. Let me clarify that. We know from what you and Russ came up with on Sanderson that he's somewhere in his mid to late fifties. Given the victim's weight and Sanderson's age, it's unlikely that he could have lifted Dazzie, unconscious, into his car or van, too easily.

"The fencing would not have been all that heavy, but everything was done so quietly that none of the neighbors heard any sounds or movement. So, yes, we think there was at least one accomplice. Who killed the victim? Romano or Sanderson? We can't say just yet. Do you have any more on Sanderson?"

"Not much, only that he's out of the country," Russ Townsend said. "We're looking into his whereabouts and should be able to get back to you before the day is out. How close do you want us to get to this guy? I mean, so far, we've talked to the security guard at Sanderson's condo complex on the harbor and a few neighbors. No one knows very much about him. Romano's fiancé gave Darlene and Kent a physical description and even located an old picture taken with Sanderson and the girlfriend."

Matt Henderson had something to add. "We're thinking that if we ask around about him at the Conley Pier in Southie, someone's going to tip Sanderson off, especially because the case is getting a lot of play by the media. With this guy's resources, he could just disappear on us, and we're not looking to have that happen.

"I'd like to nail the guys ass, and I don't want to see him getting off the hook," Henderson said, looking around the table.

"You might want to take a more general approach, you know, check out his business, what it does, without looking directly at him," Wes Symolon said. "Start on the outside and work your way into the middle. If you want to know more about his finances, maybe Kent can help you. Sanderson's a businessman, so he's bound to have some paper out there. Get as much on this guy as you can, like you said, but without attracting attention. Very good point."

"Dick, do you still want Kent and me to stay with Romano?" Darlene asked. "We checked with some contractors he hired for his house and even talked to a guy who worked on the Southie properties.

"He was a Patty – a true blooded Irishman from the old sod – and remembered very clearly that Romano had a lot of money to throw around in the late eighties and always paid the subs in cash. There's no question, Kent and I think, that Romano was stealing cars and using the proceeds to finance his real estate purchases and improvements. Kent has come up with something pretty interesting I think you'll want to hear."

"Shoot."

"I ran some numbers on the cars and figured that – even if Romano got ten percent of their retail value – he probably made somewhere around $250,000, if you take the number of license plates and multiply them times $5,000 or so. Obviously, he could have stolen more, and he probably told his friend, Mr. Dazzie, that he was making a lot less. I don't think more works because he would have run the risk of getting caught."

"Yeah. Ok. So what are you saying?"

"I'm saying that I don't think you could buy two houses with nine units between them, fix them up, and have any money left over. I think you would be coming up short.

"That consultant guy we spoke to in Weymouth gave us some very interesting information about the cost of remodeling in the early nineties. He said $35,000 to $45,000 per unit. You do the math, and it doesn't add up.

"Here's the catch. No matter what the money is on the investment property, there's no way he's able to purchase a dealership without putting down a sizeable sum. I'm guessing at least half a million or more, and then he finances the rest. Even if he re-mortgaged the Southie properties at their improved values, he's coming in awfully tight. As I see it, the numbers just don't work. Question is, how did he do it?"

The room was quiet.

"I see your point," Symolon said. "So, what's your theory?"

"My theory is that this guy had a sudden infusion of cash, a very large amount all at once, enough to buy the dealership, sell his condo, then turn an expensive dump on the ocean into a palace."

"Wasn't Romano gainfully employed all this time and taking in cash from his side business in tires and batteries?" Matt inquired. "Couldn't he have used some of the rent money to remodel the house? I agree with you, but I'm thinking those are some of the possibilities."

"What do we have on the lobster boat and car search? Anything?" Darlene asked.

"Very interestingly, they turned up nothing," McCarthy said. "We can rule out the boat, but not the car because the neighbor did see one. Romano has no alibi and admitted to us that he was at the house the night of the murder. We know he lied about knowing Sanderson, that he's covering something up.

"So, what can it be? A drug deal? Car thefts? The chances are that the statute of limitations would have run out, even if we could prove he did one or both. No, he's hiding something else, and I think it's the truck that was stolen."

"I think that the franchiser," Wes conjectured, "would take back Romano's franchise if he were ever charged and convicted of the theft and insurance fraud. He'd lose the business, and I think that's what he's trying to protect.

"By the way," he added. "Nice job, you guys."

"I forgot to tell you something," Darlene said. "Remember the other day when we were interviewing the electrical contractor who worked on Romano's house?" Everyone did. "Well," she continued, "I thanked him for being helpful and handed him my card.

"He takes my card, goes for his wallet, smiles, and gives me his own card. Says you never know when you might need a good electrician." The meeting ended with a good laugh as everyone left.

Chapter 16

He was alone in his house and home office, sitting there staring at the computer screen, dumfounded. A warning had flashed: Invalid Password. Tony Romano could not get into his bogus business account to check the balance from earlier that morning. "What the fuck's going on?" he muttered to himself. "Invalid Password. What the fuck is this?"

Tony immediately typed in the password again and got the same results. "Alright. Alright. Don't panic," he said out loud. "I can try another account."

He did, then another, another, and another. The result was the same for all of them: Invalid Password. Tony Romano could not get into his bogus accounts. "Stay cool. Think," he muttered aloud. "No one can seize your account without due process, just like the search warrant. It has to be something else. I can still go to the bank and get the balance."

Romano grabbed his things and flew out the door. He hit two banks along the way and was told the same thing. The accounts were nearly empty. Someone had taken his pocket change, and the nightmare he was living only deepened. He was tiptoeing on quicksand.

****

Rebecca Solberg warmly greeted the two new faces that had just come into the office. "Can I help you?" she asked.

"Yes. My name's Darlene Coakley of the Massachusetts State Police, and this is my partner, Kent Costigan. We are investigating the murder of Dazzie Clark and would like to talk to Dr. Pierce. Is he in?"

Rebecca was surprised. "Yes, he is," she responded, "but he's with a patient right now. He'll be but a few minutes, and then he should be free. Would that be alright?"

"Sure. We can wait," Costigan said.

The two detectives sat down on the comfortable couch and glanced around. "Beautiful office," Darlene said.

"I'll bet this cost a few bucks," Costigan observed.

A short time thereafter, Darlene noticed an elderly lady leaving Dr. Pierce's office with a younger woman, and looked over at Rebecca. "I'll check for you," she said.

Solberg then knocked on Dr. Pierce's door and told him about the two detectives in the waiting area. He was perplexed as to why they would want to talk to him but told her to show them in. Rebecca led Costigan and Coakley to Pierce's office, gently knocked on the open door, and left them to enter on their own. Costigan closed the door behind himself and Darlene. After identifying themselves and the purpose of their visit, the investigators didn't waste a minute.

"Dr. Pierce, can you tell me if Mrs. Christina Romano is a patient of yours?" Darlene began.

"Yes, I can. She is. The whole family is, actually," Pierce responded.

"Can you tell us what you are treating her for?"

"Of course not," Pierce shot back.

"We understand, Doctor, and we're not asking you to breach your doctor – patient confidentiality. We're just trying to get some background here."

"Well, I'm afraid you've come to the wrong place. There's nothing I can tell you about the Romano family because I treat each member."

"As I said, we understand, but you could tell us if you bought a car from Tony Romano, couldn't you?"

"Sure. I could tell you that. No, I didn't, but my wife did a few years back. She gets it serviced at Tony's dealership."

"Ok, then you see my point. As long as we are not discussing the medical situation, then you can talk to us, can you not?"

"As long as what you are asking has no bearing on my doctor – patient relationship, then, yes, I can talk to you."

Kent Costigan had a few questions to ask. "Doctor, other than your wife's car, have you ever had any business dealings with Tony Romano?"

"No. At least none that I can think of. Just the car. That's it."

"None?"

"As I said, just the car. Nothing else."

"Can I ask you something about billing?"

"Depends. You can ask, but I may chose not to answer."

"Ok. Let's try it. How does Tony Romano pay you?"

"I don't like it, but I'll answer it. He doesn't pay me. He has comprehensive medical insurance."

"So there's no reason why he would be paying you any money unless the treatment you provided was not covered by insurance. Is that correct?"

"Obviously."

"Not so obviously to us, Doctor."

"What do you mean? What are you getting at?"

"What I'm getting at is this. We have evidence that Tony Romano has paid you substantial amounts of cash over the last few months. Can you tell us what it was for?"

"What are you talking about? That's ridiculous."

"Then you deny that Romano has paid you anything over the last several months?"

"I've never heard of anything so ridiculous. I don't like this, and I'll have nothing else to say. If you have any further questions, you can submit them to my attorney. I'm a family physician, I'll have you know, and I won't subject myself to this line of questioning. If you have nothing else, I have another patient to see, thank you."

"No, we have nothing else for you, Doctor," Darlene said politely. "Thank you for your time. Sorry for the intrusion."

****

"How did I know I would be seeing you two guys today? How did I know?" Tony Romano asked.

"I don't know, Tony. How did you know?" Wes Symolon answered.

"Every time I turn around you guys are up my ass. How the hell can I run a business with you two around here all the time? What do you want this time?" Romano demanded.

"We want this time, Tony, what we wanted each time we have come here. We want the truth, and you haven't been giving it to us."

"What are you talking about? I've been very cooperative with you. How many times do I have to tell you, I'm not involved in this thing? I'll bet nothing turned up in my boat or car, right? Right? You're looking at the wrong guy."

"Really? Who should we be looking at, Tony?" McCarthy asked.

"I don't know. That's your fucking problem. I've got my own problems."

"You certainly do, Tony, and your problems are going to get even worse if you don't come clean with us and stop the bullshit."

"Bullshit? What bullshit? I've been straight with you, haven't I? You don't see any lawyers hanging out in the corridors do you? I could tell you to get the fuck out of here, and you would have to go, right?"

"Ok, we know you know your rights, Tony. But how about just another question or two? Nothing big. Help us clear up a few things; keep from getting the wrong idea. What do you say?"

"I say this is the last time I'm talking to you about anything. I've had just about enough, and you're starting to get on my nerves. I can only be so patient, you know."

"We're told we have a way of doing that," Symolon said. "Here's an easy one for you, Tony. Exactly when was it that you met Al Sanderson? When you sold him the car? That was it, what you said, wasn't it, Tony?"

"Hey! Come on. Ok, so I dodged you on that one. What's the big deal? The guy was married when I first knew him, and he was fucking around with my fiancé's roommate at the time. I was just looking to keep that out figuring he's still married and all. As I said, I haven't seen him for some time."

"Keep it out, Tony? Like I was going to scare up the presumed Mrs. Sanderson and tell her right away, is that it?" McCarthy said sarcastically. "Tony, I like you, but, Jesus, show us some respect, will you? This is beneath you, frankly."

"Well, what the fuck do you want me to say? I didn't say nothing, and I didn't have to. That's it. That's the end of it."

"Ok, Tony, that's fine," Symolon said. "You can have it your way. You don't have to tell us anything about Chet's Car Care in Weymouth or Manny's Muffler Pro in Hingham. We can just go down there and visit them ourselves. They'll probably give us a good deal, right?"

"I don't know what the fuck you're talking about. What's this Chet's thing and muffler place?"

"You don't know anything about them?"

"No. I know nothing about them."

"Would your bookkeeper?"

"No. She would know nothing about them either."

"Really? Your bookkeeper would know nothing about them, is that what you're saying?"

"Yeah. That's what I'm saying."

"Do you have an accountant?"

"I have a business manager. She handles all payable, and, yeah, I do have an accountant. A CPA."

"Does your business manager have medical bills she can't pay?"

"How the fuck would I know?"

"Does she have full access to your computer system?"

"Of course."

"Does anyone else?"

"No. Just the two of us."

"And she pays the bills?"

"Yeah. She pays the bills, and I sign the checks."

"Oh, you sign the checks, do you?"

"Yeah, just as I said."

"Well then, did you know she's stealing from you?"

"What? What the fuck you talking about? Get off it. You're knee deep in dog shit."

"You heard me. That's right. Tens of thousands of dollars each year of your hard earned money, Tony. No checks. It's all electronic to about a dozen businesses – like CBT Computer Training, Inc. – that don't even exist. I'll bet you're surprised," Symolon said sarcastically. "I can see it on your face."

"Then she cleans them out to pay Dr. Pierce in Cohasset. Has she been sick that often? How does she get anything done? That alternative treatment – holistic medicine stuff – can be pretty expensive, you know, and it's not covered. She's too young for Medicare. Maybe the good doc is handling it all for her. That must be it," Symolon said.

"I don't believe this. This is all bullshit. You'll do and say anything. What the fuck does Dr. Pierce have to do with anything?"

"You tell us, Tony. What does he have to do with anything?"

"He's treating my mother, which I know you know from Liz. I don't believe this bullshit your handing me. I'm done."

"I'm sure you don't believe it, Tony, because it is all bullshit, isn't it? This is the first truthful thing you have said since we came in the door."

"So what's the deal, Tony?" McCarthy interjected. "Either you or your business manager is embezzling. Simple enough, I would say."

"This conversation's over, you bastards. I'm not saying one more fucking word to you without my lawyer present. You hear me? Not one word."

"The hearing is good here, Tony, and I hope you can hear what I'm telling you. Right now, we know about your previous relationship with Sanderson and your past. The statute of limitations has probably run out. No big deal for you. You pulled it off and got out of the business.

"We think the stolen truck is your problem and the insurance fraud, but you know we have nothing on that because the guy who does, your friend, has gone to his heavenly reward," McCarthy quipped.

"You don't want us looking around the business because we might find something the franchiser won't like. You could even lose the business. Did you check the fine print in your contract about felons? The manufacturers wouldn't like it, would they?" Symolon asked.

"That's right, Tony," McCarthy emphasized. "It wouldn't look good for business, now would it? Especially once the press gets a hold of it. You know what they can do to a man's reputation, right?"

Romano fought right back. "I know what's going on here. You fucking guys are trying to hang this murder on me. It's all a set up. Well, I didn't do it. Go ahead. Charge me. My lawyer will make idiots of you two. It's all circumstantial. You've got nothing, and you know it."

"What we have, Tony, is enough to charge you now. Ok, so you were clever enough to get away with a crime a way back when and the insurance fraud. So now, you get charged and convicted of a crime you didn't commit. It all equals out. Sounds about even to me. How about you, Wes?"

"I'll take it. So what if your dying mother goes to her grave wondering if her son is a murderer? No big deal, Tony. Happens all the time. Who knows, maybe the trial will be over in time for you to attend her funeral. Some judges can be very understanding that way and might let you out for a couple of hours, in chains, of course."

"You people are bastards, absolute scum. You keep my mother out of this. She's a very sick woman, you know, and doesn't need any of this crap."

"We know how sick she is, Tony, and, if you want to help her and yourself, then you better help us out. Give us something we don't have to clear yourself. You owe it to your mother and your friend."

Romano said nothing and just glared at the two detectives.

McCarthy stood him down. "Tony, you think you're having a problem with us? Wait until the IRS shows up. Now, there's Big Brother talking. And when he does, you'll be listening. They'll come in here and check everything you've ever done in your entire life. They don't care what you stole, Tony, as long as you shared it with them. You'll be getting a bill with penalties and interest that will look like the national debt. There's no statute on back taxes, Tony."

"You guys are bastards. Total bastards."

McCarthy continued the pressure. "No, Tony, we're the nice guys compared to them. They're not going to prosecute you for income tax evasion. No, they'll keep you on the street working for them. It's cheaper that way and more profitable. You're a wealthy businessman with assets. I'm telling you, Tony, you and the IRS are going to be in a marriage that gives new meaning to 'until death do we part.' It's worse than life without parole. Eternal marriage without divorce."

"Everyone's going to know, Tony," Symolon said. "We have enough to indict you now. Maybe we'll drop in at your seaside home around two in the morning, sirens going, lights flashing, two way radios blasting, you know, wake up the whole neighborhood. Six cruisers should handle it, I should think. Don't you Dick?"

"Sounds good, Wes. And, Tony. Don't forget, the press will be all set up before we arrive, in plenty of time to make the early morning news. By the time it's over, Tony, the whole world will know you, and you won't be able to get a job selling Matchbox cars or Tonka toys."

"Get the fuck out of here. Do you hear me? Get out."

As soon as they left, Tony logged onto the computer system to check his fake accounts. This time, his password worked, and he discovered to his horror that all the money was gone from each of them and had been transferred to Dr. Adam Pierce. He was stupefied and numb with fear.

When Tony grabbed the phone and called his attorney, Jim Moran of Hingham, his heart was pounding, and he was sweating. "Jim, Tony. We have to talk. I'm in big fucking trouble."

"Don't say another word, Tony. Get in here right now."

****

Barrows was a man of his word and showed up at Rowe's Wharf for the commuter boat to Hingham. He was uncharacteristically early by a few minutes and immediately saw Lauren as he was boarding. She smiled at him when their eyes met. Graham stopped at her seat, greeted her, and then got his usual coffee for the ride home. Upon returning to his seat next to her, Graham turned to Lauren, started to say something, but stopped.

"I know you're upset with me," Lauren said, "and it's killing me. I have taken care of everything on my end, and I have the software on this zip disk. Here, take it. Everything you need is there, including test files, a help file, and some documentation."

"No, Lauren. I'm not going to take it."

"What? I don't believe it! You said you would help, Graham, and now you're going back on your word?"

"I'm not going back on my word, Lauren. I will help. Give me the disk tomorrow. I don't want it until I absolutely have to have it."

"I know how you feel, and I'm very sorry. Really, I am. You're such a man of principle, and I really admire you for it. Did you have a chance to work things out with the system manager?"

"Yes, I did, and she understands that I am doing a trial. She trusts me and didn't ask for too many details. I did arrange for her to keep the disk locked up when I'm not there, and I'm not going to install the software on the system. I'll run it from the drive."

"That sounds great. Why not look at this on the positive side, Graham? If you find anything, the problem is solved, and both Jay and I can start having a life again. If you don't, at least we have exhausted all the resources at our disposal. We did the very best we could do. What's so wrong about that?"

"As I said before, it's the principle of the thing that bothers me. It's just my way. I would like to look at this on the positive side. Let's say the problem is solved, what kind of a life will you and Jay then have?"

Lauren took her time before answering. "In all honesty, I can't really say for sure. I didn't grow up in a home where there was chaos all the time. I have learned some things about Jay and myself that I did not know before or failed to recognize. I had never even thought of the possibility of someone like you coming into my life. Naturally, I worry about the children. I don't know. We'll have to wait and see."

"I shouldn't say this, Lauren, but I hope I won't have to wait very long."

Lauren beamed. "You're so sweet, Graham. I don't know what I would have done without you." She then gently kissed him on the cheek.

"Better be careful," Graham warned. "There are a lot of prying eyes on this boat."

"None more prying than mine," she returned.

****

"Did you get the $10,000 I wired last Friday?"

"Yes, I did, thank you. But now I'm going to need another $25,000."

"Another $25,000? Jesus, that's worse than a contractor, but at least I already know he's going to fuck me over," Tony Romano said dryly.

"Well, Tony, with a contractor, you can get yourself into a real mess," Criminal Defense Attorney Jim Moran said smartly. "I'm trying to get you out of one. I told you to keep your mouth shut, and you went against my advice. All you've done is make it a lot more difficult for me to help you. So what happened today to make things any different from the other day?"

"For starters, these two detectives from the State Police showed up and made all sorts of allegations. They said they are ready to indict me for murdering my best friend, Dazzie. They threatened me with the IRS, if I don't cooperate with them. And they said some things about my mother that really pissed me off."

"Your mother? How did she get mixed up in this?"

"She's not. What's wrong with you? They're saying that they know she's dying, and they're telling me I'm never going to see her again because they're going to put me away."

"Whoa. Whoa. Wait a minute. I'm not following you at all. Why don't you back up and start from the beginning. This IRS thing. Where's that coming from? This is a homicide investigation, not a white collar crime."

"Yeah. Right. You know, I thought I would show good faith with them and cooperate because I am absolutely not involved with this murder. I even tell them I have no alibi. I figure I have nothing to worry about because there's no way they can connect me. I simply didn't do it. Then they start asking around, and they find out some things about my past. Shit I was involved in about ten years ago."

"No alibi," Jim Moran said, looking down at the floor and shaking his head. Looking up, he asked, "Were you ever charged for this stuff in the past?"

"No. I wasn't. No one was. No one even knew."

"So, the statute of limitations is up. Even if you told them now, there probably isn't much they could do about it. Drugs would be an iffy. So how is that a problem?"

"How is it a problem? They are saying that the IRS would like to know about my activities back then. They can sick the IRS on me, you know, send out an army to find an extra ten cents I didn't report or some goddamn thing."

"So, either you cooperate or you get audited? Is that what they are threatening?"

"Something like that."

"And?"

"And, I could have some problems there because of that thing I told you I did in the past."

"Ok, you get audited, some things turn up and you're fined and penalized. You hire attorneys and accountants to help you straighten it out and get the best deal. It's not a happy thought, but a man in your financial position certainly can handle it. We're talking about money here, Tony, not your freedom. Let's keep things in perspective."

"I don't want to lose everything I have spent my entire life working for."

"I don't see how you're going to lose everything, Tony. You'll lose some, maybe even a lot, but not everything."

"There's more to it than that. They made some threats about a truck that was stolen off my property and covered by an insurance claim. They're talking insurance fraud."

"Can they prove it?"

Romano said nothing. "Tony, I'm your lawyer. Can they prove it?"

"If they talked to the right people they could."

"And, one of those people isn't talking anymore, right?"

"Right."

"And the guy who can't talk anymore knew the guy who can?"

"That's about the size of it."

"And the guy who can does nothing unless you do something, right?"

"Right. And I was planning on doing nothing, so he's got no gripe with me."

"Ok. I'm with you so far. We've got a fight on our hands, but we've also got some wiggle room."

"That's what I've been thinking all along. I know for a fact that my lobster boat and car show up nothing because I'm not involved. My car, well, maybe, but I don't think it's a problem either because I gave Dazzie plenty of rides. You know, I helped him get to work. No way they find Sanderson in the car or on the boat."

"Understood. But you're still worried about Sanderson, the guy who could talk, right?"

"Yeah. I am, even though I had nothing to do with him. The license plates on the body were meant as a message, and I'm thinking to me."

"True, but they also could have been for someone else, no? Maybe Dazzie had help, and that's who the message is for."

"There's some possibility there, although I hadn't thought of it until just now. See, the point is, I didn't want the murder solved because I didn't want Sanderson to be drawn in because he knows so much about me."

"If he thinks it's his ass or mine, you know whose ass he's going to grab. He thinks he can pin the tail on the donkey. You know, he goes down, and I go down with him. That's what I was thinking."

"Maybe not. He only takes you down if he thinks you deserved the message."

"Yes, he does, no matter what, even though I didn't do the murder. I wasn't even there, and I didn't know it was going to happen. I get involved in a fraud, and the franchiser seizes the business. Forget a murder. So, the way it plays out, I can lose the business, all my real estate investments, stocks, house, everything. Someone's already taken some of my money."

"So, the bottom line is, if you give them what they want, which is the perpetrator, you lose everything, but you're still on the street. They're playing very, very tough with you. What's this thing about missing money? What money?"

"Another problem. You want to hear about it?"

"If you think it matters, why not? I'm your attorney, Tony, not your priest."

"I had a little thing going at work where I would salt away some money. I found you could move money around, if you were real careful, and then take it out as cash. You had to be smart about it, not obvious, because the banks routinely monitor checking accounts for any irregularities, so I am told. Everything was done electronically."

"Ok. I'm getting it. So what happened?"

"So, today, I needed some extra cash to help out Dazzie's mother and father. They don't have much, and I figure they're in the hole for the funeral. I go to the bank to cash a check drawn on my account there, and I'm told I don't have enough money to cover it."

"Then what?"

"I figure with the death of my friend and the news about my mother – she has a terminal illness, which is another thing I find out the same day Dazzie's found – and the police dropping in that I had the wrong account. Later today, I check the account, and I can't get into it because my password's wrong."

"Your password's wrong?"

"Yeah. My fucking password. So I immediately go to a couple of banks on the way to work, talk to the managers, and ask them to check the balance. I'm not about to say anything about the password to them. It's the same story. Minimum balance."

"Then, when I get to work, these two guys from the State Police show up again, doing their thing, and tell me someone's stealing from my business along with everything else."

"In addition to your salt fund?"

"No, they're playing like, hey, Tony, we know the deal. You've been stealing from yourself and paying off your mother's doc with the money, treating him like he's a contractor. That's what you do, right? You know what I'm saying? For something that's not covered. Like, a side job under the table. I'm telling you on her future grave, God forgive me, that there's no way I'm paying him anything. I'd have no reason. My mother's on Medicare, and I have my own insurance."

"Alright. These transfers, when did they take place?"

"You know right before I called you? Well, I get back on the computer at work, try the password, and I get in. I can't believe it, so I start checking on the accounts, and it's all the same. Somewhere around $60,000 is gone, and it's all gone to the doc."

"All today? All the money was transferred today?"

"No. That's the thing. It's been going on for awhile, since this past January."

"And he never called you to tell you about it? And you never picked up the error?"

"No, he never called or mentioned it, and I've seen him several times over the last few months. I don't get it."

"Neither do I. How come you didn't pick it up sooner?"

"It's like this. What's the point of balancing all those accounts if I'm going to empty them out, a different one every month? It would be a waste of time. I knew what I had. The older the account, the more money it would have in it. That way, I wouldn't have to remember everything. I could do everything on line."

Jim Moran was perplexed. "Tony, I've heard a few strange tales in my day, but this is one of the weirdest. About the only thing I can think of is that somebody at work did it, someone you really pissed off. I don't know how, and I don't know why, but it's about the only thing I can come up with."

"I got an idea who could have done it. We had this real problem with the computer system, which is how the truck came about in the first place, and orders and inventory were getting fucked up. I went ballistic and demanded that the manufacturer fix it or else.

"So they do. They send a real hotshot, and he wants to blame me for the problem. Says security's all fucked up, changes the passwords, and makes me assign computer duties to one of my people. So for the whole time he was there, I let him know how pissed I was. I really busted his balls. He was a fucking nerd, anyway. So, I figure he saw something and took his shot."

"Setting that aside for the moment, Tony, the larger problem you have," Moran said, "is with an indictment. They probably have already issued a warrant to search your business records and bank accounts. You can bet that they won't be secretive about it, either. They are right about one thing, you'll be getting a lot of attention."

"So what do I do? As I said, I don't want to lose everything. I don't want to hurt the business. I got some good people working there. Obviously, someone's setting me up. Even an idiot can see that. What are my options?"

"You know, Tony," Moran replied, "I heard a guy say once that when you have a man by the balls his mind and heart will soon follow. These people are real nutcrackers, and you're in the proverbial rock and a hard place. Let me play out a few scenarios for you. You want a coffee or something to drink?"

Before continuing with the discussion, the two men took a break. Moran made a phone call, and Tony went to the men's room. When he returned, he looked like a man who was about ready to cry.

"Alright, Jim, alright. Why don't you just lay it all out for me, and I can decide. Like I said, what are my options?"

Jim Moran studied his client, shifted in his chair, and then laid out the options. "If you get indicted for the murder, it could be as the principal or an accessory. You have money missing from the business and potential insurance fraud, but only if they can turn Sanderson. I think you have a fifty-fifty chance of beating the murder rap, but you never know what a jury might be thinking. At minimum, Tony, you're going to lose the business and, most likely, all your assets. The IRS will become your partner for life. Of course, you could still lose your freedom along with everything else. I say we go for blanket immunity, assuming, of course, that you have something substantial to give them. Do you?"

"Yeah, I got something substantial."

"Great. What is it?"

"I know who committed the crime. I saw him at the scene."

"You were at the scene of the crime, Tony? That's a different story. It makes you an accessory. I thought you said you had nothing to do with it."

Romano then explained to his lawyer that he did not witness the murder, that he probably arrived there either just before or after it happened. As he had told the police, he was at the Clarke residence, had rung the bell, found no one home, but then left.

Tony did not see Dazzie's Harley that night, which would have been parked near the front door, assumed he was gone, and then left himself. As he was leaving, he saw a dark truck parked at the corner, and two men were sitting in it. He thought it was strange and doubled back.

He then saw the truck backing into Dazzie's driveway, lights out, and recognized Al Sanderson when the light inside the cab turned on as he open the door, thus revealing the faces of the two occupants.

"So you're a witness that Sanderson was there. Why did you leave, Tony?" Jim Moran asked.

"I left because I didn't want to have anything to do with Sanderson. That part of my life was over, and he had been pressuring me for a couple of years to do some more deals, especially construction equipment. I had told him I was no longer interested but that Dazzie might be."

"So Dazzie took over the business?"

"Right. Dazzie never said nothing to me, but he must have known I was getting a much bigger payday than he did back around ten years ago. He wanted in on the action, the big time, I guess, and went for it."

"I think the key here is the second guy in the truck. Did you recognize him, too?"

"Yeah, I know who he is and that he worked for Sanderson. I'd say he's been with him for a very long time."

"I think we've got something, Tony. The police suspect Sanderson and probably are looking for an accomplice. They may figure it's you. No one's going to be surprised to find your fingerprints at the crime scene because they are probably all over the house, too. Plus, fingerprints don't tell you when you were there, just that you were. No, this is good. Now they know to look for someone else, and you can point them in the right direction. Let's hope the trace evidence turns up something. They will probably try to get the driver to turn, too."

"So what do we do now?"

"We go to the District Attorney's Office and make our best deal. I'll be looking for blanket immunity because, in the event you testify against Sanderson, you can spill your guts out, and it's all covered. That way, they won't be coming back after you later with more charges.

"They may be able to help you with the Massachusetts Department of Revenue, but you may still have to worry about the Feds. My advice is that you make the deal to save your freedom."

"What about my mother?"

"You know, Tony, sometimes mothers know a lot more than we give them credit for. You're her son, and she is still going to love you no matter what. You don't have to get into all the details with her.

"You tell her you made a terrible mistake but did your best to correct it by helping solve the murder of your friend. That's what I would go with, if I were you. In the end, you did the right thing, and that's what a mother will want to remember."

Jim could see that Tony was on the verge of tears. "You know, Tony, I think we could have weathered the murder and maybe done something with the IRS. But the stealing from yourself thing, well, that's what brings the whole house of cards down. That's what makes it a double whammy because the franchiser doesn't need a trial to take away your business. That's what you were trying to prevent is the way I see it."

Chapter 17

It was dark now along Nantasket Beach, but people were still walking the beach, some couples, some alone. "I wouldn't mind a nice walk along the beach," Darlene Coakley said as she walked towards a waterfront condominium. "I can't imagine what it must be like to live on the water."

When she and her partner, Kent Costigan, knocked on the door, they did not have to wait long for an answer. Rebecca opened it and recognized the pair immediately. They had been at Dr. Pierce's office earlier that same day. The detectives formally introduced themselves and the purpose of their visit.

Although the fear and confusion on Rebecca's face was clearly visible, she graciously let them into her apartment and asked if there was anything she could get them. Costigan accepted a glass of cold water with ice and began the interview.

The three of them were sitting in the living room from which the view of the ocean was spectacular. "You probably don't understand why we are here, Mrs. Solberg, but our investigation into the murder of Dazzie Clarke has had, like most cases do, a lot of twists and turns."

"I understand," Rebecca said, "but I really don't know what I can do to help you. I barely knew Dazzie Clarke, other than he and Tony Romano – whom I have known all my life – were best friends. Beyond that, there's not much I can say."

"We would like to ask you some questions about Tony Romano and Dr. Pierce," Costigan said. "We know his mother's being treated by the doctor, and we know that Tony and his father also see him at various times. We do not want you to violate any doctor – patient relationship that also applies to you as an employee of Dr. Pierce."

"I see. As long as I can tell you without breaching that confidentiality, I would be willing to answer any questions you might have."

"Thank you, Mrs. Solberg," Darlene said. "Can you tell us who in the office handles your record keeping?"

"You mean medical records?"

"No. I'm sorry. I should have been more specific. I meant the books. Who does the bookkeeping?"

"That's easy. I do. It's one of many things I do for the doctor."

"Fine. Is the bookkeeping done on a computer?"

"Yes, of course. We use a common accounting package adapted to a medical practice. It's quite easy to use and very flexible."

"Do you, does Dr. Pierce allow you to see everything in the accounting package? Are you, for example, restricted from seeing the balance sheets or profit and loss statements?"

"Oh no. Absolutely not. He trusts me completely and lets me do whatever I need on the system. He's like most doctors in that he hates doing the bookwork. I handle everything for him."

"So you know how much money is in the checking account, what's payable, who owes, and so forth?"

"Yes. Yes, I do."

"Ok. So at the end of each quarter, you could give the doctor reports on payroll for DET, DOR, and the IRS, yes?"

"Yes, and any other reports he might ask for, you know, receivables from Medicare, insurance companies and such. I would send the payroll reports to Dr. Pierce's accountant."

"And, presumably, you would reconcile the accounting system with the bank statements, would you not?"

"This will probably surprise you. That's the one thing Dr. Pierce likes to do himself. I have worked for many doctors over the years, and they were the same way. For some strange reason, they like to balance the checkbook themselves."

"Really? Do you know how he does that?"

"Yes. He set up a spreadsheet to balance the bank statement. Then he checks with the accounting system to see what the difference is. For the most part, all I do is subtract the bank fees or chase down a deposit slip to confirm the amounts. I keep telling him that he has better cash flow than he thinks, but he just shrugs or smiles at me."

"Is it reasonable to assume," Costigan said, "that you would know the status of the checking account at all times?"

"It's reasonable, but not right. Dr. Pierce has a bad habit I can't get him to break, and it's waiting until the end of the quarter to balance his checkbook. I get after him, of course, but it does not seem to matter."

Costigan and Coakley looked at each other. "Don't seem so surprised," Rebecca said. "That, too, happens all the time."

"Mrs. Solberg, would you know about any deposits that were made electronically," Darlene asked.

"If Dr. Clarke told me about them I would. Sure. We don't have that many, and, once again, that's something that he's not too good about. He gets so wrapped up in his work that he can easily forget about everything else. Doctors are not the best businessmen in the world, and all of them really, really hate paper work because there's so much of it."

"So, they put it off?"

"Right. Exactly. They put it off. And then he's under pressure to get it done."

"Would you know whether or not Tony Romano electronically deposited large sums of money into Dr. Pierce's account?"

"I can't imagine why he would, but, yes, if Dr. Pierce told me so."

"And Dr. Pierce never has, is that right?"

"Yes, that's right."

"Do you have – or have you had – any questions about the way Dr. Pierce handles the business side of his practice? Anything that seemed irregular or suspicious?"

Rebecca froze and seemed dazed by the question. Darlene noticed her reaction and gently said, "Mrs. Solberg, we're not accusing him of anything, but we are investigating a murder case. If there's anything that you can tell us, anything that seemed a little out of the ordinary, then I wish you would tell us now."

Costigan and Coakley waited what seemed like an eternity before Rebecca answered. "I don't know what to say. I really don't know how to answer the question."

Darlene gently pressed. "Mrs. Solberg, if there's anything that you know that will help us, please tell us. I can understand that this may be difficult for you, but it could get much more difficult later if certain things come out. We're trying to get to the bottom of something, and we're asking for your help."

Rebecca shook her head slowly back and forth. "There was something I overheard Dr. Pierce telling his wife a few months after I started working there. He's very angry about the condition of medicine today, especially HMO's, insurance companies, and government regulations."

"Did you ever talk to him about what you overheard?"

"No. There really wasn't any way I could."

"Ok. Was there something he said or did?"

"Well, he. Listen, I don't want to cause anyone any trouble here. Is this really necessary?"

"If it wasn't necessary, Mrs. Solberg, we wouldn't be asking. You started to tell us he said something. Can you tell us what it was?"

"I really don't like this, and it was just something I overhead."

Coakley and Costigan waited and said nothing.

"He said something about how unfair Medicare is to the doctor and that he should take matters into his own hands, just like a lot of doctors do. He made it seem like he would be getting back what Medicare was taking away anyway. He said it would be the right thing to do, that it was a matter of principle."

"Fine. Understood. As a result of what he said, do you know if he did anything?"

"I am really, really ashamed to tell you this, but, no, as best as I could determine he did nothing of the kind. I got really worried at the time and did something terribly foolish. I was trying to look out for him. I finally concluded that it was all about nothing and gave up looking."

"What did you do?" Costigan asked.

Rebecca rolled her eyes and was very reluctant to continue. "I started keeping two sets of books. One to track what I knew was going on and the other what I suspected. There were a few irregularities, tests, extra appointments in the office, but nothing all that significant. I got rid of the second set today."

"Today? You got rid of the second set of books today? Well, that doesn't look very good. When today did you do it?"

"A short time after I got to work. It was on a separate drive, and I just deleted the file."

"Is the disk still at the office?"

"Yes."

"Ok. No problem. We can probably recover the file with a utility."

"If you need the file, I have a copy of it," Rebecca volunteered, now half frightened out of her wits. "I e-mailed it to myself from the office to my home computer and then back. I sometimes would do the bookkeeping here instead of going into the office. Usually over the weekend. I have both sets."

"Would you be willing to give us copies of the files?" She would, and from that moment on, Rebecca could only hope and pray that none of it would mean anything and that Dr. Pierce would never find out.

****

Rumors were swirling the next morning that there had been a major break in the Clarke case. To prevent the press from picking up the scent, especially because the chief suspect was still out of the country, Symolon and McCarthy called a meeting of the investigative team at eight in the morning to give everyone a heads up.

"You probably have heard some rumors about the Clarke homicide, and I do want to be the first to tell you that we have had a major break in the case," McCarthy said. "Mr. Romano came forward last night with his attorney and provided the District Attorney's office with information that implicates Al Sanderson and another individual in the death of Mr. Clarke. The District Attorney's Office intends to grant Mr. Romano blanket immunity in exchange for his testimony. They believe, after all, that he was not involved.

"Wes and I intend to interview Mr. Romano sometime this morning, and we'll get back to you with what we have learned. For the moment, that's all I have, other than to let you know that all of you did an excellent job in solving this case, and we're all very grateful. You should be proud of yourselves."

"Dick, when you do meet with him," Kent Costigan said, "will you ask him about the money transfer? That thing's driving me nuts. He's got his blanket immunity, so I can't see what the problem would be."

"Sure, I will, Kent. You still stuck on this invisible hand theory? Last time I heard, Romano says he didn't do it."

"He can say what he wants, Dick, but his home phone records say that he did."

****

It was a quiet, intimate, little Italian restaurant in the North End of Boston, off the beaten track and down by Canal St. near the Fleet Center. Graham Barrows was waiting there to meet Lauren Parker at the end of a very long and difficult week for him. He was turning the glass containing his traditional drink, a scotch and soda, and sitting at a table for two by the window fronting the street.

Graham spotted Lauren as she came into the restaurant and stood to greet her. The two embraced, and then Lauren took off her coat and hung it on a nearby hook. "You look smashing," Graham said while seating her. "Positively radiant. Sorry I haven't seen you on the boat much this week."

"You look pretty smashing yourself. Very gallant. I like the tie. Very colorful, but very non-British," she said.

"Would you care for a drink?" Graham asked her.

"I most certainly would. A nice, dry red wine sounds good."

Barrows got the attention of the waiter and ordered for Lauren her glass of cabernet sauvignon. As soon as it came to the table, he raised his glass to hers and said, "Cheers."

Lauren smiled at him as she usually did and put the glass to her lips. "Very nice," she said. "Very nice, indeed."

"Are you ready to order?" Graham asked, handing her a menu. "The crab cakes here are exceptional. Would you care to try a side order?"

"A side order? Ah, yes, a side order," she said. "Why not?"

"Aren't we being playful tonight," Barrows observed. "All is well, I trust?"

"It is now, Graham. What will you be having?"

"I'm not sure. The selection here is quite good. I'm inclined towards the chicken marsala. How about you?"

As the waiter prepared the table, filled the glasses with water, and served the bread, Graham and Lauren passed the time in gentle conversation. The small restaurant was full, but they felt as though they were the only couple in it. Operatic music played softly in the background, and a small candle flickered on the table set with white linen.

Since everything was cooked to order, Graham and Lauren knew they would have a long wait before they dined. They were holding hands across the table, and the waiter would see to it that their glasses were always kept full.

"So, what's this good news you have for me, Graham? You were so cryptic over the phone. Do we have a solution to the problem?"

"Which problem, Lauren?"

She smiled. "You know the one. Come on. Don't tease me, now."

"You're right, I do know the one, Lauren. The salami thing. First things first. I am returning your disk. I hope something like this never comes between us again."

"You're not alone on that, Graham. I have felt awful about it all week long. Awful and nervous. Did you find anything?"

"Lauren, what I am going to tell you is the literal truth. I remembered what you said last week about lying to Jay, so I am going to tell you something that you can and should absolutely believe in. You won't be lying to him."

"God, Graham, you drive me crazy when you're like this. You're so serious. Lighten up. We're not sitting in a den of spies, you know," Lauren said laughing.

"Lauren, this is a serious matter. So listen very carefully to what I am telling you. I know what is going on, and I have finally done something about it. You can tell Jay that his problem is over."

"It is? Oh, God, Graham, I could kiss you! How did you find out? What did you do to fix it?"

"I have to be careful with what I tell you. Remember, you're not supposed to know how this application works. You told me so when we met the first time."

"That's true, and you've never asked me anything about it since."

THE INDEPENDENT CONTRACTOR

"Do we understand each other?"

"I think we do," Lauren said almost wanting to laugh.

"I know Jay's becoming interested in the history of World War II. We discussed the Enigma Machine and encryption when we met that time at the restaurant. When he asks you, I want you to tell him the solution to the problem is simple and based on a little known fact about Nazi intelligence gathering operations during the war."

"Ok. Then what?"

"No. No. I haven't told you. Here's what I want you to say. Tell him that the Germans had an absolutely foolproof method to determine the identity of an agent sending Morse code. Tell him that the person on the receiving end recognized a subtle pattern from the sender, something like his fingerprints in sound, only better. They recognized his habits in the way the message was sent."

"Is this true?"

"Every word of it. Tell him the identity of anyone using a computer can be falsified. The one thing you can't fake is your habits because you are not always aware of them. So here's what you say. The solution is to recognize the person's habits, not a password. There is no security at the door because everyone gets in.

"Once there, the system analyzes your habits, how quickly you type, what characters you hit incorrectly more than once or twice, the applications you open and in what sequence, how long and when you use them. The computer knows more about you than you know about yourself. One character alone tells the computer something!"

Graham stopped his explanation to make sure that Lauren was following him. Satisfied that she was, he continued. "It's not very different from what happens when you go to a WEB site to buy something. The site sets what is called, cookies, to develop information about your shopping habits and interests. It's how the advertisers target you as a customer. They have a profile on you."

"Is that why I suddenly get catalogues about products from stores I have never been to?" Lauren asked.

"Yes, in part, I'm sure. Someone is watching you and gathering a lot of information about who you are and what you do."

Barrows continued. "This system develops and maintains a profile of your work habits. If you do something that is not in the profile, you can't get out. You're trapped! The only way into the system is through the front door. There is no key. The problem is in getting out."

"Well, I have to admit, this is pretty fascinating. Ingenious really. But, you're not telling me everything, are you?"

"No. I'm not, for obvious reasons. You can fill in between the lines. It is to your advantage not to know everything. If he asks you for more detailed answers, you can truthfully say you don't know. He already thinks I have a conspiratorial side to me."

Lauren laughed. "He does? I'll have to say this much about Jay. He's a pretty sharp observer. I think it's really funny. One thing, though. Is this it? Is this thing ever going to come back?"

"Lauren, I can tell you with certainty that this thing is never coming back. The problem is solved. He does not need to know how. You don't either. Just tell him that the application works. It's really quite amazing."

"I don't know what I can ever do to repay you. Jay's not expecting me home until late, you know. I would love to just linger, you know, walk and talk."

"Then linger, walk, and talk we shall. How do you feel now?"

"I feel like an enormous burden has been lifted from my shoulders. I feel very warm inside. I find that I love being with you."

"That really pleases me, Lauren. And I kept my word."

"Yes, you did, Graham. You most certainly did."

****

The article consisted of a few paragraphs and was buried deep inside the pages of a major Boston newspaper. A prominent doctor from Cohasset was being investigated for Medicare fraud the article indicated. "Unnamed sources" from the Massachusetts Department of Revenue said the inquiry came about as a result of an investigation into the recent homicide of a suspected car thief and drug peddler from Hull.

Although money laundering by the doctor was not suspected, authorities said, "that possibility had not yet been ruled out."

The local papers would follow up the story and try to run with it, but there just wasn't enough proof to connect the dots. It was tantalizing – revered doctor in affluent community leading a double life involving Medicare fraud and money laundering – but speculative.

Dr. Pierce, the innocent, principled man of honor and "highly respected member of the community" had been given a black eye on the first day of spring, 1999.

****

THE INDEPENDENT CONTRACTOR

He walked down the gangplank pleased with himself and relieved that his ship had arrived on time and was now berthed at the Conley Pier in South Boston for unloading and reloading. His import – export business could not have been better, and it was a heady time.

Al Sanderson and his associate, Mike Norris, were not expecting the welcoming party provided by the Massachusetts State Police as swarms of cruisers – sirens blaring, lights flashing, and radios screaming – descended upon the pair and took them into custody for the murder of Dazzie Clarke.

They looked completely surprised, as no advance warning had been given, and the press was not there to record and repackage the historic moment. The authorities then seized the ship and began an exhaustive search, which turned up drugs and other contraband.

The incident sent a shiver down the spines of many people who witnessed it. Uncontrolled and outrageous rumors flared up and down the Port of Boston for the next several days after the arrests. In a few more weeks, everything would quiet down, and it would be back to business as usual.

The cameras were rolling several hours later when the State Police staged Act II at a law firm on State Street. A prominent attorney "with connections to important people in high places" was arrested for money laundering and racketeering. He didn't know what had hit him and had never given so much as a thought to the day almost seven years ago when he accepted from Tony Romano a brown paper bag containing $500,000 in cash.

It was three weeks to the day since Tony Romano had been given his blanket immunity. He had added the attorney as a sweetener in the deal; the "legal community" was duly shocked by the news.

****

Lauren Parker would miss her commuter boat trip into Boston, but she wasn't worried. She was headed for Crow's Point and an impromptu meeting with a very special man.

When she turned into Graham Barrows' driveway, Lauren was happy and full of expectation. It was a magnificent morning in early spring, which in New England is not marked by the calendar. The deep blue water of inner Hingham Harbor was calm and the sky cloudless. In another few weeks, the earth would explode with renewed life, and vibrant – nearly iridescent – color would return to the drab landscape.

"Good morning, Lauren. Sad to say it's been awhile. How are you?"

"I'm fine," she answered. "It's good to see you again, Kevin. Where's Graham?"

Sweeney looked at Lauren, but said nothing. He grimly stepped aside to let her see the House For Sale sign that had been hung on a post near the driveway.

"What's this, Kevin? What's going on?"

"I'm sorry, Lauren. I'm really sorry," Kevin said. "This is all my fault. I am so sorry."

"Sorry? What are you talking about, Kevin? Sorry for what?"

"He's gone, Lauren. Graham's gone. All the furniture inside the house is gone, Lauren. He's just up and disappeared. I never should have told him about you."

It suddenly hit her, and it wasn't pretty. Lauren was first seized by fear then rage. The expression on her face was wild. She clenched her fists, crossed her arms across her body, bent at the waist, and alternated between screaming and sobbing.

"No! No! No, Kevin. No! He wouldn't do this to me. He couldn't," she said hysterically. "He loved me. I know it. I just know it."

Kevin immediately went to Lauren and crouched down to hold and comfort her. The enormity of Graham's betrayal fell upon both of them, and each was grief stricken and outraged. Neither had seen it coming. Kevin helped Lauren to her feet and held her for several very long minutes until she calmed down.

"When did you know?" she asked Kevin, as he gently stroked her back.

"Yesterday, when I drove down to look at my project on the other side of that hill over there," Kevin said. "I never drive this far because I take a side street that is more direct. It was a beautiful morning, so I decided to drive around. I saw the moving van, asked around, tried calling Graham, even sent him an e-mail, which he didn't answer. That's when I knew."

"Do you know what he's done to me, Kevin? Do you know?" Lauren asked as she began to sob again. Kevin just held her and rocked back and forth. "It's all my fault, Lauren. It's all my fault," Kevin said again.

Both of Lauren's hands were tucked under her chin, and Kevin just held her, until her whimpering and shaking became less and less noticeable. "Are you going to be alright?" he asked Lauren, lightly loosening his hold on her.

She seemed to say nothing for a very long time. "I don't believe it," Lauren said. "I just don't believe he could have done this to me."

"Is there some way I can help you? Is there something I can do? Would you like to get a coffee or something?" Kevin asked, trying to find something – anything – to relieve her anguish.

He felt her go limp in his arms. "Come on," Sweeney said. "Let's just go for a short ride in my car, and maybe we can talk. I don't know what I can do, and I'm feeling a little helpless here. Why don't we just do that?"

"Ok," she said softly. "I must look awful."

"No. No, Lauren, you don't. You always look lovely. Really."

She didn't. Her eyes were red and swollen, and her makeup had run down her face. She walked slowly to her Land Rover, retrieved her handbag, and came back to where Kevin was standing.

He then helped her into his car, backed down the driveway, and headed off to nowhere in particular.

"Did he tell you that he refused to make love to me, Kevin? Did he tell you that?"

"Lauren, really," Kevin protested. "That's none of my business. That's really not something you should be telling me."

"And each time he turned me down, I wanted him more. That's how he did it, Kevin. He let me in just enough and kept me there. Just like he said, once I was in, I couldn't get out. I was in too deep. That was the system that worked so well."

Kevin was uncomfortable. "Lauren, what went on between you and Graham is your business. If talking helps, I'll listen, but I would really rather not know. It's too private and personal."

"Let me ask you this, Kevin. A woman meets a man who is handsome, cultured, charming, funny, intelligent, and very worldly. He knows how to talk to her, what to say, how to say it. He knows all the little, silly things she likes or dislikes. He listens to her, encourages her, supports her, and is there when she needs him. What kind of a man would you say he is?"

"Well, I would say that he's a man who knows how to treat a woman and make her feel special, very much like a lady."

"Right. And what if that same man won't let the woman do anything that he thinks is not good or right for her?"

"I would say he is very protective of her and really cares about the woman."

"Would you say he loves her?"

"I don't know if I would go that far, Lauren, but I would think that it was possible, especially if he was also kind and considerate."

"Alright. I understand. Do you think that this woman would trust him, even though he flirts with her and she with him?"

"Well, sure. I think she would most definitely trust him. No question, especially if the flirting is harmless."

"You may not realize it, Kevin, but you just confirmed everything I felt and believed about Graham. Do you have any idea how a woman is going to react to a man to whom she's very attracted – and she knows he's attracted to her – but he's not going to let it get out of hand for her sake, not his own?"

"She's probably going to think that he's unselfish and really, really cares about her. She's probably going to trust him completely."

"Which is exactly what I did, Kevin. I gave him the proprietary software to my company. I pressured him into taking it. I even went so far as to tell him to trust me that I knew what I was doing and that he was helping me. Can you believe it? Trust me?"

"I don't know what to say."

"Jay was never the target, Kevin. I was. There never was any salami programming scheme or needle in a haystack. Graham was after that software all along, but he needed to convince me that he wasn't. So he waited, and waited some more, and played me like a virtuoso. Everything he told me was literally true. He didn't try to talk me into anything. He got me to do it to myself.

"And the more he warned me about the danger of handing over the software, the more I trusted him. He put it right in my face, even hinted that I was placing our relationship at risk.

"It was all a very, very clever game, Kevin, and I feel like such a total idiot that I don't know how I'll ever be able to live with myself after this. The literal truth was, literally, nothing but an elaborate deception. I was completely fooled, and I feel violated. Was his wife in on it, too?"

"No, Lauren, of that much I'm sure. Doubtless, she saw in him things you and I did not. I got to know her pretty well when I was doing the remodeling, and I sensed the tension every now and then. It was nothing obvious, you know, under the surface. Normal is what I thought. Remodeling has a way of bringing out either the best or worst in people, and seldom is it in between. I've always maintained that it's about relationships, not construction."

"You know, Kevin, I never even thought to ask you. How are you with all of this?"

"I'm devastated, Lauren. I don't deal well with people who turn their backs on me or use me. It's the main reason, I think, why I take such a long time to develop friends and can never say, 'Goodbye.' In my business, you really get to know the clients and subs, and I always wind up liking them. Well, not all of them. It really hurts."

"I wonder where he is, Kevin, what he's doing. How does he look himself in the mirror? Why do you think he did it?"

Kevin blew his breath out. "Greed, Lauren. Greed. What else could it be? He stands to make a fortune, if that's what he was after."

"I can't go into work today. I don't know how I can face the owners. I've betrayed them, too, you know. I'm no better than Graham."

"Lauren, I always try to see the silver lining in the dark cloud. Most people think that I'm one of those naïve optimists, that I have no idea about the real world. All you know at this point is that Graham is gone. You don't know for a fact that he stole your company's secrets. I think that what we both do from here on in is believe in the doubt. At least we'll have hope that way and can get on with our lives."

"Believe in the doubt? I don't know if I can do that. You are naïve, Kevin, but I always loved that boyish innocence about you. It's part of your charm, what makes you the sweet and gentle man that you are."

"Lauren, would you mind it very much if I called on you sometime in the near future? I'm really worried about you and how you're feeling at the moment. It would really help me if I knew you were alright."

"Sure, Kevin. I won't mind. You were always great to talk to. You don't have to worry about Jay. He told me you and he talked around Christmas. The ferry was a great idea, Kevin. Too bad it will never get built."

"Never get built? Why not, Lauren?"

"Because Jay and I are separating, Kevin."

Sweeney looked as though he had been shot through the heart. "Don't worry, Kevin. It may be the best thing for the whole family in the long run. It's a long story, but once I told him that the problems he was having in work were over and what I had done to help him, he became very angry and upset."

"Angry and upset? Are you serious? Didn't he believe you?"

"He believed me alright. Graham had seen to that. A couple of days before I gave the software to Graham, I told Jay that I knew about a relationship he was having with a woman at work.

"He turned on me and said it was nothing, that he and this woman had really done nothing but talk dirty online. Then he asked me if it was something I would hang over his head for the rest of his life.

"I never told Jay about my involvement with Graham, so I was feeling guilty myself. I said I forgave him, but he didn't believe me.

"I asked him to go to counseling, but Jay thinks psychologists are mind Nazis. He said that he didn't think that he could live his life and be married at the same time to a woman whose shoulders he was standing on. Jay blamed all his success at work on me. Imagine. He blames me for his success.

"I had saved him one more time, he said, and he just didn't think he could take it anymore. I thought I was helping him and maybe our marriage by doing what I did. I thought it proved I had forgiven him," Lauren finally concluded.

Kevin just stared straight ahead. His desultory ride had just taken them past the intersection off Route 3A to World's End in Hingham.

Chapter 18

It was the second time in nearly eight weeks that two strangers drove up Kevin Sweeney's long driveway early in the morning, only it wasn't a Saturday, and he and Marie were not having their traditional breakfast. Marie was not even home.

Sweeney was in the Bunker Office waiting but had kept the door open to hear the bell ring. When it did, he anxiously raced up the stairs to answer it and saw through the sidelight of the front door a man and woman standing outside.

Immediately Kevin opened the door and nervously greeted them even though he had never met either one previously. He recognized the voice of the man because he had spoken to the agent over the phone once before. The introductions were quick, and Kevin knew why they had come to see him.

Kevin led them down the hall and showed them the door to his basement office. The agents went before him, and Sweeney warned them about the last step, which was difficult to maneuver. "Be careful, or you'll bang your heads on the ceiling," he said.

Standing with her associate in the room where Kevin kept all his books, the female agent broke the ice by saying how beautiful everything looked. "You can really smell the pine. I love that smell," she said. Kevin stood there for a moment and looked around at everything, especially all the framed articles about his company that were hanging on the walls.

He was overcome with sadness because he knew then and there that it might all be coming to an end. This business for which he harbored a love – hate relationship, the crowning jewel of his professional life, the main recipient of all his attention, creativity, energy, and time, but not the dazzling financial success he had hoped for could soon be gathering dust.

In a second room, which was under the kitchen on the first floor, Kevin introduced the agents to Criminal Defense Attorney Jim Morris and his associate, Bob MacPherson. The four exchanged professional pleasantries then sat down around the conference table.

"Jim, I sent you all the paperwork," Neal Doherty, the agent, began. "Is everything in order?"

"Yes, it is Neal. I've gone over everything with my associate and Mr. Sweeney here, and I think we have a workable agreement. Incidentally, I want to thank you and Dusty for meeting us here. I know it's very unusual, that you like to do everything downtown."

"No problem. Great," Dusty Rose said. "Why don't we get everything all signed then and get started?"

"That's quite a name you have there, Dusty," MacPherson said. "Were you named after a color or a plant?"

Everyone laughed. "I think my father called me Dusty. My real name is Cynthia, but Cindy didn't seem to work as well as Dusty, so it stuck."

Turning to Sweeney, Doherty said, "Kevin. Understandably we have a lot of questions for you, and I thought I could begin the meeting by telling you, firstly, that we have done our homework and been very thorough about it, as you might expect.

"This is very complicated, and we need to get a better handle on it. If Jim and Bob have no objections, I would like to just fire away and, Dusty, you can jump in whenever you want to."

"Fine with me," she said.

Morris also responded to the suggestion. "I have no objections, unless you do Bob."

"None here," MacPherson said.

"Ok. Then we all agree," Doherty said. "Kevin, do you have a copier?"

"Yes, I do. It's right over there in my office. How many do you want? While I'm up, does anyone want any coffee?" A few people said they would.

"A couple will be fine," Neal said. "You can keep one for your records and Jim's."

After the signed copies were made and given to the appropriate parties and the coffee served, Doherty started the interview. "Kevin, we seem to have a number of people – Tony Romano, Dr. Adam Pierce, and the Parkers – and all of them have had something awful happen in their lives recently. Although these people have crossed paths with each other, they really only have one thing in common. They are all former clients of yours."

"That's true, Neal." Kevin said. "They are all former clients of mine."

"As such, Kevin, if you look at the big picture, Romano either has lost or may lose everything but his freedom, Pierce has lost his impeccable reputation, which is to say it's been stained, and Jay Parker may lose his family. Is that how you see it?"

"I don't quite think of it that way, but I can see your point. I see three men who are very wealthy, selfish, self-righteous, and self-centered. One inherited his fortune, one stole it, and another actually worked for his.

"As long as these men get what they want – and are capable of corrupting their intellects sufficiently to do it – they don't care about anything else or whom they hurt. No, the way I see it, justice has been served."

"Really? That's pretty cold, Kevin, and you seem like such a warm and caring guy," Dusty said. "What did these people do to deserve their fate? Their wealth and power? Does the punishment really fit the crime?"

"You can't be serious," Sweeney responded. "Tony Romano is not a nice guy who looks out for his mother and his friends. He's an evil man who took what did not belong to him and then brought drugs into this country. Do you have any idea how corrupting to this society drugs can be? They permeate every level of our society, and I positively hate them. I hate them. I hate what they are doing to this country. They are a plague upon the nation's house." Kevin was getting angry and upset.

"Romano didn't care who he used to get ahead, including his friend who may have died because of him, myself, and a contractor who did him no wrong. Romano got exactly what he deserved, and he did it all to himself."

"Alright. Alright, I get your point, and I partly agree with you," Dusty said. "What about Dr. Pierce? What did he do that was so terrible?"

Kevin sipped on his coffee before answering. "You know, you seem to have a nice job, and I'm sure it provides you with a decent living. Do you have any idea of what it is like to struggle every day or your life? If you don't, I certainly do, and Pierce didn't hesitate to reduce my fee by $3,000 simply because he believed the blasting that had to be done on his addition was not his responsibility. 'I'm not paying for it,' he says. 'This is a surprise, and you know I hate surprises.'

"Well, guess what Doc? Your medical bill would probably surprise a lot of people, too. Welcome to residential remodeling.

"Suddenly he treats me as though I'm the general contractor and should have allowed for it. 'You should have known,' he says, as though he knows everything there is to know about his own practice. Come off it. Everything was black or white with that guy and nothing in between. I wonder what he could tell me about the art of medicine."

Dusty backed off and Doherty took over. "I can understand that you're upset about Romano and Pierce, but what did the Parkers ever do to you?"

"Lauren Parker is a sweetheart, and she never did anything to me. Her husband seemed like a decent guy at first, but he turned out to be an asshole. He arbitrarily decides not to pay one of the contractors because the guy messed up his patio. Lauren had approved the work and knew what the result would be before we started. Everything was in the specifications, just like it was with Pierce.

"The contractor figures he's all set because the wife has told him to go ahead. He does the work and asks to get paid. The husband steps in, does his guy act, and refuses to pay the contractor. He was wrong, dead wrong and puts his wife between himself and the contractor. No guy is going to respect that. About the only nice thing I can say about the husband is that he was great with his kids."

"Speaking of which, Kevin, what did Lauren Parker and her children have to do with this?"

"That's another matter, and something we can get into later," Sweeney answered.

"You're coming across as a bastard, a self-righteous son of a bitch yourself," Doherty responded. "You're no better than the people you pillory."

"I know," Sweeney responded while taking a deep breath. "I had a few things I wanted to protect, too. I got close to the guys and tried to look out for them. They're like a family to me, which is not the way a business is supposed to be run."

"And we can probably guess how you feel about family," Dusty said.

"Right."

"Alright, Kevin, let's get right straight to the point. It's all circumstantial, but you definitely had something to do with what happens to Romano, Parker, and Pierce, didn't you? Isn't that right?"

Sweeney defiantly looked Doherty straight in the eye. "Yes, I did," Kevin said. "There, I said it. That's what you wanted to know, right?"

"That plus one other thing, Kevin. How? How did you do it?"

"How about if we all take a break before I get into it?" Sweeney said. "All this coffee I've been drinking is building up. There's a bathroom right at the top of the stairs on the first floor and another on the second. I think I need to stretch."

The meeting broke up, and Kevin waited before going to the bathroom. "How do you think it's going?" he asked Jim Morris.

"I think it's going pretty good. You're doing a good job. Just try to be clear about everything so that they understand. I'm not worried about how it's going to end at all. Just make your case."

A short time later, everyone reconvened at the table. "Before I tell you exactly how I did it, I would just like to ask a question of my own. Is that alright?"

"Sure," Dusty said. "Go ahead."

"Every person in this room right now thinks that there has been a massive breakdown in security on the Internet, right?"

Everyone nodded in agreement.

"Ok, I just wanted to be sure."

"I don't mean to be teasing you along, but here's what you need to understand. Whenever I go into a house to work with a client, I learn a lot of things about what goes on there. For example, I know when the mailman comes and what he delivers, what birthday or anniversary cards, bills from what stores, and what dividend checks.

"I also know where you keep your spare key, what you had for breakfast, lunch, or dinner, your schedules, the children's, and so on. If you leave your laundry out, Dusty, I'm going to know what bra and panties you wore to work, what they look like, sexy or steel belted radials.

"I'm not intentionally violating your privacy, mind you. You left the dishes in the sink and the laundry on top of the washer. The plumber has work to do in those areas, and all your stuff's hanging around because you were too busy, too tired, or too lazy to do it yourself. You never gave it a thought. We see your tampon wrappers in the wastebasket, and that tells us something, too."

Dusty sat upright in her chair.

"And you're not too careful about your medications because you leave them on the window sill or in the medicine cabinet, which is on a wall we're going take down that day. We work for a lot of doctors and discuss these things with them every now and then. And we remember things about blood thinners, depression, and not being able to get it up."

Neal Doherty shifted in his chair.

"I know what magazines your husband reads, Dusty, while shitting on the toilet. I know your neighbor up the street is retired, and I know he's going to check on the job every day and tell me what he thinks about it. He's going to be a goddamn expert on building. I'm going to know that he's a veteran, living on social security and a small pension, all the jobs he's worked, that he has a son who visits him every now and then, a daughter, too, and grandchildren he's crazy about.

"I'm also going to know his wife died a year ago, and I'm not going to be wondering why he's always dropping in. He's going to tell me his life's story because he has nothing else to do, and he doesn't want his memory to be forgotten. And I'm going to listen, even though I can give him a print out because I have heard that story so many times before. And he's going to love me simply because I'll listen.

"So, you see, there's very little about you I don't know right down to the smallest details, including your pets, because, if I don't discover them on my own in your house, someone else who is lonesome is going to tell me. Then he's going to talk about every single house in the neighborhood, what was done to it, how much people paid, and so on."

Everyone seemed to be sitting upright in the chairs.

"But he's not the only guy I'm going to be listening to. All the subs will be talking to me, too, telling me things about you that they found out, things like how you and your husband get along, who's the top dog, how quick or slow you are to pay. They will be talking to your au pair, house cleaner, and the guys who take care of your landscaping.

"Your hired help identifies with me and the contractors more so than they do you, so they'll tell us even more. Usually, it's just every day stuff, but sometimes they have more to say than you would want. That's when we find out who's moody or has a temper, who's cheap or a spender, what you argue about, you know, things like that."

There was heavy silence in the room.

"The contractors?" Kevin continued. "What about them? Let me tell you. Take Stevie Bear, for example. He's a good-looking guy, Dusty, and you like the attention he is giving you.

"He listens to what you have to say, and he asks for your opinion. So, you spend a little more on the lighting than you had planned. The next day, Stevie picks up on your mood and asks if you got kicked out of the big bed last night. You think he's funny, and he is, so you let down your guard. You have forgotten that he's a very, very good business man and that in the heart of every man lurks a lecher."

Dusty blinked.

"So, I'm telling you what I tell all my clients. Building or remodeling is not just about construction. It's about relationships and decision making, and I get to see it all.

"And it doesn't end there. You leave all your stock and bond certificates on a shelf in the closet, and the electrician has to get a wire up there to the second floor. The damn box falls on the floor, and he has to clean it up, trying to make everything look like it did before. So he notices things and tells me what I already know. You have a lot more money than you are letting on. You don't want me or anyone else to know.

"He or someone else hears the phone ring, and it's recording a message from your mother, sister, friend, doctor, dentist, colleague, attorney, or anyone else. The radio is on, but he still hears the message. He hears the hang ups, too."

Kevin paused. All eyes were on him, so he continued. "Oh, yeah, I almost forgot something else about the home phone. You left out the recording device manual, which can be used to get your remote access code. Someone could listen to all your messages, just like you.

"And your computer? You think that just because it's in your house, it's safe, and you don't need a password to get into it. So you put your life on it, your personal accounting, credit card numbers, pin numbers, personal information managers, bookmarks, and passwords, and you put them in a file so that you won't forget them. Did I mention recipes? You have them there, too. You even asked me to help you set up your system because you know I know something about computers.

"You leave your house in the morning hoping the guys will even show up, and you may even leave them a key to come in the front door. And the guys are always respectful, and you like them. Once the security system is operational after the job is over, you set it and go about your business. Everything inside is secure, but you forget that the person who installed it, my good friend, Stevie Bear, the electrician, knows the security settings or a work around.

"One day you do something I don't like, something for which I have no recourse. So, I make use of what I have at hand, what has been given to me, and I copy all of your software onto the drive of my laptop. I'm not feeling good about what I'm doing, but I don't feel so good about you either. You buy the same software that everyone else does, which makes it easy for me because I don't have to learn a new application. Call it an advantage of standardization."

"Are you saying that you stole PC software from Pierce, Parker, and Romano? You had their software?" Doherty asked.

"Stole? Hmm. That's a harsh word. Let's just say that I kept it until the bill came due. How did I work it out? You took something from me, and I took something from you. Everything is equal."

"And this massive security breakdown on the Internet never happened? It was all in the home?" Dusty asked wide-eyed.

"Yep. It was all in the home. You've been off trying to figure out where the failure happened. You've been looking in the wrong place all along. The breach came in the house. You left the door wide open, and I just came waltzing in. I hammered your privacy, destroyed it."

The two agents stared at Morris and McIntyre. "So now we're adding software theft and invasion of privacy to the list, right?"

Neither said anything and just shrugged.

"What's more, I didn't even have to leave my office to know what was going on."

"What's that again? You didn't have to leave your office? All of this took place right here?" Dusty asked.

"That's right. See that computer sitting right over there on my desk? I used it to see everything Romano, Pierce, or Parker were doing from their computers. Remember what I said about knowing all their personal habits?

"Whenever I called Parker late at night, I knew he was online because the phone was always ringing, and they had call waiting. Lauren wasn't much of a phone person, so I knew it had to be him. I could see every keystroke in real time. I even set up it so that every time he went on the Internet, I would get a file with every keystroke in it. The file would then automatically delete itself from his system so that he would not notice a large decrease in disk space. I didn't want him to notice anything different."

This news was startling to the agents who thought they had heard it all. "So, the real crime here, Kevin, is a computer crime you committed. You were responsible for Parker's credit card problems, the e-mail intercepts, all the problems Romano was having with his computer at work, and the transfer of funds from Romano's into Pierce's account. Is this what you are admitting to?"

"Not quite. If you're talking about the e-mail that Andrea Wilson received from Jay about her transfer, I didn't do it. Jay did. I knew about it, of course, because I checked his SENT mail on Netscape. That's how I knew about what was going on between Jay and Andrea, and Jay and Lauren. I even checked his TRASH folder. I knew Lauren was going to the Museum of Fine Arts the night she did and passed that information along to Graham Barrows."

"Graham Barrows. Why Graham Barrows?" Doherty asked.

"Well, he was in on the caper with me and understood my frustration. When I told Graham that Pierce, Parker, and Romano were beyond my reach because they had the money to exhaust either my or the contractors' resources, he said he didn't think so at all. He's the one who wrote the code I put on all the PC's. It really started out as a lark – Romano was the first one – but things kind of got out of hand."

"What code are you talking about? Didn't they have virus protection?"

"Sure they did, but I disabled it and then installed the code Graham had written. It was an invisible file that could not be opened by any application on the system and would not be seen in any directory. I knew it could be done because the company that Graham and I had worked at did it more than twenty years ago."

"Did what?" Rose asked.

"Networked all the computers together," Kevin explained. "I was in training, and I could watch from my terminal in another room what you were doing on yours. So, in a way, Romano, Parker, and Pierce were sitting on a sub-network they knew nothing about. It was pretty neat."

"Pretty neat! It was pretty neat? Is that all this was to you, Kevin, a neat little game? God! That's terrible. Really terrible," Dusty Rose said. "I'm sure we can get into the technical aspects later, Kevin, but in the meantime, Jay Parker's credit problems. How was that done?" she then asked.

"It was so easy, this will drive you nuts. Remember now, I know all about Tony Romano, when he's home and when he's not, if he's at his parents or walking the beach, if Liz is there with him for the weekend. Naturally, I have a key to the front door. I also know the security system code because Steve, the electrician, installed the unit and helped Romano set it up. No problem so far, only Romano or his fiancé can't remember the number, so they write it down on the inside back cover of the personal phone book, and Steve knows about it."

Dusty looked puzzled. "So you what? You did what? You went to Romano's house? You broke into his house?"

"Jim, make sure you add breaking and entering to the list," Neal Doherty interrupted.

Jim Morris still said nothing, and Sweeney continued.

"Exactly. I just slipped in, turned on his computer, and went about my business. I got into Romano's business and put through a credit authorization that maxed out Parker's card. I knew the amount of credit left on the card because I called to confirm it."

"A credit authorization? What is that?" Doherty asked.

"All it does, really, is set aside the amount of credit indicated until the purchase is made. If nothing happens and the purchase does not go through, it's automatically deleted, and the credit line is restored. The beauty of the credit authorization is that it ties up the card then disappears, which was the whole point in the first place."

"The whole point?" Doherty inquired. "Just another neat little thing, a clever little trick?"

"Yes, that's the whole point. All I wanted to do was piss Jay off, you know, have him be inconvenienced. Once he started to order online, I got those numbers, too. When he went back to his old card, it went through. So the problem was intermittent and with almost any card. I figured it would drive him absolutely nuts.

"Another thing. It's almost impossible to track down the credit authorization. It simply expires, and the credit card company doesn't care. By the time the problem has been checked into, it's gone. At least, that's my understanding of how it works. Later on, of course, Graham helped me with Jay and persuaded him that the credit card problem had worked itself out. We thought we could unnerve him a bit. It was all psychological."

Neal and Dusty looked at each other again, which was becoming a habit by this time.

"Kevin, you're in Romano's house when he's not there, and you're screwing around with Parker's credit cards and Romano's business computer, right? Exactly what did you do on the business computer? Breaking into computers is a crime you know."

"I know. Oh, I just changed a few numbers in his inventory, some of the equipment that had been ordered for cars. I also ordered an expensive truck to see what would happen, and the damn thing showed up. That's the truck, which, if I understand correctly, Romano had illegally removed from his property. So I ordered another one to see what he would do. Really piss him off."

"For the fun of it, in other words. And you weren't worried about getting caught?" Rose asked incredulously.

"No. Not at all. I mean, I'm in his house taking care of business, and I'm using his password. If there's any audit trail, which I did not bother to check on the business system, it's going to point to him. My thinking is it must have driven him crazy. I had heard that he went ballistic over the computer problems he was having and that the manufacturer was blaming him for them. Everything was working great.

"I figured as much because they changed all the passwords at the dealership. So I backed off for a while, even on the credit cards, to let him feel safe and secure again. If someone figured out what was going on and checked the phone records, Romano's number would have shown up on the line to his ISP – you know, Internet Service Provider – especially because he had Caller ID, which works both ways."

"Which explains the money transfers, Kevin. You were in his house when the money was transferred from Romano's accounts to Pierce's. Isn't that right?" Doherty wanted to know. "That's why Kent Costigan thought there was an invisible hand in all this, especially the tip that was sent to the State Police."

"Right. So far, so good," Kevin said.

"He knew Romano had blanket immunity," Doherty said, "but Romano still claimed he never put the money into Pierce's account. Pierce denied he had ever authorized it, which triggered the DOR investigation because the State Police don't believe either one of them. Then the media picks up the story from a source at the DOR."

"Yes, all the serious stuff I did right from Romano's house, which is why all the evidence against me is circumstantial. No one is going to find my phone records connecting me to Pierce, Romano, or Parker. The whole thing worked like a charm. I emptied out all his accounts the morning of Dazzie's funeral because I knew Tony would either be at the beach for his usual walk or going to the funeral.

"I added another twist and changed his password so that he could not get into the accounts. Later that day, I changed it back. I can only imagine what was going through his mind. You know, like, what's it like for you, Tony boy, to really, really worry about your money? You have more money than you can ever spend in a lifetime."

"Jesus, this is unbelievable. So, once again it was you. You tipped off the State Police. The material they received, I'll bet came right off Romano's printer," Rose asked.

"Yes, I did, and you're right. If they checked the printer, they would have found out it was Romano's. I'm assuming that even a laser printer has unusual characteristics much like a typewriter does," Kevin said. "I used surgical gloves I got from Dr. Pierce's to hide my fingerprints. I was worried they would transfer to paper or equipment he could prove he bought recently. Otherwise, I didn't care because my fingerprints were probably all over the house legitimately."

"Very clever, Kevin, but why did you transfer the money in the first place?" Rose probed.

"Originally, Dusty, I transferred the money to piss Romano off. But I also knew that Dr. Pierce was not all that good about balancing his check book because when I was down there working on his project, he told me so. He was busy doing it then and didn't have much time for me. I have the same habit, and I think most small business owners do, too. Anyway, I set up a spreadsheet on the computer to help him out."

"But why transfer the money to Dr. Pierce? Why not just take it yourself? Oh, and by the way. Unauthorized transfers of money, especially the amount you moved, would be grand larceny. A very serious charge, Kevin."

"I realize. Myself? Transfer the money to myself? That would be silly, as subsequent events proved. I just thought it would be interesting to see Romano and Pierce go at it. 'Why did you take my money?' Romano says. 'I didn't take your money,' Pierce contradicts with righteous indignation. Yeah, that would have been interesting. Naturally, Pierce does not know that I have his PIN and account numbers. I got them right off his system."

"It figures," Dusty said impassively. "I almost forgot. You've become God, all knowing, all-powerful, and you get to play with your victims. Cat and mouse, only they don't sense the danger."

"There's one key thing I want to tell you about Romano," Kevin said. "When I first started my business, I wanted to franchise it, so I hired a franchise attorney to help me. He told me about the Uniform Franchise

Agreement required by the SEC, and he also said that all franchisers have in their contracts something about frauds or being a felon.

"It didn't take much for me to realize that there must have been a similar clause in Romano's contracts with his manufacturers. In other words, he could be more worried about them than the police. The franchisers could take his business, and he would never get another one like it."

Doherty stopped Kevin. "You've thought of just about everything, haven't you? You have an answer for everything."

"I'm just trying to lay everything all out there for you. I want to make sure you understand my thinking. Anyway, I figured that the investigators would look into Romano's embezzlement once they knew about it. I also figured that they would not believe Dr. Pierce because he was in a position to arrange for the holistic treatments Romano's mother would be receiving. I had seen a list of providers Rebecca had sent Tony by e-mail.

"Their argument would be that Romano's paying Pierce under the table to take care of things, much like he did with a few subcontractors. Same MO as before. I thought it would be a nice touch. Show Romano's consistency and the skepticism of the police. Even they were not about to believe the truth."

"A nice touch, Kevin. Is that all you can say?" Doherty asked.

"No, I can say more if you want to know the whole story."

"Alright, Kevin. What else could there be?" Rose asked.

"Well, I knew about the two sets of books because I saw Rebecca, Pierce's medical secretary, e-mail them to herself. So I took a look at the balance sheets and saw a difference of around ten percent. I read Pierce's e-mail and knew how he felt about a lot of things, especially Medicare. Being the self righteous son of a bitch I think he is, I figure he's playing with Medicare."

"You think he's playing with Medicare? You think he's committing Medicare fraud?"

"Something like that. I mean, who keeps two sets of books? There was only one on the system and an identical backup. Something was going on, so I used what was handed to me. I worked with what I had."

"Which was?" Doherty asked.

"To connect Pierce and Romano and cast aspersions on Pierce. If he's guilty, he gets caught. If he's not, some people will hear about the investigation anyway, maybe in the papers, and his sterling reputation is tarnished. Either way, I win."

"You win? What kind of person are you? I don't know who is worse here, you or Romano?" Dusty said indignantly.

"You are a devious son of a bitch, Kevin, I'll have to tell you that. Smart, but devious. About the only thing worthwhile that has come out of this is that the embezzlement, as it turns out, was the one thing Romano was most afraid of. It's the one thing that could have cost him the business. He was not afraid of the police; he was afraid of the franchiser," Neal observed.

"Kevin, you mentioned earlier that Barrows helped you with some code that you installed on all the PC's," Dusty said. "What happened to the code? It could still be on the computers, and the trail would lead back to you."

"Not quite," Sweeney said. "I took two precautions. When everything happened with Romano, I simply removed the code from his system, then everyone else's. If you want to get into it later, I can tell you how I got around the virus protection on the other two systems."

"Sure. We can talk about that later. I thought that – even if you delete a file – you can recover it, right?" Dusty asked.

"Yes and no. Here's what I did. I had helped Romano, Pierce, and Parker with their systems and told them about the importance of running utilities that kept their data clean. Most people do not realize that when you delete a file, only the pointer to the file has been removed, but the data remains.

"If the data is going to be overwritten anyway, it makes no sense to clear it out. In a way, it's extra work. So the utility wrote zeros or ones to any file where the pointers had been removed, thus removing the data in them," Sweeney explained. "Any computer guru working for the government, as you know, would know how to resurrect the data and reconstruct the file.

"The utility would erase the data, the electronic debris that was hanging around, and you would wind up with nothing. As an extra precaution, I reduced the number of files that could be recovered from fifty to twenty-five. It's been at least a couple of months now, so, if they ran the utilities or used their systems, I don't think you could ever find anything."

The room was so quiet you could hear a pin drop on the carpet.

"Kevin, probably the most serious charge against you is that you interfered in a criminal investigation. It's a major problem, you realize," Doherty said.

"I know it is, but I truly thought I was helping the investigation. I don't think that the investigators knew what made Romano tick. It was money. Threaten his money, and you threaten his life. I knew all about Romano's embezzlement because I had helped him set up some invoices. He told me at the time that he was starting a new side business for custom car care.

"Don't forget, I saw him do the invoicing and billing on the dealership's accounting system from his home. I had the same access to it as Tony did, so

I looked, printed out a list of vendors, and checked into them. It wasn't hard to figure out."

Rose was puzzled. "There's something missing, Kevin. You could see what he was doing on the computer from right over there, from that computer on your desk. How did you know about the electronic payments? I don't understand."

"It's like this. The accounting system was not tied into the bank. In order to make a payment from the dealership to one of the fake businesses, Tony had to open up the application from the bank and go on line. He had electronic access to all his phony accounts. I had that software, too. What he knew, I knew."

"It's quite a story, Kevin," Dusty said. "You're a very cynical, angry, and dangerous man. There's just one more thing I wanted to know. Why Lauren and the children? Please, tell me why?"

"It's just the way things turned out, Dusty. It was not part of the original plan. The salami programming notion was Graham's idea, and he thought it would be fun to throw Jay off guard because I said he was so sure of himself and arrogant. I gave Graham all the background on the Nazi stuff and the Brink's Robbery. It was quite a smokescreen, I think you'll have to admit. Very convincing."

Dusty and Neal simply shook their heads. "There was only one problem," Sweeney continued. "I had not planned on Graham's becoming involved with Lauren, and his betrayal of her and me I never saw coming. I would never have hurt Lauren or the children. I really cared about them."

"I can sense that you do, Kevin," Dusty admitted. "Why then did you send her the cyber sex stuff about her husband?"

"I never did, and I never knew about it. I can only assume that Graham did, that he was doing to me what I was doing to Romano, Pierce, and Parker."

"Meaning?"

"He was watching me. Graham probably set the whole thing up right in front of me when we were testing the software he wrote. For all I know, he could still be watching."

"Really? And he used the cyber sex material to send Lauren in his direction?"

"I would think so. She certainly stepped over the line, and it's easy to see why. I must say that he played his shining white knight role to perfection."

"And the connection of Jay to the money laundering. If the salami programming scheme was operational, Jay could be implicated perhaps. Whose idea was that?"

"Definitely not mine. Eddie Matros told the State Police that Parker had paid Romano cash for the car. Matros found out about it from Steve Bonnano when we were all out to eat one time around Thanksgiving. Steve was busting Matros' balls and made a comment about the sound system Parker installed in his car at Eddie's expense.

"You never know how these things can come back to haunt you," Kevin said with indifference.

"At any rate," he continued, "Parker thinks he's being drawn into some money laundering deal because of the salami programming scheme and the connection to Romano, and he panics when he's investigated. Graham could never have planned on Jay's being fingerprinted, which was done because Jay drove the same make, model, and color car as the one seen by the neighbor who lived next door to Dazzie's parents. I must admit, I would have liked to have seen the look on Jay's face when the veneer cracked.

"What Graham did do was make the most of what had been handed to him by myself, the police, and Lauren. She was desperate and in a terrible conflict. I think she loved Graham but did not want to admit it. He was like the flame that attracts the moth. It had to be devastating."

"That's an understatement," Neal Doherty said.

"I can only wonder what went through her mind. Other than me, whom could Lauren talk to?" Kevin asserted. "She certainly could not say anything to the owners of her company. You know something, but there's no way you can confirm your suspicions because you'll run the risk of giving away more than you'll get in return. So you carry them around with you."

"Right. You're trapped by what you know," Doherty observed.

"Well, yes. I guess you can say that she was. And don't forget. An accumulation of facts does not always lead you to the truth. As I said, though, I did have tender feelings for Lauren and the children. That part is difficult."

"You have a very strange way of showing your feelings, Kevin," Rose said. "I can't imagine what you could do to someone you hate."

"Listen, I was very nice about the whole thing." Sweeney countered. "I left my calling card before I did anything. You know, something of a warning," Sweeney said.

"Your calling card?"

"Right. The nails in the tires. That's what gets everything going."

"Exactly. Now we've got malicious damage to add to the list, Jim. I just don't know what we're going to do with this guy."

"Well, I do," Morris fired back at Doherty. "You're going to honor the blanket immunity."

"Now that you know the whole story, my involvement, and my motivation," Sweeney said, "what do you think? Is it a perfect crime?"

"That's it? That's all you're worried about? That you may or may not have committed a perfect crime?" Rose asked incredulously.

"Well, no, that's not all," Kevin answered.

"Alright. What else then?"

"Did Graham commit one, too?"

"I don't get it. What do you mean?" Doherty asked.

"It's like this. The main reason I'm even talking to you right now is that I was afraid that you would find out that I was eating salami. I figured I had better come forward first before you came to me."

"When did you find out that the salami programming scheme was directed at you?" Rose asked.

"When I finally sat down to do my accounting," Sweeney answered, "about a week ago and found myself with a small fortune on my hands. Graham knew my habits, too."

"Why do you think Barrows did it?"

"I can only speculate, but I think he did it to tempt me. I am sure he thought I would condemn him. So, to see what I would do, he dangles all this money in my face at a time when he knows I'm struggling with a lot of things.

"I can almost hear him say, 'What would you do if you had a chance to make a billion?' If I did nothing, I would be his equal. It was a brilliant plan pulled off by a master, better than the Phantom Shitter."

"Phantom Shitter?" Doherty asked.

"Right. Phantom shitter. It's an old Coastie story of mine. Someone who comes in the middle of the night, does his dirty business, and then disappears. A real symbol of mischief." Sweeney explained. "Graham enjoyed the mental games, called them a conundrum."

"What would you call them, Kevin?" Rose asked.

"I'd call them 'busting your balls, your chops, or ranking.' It's pretty amazing. He did to me what I was doing to everyone else and nailed me with my own principles. Otherwise, it's all about greed."

Chapter 19

It was now June 1999, the most beautiful time of the year in New England. Poets had written about it. "And what is so rare as a day in June? Then, if ever, come more perfect days."

Builders loved them, too, and most contractors were benefiting from a serious shortage of skilled labor that had driven up the cost of building and remodeling that spring. Demand far exceeded supply, and the contractors were making a very decent living.

The guys had what many people coveted: outside jobs in the good weather. Homeowners seemed grateful just to have a warm body to do the work and were willing to wait six months to a year before starting their projects.

Stephanie Lahey and her fiancé, Jason, got married that very month and everything went, well, just perfectly. Dr. Pierce, his wife, and Rebecca Solberg and Barry Sobilof attended and had a wonderful time. Their romance was well on its way to marriage, although it had recently hit a few bumps in the road.

Rebecca was tortured by what had happened to Dr. Adam Pierce and the possible role she may have played in his public embarrassment. She had confided as much to Barry, and he advised her to let it go. "What's done is done," he had said. "You never intended to hurt him in the first place, so let it go at that." It was good advice, and it sustained her through a difficult time.

Dr. Pierce never questioned what had happened to him or why. As it turned out, he was innocent of any Medicare wrongdoing and saw to it that the extra money in his accounts was quickly returned to Tony Romano's dealership. From then on, Dr. Pierce had Rebecca do all the bookkeeping, including the balancing of the checkbook. He dismissed the rumors swirling about him with a cavalier wave of the hand and blamed the whole incident on poor police work. His practice would continue to do well, and he did not lose a single patient as a result.

Not one, except, of course, for Mrs. Christina Romano. In addition to her illness, her system may have been weakened further by the trouble her son, Tony, found himself in. Perhaps in the end, it was too much for her, and she simply gave up. No one will ever know.

Her funeral in St. Ann's Church, Hull, was well attended, and even Tony was there.

The star witness in the prosecution of Al Sanderson and Mike Norris had cut himself quite a deal. As his defense attorney had wisely suggested, Tony spilled his guts to the prosecutors and would do so again in the trial itself. He would have a clean slate and a chance to start all over again without the worry of another criminal prosecution.

Romano did get married, but not to Liz Jensen. He took as his bride the IRS, which was unraveling Tony's estate and complicated finances. Romano had his attorney working on the case, and it remained to be seen how much of his considerable fortune Tony would get to keep.

Although he was now unemployed, Romano did not attempt to collect unemployment. The business was gone, but not to the franchiser; even he would have to stand in line behind the IRS.

Jay and Lauren Parker had separated and, most likely, would get divorced. Lauren never discussed Graham Barrows with Jay or his crushing betrayal of her. She would eventually take her company public and become, just as she said, set for life.

Lauren would then leave her company and become a stay at home mom, mainly because she wanted to be with her children. She also had had enough of the pressure of big business. Ironically, as word of her stunning success – the company raised billions in the IPO – became well known amongst the "Investment Community," she found herself in greater demand. Turning down potential employers drove her professional stock up even further.

Still, her children would need her now more than ever, and she would be there for them in the same beautiful home Kevin Sweeney had helped remodel.

Jay Parker had found real success in a most unlikely place. At Kevin Sweeney's urging, Jay had given a marketing overview a couple of years ago to a group of unemployed entrepreneurs involved in the program sponsored by the Commonwealth of Massachusetts where Kevin had once been a part-time instructor. After class, Jay met two people who had an idea about a new product for the Internet.

Parker listened, learned, and helped arrange the financing of the startup, which eventually went public with an offering that also raised billions. Maybe he had an eye for success, after all, because the company did not become a dot bomb.

Although Jay's marriage may have failed, his relationship with his children did not, and he continued to see them regularly. Not being around Lauren as much seemed to help him get along better with her. Jay still loved Lauren, and always would, but realized that he could not live with her. He did not miss her controlling ways, which were in conflict with his own.

He was also getting along now much better with his father, as they had managed to reconcile many of their differences. For the first time in the lives of either man, they actually were talking and listening to each other, father to son, man to man. There was real hope that their relationship would grow and become more mature, loving, and respectful.

Although the whereabouts of Graham Barrows were uncertain, there were several rumors circulating that he was living in Copenhagen and working for a software start-up involved with some Internet product. No one, perhaps, would ever know what, if anything, he did to Lauren or why. It would forever remain a mystery.

Marie Sweeney was still busy at school and planning her life without the two children at home. It was not easy for her, and she felt the same sense of pain and loss when Lisa left that Kevin did with Mark. That special time when they all lived together as a family under the same roof was gone. "You don't cry when they leave," a friend had told Marie. "You cry when they come back."

Marie and Kevin did not feel that way even though they still had each other. Their hearts ached, but they would adjust to the transformation as most parents do.

Kevin Sweeney was a much changed and chastened man after the Romano, Pierce, and Parker caper. He had been in a terrible car accident that almost cost him his life when an eighteen-wheel truck plowed into the passenger side of his Grand Am and completely destroyed it.

Although Kevin walked away from the accident unscathed, he did suffer for weeks from ugly bruises to the right side of his body. The night the accident happened, Kevin shook and trembled in his bed, and Marie held him while he wept in her arms.

Marie knew her husband would be ok and told Mark as much when he had called the house frantic about his father. "He's doing better," she said. "He's stacking his french fries." Until his wife had mentioned it, Kevin never realized that he stacked his food in neat little piles, especially anything with some length to it, like asparagus or green beans.

Even without the accident, Sweeney had much reflection to do. "Where did I go wrong?" he thought to himself more than once over the ensuing months. "Maybe Lisa is right. Maybe I should just go back to teaching English."

Realistically, that option was out of the question because Kevin could never go back; he had to go forward. His business was actually progressing, and Sweeney had recently published in *The Boston Globe* an article about remodeling.

No one would ever find out about the vengeful game Sweeney had played on his unsuspecting clients or his close call with the law. The government was not interested in prosecuting Kevin or Graham Barrows because all the evidence was circumstantial and the money had been returned in each case. Sweeney's invisible hand had actually helped the State Police by pushing Tony Romano over the edge.

Security at the investment firm was increased, of course, but not so much as to draw attention to the singular success of the salami programming scheme. It was correctly assumed that a man with Graham Barrow's technical skills would leave no virtual fingerprints buried deep inside the software.

No one was going to find the needle in the haystack that Barrows had placed there since it would take all the king's horses and all the king's men to put the cracked software together again.

Everything that had happened to Sweeney was nothing but a bittersweet scare, and he could now relax and set his sights on the future.

Even so, the Barrows affair nagged at him. Graham had busted his balls with little chance for rebuttal, and Sweeney wasn't a man who ignored a challenge to his principles. Righting a wrong is what got him started in the misadventure in the first place.

"What would be the point of my pursuing it any further?" Kevin would ask himself. "On the other hand, Graham doesn't know I stole his software from his home office computer, nor does anyone else."

Kevin still loved ranking or busting your balls, and the temptation to play the game with Graham, a crafty master and the ultimate Phantom Shitter, was very appealing. The stolen software was yet another trump card Sweeney had up his sleeve, and Kevin knew exactly how and when to play it.

Printed in the United States
3113